# Welcome to the Dungeon

It is a road where travelers pass through flaming geysers on an endless journey to nowhere.

It is a bridge of worm-eaten boards that dangles its captives over a bottomless chasm.

It is a mist of reverie out of which winged demons and fantastical creatures spring to life.

It is a palace that offers mysterious hospitality and provides more questions than answers.

From the lake of fire to the edge of the unknown, this is the quest of Clive Folliot, explorer and hero!

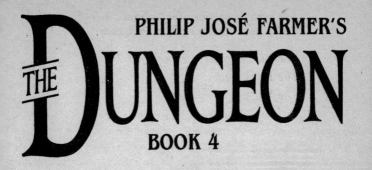

# PHILIP JOSÉ FARMER'S
# THE DUNGEON

## BOOK 4

# THE
# LAKE
# OF FIRE
■
## Robin W. Bailey

**A BYRON PREISS BOOK**

BANTAM BOOKS
NEW YORK · TORONTO · LONDON · SYDNEY · AUCKLAND

THE LAKE OF FIRE

A Bantam Spectra Book / October 1989

Special thanks to Lou Aronica, Betsy Mitchell, Richard Curtis,
David M. Harris, and Mary Higgins.

Cover and interior art by Robert Gould.
Book and cover design by Alex Jay / Studio J.

THE DUNGEON is a trademark of Byron Preiss Visual Publications, Inc.

ISBN 0-553-28185-2

Published simultaneously in the United States and Canada

Bantam Books are published by Bantam Books, a division of Bantam
Doubleday Dell Publishing Group, Inc. Its trademark, consisting of the
words "Bantam Books" and the portrayal of a rooster, is Registered in
U.S. Patent and Trademark Office and in other countries. Marca Registrada.
Bantam Books, 666 Fifth Avenue, New York, New York 10103.

PRINTED IN THE UNITED STATES OF AMERICA

0  9  8  7  6  5  4  3  2  1

This book's dedicated with great affection to the incomparable Piranha Brothers: Bob Anesi, Vernon Nelson, Brad Strong, Brad Rainke, Rex Reeve, Steve Piland, Ellis Thigpen, David Stagg, Tom Ryan, Jonathan Nye, David Canaday, Mike Seimer, Mike Spenser, Forest Lewis, Rick Axsom, Tony Porter, David McGuire, Bryce Watterson, Pete Van Allen, Charlie Pierce, Jeff Diehl.

It's also for the incomparable spectators: Arthur Butler, Dennis Mitchell, Wayne Burge, Fred Pond, and Greg Hancks.

For Bob Johns, who provided technical assistance.

And always, for Diana.

# · Foreword ·

First you go down. Then, you go up.

That is the opposite of what Heraclitus, the ancient Greek philosopher, said. He stated that it was a physical law that what went up had to come back down.

We know now that that is not entirely true. A rocket sent out of the solar system is not going to fall back.

Nor are the first two lines of this text entirely valid. But I am speaking of a general rule re the heroes of fiction. (By *heroes*, I also mean *heroines*.) They descend into a hell, and then, because they are fighters, they battle their way upward. This applies to both their psychic and physical struggles.

"Easy is the way down to Hell." But, oh, that way up!

So says Virgil, the ancient Roman writer (70–19 B.C.). *Facilis descensus Averni*. He was referring to the descent into the Roman underworld. Of course, he was not thinking about such an event over two thousand years later. That is, down into The Dungeonworld and the battling of a heroic band to climb out of it. At least, I do not think so. However, I would not be surprised if, in the course of the next two volumes of *The Dungeon*, our band ran into Virgil, snatched away from his sunny Mediterranean into the gloomy and peril-soaked Subterranean by its mysterious and malignant rulers. And then returned later to his own time and place. Perhaps Virgil, whose spirit was to guide Dante through Inferno, could aid our band in their search for the escape exit from the Dungeon. After all, the Dungeon, unlike Dante's underworld, does have hope for those who enter its ivory gates.

Upward go our heroes, though not only in a physical sense. In the sense of the light shed on the many enigmas and puzzles they encounter, they are also ascending. But this light brings with it more shadows. Every answer hurls more questions into their faces and strikes their hearts. Shriek, the female sentient spideroid, who is a walking pharmaceutical factory and missile launcher, is also telepathic. She detects two powerful telepathic observers of the band, though she knows neither where they are nor their identities.

I have no more idea than you or Shriek who these two are. But I suspect that one of the observers is evil; the other, good. Perhaps, they belong to two superraces not unlike the Boskonians and the Arisians. These were the supreme evil and supreme good powers, respectively, of the universe created by Doctor E. E. Smith in his Lensman series. They manipulated the lesser beings in their warfare against each other.

I could be wrong. Perhaps Richard Lupoff, who wrote the first book in *The Dungeon* series and will write the final (the sixth) will present another concept.

However it goes in succeeding books, we do know that when Clive Folliot, our main hero, enters this next level of The Dungeonworld, the diary of his twin, Neville, asks: "What will you do when you meet Hell's Sire?" Thus, Clive's destiny is to have a terrible confrontation with the prince of this underworld, in this volume or a later one. Whether or not this superformidable enemy, as powerful and malicious as Satan Himself, will be a clone of the Chief (W)retch or The Original, I do not know. At this point, what with all of the many surprises that have occurred, I'm not sure of anything. It's possible that Clive Folliot himself, User Annie, Sergeant Smythe, Sidi Bombay, and Shriek (and others) are clones. Anything can happen. Unlike the Hell of Dante, The Dungeonworld is open-ended, not a closed system. But it sure as hell has a lot of negative feedback—suffering and frustrating—for our heroes.

The parallel of this underworld to Dante's is obvious. And, as I have said in previous forewords, certain parallels—not strained—exist between The Dungeonworld and the worlds of Baum and Carroll. The main characters of *The Wonderful Wizard of Oz* are searching for something they lack or believe they lack. So are our heroes. All, like Dorothy, want to get back to their homeworlds. And the appearance and then fading away of some of the people and things our heroes encounter or their dissolving into other people and things reminds me of *Alice's Adventures in Wonderland* and *Through the Looking Glass*.

One of the major differences between our heroes and Baum's and Carroll's is that the latter do not bleed, sweat, fart, or suffer intensely. They also do not think about carnal lusts, sex, sexism, and racism. These elements are not necessary for their works and would ruin them if they were in them. But this is 1988, and *The Dungeon*, though fictional, is in "real" time.

"Real" time is a wearing down of things living and nonliving. An erosion, in short, like winds or waves grinding away rocks. This temporal erosion confuses and deceives us. If it were not for time, we would be fully aware of that unerodable part of us, that which exists after time has ceased to exist. We are incessantly bombarded by X rays and other radiation, pierced by neutrinos, and bent by gravitons. But the chronons, those wave-particles of time that surround and infiltrate us, most injure us. Chronons blanket with darkness that mental-spiritual light in us that does not know time.

The real essence of time is the never-ending smash of chronons. Helplessly, we are hurled along a path that would not exist if we could live within that glowing ball of timelessness that all of us have within us but of which we are either completely unaware or dimly aware.

Time was invented by The Devil, Some Thing, anyway, and this invention prevents us from knowing and using our timelessness. So, we erode—in this world.

Nevertheless, the timeless *Alice* books have enormously affected the fiction of our fake-real time world. This is not just because the more perceptive readers of them have a hemi-semi-demi-awareness of the timelessness embedded in the books. There is also the adventure, the like of which we did not have before Carroll wrote about it. There are his wild and distinctively individual characters. And there is the sense of Alice and all beings in the two books as pawns on a giant chessboard. That resonates with the feeling that I, and perhaps many of you, have of being pawns. (Though we are also pawns with, perhaps, free will.) Along with this goes the question of the identity and gamesmanship of the two Chess Players.

Aside from the Bible and Shakespeare's works, Carroll's *Alice* books and *The Hunting of the Snark* have inspired more references in literature and given rise to more plots and characters than any others you can name. Many mainstream, science-fiction, fantasy, and mystery books show evidence of this. There are Carrollian threads woven throughout the Dungeonworld books, some consciously put there. For instance, Clive and Neville Folliot, twins, are a sort of nonsilly Tweedledee and Tweedledum. Though, it can be said that their prejudices seem rather silly to us. Some of us. There are millions, perhaps billions, who in 1988 cherish the prudishness, racism, sexism, and superstitions of Clive and Neville. Neville may or may not be an evil twin, but Amos and Lorena Ransome, also twins, are undoubtedly evil. How could they not be, since they are so closely associated with the ironically named Philo B. Goode? Whom we may discover is the true Hell's Sire mentioned in Neville's pop-up diary. Or he may be a twin (or clone) of Hell's Sire.

Another Carrollian parallel, found in this very book, is the presence of the frogmen servants in Baron Tewkesbury's electronic gingerbread house. Remember the batrachoid

Footman who met Alice at the doorway of the Duchess's house? Bailey's Footmen, however, are tools of evil. So are the Wonderland robot characters misused by a murderess in the final book of my *Riverworld* series. Bailey must be aware of these and of the many other resonances à la Carroll in my works. Thus, writing this *Dungeon* novel in the spirit of my fiction, Bailey moves his frogmen along the chessboard derived both from Carroll and myself. But they are also moved by Bailey's own spirit and are far from being just derivative.

In the spirit of my writings, *The Dungeon* is a nexus where people and things from all times and places are collected by some unknown power for unknown reasons. But that nexus concept may have come to me (I really don't know) from the Sargasso Sea, which figured in so many pulp-magazine stories and hardcover adventure books in the late nineteenth and early twentieth century. (The last Sargasso Sea story I remember reading was a Doc Savage novel, *The Sargasso Ogre*, first printed in 1933.)

For those who have not heard of the Sargasso Sea, it does exist. It is an area of the Atlantic that encompasses the Bermuda Islands. Its surface is strewn with floating gulfweed, and it is a biological desert. The legends of early mariners related that this sea had trapped in its smooth and weed-filled waters many ships that had ventured into it. These ranged from fifteenth-century Spanish galleons to the ships then currently sailed by the storytellers. In the twentieth-century legend, the sea had also ensnared in its weeds abandoned steamers.

When I was young, the stories I read about the Sargasso Sea delighted me. I believed them. Then I found out that the stories were not true, in that this sea did not trap ships. However, this did not spoil the stories for me any more than knowing that Burroughs's Barsoom (Mars) did not exist. Not in this continuum, that is. Nor did that keep new writers from using some form of the sea in their plots. I used it myself, in *Venus on the Half-Shell*, though that sea was a nexus in outer space that attracted wrecked and abandoned spaceships.

The writers of *The Dungeon* series have been faithful to the spirit of my works in using both the pulp and classical themes used in my fiction. But I must stress that these writers have added a great deal of their own originality while paying homage to my spirit.

Our motto: Ever upward, onward, and outward!

—Philip José Farmer

## · CHAPTER ONE ·

# Descent and Fall

Clive Folliot tried to stifle a yawn as the small horseless cart that bore his companions and him continued down the seemingly endless corridor between levels six and seven. The walls and floors were a sparkling, featureless white, as was most of the ceiling. He'd long ago given up trying to count the strange light-panels overhead, which provided an eye-aching illumination.

He longed to stretch his legs, but there was no room in the back of the tiny cart. Instead, he reached down with one hand and tried to massage away a cramp. How far to the end of this blasted passage, anyway? His stomach rumbled. *Not now*, he told it silently with no idea when he'd see his next meal.

He regarded his companions and let go a little sigh. They'd come through so much together as they'd descended the Dungeon's levels, faced one danger after another. It amazed him that they were all still alive.

He looked down at Annabelle. She slept with her head on his shoulder, her features peacefully composed. It pleased him to know that she was his great-great-granddaughter, a fact that filled him with pride. She had handled herself well through all their trials. It troubled him, though, that she reminded him so much of Miss Annabella Leighton, his mistress, whom he'd left behind in Plantagenet Court. In London. On Earth. Wherever that was.

He brushed a lock of short, dark hair from Annabelle's forehead and put on a weak smile.

Across from him, with his legs folded lotus-style, sat Sidi Bombay, the Indian guide who had been at his side even before they crossed the Shimmering Gate in Equatorial Africa. Well, his usefulness as a guide had been minimal in the Dungeon, but he had proved himself in other ways. Strange, to look now at the Indian. He had entered the Dungeon an old man, but an incident on the second level had aged him backward. Sidi was Clive's age, now, or even a little younger. And it bothered Clive that Annabelle and Sidi seemed to share a growing attraction.

Beside Sidi sat Tomàs, the Portuguese sailor from the fifteenth century. He'd drawn up his knees to make more room for the others, wrapping his arms around them. His head rested on his knees where it had been for some time, and Clive wondered if the man could possibly sleep in that position. Clive hadn't made up his mind about Tomàs, yet. He'd stuck with them and come in handy a time or two. Yet, Clive didn't particularly want the man at his back.

His former batman, Quartermaster Sergeant Horace Hamilton Smythe, sat behind the steering wheel, in one of the two front seats. The man was a rock. He'd been driving for what seemed like hours without one complaint or any indication of discomfort. Smythe had been with him through many a campaign in Her Majesty's service back on Earth, but only down here, in the terrors of the Dungeon, had Clive Folliot learned to call him friend.

He looked to the passenger beside Smythe, and his lips drew into a taut line. Chang Guafe was a cyborg, Annabelle had explained to him with her twenty-first-century knowledge. Yet, he didn't look to Clive like any of the other cyborgs he'd encountered on the Q'oonan level. Other than two arms and legs, a torso, and a head, there was nothing symmetrical about Chang's construction. He wasn't even human, but an alien from some distant planet. Chang Guafe chose that moment to look over his shoulder, and their gazes met for just an instant. Clive found those ruby lenses that served for eyes completely unreadable, yet he waited until the cyborg looked away before giving in to a shiver.

Perched on the hood of the cart sat the strangest member of their company: Shriek, as everyone had come to call her, an evolved spider from another alien race. She had four arms and four legs and six eyes, and all the other attributes of a spider as far as anyone could tell. Oddly, Clive found that he'd developed a kind of fondness for the creature. They had touched minds in a weird sort of mental linkup and shared each other's histories and experiences, their very essences. Though undoubtedly, to his way of thinking, the most enigmatic of their company, she seemed also the most sublime, and he trusted her.

He yawned again and looked down at the bottom of the cart. Scrunched between them lay the unconscious form of his brother, Neville Folliot, whom he'd come so far and through so much to find. His twin, Clive reminded himself, though at the moment he felt nothing but a vast distance and detachment toward his brother. Oh, he'd felt bad enough, yes, when he killed a clone, thinking it was Neville. But that was then, and this was now. Neville had led them a not-so-merry chase, and when the blighter woke up, Clive intended to have some answers if it meant choking them out of his brother.

Something nudged his elbow where it rested on the side of the cart, and he heard a sniffing. Clive craned his neck around and raised an inquiring eyebrow. He'd almost forgotten Finnbogg.

"Not sleep?" Finnbogg asked softly in a gruff voice, his shaggy head bobbing up and down as he trotted alongside the cart.

"I'm okay," Clive assured him, reaching back to give Finnbogg a quick scratch between the ears.

That made Finnbogg smile. "Okay," he repeated, and then romped ahead of the cart to play scout. What there was to scout for in this featureless corridor, Clive couldn't imagine, but he watched over Smythe's shoulder as the creature ran ahead.

He smiled to himself despite his fatigue. If Shriek was an evolved spider, then Finnbogg was an evolved bulldog. Four feet of sheer canine muscle, the ferocious little being had pulled them out of more than one sticky situation. And if nothing else, he was the sense of humor the group so badly needed. Clive had long ago decided that an entire planet of Finnboggs was something he'd love the chance to see.

But he shared another bond with Finnbogg. As Clive had come to the Dungeon seeking his lost brother, so Finnbogg had come to find his missing littermate, his own brother. Clive realized with a start that he'd been fortunate in finding Neville. Finnbogg had been on the trail ten thousand years.

"Here's a piece of bad luck, Major," Quartermaster Horace Hamilton Smythe said suddenly without a trace of annoyance or panic in his voice.

"Another piece of bad luck is not what we need, Horace," Clive answered, rousing himself to see what the trouble was. As gently as he could, he eased Annabelle's head from his shoulder, inadvertently waking her in the process.

She batted her eyes, then rubbed them with one hand and tried to shield them from the overhead light. "What's wrong?" she asked, sitting straighter.

Sidi's eyes snapped opened and he regarded them placidly, not speaking, but waiting.

Clive leaned over the driver's seat and put his mouth close to Smythe's ear. He determined to remain calm whatever Smythe's news might be.

"Bad luck, he say? *Bad luck?*" That came from Tomàs in the back. So he hadn't been asleep after all, or not very deeply. "*Madre*, your man got some sense of humor."

Clive tuned out the Portuguese's grumbling.

"What is it, Horace?" Clive said quietly, peering ahead down the long corridor. He perceived no threat at all.

"Don't you feel it, sah?" Horace Hamilton Smythe said. "We're slowing down, and no matter how I step on that thing"—he pointed to a flat black pedal under his right foot—"we're not keeping speed."

Chang Guafe placed the palm of his left hand against the cart's dashboard. "Sensors reveal the power cell is depleted," the cyborg announced, his voice cold and mechanical, and to Clive's mind, chilling.

Clive pursed his lips, frowning. Damn all these mechanical contrivances. A good horse or even a mule wouldn't have let them down before the journey was over. And Annabelle had called this progress? Well, what about efficiency and reliability? He hoped they counted for something, too, in her world of the future. "Then I guess we walk," he said finally with some irritation. "And the next time we steal a cart, let's make sure we get something with four legs, too." Then he shot an embarrassed glance forward. "Oh, sorry, Shriek."

They clambered out of the cart amid a chorus of groans and joint creaks and bone pops. Clive was almost maliciously gladdened to discover he wasn't the only one who felt like a skin sock stuffed with gravel. He stretched with both arms over his head, and his vertebrae cracked into place one at a time. "A little trick I picked up while on duty in your country," he explained to Sidi Bombay when the Indian looked at him. Sidi put on a big smile and popped his back in the exact same manner.

"Enough of this exotic macho bullshit," Annabelle grumbled. "Somebody's got to carry this scrodhead, here." She pointed to the unconscious Neville Folliot.

As if his name had been spoken, Neville Folliot opened his eyes and sat up. He looked around, a big smile beaming on his face. "Are we there, yet?" he said cheerily. "I've had the nicest nap. Ready to face anything, I am!"

"Neville!" Clive shouted, turning to face his brother. A surge of relief and joy swept through him followed by a greater surge of annoyance.

"Bet this hacker's been awake the whole time," Annabelle accused, folding her arms across her chest, regarding Neville Folliot disdainfully. "Thought I felt him stir once or twice."

"*Seu irmão*—your brother—he is a big pretender," Tomàs mumbled, standing at the edge of the company apart from the rest. His dark eyes darted to each of them as if seeking approval for his contribution.

Neville Folliot nodded as he looked each of them over. "A very charming party, indeed, little brother," he said to Clive, grinning, "and very charming guests!" He brushed a finger along Annabelle's cheek, his smile widening as he looked into her eyes.

Suddenly, his hair crackled and stood straight on end, his eyes snapped wide with surprise and pain, and his entire body stiffened as he found himself flung three feet through the air. He crashed to the floor and lay there, stunned for a moment. Then, slowly he lifted his head and stared with puzzlement.

"You'll smoke a turd before you touch me again," Annabelle warned with a nasty little grin of her own as she fingered the array of small metal implants on her left forearm, the controls of her Baalbec A-9. Though the unit had numerous functions, its self-defense mode was formidable, as she had demonstrated time and again.

"You'll find your great-great-grandniece is not quite like the women you're used to," Clive Folliot told his brother with more than a fair share of smug satisfaction. In fact, Neville looked pretty good flat on his back like that, taken down a peg, as it were. And it delighted Clive that it had been Annabelle who'd done it.

Neville rose to his feet, rubbing his backside with one hand, watching Annabelle ruefully. "Grandniece, you say? From our future, then," he observed, proving he understood the nature of the Dungeon as well as any of them. "I'm not sure I like the change." Yet, he managed a wink in Annabelle's direction. "Then again, I might. Grandniece, you say? The devil take you, little brother! How about your hand, and it's good to see you, too!"

Finnbogg came bounding into their midst, alerted by the sound of the Baalbec A-9's zap. He looked at Neville and growled, rising on his hind legs. "Annie okay? Clive okay?" He growled again without taking his eyes from Neville. "Okay, okay?"

Annabelle put her hand on Finnbogg's head and scratched. "Okay, Finnbogg," she said, calming the creature. "Neville had a bug in his system, but he's user-friendly now." She gave Neville Folliot a piercing glare. "Aren't you, Uncle Neville?"

Neville made a sweeping bow. "As you say, dear lady." He turned to Clive. "Now, little brother, let's get this show back on the road, as they say, and you can make proper introductions as we go along. It'll help pass the time."

A deep crease formed between Clive's brows as he frowned. He knew that tone too well, and he didn't much like it. But Neville was right, they couldn't very well stay here. The others looked at him expectantly. At least he seemed to have their support. "Very well," he said, "let's go."

"*Ai!* Hope we find something to eat soon," Tomàs grumbled, following behind the rest. "And drink. I'm thirsty. Cart no fit place to sleep, either. Wish to get home. No place like home. . . ."

Clive tuned him out.

Clive filled in his brother, Neville, on all his adventures, beginning with the trip to Equatorial Africa, explaining how concerned their father, Baron Tewkesbury, had been for his missing son and how determined that Clive should find him. Father was fine, by the way, and codgerly as ever. He told of meeting his companions as he introduced them, and of the various races and peoples they'd encountered. The only thing he left out was his duel with Neville's clone on the level they'd just departed. He fully intended to forget that altogether.

He began to question his brother. "What is going on

here?" he said. "When Smythe and Sidi and I first got here, we found your body in a coffin. We also found a monster on a bridge with your face. We've found people impersonating you, and met a creature who—" He shut up suddenly, on the verge of mentioning the clone. "We've seen you half a dozen times around one corner or another."

"And how do you explain this?" Annabelle said suspiciously, taking Neville's diary from the inside of her jacket. "It turns up in the strangest places and says the strangest things."

"It has been a source of much trouble and misinformation," Chang Guafe agreed, his head rotating toward the book and away again.

Neville Folliot glanced back over his shoulder as he had done several times before. "I would love to answer all your questions and promise to do so at a convenient opportunity—"

"Neville!" Clive snapped, exasperated at being put off.

"Now look, scrodhead, we're tired—"

"Yes, I'm sure you are," Neville persisted as he turned to point the way they had come, "but doesn't it look to you as though the other end of this corridor is rushing at us awfully quickly?"

Annabelle gave a little scream.

"Good God!" Clive cried.

"Focusing sensors," Chang Guafe reported. "Confirming."

"*Christo!*" Tomàs turned on his heel and started to run without another word to the others.

Clive stood rooted to the spot, unable to believe what he saw even after all this time in the Dungeon. It couldn't be the same doorway they'd come through. Yet it was! The sound of huge hammering fists convinced him. It was the same door, and the Lords of Thunder battled to get through. The Lords of Thunder were still after them!

"Finnbogg, take Annabelle!" Clive shouted, taking Annabelle's hand as the beast came beside him.

"Hey, Clive-o, I can run as well as—"

"Just get on!" he snapped, practically lifting her onto

Finnbogg's back as Finnbogg settled on all fours. "Now go!"

"Good advice for us all, sah!" said Horace Hamilton Smythe, tugging at his sleeve.

Clive Folliot hesitated long enough to shoot one more frantic glance at the doorway that hurtled toward them. "Damn you!" he shouted at the Lords of Thunder. "Damn you!" That one was for the Dungeonmasters, whoever the unknown, faceless bastards were that so manipulated them.

He started to run. Far ahead, he spied Finnbogg, Annabelle clutching wildly to his back. The beast had already passed Tomàs. If there was a doorway ahead, an exit from this corridor, Finnbogg and Annabelle would reach it first.

Shriek scuttled on ahead with spidery speed. Chang Guafe, too, ran with mechanical precision, who knew what energy powering his limbs. Clive had seen the cyborg fight often enough to know Chang never tired. They would swiftly overtake Tomàs.

That left, then, the humans. Poor frail humans. Smythe fell into place at his right side, Sidi Bombay at his left. Clive became aware of a slapping at his left leg that interfered with his stride. His sword, he realized, unbuckling it and carrying it in his hand. Smythe did the same.

They ran at a swift pace, encouraging each other. Quickly, they were upon Tomàs. "Come on, sailor!" Smythe cried desperately, catching the little Portuguese's arm and half-dragging him. "Run! Show us a navy man's better than a queen's army regular!"

Tomàs gasped and clutched his side, but somewhere within he found a reservoir of strength and matched them. The fear on his small round face, though, was pitiful to see. "*Caminho cerrado! Caminho cerrado!*" he muttered through tortured breaths, but Clive didn't understand his language.

"Run!" Clive screamed over the furious pounding that now filled the passage.

Far ahead he saw the others, and a rush of joy and relief surged through him. A door, they'd found the door, the way out! Ignoring the pain in his side and the fire in his chest, he put on a burst of speed.

It was a huge iron door with a huge iron ring. Shriek, Finnbogg, and Chang Guafe all bent their massive strengths to opening it, yet it resisted all their efforts while Annabelle stood by, her fists clenching and unclenching.

To Clive's surprise, his brother stood beside her.

"How the hell did you get here so fast?" Clive demanded, embarrassed to admit that in the panic he'd seen to the welfare of his companions first and nearly forgotten his brother.

"Clung to Shriek's underbelly," he said, pleased with himself. Insufferably, thought Clive, strapping his sword around his waist again. "Will your friends be able to open that door in time, do you think?"

Clive shot him a withering look, offended by the very idea that Neville had allowed himself to be carried by a lady, even an alien lady.

Suddenly, there came a loud wrenching of metal as one corner of the huge door tore away from its jamb. Shriek raised up to her full impressive height, gripped the torn corner with her four hands, and braced two of her legs against the wall. Finnbogg gave a powerful leap, caught the top of the tear, and swung his own feet up against the wall above the door. He used his body as a fulcrum, pushing down and out while Shriek pulled down and out. The metal began to rip like paper. Chang Guafe thrust his fingers into a jagged tear that raced clear to the floor. A nerve-grating noise warned of impending success.

"Hurry!" Annabelle screamed, staring back down the corridor.

"Crush us! *Madre!* Crush us!" Tomàs sank to his knees and huddled into himself.

"Care to wager a pay packet on their success, little brother?" Neville whispered with a nonchalance that Clive refused to believe, so he ignored his brother.

With a last grinding squeal the door crumpled.

"Ooops" was the last thing Finnbogg said before he tumbled through the opening into the darkness beyond.

"Finnbogg!" Annabelle screamed, rushing to the edge. Then, she threw up her hands to protect her face, giving another cry of startlement, and nearly lost her balance.

Chang Guafe caught her around the waist and pulled her back from the brink.

Clive hurried to the doorway and stumbled back. "It's like a blast furnace!" he shouted in exasperation. He crept to the edge again, grimacing against the heat. "Finnbogg!" he called. "Finnbogg!"

Blackness and heat were all that filled the doorway, a vast yawning emptiness, frightening in its immensity.

"Sensor confusion," Chang Guafe stated.

"Great," Horace Hamilton Smythe snapped. "Finnbogg's gone, and now he's blind!"

"Not blind," Chang Guafe contradicted. "Unable to determine physical nature of environment which confronts us."

"Oh, pardon me," the quartermaster answered sarcastically.

Clive stared into level seven and beat his fist on the side of the door. "Can we survive in there?" he wondered aloud.

Something settled on his shoulder with feathery softness, and he felt Shriek's mind-touch. *Survival always possible is, Being Clive, especially with leader you.*

"I don't see that we have much choice, Englishman," Sidi Bombay said, coming to the edge.

Horace Hamilton Smythe joined them, shielding his eyes against the heat. "He's right, sah!" He jerked a thumb back over his shoulder. "It's either jump, it is, or get shot out like human cannonballs! The other end's coming fast on us!"

Clive looked back, and his eyes widened. There was no more time to hesitate. "Join hands!" he ordered. "We go, and we all go at once!"

"Well done, little brother!" Neville said, giving a small

round of applause before linking hands with Annabelle and Tomàs. Together, they crept to the brink and collectively drew a deep breath.

"Heigh-ho, Finnbogg!" Neville shouted cheerily, always trying to claim the last word. "Here we come!"

"What a jerk," Annabelle muttered.

Then, they jumped.

## • CHAPTER TWO •

# The Land of Darkness

How long or how far they tumbled Clive couldn't tell. He clung for dearest life to the two hands in his and hoped the others did the same. His eyes were open—at least he thought they were—but there was nothing to see, not even his companions. He listened, but there was nothing to hear. Except for the touch of the hands he held, all his senses failed him.

Suddenly there was solid ground under his feet. He couldn't say that he landed or that he hit bottom. It was just there under him. He didn't collapse from impact. There was no jolt, no shock to his knees or spine. It was as if the ground had been there all the time, and he had only just become aware of it, and considering the loss of his senses, he had to concede that, indeed, was possible.

But his eyes still refused to function. Was he blind? He squeezed the hands he held for reassurance. "Annabelle?" he called softly.

There was a pause before Annabelle returned his squeeze. "I can't see, Clive-o." She tried to sound hopeful, but a note of fear colored her voice.

"Nor I, little brother," Neville added, subdued.

Tomàs muttered under his breath, "*Ai, bento Maria!* Holy Mary!"

Clive tried to remember where the cyborg stood in their line and turned his head that way. Perhaps the cyborg's sensors would prove more reliable than human eyes. "Chang Guafe, can you see anything?"

"Negative, Clive Folliot. Visual-input systems remain inoperative. Running a complete light-spectrum scan."

*Whatever that means,* Clive thought to himself. Sweat began to trickle into his eyes. He tried to blink it back, then shook his head to hurl the droplets away. No use. The salt of his own perspiration stung like fire. He almost let go of Annabelle's hand, but he feared to do that. Until they knew what they were facing, he didn't want anybody to let go of anyone.

"Hold this a moment," he said to Annabelle, and he wrapped her fingers around a piece of his shirttail. Only then did he draw his sleeve across his eyes.

He took her hand again. "Now look, everybody keep hold of everybody," he said. "Don't let go, no matter what. There's got to be something down here, some clue as to which way we should go."

"But how are you going to find it in the dark, little brother?"

Clive almost snarled. He could just imagine the sneer on his twin's face. He could certainly hear it in that disparaging tone.

"I have a suggestion, sah," said Horace Hamilton Smythe, squeezing Clive's other hand.

"Yes, Smythe, speak up." Good old Smythe, he always had an idea.

"Let's lay your brother on his back, sah, give him a good spin, and go in the direction his head points when he stops."

Annabelle chuckled at that.

There was no amusement in Neville's voice, though. "I say, Smythe, you seem to have forgotten your manners, not to mention your proper station. Not good form for one of the queen's career men, I should think."

Annabelle chuckled again. "You've got a lot to learn, chipchewer. Attitudes like yours die hard, but don't make me sorry I hauled your butt out of that coffin thing back up there. Maybe I should have left you for the Lords."

Chang Guafe interrupted what Clive feared would turn into a serious argument. "Targeting," he announced suddenly. "Operational in the infrared spectrum." Twin beams of ruby light lanced outward from the cyborg's optic lenses, extending perhaps four or five feet before diffusing in the darkness. "Now indicating appropriate direction."

A chorus of grateful noises arose in response to Chang Guafe's beams. At least, that meant they weren't blind. One by one, Chang faced them, illuminating each face as he did so. Still, there was only darkness around them. They couldn't even be sure exactly what it was they stood on. The ground was just as black as everything else.

"*Obrigado, obrigado!*" Tomàs muttered, releasing his grip on Shriek long enough to cross himself. "Thank you!"

"Exactly what did you see, Chang?" Clive asked when everyone settled down again.

"A major heat source in the distance," he answered.

Annabelle interrupted. "The cause of all this heat, Tin Man? It's southern California in July down here. I'm melting!"

"Affirmative," he answered. "Also, a smaller heat source in proximity." He trained his eye beams in the proper direction. "Suggest we investigate."

"I agree," Clive said. "Let's not leave something at our backs without knowing what it is. Lead on, Chang Guafe."

"By all means, lead on," Neville chimed in.

They began to walk in a line, holding hands, stepping carefully. Their footsteps made no sound, yet the ground seemed completely solid. It was the eeriest thing Clive had yet encountered, he thought, resisting the desire to hold his hands out in front of him, fearing that any moment he might collide with something or trip on something or fall into something. Those two ruby lances of light were the only thing for the eyes to focus on, and just a bit of Chang's face where the light glinted briefly on the metal.

Clive heard a muttering. At first he thought it must be

Tomàs and more of his ever-running litany, but then he realized it was Annabelle right beside him.

"Lions, and tigers, and bears, oh, my!" she whispered. "Lions, and tigers, and bears . . ."

"What's that?" Clive said, wiggling his fingers among hers, leaning his head a bit closer to where he thought her mouth was.

"Oh, nothing," she said, sounding embarrassed, as if she hadn't realized she had been talking at all. "Just got the willies, that's all. Place gives me the creeps, Clive. It's like walking in space, only there aren't any stars."

He squeezed her hand again, then slid his palm up her arm without breaking contact between them and draped his arm around her shoulders.

"Clive?" she whispered again. "I think the Baalbec could give us a little more light."

"No," he told her firmly. "That's powered off your own body heat. It might drain you too much. We may have to risk it later, but for now we'll just follow Chang's light."

"Yes, Granddaddy," she answered meekly.

"Audio sensors receiving," Chang Guafe reported.

Clive gave a little start. The cyborg's voice just had that effect on him, especially in this infernal darkness. He drew a deep breath and determined to get his nerves under control. "What is it?" he asked. "What do you hear?"

Chang Guafe modulated his voice. "Camptown races five miles long, doodah, doodah!" he sang in a familiar manner.

"Finnbogg!" Smythe and Annabelle cried as one. "That's Finnbogg's voice!"

Indeed, moments later they all could hear the alien canine's crusty intonations roaring up from the gloom ahead, and they all joined in. "Goin' to run all night," they sang heartily with a little more bounce in their steps, "goin' to run all day!"

Only Shriek did not sing, because her vocal apparatus had such limited capability. But her thoughts brushed against Clive's mind. *What noise be this, Being Clive?* she asked curiously, amused. *Happiness, sense I do, and joy. Some ritual chant?*

*Yes, Shriek,* he answered gladly, *a ritual chant for the friend who was lost, then found.*

*Friend?* she inquired. *The Finnbogg being?*

He heard the echo of their song in Shriek's mind as she tried out the melody, struggled to make sense of it, and realized that, in her own way, she had joined in.

Finnbogg's voice stopped suddenly. "Annie!" His shout rose up out of the dark. "Smell Annie! Smell Clive! Smell Horace!" He pronounced it like "horse." He gave a long howl, then paused. "Ugh!" His voice rose again. "Smell Neville!"

"A fine thing," Neville said defensively. "After all, I taught him that song! Picked it up during a trip to America, I did."

For an instant two bright eyes gleamed at them as Chang Guafe's beams reflected on Finnbogg's face. Finnbogg threw up his hands and bounded at them. "Finnbogg friends!" he cried. "Happy reunion!" He rubbed up against Annie's leg and licked Clive's hand. Dropping the link, they clustered around the canine, everybody petting and scratching him at once, and Finnbogg preened in the sudden attention.

"Knew Finnbogg friends come!" Finnbogg said, grinning as he gratefully accepted a scratch on his left ear from Sidi Bombay. "So just sit down and sing Finnbogg! Friends hear and come. You hear Finnbogg sing? Sing good!"

"Sure, sure!" Annabelle assured him, rubbing his throat with long strokes. "Finnbogg hear Finnbogg friends sing back?"

"Ummm. Annie rub good. Annie smell good. Everybody smell good!" Finnbogg gave another long howl, and they all laughed, all but Neville and Tomàs, who stood a little apart.

"*Basta!*" Tomàs said abruptly. "Look there!"

Clive straightened. He could imagine the little Portuguese pointing, but he couldn't see the arm. He turned slowly, scanning the darkness. Far in the distance he spied an orange glow and the barest hint of what he thought were flames. The air, too, had gotten noticeably warmer.

"I've got a bad feeling about this," Annabelle said, coming to his side again.

"Chang Guafe?" Clive said over his shoulder.

"It is the major heat source I reported," the cyborg answered. "Indications are that it has just doubled in size and temperature output."

Clive turned to his brother. It galled him to have to ask Neville for advice. Neville had always lorded it over him, played the superior, and all because he'd been born a few minutes earlier, on one side of midnight, and Clive the other. But now his friends' lives might be at stake, and he swallowed his pride. "Do you know anything about this?" he asked as civilly as possible.

Chang Guafe's eyebeams happened to play over Neville's face. Of course, he wore that sarcastic smile. "No, nothing," he said. "You're now as deep into the Dungeon as I've been, so this is new for all of us, I'm afraid."

Sidi Bombay stepped between them and gave Neville a long, hard look. Then, he turned back to Clive. "Just an impulse, Englishman," he said calmly, "but check his diary. See if there's an entry."

"What diary?" Neville said with feigned exasperation. "All of you keep talking about my diary. I've never kept a diary in my life! And I've certainly been too busy down here just staying alive to start!"

Annabelle took the book from inside her jacket and passed it to Clive. "Sure, chipchewer," she said with a sneer. "Your program need another debugging?" She ran a finger over the Baalbec implants. "You know something about this place, you better upload."

Finnbogg gave a low snarl.

"Am I being threatened?" Neville said, laying a hand to his bosom in an exaggerated display of shock.

"Annabelle," Clive said. "You said the Baalbec could provide a little light. Chang's eyebeams are insufficient for reading."

Annabelle nodded. "Right up, Clive. Boy, I can't believe you came so far to find this piece of scrod!" She touched two of the implants on her forearm. An instant later she began to glow a with soft green light like a human firefly. "It's great for finding keyholes," she added with a grin. "Don't get too close, though, it still packs a zap."

Clive crept to the border of her light, opened the book, and thumbed the pages until he came to the last entry. He hesitated an instant, glanced up at his brother, then read aloud: " 'Out of the frying pan, into the fire; well done, little brother, well done. How will you feel when you meet Hell's Sire? Well done, little brother, well done.' "

" 'E's a bleedin' poet an' claims 'e don't know it!" Smythe said, putting on his best cockney.

"But I never wrote that!" Neville Folliot exclaimed in apparent indignation. "Here, let me see that bloody book!" He snatched it from Clive's hand and turned so Annabelle's light shone on the page. "Why, it's even in my hand! But I swear I never wrote this." He turned back to his brother. "Clive Folliot, you know I never. Why, I'm twice as good at poesy as the author of this bit of doggerel!"

Shriek quietly maneuvered behind the elder Folliot, and Chang Guafe moved to his right. Tomàs and Smythe stood shoulder to shoulder on Neville's left flank, looking like starved men regarding a good steak.

Sidi Bombay spoke up from the sidelines. "Actually, Major Folliot, I believe your brother, Neville."

All eyes turned toward the Indian.

"You do?" said Neville, as surprised as any of them.

Sidi Bombay folded his arms across his chest, closed his eyes, and bobbed his head up and down. He pursed his lips until they became a little brown pucker and touched them with a fingertip. "This book, which we are to assume is the diary of Neville Folliot's journeys, has turned up time and time again in places where your brother should never have been. And please to recall how every time you open it—or on some occasions, it opens itself—there is a new entry, whether or not it has left the possession of this party. Therefore, it is not reasonable to believe it is authentic."

"*Ora Bolas!*" Tomàs snapped.

"What's that?" Horace Hamilton Smythe said, raising an eyebrow.

Tomàs jerked a thumb toward Annabelle. "As she might say, 'shit of bulls'! Is his own writing, no?"

Sidi Bombay opened his eyes. "Handwriting can be duplicated. I believe this has happened. The question now becomes *who*? Who has done this, and to what purpose? Obviously, we are being led."

"Where led?" Finnbogg growled.

Neville pointed toward the fireglow in the distance. "Obviously, there. What else can it mean, 'when you meet Hell's Sire'? An invitation, if ever I heard one."

"And I know how you love parties," Clive responded caustically. "Do you think we should attend this one?"

Neville's saccharine smile returned. "Do we have any choice, little brother? That seems to be the only feature in this otherwise very dreary place. If there's a gate or doorway to the next level or to home, then it's got to be there."

Shriek's thoughts suddenly blossomed in Clive's head. *And if correct is the Bombay being, Being Clive? If led we are by secret Dungeonmasters, might they not also in strangeglowfireplace be?*

*You are right, of course, Shriek,* Clive conceded. Then, he said aloud, knowing Shriek would still understand, "I'm getting a little tired of being manipulated. Let's take it to them for a change."

"*Muito falar e pouca ação,*" Tomàs grumbled.

"Much talk and little action," Annabelle translated, much to the Portuguese's obvious surprise. She gave him a wink. "I'm beginning to crack your program, user."

*Light from the Annabelle being dimming is*, Shriek mind-whispered to Clive. The spider-alien was correct. The halo surrounding his great-great-granddaughter was only half as bright now.

"Annabelle, turn off the Baalbec," Clive instructed. "You're tiring."

"I'm all right, Clive-o," she told him, but she switched off anyway, plunging them into darkness again. "It works off my metabolic body heat, remember? The harder I work, the more heat the Baalbec has available to convert to power. Until I acclimate to this temperature, I can even use it as a siphon to delay the effects of heat stress."

Clive shook his head. "The harder you work, the harder the Baalbec works. It all adds up to a strain on your system, and that means exhaustion. We'll get by without it for now."

They had Chang Guafe's eyebeams to point the way, and the fireglow in the distance was now an easy mark to aim for. Still, Clive insisted they join hands again before they started off.

"You're turning into something of a worrier, Granddad," Annabelle said quietly, her hand in his.

"And you're using that 'granddad' business a bit liberally, aren't you?"

She nodded in Neville's direction. "A lot more aware of family relationships, lately," she confessed. "Before, we were just looking for your brother and a way out of this mess. Now, it seems there's more. Some—dare I say it?" She gave his hand a playful squeeze. "Plot?"

They continued walking. The orange glow slowly stretched out toward them across the vast dark expanse. Plainly now they could see the flames that leaped soaring and crackling into the air, searing white-hot tongues that might have licked the stars had there been any. A hot wind that stank of sulphur blew upon their faces and whipped their garments. It stung the eyes, and the humans in the company began to move in half-crouches, bent over against the scorching bluster. Even Finnbogg cowered down onto all fours. Only Shriek and Chang Guafe appeared unaffected.

Horace Hamilton Smythe stopped abruptly. "Do you hear that?" he asked.

At first, Clive thought it was singing.

"Begging the major's pardon, I don't think so, I don't," Smythe responded. They resumed their march.

It was Clive who stopped next. "What the hell is that?" he said suddenly with uncharacteristic crudeness.

"Just that, little brother," Neville answered quietly. "Hell, just as the book said."

They listened, rooted where they stood, to the terrible din that drifted to them. Lamentations and wails, cries and screams, moans and groans and shrieks: It chilled the blood in Clive's veins. Another groan sounded right beside him, and he nearly jumped out of his skin.

"You're crushing my hand!" Annabelle said, jerking free of his grip.

"Sorry," he apologized. "Guess it all got to me."

"I think it's supposed to get to you," Neville muttered. "Somebody's trying to soften us up."

"Friends of yours, maybe?" Annabelle said.

Neville didn't answer, and they started forward again.

The light from the fireglow was now bright enough for them to see easily. A huge black wall surrounded the fire, extending as far as even Chang Guafe could determine. Straight in their path lay an immense gate with double doors. The doors stood open invitingly, and through them Clive and his friends could see only fire.

As they drew closer, though, it became clearer that a path wound among the flames, a path of black-charred stone around which a pale smoke curled and eddied. Just outside the gate they stopped.

Annabelle looked up and groaned. "Oh, give me a break already!" She pointed overhead to the tall letters carved in the blocks that made the lintel. "Somebody's been working overtime at the scrodding funny farm! Is this supposed to be some kind of joke?" She whirled toward Clive, then

Neville. "I'm getting awfully goddamned tired of being fucked with, Folliot!"

Clive was unprepared for her angry explosion, but before he could say anything Tomàs fell to his knees in a heap. "*Ave Maria, cheia de graça!*" the Portuguese prayed at the top of his blubbering voice as tears streamed down his face. "*Ai, Christo, bendizo Christo!*"

Sidi Bombay ran to the little sailor's side and knelt beside him. Clive, too, went to his aid. "Get up, Tomàs, get up! It's all right. We're still all right!" He tugged on Tomàs's arm to no avail.

"*Analdiçoado!*" Tomàs screamed in terror. "Damned!"

"What a scrodhead!" Annabelle shouted, flinging up her arms. "You can't believe any of this is real. Come on!"

Clive snapped, "Annabelle, shut up!" He glanced at the Indian and whispered, "Sidi, take care of her. She's as hysterical as Tomàs."

Sidi Bombay went to Annabelle and slipped an arm around her shoulder. She shrugged him off angrily and paced off a bit, but at least she quieted.

"Tomàs," Clive continued, laying a hand atop Tomàs's head and gently rumpling his hair. "We must go on. Get hold of yourself!"

Tomàs caught Clive's hands and interlocked his fingers. "*Mi alma!*" he muttered. "My soul!" He let himself be lifted to his feet, but when he looked up, Clive thought he had never seen such pain and fear in a man's gaze before. "I'll stay beside you," Clive assured him, "right beside you."

Tomàs took a faltering step toward the gate, his entire body trembling like a leaf in the worst hurricane.

Suddenly Clive felt Shriek inside his mind. *Noting human reactions am I, Being Clive,* she said. *All right well are you?*

*I'm a man of reason, Shriek,* he answered with all the calm he could muster.

*What, then, writing on gate that upset the Annabelle being is?*

He looked up and translated for the spidery alien: "Abandon Hope All Ye Who Enter."

He glanced around for his brother. Neville stood in the gateway waiting for them, hands braced on his hips, the perfect image of the queen's military man. The fireglow even gleamed on his brass buttons. There was more than a hint of impatience in his stance as he regarded Clive's company.

"Smythe?" Clive called, looking around.

"Here, sah."

"Finnbogg?"

The alien canine turned toward him, tongue lolling. "Okay, Clive, okay, okay."

"Stay close to Annie, then," he instructed. "Keep an eye on her."

"Keep nose on her," Finnbogg assured. "Annie smell good."

He called to the last two, the strangest members of his strange troupe. Chang Guafe and Shriek both nodded and moved in closer on each of the company's flanks.

"Then let's go," Clive said, drawing a deep breath that threatened to sear his lungs. He wrapped an arm tighter about Tomàs, drawing the little man closer. "Let's go together."

# · CHAPTER THREE ·

# Inferno

"Perhaps it's because I lost my turban." Sidi Bombay tried to inject a note of humor as they passed under the foreboding gateway. "God abhors a bare head."

The pathway was a craggy road of broken, blackened rock perhaps ten feet wide. Geysers of flames shot high on either side, spitting and leaping into the air like prominences shot from the sun. The ground itself seemed to burn with a low, blue fire that wavered hypnotically. Only the road offered safety.

Far in the distance Clive noted a feature that he quickly dubbed the Burning Mountains. Beautiful and terrible, they swelled on the far horizon, yellow and orange and red, with peaks so sharp they seemed to spear the darkness. They, too, wavered and danced with heat radiance so they were hard to look at for long.

Sweat ran down his face and neck, down his chest, making his garments sodden. He considered removing his shirt, but the skin of his face felt tight and tender already from the heat, and his hands felt as if they were slowly crisping.

"You don't seem to have much to say, Brother," he said to Neville Folliot, reflecting that his brother looked almost ridiculous in his crisp military uniform with its red coat and shoulder braids and brass buttons. He couldn't have entered the Dungeon in that outfit and must have had it made for him by the servants of the Lords of Thunder.

Neville stared straight ahead. "It is a sight that commands awe," he answered quietly. "If we get back home, little brother, I may amend my ways and return to the bosom of the church."

"Please!" Horace Hamilton Smythe interrupted. "We're going to get thirsty enough as it is. Don't make me waste what little spittle I've got left."

Neville shot the quartermaster a look of surprise, arching an eyebrow. "Smythe!" he said. "I really never knew you disliked me so!"

"Dislike you, sah?" Horace Hamilton Smythe responded with uncharacteristic bluntness. "I don't know you well enough to dislike you, having only met you a couple of times as your brother's batman. But that's enough to disapprove of you. I've been around in the queen's service, sah, and I know your reputation."

Neville Folliot looked at his brother with something of a frown, but he still addressed himself to Smythe. "Well, it's not your place, now is it, to approve or disapprove? After all, I am the Tewkesbury heir, and you? Well . . ." Neville turned up his nose and shrugged his shoulders.

"Let's move on," Clive suggested. "There's no point in lingering here." But Neville's words played over and over again in his mind. It was true, now that he'd found Neville alive, Clive had cut himself out of his inheritance. Neville had always been Father's favorite, while Father had always hated Clive, blaming him for their mother's death because he'd been the last from the womb.

Yet, even as he turned that over in his thoughts, it seemed like such a dreary old song. He just didn't care anymore. Right now he had good friends counting on him to lead them out of this mess, one of them his own great-great-granddaughter. Let Neville keep the money, and damn his father, and that was that.

Suddenly over the rush and crackle of the flames Clive heard another sound and called for a stop. He peered up, but it was hard to see. The brightness of the fires hurt his eyes, though he shielded them as best he could.

"Do you hear that, Chang Guafe?" he asked. The cyborg's sensors were far more acute than Clive's human senses.

"Affirmative," the machine man answered. "Unable to identify. Wait." He craned his neck and looked into the sky. "Something approaches from above."

They appeared right out of the flames, huge leathery batwings beating the heat currents as they soared downward toward the company and began to circle overhead. *Demons* was the only word Clive could find for the horrid monstrosities as he untangled himself from Tomàs and whipped his saber free from the scabbard.

"My God, sah!" Horace Hamilton Smythe exclaimed, taking his place at Clive's right side. His own sword was in his right hand, and in his left he carried the small stasis ray box he'd taken from the servants of the Lords of Thunder.

"Looks like we're in for a bit of a row," Neville said, stepping to Clive's left side. He brandished his own saber and gave Clive a wink.

Clive whispered to Smythe from the corner of his mouth, never taking his eyes off the winged threat above. "Give one of those to someone who doesn't have a weapon," he said. "Personally, I trust your sword arm."

"Sidi?" Smythe said without looking behind him, and he held out the stasis ray to the small Indian.

Above, one of the demons separated from the rest, folded its wings, and dropped feet first to the ground to stand before the company. Though otherwise gross in its monstrous nakedness, a hood covered its head and face.

"Welcome to Pandemonium, Clive Folliot," the creature said as it swept back the concealing garment.

"Philo B. Goode!" Clive stared at the familiar face. Despite the fangs that curled from the corners of its lips and the eyes that were slitted like a cat's, there was no mistaking the visage of the man who had tried to cheat him at cards aboard the *Empress Philippa* during the journey to Africa and whom he had seen on several occasions running loose throughout the Dungeon.

Philo B. Goode threw back his head and laughed a horrible laugh. "Ah, but down here, my good Folliot, I am known as Beelzebub!"

"The Lord of Lies!" Horace Hamilton Smythe interjected. "Hmmmph! It figures!"

Beelzebub looked down on the shorter quartermaster and smiled, showing the full razor-sharpness of his fangs. "Nice to see you, too, Sergeant Smythe. It's been a while since New Orleans, hasn't it?"

"I thought I killed you, then," Smythe said with some bitterness.

Beelzebub's smile widened until the flames reflected on the pearl whiteness of his teeth. "And so you did, and now I'm in hell. And you must join me, too, in spirit as well as in body!"

He threw back his head and gave a shrill scream as he leaped into the air, wings spreading, lifting high even as the other demons folded theirs and plummeted, screaming, down upon the company.

Clive steeled himself and thrust his sword through the chest of the nearest creature before its clawed feet ever touched the ground. Its scream took on a shriller note of terror all its own, and Clive ripped downward through its belly and jerked his blade free. Much to his relief, the creature crumpled at his feet and sprawled upon the road, bleeding a thick, black ichor.

"They can be hurt!" he shouted triumphantly. But Smythe and Neville had already learned that. The others, too, apparently. Behind him, he heard the hum of Sidi's stasis ray and saw one of the demons stop in midreach. To his surprise, it was Tomàs who gave a furious cry, leaped, and kicked the monster across the road and into one of the flaming geysers, where it sputtered and exploded. The little Portuguese stood there for a dangerous moment, shouting invectives in his native tongue.

It nearly cost him his life. A demon dropped out of the sky behind him and raised a clawed hand that might have severed Tomàs's head from his shoulders, but before the creature could strike, two of Shriek's envenomed hair-spikes suddenly sprouted from its back. It gave a hideous cry of pain and tried to reach back to pull the spikes free. It was too late. The venom did its work swiftly. The demon fell to the road, swelling and darkening as it twitched and kicked. Its flesh cracked open, and black blood oozed from its eyes and nostrils and mouth. It died horribly, but quickly.

Clive and Neville and Smythe worked as a front line, their sabers rising and falling, thrusting and cutting as the demons came at them. Overhead, the monster that called itself Beelzebub and looked like Philo B. Goode shouted curses at his minions and at Clive's company while his great beating wings kept him a safe distance away.

A loud zap behind Clive caused him to turn. *Annabelle!* he screamed inwardly, searching for her in the fray, fearing for his offspring. He should have kept a closer eye on her!

He needn't have worried. Many times she had proven herself on this journey. He watched as a demon lunged at her from the sky. She waited, waited, then at the last moment stabbed one of the implants on her forearm, and the Baalbec A-9 snapped on at full strength, stunning the monster. Finnbogg leaped on it, rending it with his own clawed hands and bared fangs. They made quite a team, Annabelle and Finnbogg. So did Tomàs and Sidi, he realized. So did Sergeant Smythe and Neville and himself.

That left Shriek, a deadly force all by herself. She didn't wait for the demons to land, but hurled her hair-spikes into the air by the handfuls, taking a devastating toll, and bodies rained about her.

And Chang Guafe. A mound of demon flesh piled at his feet. He had no weapons but his own armored strength. The creatures came at him, and their claws slid off his steel-sheathed body. He caught them in his hands and twisted their necks, stripped the wings from their backs, crushed their skulls. He moved like a juggernaut, unstoppable, like the golem of ancient Hebrew legend.

As Clive watched his friends, an angry passion surged through him. He felt stronger than he ever had, and more powerful. They had been through too much, suffered and experienced too much. And for this moment, at least, Philo B. Goode had picked the wrong time for a fight. As Annabelle had said, they were tired of being fucked with, whatever that meant.

He shook his saber at the sky. "Come on down here, Goode, or Beelzebub, or whatever you call yourself! Come down!"

The demon commander scowled and raked his claws through empty air. "You have this round, Major Folliot, you and your brother and your friends! But the minions of Hell are numberless, and the way is far to the Palace of the Morning Star! We will meet again!"

Shriek drew back to hurl a hair-spike, but before she could release it, a brown streak hurtled upward through the air, growling. Philo B. Goode gave a startled scream of his own as Finnbogg, at the apex of his leap, clamped powerful jaws shut on his ankle. The scream drew out into a long shrill note as he tried to shake the alien canine, flying high in a loop-the-loop, through a series of sharp twists and turns, and finally through the heart of a geyser of fire.

Finnbogg gave a yelp as they emerged and let go, falling ungracefully right at the edge of the road. Annabelle and Smythe ran to his side, Annabelle throwing her arms around him. "Good Finnbogg!" she cried, stroking him between the ears.

"Heh, heh, heh!" Finbogg answered with a gruff chortle. Then, "Phooey! Fly-thing not taste so good, but make a satisfactory snap, crackle, pop, in mouth!"

High in the air, Beelzebub/Goode glared down at them, cradling his broken foot. "Go, for now!" he raged. "But I have many surprises in store for you. Especially for you!"

He jabbed a long finger at Annabelle and then began to climb higher and higher into the sky until he disappeared from sight.

"And your little dog, too!" Annabelle mumbled as she scratched Finnbogg's right ear and watched Philo B. Goode depart.

"Hell hath no fury . . ." Neville started and left it there. He turned to Clive. "Well, little brother, I'm quite impressed. Quite impressed, indeed. These are some companions. I actually think we may stand a chance of finding our way home with friends such as these!"

"You handled yourself well, Neville," was all Clive said. He turned to see to his friends. All seemed well enough except, to his surprise and consternation, Chang Guafe. The cyborg was not entirely sheathed in metal, and the places where flesh was exposed were scored with seeping wounds.

"No cause for alarm," the cyborg told him as Clive examined his scratches and cuts. Some of them looked deep, and skin hung in ribbons. "Injuries well within design parameters. Damage-control systems functional and operating." Even as the others gathered around to watch, the bleeding stopped and clotted. "Antibiotics flooding system," Chang Guafe reported. "Healing in progress."

Well, that was that. "Let's get on the road, then," Clive said. "I believe I heard Goode say something about a Palace of the Morning Star and not letting us get there. That would seem to be our destination, then. Perhaps we'll find the next gate there."

"I believe you should check on Miss Annabelle, Englishman," Sidi Bombay whispered, leaning close. "She doesn't look well."

Clive felt a moment of terror grip his chest as he pushed through them. Had he missed something? Had Annabelle suffered some secret hurt and kept her mouth shut?

He found her sitting cross-legged on the side of the road with Finnbogg's head in her lap right where he had last seen her. She did look pale and as she would have said, "out of it." He touched her shoulder, then her cheek. Her skin was cool.

"Are you all right, Annabelle?" he asked.

Finnbogg rolled his huge brown eyes upward without lifting his head. "Okay, Annie?" he joined in. "Annie okay? Want Finnbogg to sing?"

Annabelle forced a smile. "That's okay, Finnbogg. I'm fine." She looked at Clive, and the smile faded. "The Baalbec," she said softly. "It took a bit out of me using it that much at that power level. I'll be fine, though. I'm just a little wobbly right now."

Clive helped her to her feet and supported her for a moment. "Finnbogg, will you carry Annie? I don't think it's wise to stop here."

Finnbogg sprang to his feet, then dropped to all fours again, and offered his back. "Happy to carry Annie. Finnbogg strong, and Annie smell nice, like littermates."

"There now, doesn't that make you feel better?" Clive said, helping Annabelle to straddle Finnbogg, making sure she could balance properly. "You smell just like his littermates."

"Want to know what you smell like, Clive-o?" she said with a gleam in her eye.

He turned back to the others and waved an arm. "Chang, can you monitor the sky with your sensors? They may try to attack us that way again."

"I am fully functional," the cyborg answered, "and monitoring."

Clive turned to Tomàs as they began to walk. "You did very well, my friend," he said. "Glad to have you back with us."

The expression the little Portuguese wore was one of near anger. "The *demonios* bled and died!" he answered through clenched teeth. "If this was truly *o inferno* that could not be. Before when I wandered through the Dungeon, I took things as they came to me. But now, I begin to think someone plays a deliberate game." He gave Clive a stare that was almost chilling. "I do not like games,

Englishman, especially when someone plays them with my faith." He looked down and made the sign of the cross, but as part of the last motion he drew a thumb across his throat and once more gave that cold, hard look ahead.

Clive only nodded.

For a while they walked with their weapons ready. Smythe was the first to sheathe his, noting that the grip was almost too hot to hold for long. Clive hadn't noticed during the battle, but Smythe was right. The metal was very warm to the touch. In fact, he was very warm, too. He ran his tongue over his lips. They were parched and dry. *Now, why did you do that?* he asked himself. *All you're going to do is think about how thirsty you are.*

Almost as if to tantalize him, the scenery changed. The huge roaring plumes of fire remained, but the burning ground came to an end, and they stood on the bank of an immense lake of brackish, black water. Its surface rippled and shimmered with firelight, and the water bubbled, frothed, and steamed. The air turned heavy and moist, in some ways a welcome relief from the searing, dry wind and heat they had encountered before.

But the sight of so much water made Clive thirstier. He could see the same thirst in the eyes of his human comrades.

"Will you take water from my mouth?" Chang Guafe asked, coming to his side.

"What?" Clive was uncertain of his meaning.

Chang Guafe said no more but knelt down by the roadside and plunged his head into the boiling lake. Horrified, Clive Folliot dropped down beside him, caught his shoulder, and tried desperately to pull him back up. The cyborg merely shrugged him off, and when he raised up again, his metal plating gleamed clean.

"Chang, are you all . . . !"

Before he could say more the cyborg caught his head in a viselike grip and pressed metal lips to Clive's. Clive resisted for an instant, uncomprehending, until he tasted the liquid that seeped between his lips. It was warm, but it was water!

Nevertheless, he pushed away, flustered, and shot a red-faced look around at the others. Neville's and Smythe's faces registered pure shock and bordered on outrage. Annabelle giggled, and because she did, Finnbogg did also. Only Sidi, Tomàs, and of course Shriek stood by quietly.

"The water can be consumed," Chang Guafe assured him. "I have analyzed its various compounds. The high sulphur content flavors it somewhat, but will not harm."

"That doesn't have anything to do with it!" Clive Folliot shouted. "A man doesn't do that to another man, even if he is some alien cyborg!"

Chang Guafe was unruffled. "Your life-form requires liquid sustenance. However, your flesh cannot tolerate this temperature extreme, and you have no container in which to collect and cool it." He continued with mechanized patience. "I can take and cool it in my mouth and pass it to you in the manner I have demonstrated. There is no other way."

"But, but . . . !" Clive looked to the others for help. He was thirsty as hell, appropriately. But this was an embarrassment, immoral! He wouldn't do it, he wouldn't!

Annabelle slipped off Finnbogg's back, came to Clive, and pushed him out of the way. "Oh, Clive, don't be a scrodhead! It looks kind of fun and kinky to me." She turned to Chang Guafe. "Down on your knees, cowboy. Fill 'er up, and give me everything you've got."

The cyborg's ruby eyes focused on her. "You will take liquid sustenance?"

Annabelle grinned. "I think that's what I said."

He bent down, plunged his head underwater, and surfaced again, then waited a moment while the water cooled in his mouth. He nodded when he was ready.

Annabelle's grin widened as she glanced at Clive. She locked her arms around the cyborg's neck, pulled him close, and set her lips right against his.

"No need to make a spectacle of it!" Clive snapped nervously. "It's broad daylight!" Well, it wasn't really daylight, but it was bright enough.

Annabelle backed away and licked her lips. She winked at Clive and said to Chang Guafe, "I think you enjoyed that, Tin Man!"

"I register alpha waves cerebrally when I serve good friends," the cyborg answered.

"I'll bet you do," Annabelle returned.

Sidi Bombay stepped up next. "I'm only a miserable savage," he said to Clive. "Completely uncivilized by the standards of your empire. What can you expect of me?"

Clive had to turn away from what followed.

Tomàs moved up next, and Clive groaned and closed his eyes. He, at least, had been a sailor. One might expect such behavior from a seaman.

"Begging the major's pardon," Smythe said apologetically, "but I'm just too thirsty to care how I wet my whistle, I am."

Clive grabbed his shoulder. "Not you, too, Horace!"

Horace Hamilton Smythe merely shrugged and stepped closer to Chang Guafe.

Neville Folliot came next. "You do think of me as a black sheep, after all, little brother."

Chang Guafe waited for Clive. "Will you not be reasonable?" the cyborg said. "There is no other way, and my sensors register a dangerous depletion in your bodily reserves."

Clive groaned again and looked at the others. As one, they folded their arms and grinned at him. It was a conspiracy! What was he to do? He bit his lip, trapped, and nodded. But he squeezed his eyes shut when Chang's lips met his, and he tried to think of his mistress, Annabella Leighton, in Plantagenet Court.

"That's it, little brother," Neville snickered. "Close your eyes and think of England."

"Don't worry," his granddaughter said laughingly over his shoulder. "It's just a phase."

A hearty round of laughter greeted him as he stepped away from Chang Guafe. Even Shriek chittered with the rest. Red-faced, he accepted their teasing. The water had refreshed him, he had to admit. When they stopped laughing, he turned back to Chang Guafe.

"We're just good friends," he said firmly. Then, he gave a laugh, too, and clapped the cyborg on the arm. "You must do something about your breath," he whispered just loud enough for the others to hear.

"It's the antibiotics," Chang Guafe told him, and even the cyborg laughed.

The road snaked across the lake, vanishing in the steam and mist that swirled over it. Clive insisted that Annabelle take her place again on Finnbogg's back, and she finally gave in. It wasn't as if Finnbogg minded. He lifted his head and began to sing.

"Oh, you take the high road, and I'll take the low road . . .!"

"Doesn't look much like Scotland to me, little brother," Neville confided.

"Oh, I don't know, guv," Horace Hamilton Smythe said, putting on his best cockney. "There's some good Englishmen what might think of it like that. Not a good pub in the whole bleedin' country, if you ask me, which you didn't."

The mist began to swirl up about their feet, hot and cloying, soaking through their trousers, seeping into their boots. Clive stamped on the ground to make sure it was still solid, that they weren't beginning to wade in muck or water. The road, though, was still the road, hard rock.

As they continued, the road took a sudden right turn, and they followed without a choice. Then, it turned left and doubled back on itself yet again. Suddenly, they came to a fork in the way and stopped.

"Finnbogg got a bad feeling about this!"

They all stared in surprise at the alien canine, and Annabelle gave a little whoop, then covered her mouth, though her eyes still twinkled. She scratched Finnbogg's ears. "I've got a bad feeling about this, too," she admitted.

"You don't think it could be another maze?" Horace

Hamilton Smythe asked, frowning, scratching the stubble on his chin. "Not another one, please."

"If it is," Clive said uncertainly, "at least we've got Neville. Mazes are a specialty of his."

"You've done well enough, yourself, sah, with the mazes we've encountered," Smythe commented.

Neville looked around kind of nervously and pursed his lips. "Are you referring to that hedge maze when we were kids? I've got a confession to make, little brother. I never solved its puzzle. I just crawled between the bushes in a straight line. Knew that would take me out eventually."

Clive's jaw dropped. "You cheated?"

Neville looked indignant. "Well, I wouldn't say it like that! I just played the game by my own rules!"

"We could apply the same rule if this is a maze," Annabelle reminded them. "The Baalbec took us all underwater once before and let us breathe."

"Negative," Chang Guafe said. "The Baalbec can electrolyze water into oxygen and hydrogen, yes, allowing you to walk underwater. It has demonstrated no capacity for ambient heat transference, however. In these waters you would be steamed to death within its field."

"Not a pleasant prospect," said Sidi Bombay.

"Then what?" Clive said in exasperation. "Which way to the Palace of the Morning Star?"

"This way, Clive Folliot."

They turned to stare in startlement down the left fork. A raspy-voiced figure sat cross-legged on the ground, shrouded in the swirling mist, at the center of what appeared to be a narrow crossroad. It was hard to see much about him until they drew closer. He wore an old suit that was mostly tatters and a high, black top hat. His skin was very pale, almost alabaster, and thin as tissue. His hands were mostly bone, the knuckles grossly swollen, and his feet were bare. The red-glowing tip of a stubby cigar flared briefly as he put it to his lips and inhaled. "Got to give these up," he muttered to himself as he stared at the butt with an expression of disgust. He flicked it away, raised his arm toward them, and beckoned with one crooked finger.

Clive stopped and laid one hand on the hilt of his saber as he peered at the figure. "Who are you?" he said in a barely audible whisper. Then he repeated the question.

The figure stared back, still beckoning with that thin, impossibly long finger. "I am called Baron Samedi."

## • CHAPTER FOUR •

# A Guide by the Lake of Fire

"I say, chap," Neville spoke up sharply, "you're a bit out of place, aren't you?" He waved an arm around to indicate the landscape, if it could be called that. "I mean, a god of voudoun in a biblical hell?"

Samedi shrugged, a particularly gruesome gesture as Clive could almost hear the bones rattle inside that dry fleshly casing. "Hey, Jack, it's not my nightmare," came the raspy answer, and the thing smiled a smile that showed the roots of his teeth and colorless, receding gums. "Come." He turned and started along the mist-enshrouded pathway.

But Clive hesitated. "What did you mean, 'a god of voudoun'?" he asked his brother. "Who is he?"

"I spent some time in New Orleans," Neville answered, "and picked up something of the local voudoun practices while I was there. Voodoo, a lot of people call it. Just curiosity, really, and the fact that I met this really lovely girl who turned out to be something of a priestess, a mamaloi, she called herself. Anyway, this Baron Samedi fellow is sort of a spirit of the dead. You can find him at any crossroads, they say." He indicated the narrow paths that snaked off across the water and vanished in four different directions into the fog. "I guess this qualifies."

Sergeant Horace Hamilton Smythe stepped forward. "I spent time in New Orleans, too, sah, and I heard talk about this Baron Samedi, too, I did. Not a very pleasant fellow, the way I heard it. Turns men into zombies, he does."

"Whatever he is," Annabelle said, joining them, "he's a definite bug. He doesn't fit in this program. Somebody's made a mistake."

"But is it a mistake in our favor, beautiful lady?" said Sidi Bombay with a look of cautious doubt.

Ahead, Baron Samedi stopped, turned slowly, and beckoned to them again, crooking his finger and smiling. The tilt of that old black top hat gave him almost a comical look at a distance, when one couldn't quite see the pallor of his skin stretched taut over those cheekbones. "Come," he called.

*Being Clive*. Shriek's thoughts touched his with the gentleness of a single falling snowflake. *Choice is to wander maze pattern without Samedi being and perhaps lost be, or follow it, we. Destination it must have specific.*

Chang Guafe spoke up then. "I hear and agree with Shriek," he said. "If it will help you to decide, Clive Folliot, then my sensors reveal it is no spirit which confronts us. This ragged creature maintains a near-human heartbeat and radiates a body temperature of one hundred and five degrees. That is higher than human-normal, but no doubt allows it to function more comfortably in this heat extreme. I can probe deeper. . . ."

"No need," Clive said, holding up a hand. "I am convinced. As Shriek said, we really don't have much of a choice. But stay close together, and be ready for anything."

"Sound advice, little brother," Neville Folliot approved.

They followed the shambling figure of Baron Samedi through the thin mist. The path turned rockier. On either side now new pathways began to branch off, some wider, smoother, more inviting, but Samedi moved with surety, choosing the course without hesitation.

The path began to narrow and slope at odd angles. This mist made the black rock slick in places, and footing became uncertain. They were forced to walk single file.

On either side of the crazy, twisting road the bubbling black lake water lapped against the stone.

Clive's khakis clung to him, sodden with sweat and the dampness of the mist. At last, he cast propriety to the winds and dared to unbutton his shirt as low as his waistband. He might have removed it entirely, but that would have been stretching decency's boundaries too far with Annabelle and Shriek right behind him.

Out on the lake, a geyser of fire exploded upward from the surface. A blast of heat rolled across them, and the sudden flare of brightness caused Tomàs to cry out in astonishment and Neville to throw an arm across his eyes. The mist swirled in agitation, and the water lapped over their feet.

Barefooted, Sidi Bombay gave a shout of fear, but before the liquid could scald him Chang Guafe picked him up bodily under the arms and held him dangling in the air. The temperature of the water didn't seem to bother Shriek, whose four feet were also bare. Nor Finnbogg, who stood on somewhat higher ground.

"My thanks and gratitude, noble alien," said Sidi Bombay when the waves subsided and the geyser had disappeared. Chang Guafe merely nodded and set him down again.

"Come." Baron Samedi stood safely on a rock ahead of them, beckoning.

"Somewhat of a limited vocabulary, that chap," Neville muttered to his brother as they started up again. "Don't care much for his tailor, either."

The pathway took a sharp upward slant, and some of them had to help the others. For a change, it was particularly Chang Guafe who needed help. His metal-shod feet slipped and scraped on the damp stone, which had become obsidian-smooth, and more than once he fell to his knees. Clive discovered, to his surprise, what an expression of frustration looked like on a metal face. It might have been amusing had the situation not been so grim.

"Look here, isn't there an easier way?" Neville Folliot called ahead.

Samedi turned with a wide grin on his ashen face. "An easy road through hell? What a novel idea."

It was such a perfect imitation of his brother's voice and tone that Clive Folliot had to cover his mouth with a hand to keep from chortling.

"Well," said Annabelle with more than a trace of sarcasm, "his vocabulary is improving."

"If not his manner," Neville answered indignantly.

More geysers of flame erupted on their left and right, but now the path was too high above the lake to be flooded by the resulting waves. Hot winds whipped at them and tore at their clothes, and in the strange, wild flickerings they looked an odd company, indeed.

At the peak of their climb, Samedi stopped and reached into the pocket of his baggy old suit. His fingers unfolded to reveal a large lump of dirty wax. "Now, dudes, get this. You wear this stuff in your ears, see. We comin' up on the Lake of Lamentations, and you don't even want to hear that soulful sound, or the blues might hit you so bad you'd do somethin' real dumb, like throw yourselves into the water or somethin', dig it?"

Clive looked around, funny-faced. "What'd he say?"

"I say, that's very classical." Neville reached out to take his portion of the wax and began making small balls of it. "I guess that makes me Ulysses, braving dangers, trying to find the way home."

"So pass the wax, hero," Annabelle snapped. "You're not the only one on this ship, you know."

Clive ignored them both as he accepted his share. "The Lake of Lamentations?" he said to Samedi. He tried to remember his Bible verses, though he'd never paid much attention to that sort of thing. "You mean the Lake of Fire?"

Samedi made a sweeping gesture. "This all the Lake of Fire, brother!" He slapped his thigh. "But part is also the Lake of Lamentations. Don' pay no attention to what you see out there, either, and jus' tune your ears out completely. An' lemme tell you this, too, you step off that pathway an' you gonna be a sorry sucker! It ain't far where we're goin' when we get to the other side."

Clive immediately thought of Chang Guafe. "You don't have ears for the wax," he said.

"I will deactivate audio sensors," he answered. "I will not be in danger."

"Shriek, what about you?"

*Hear, I do not as human beings think of it. Vibrations feel I on spike-hairs. Wax, nothing can help. Fine, will I be, though.*

Baron Samedi beckoned and turned away to lead.

"Not yet!" Clive called. Samedi halted and regarded him patiently.

Clive turned back to Shriek. "Samedi says we mustn't step off the path, so I'd like us all responsible for each of us. The strong support the weak, and the entire group supports the strong, and all that. Can you web us together?"

Horace Hamilton Smythe clapped him on the shoulder. "Good idea, sah! A lifeline!"

*Slender thread spin I,* Shriek answered, *strong enough all to help.*

"Then do it now," Clive suggested.

But Neville protested. "Now wait a minute, I . . ."

Annabelle seemed to have appointed herself to keep Neville humble. "Oh, shut up, Neville," she said caustically. "Even Ulysses allowed himself to be bound."

Shriek moved carefully among them on the narrow path, circling each of them once, spinning a graceful strand around each waist. At first, the filament was sticky and wet, but in the hot wind it quickly dried, becoming a fine, strong line. Lastly, she approached Baron Samedi, who held up a hand and shook his head.

With deft agility and speed, she ensnared him before he could protest further. *Go down we, go down Samedi being,* she said.

"Looks like you done made Death your prisoner," Baron

Samedi rasped with some amusement, plucking the line with one finger as if it were a harp string.

"Turnabout's fair play, I say," Horace Hamilton Smythe muttered under his breath just behind Clive.

The road began to descend again, turning downward toward the lake's surface. The rock, so smooth on the way up, was cracked and battered now, providing surer footing.

Clive glanced at the small balls of wax on his palm and listened as the road descended almost to the level of the lake. If a geyser erupted, they would certainly all have scalded feet, he realized. He looked at the balls of wax again. The others had put theirs in their ears already.

A sound shivered on the misty air, a high plaintive cry, very distant. Still, it cut through him like a rusty sawblade. Another followed it. He remembered the screaming they had heard outside the Dantean Gate, as he had come to think of it, the shrill cries that had so terrified the company. They, at last, had faded, and he had almost forgotten them.

These were worse by far. They abraded the very edges of his soul! What creatures could know such torment? A sudden shriek tore at his nerves. He jumped, and before he could stop himself, he dropped one of the precious earplugs. It bounced on the rocky path and plopped into the water. He stared at the ripples, but the line compelled him onward.

"Horace!" he called over his shoulder. But there was no answer from Horace Hamilton Smythe, who had already stopped his ears.

*Calm, Being Clive!* Shriek's thoughts blossomed in his mind, soothing. *What remains, divide. Enough it may be.*

She was right, of course. There was nothing else he could do. Quickly, he tore the wax in half and made new balls. They looked so small, and his hands trembled as he rolled them. Another shriek sounded as if it came from right beside him, and he jumped again, but this time he closed his fist tight and the plugs did not get away. As fast as he could, he pushed them inside his ears.

He could still hear, he discovered, but at least the cries were muffled.

Something splashed out on the lake's surface. He caught the motion in the corner of his eye and stared. A hand! It was a hand that thrashed the water! And a head! A face broke the surface. A mouth opened in an almost soundless scream before the apparition went under again.

He knew that face!

"Du Maurier!" he shouted, terror roiling in his breast. "George, my God!"

But the line compelled him onward. He stared over his shoulder where his old friend thrashed and drowned without help or hope.

He didn't believe it, he told himself. He just bloody well didn't believe it! Somebody was playing tricks with them. George du Maurier was home in his London flat, sipping tea over his philosophy books and newspapers. That couldn't have been George!

Another motion caught his attention. A body bobbed up right beside the path at his feet. He glared at the bearded face as it opened its mouth and screamed. That terrible sound knifed even through the earwax. Weakly, as if the spirit were draining from him, Clive stumbled to one knee, and for an instant he came face-to-face with Maurice Carstairs, his former patron at *The London Illustrated Recorder and Dispatch,* the man who had funded the first leg of his journey to Africa.

But the line compelled him on.

He glanced over his shoulder, turning to his good friend Horace Hamilton Smythe for help, but Smythe only stared out over the water, tears streaming down his face as some great emotion wracked him. He wrung his hands around and around the line that bound him as if a part of him sought escape. Still, the sergeant walked on and left behind whatever part of his soul the lake called to.

Clive turned his gaze forward and tried to focus his attention on Samedi's top hat. *Don't look anywhere else,* he told himself. *It's all a trick, it's not real!*

There was a powerful tug on the line and a sudden splash. He felt himself pulled toward the lake and balanced precipitously on one leg until he braced himself. One toe slid into the water, and only his boot saved him from a burn as the water bubbled up. Still, the line shivered and vibrated and snapped taut around his waist.

"Finnbogg littermate!" The alien canine's roar cut plainly through the wax. "Stop! Finnbogg littermate! Need Finnbogg!"

His plaintive howl hurt Clive more than he knew he could be hurt, and the desperate sight of Chang Guafe and Shriek dragging Finnbogg back onto the rocky path moved him to pity and to anger. No one had the right to do this, no one!

He glanced at Annabelle before he turned around again. There was fear in her eyes, concern and puzzlement. He wondered what horrors she might be experiencing. But she was behind Horace and behind Neville, and he couldn't get to her, couldn't put a comforting arm around her.

On his right a geyser of fire shot into the sky, a tube of flame, carrying upward with it thousands of naked souls that writhed and squirmed over each other like snakes in a pit.

Dear God! He saw *her* there, screaming and crying, anguished tears streaming down her beautiful face as she clawed and scratched and dragged herself over and under the others, as they pressed and smothered and squirmed over her. As he watched, the fire caught in her lovely hair, setting her head ablaze. Her skin began to melt and burn, and her eyes exploded in their sockets. Flesh blackened, exposing bone, which blackened. Still, she churned and struggled with the rest, knowing no respite, no release.

"Annabella!" Clive choked. He had known she would come. The pattern of the lake was plain enough to see. It preyed upon the memories of their friends and loved ones. From the first instant he'd realized that, he'd prepared himself for this moment. Annabella Leighton was safe and sound back in Plantagenet Court, teaching literature to high-born young girls, eating crumpets, and waiting for his return. That thing in the flame, whatever it was, was not his sweet Annabella Leighton. Still, he choked again and muttered, "Annabella!"

*Being Clive?*" Shriek's mind-voice interrupted his grief. *Finnbogg being badly burned is. Jumped in hot lake did. Need treatment. Need help. Swiftly go must we to other side.*

Clive did his best to snap out of it. Finnbogg was hurt. He had to concentrate on that. All of his friends were in danger if they lingered out here. He tore his gaze away from the geyser and clenched his fists.

*Tell everybody, Shriek,* he said suddenly, *tell them to run. Tell them to hold on to the line and don't think of anything else except running.*

*Slippery wet road is. Treacherous could be.*

*The greater danger is out here,* he snapped. *Tell them!*

He stared at the back of the figure before him. Baron Samedi kept up his relentless shambling pace, eyeing the ground before him as he walked without looking back.

"Samedi, you old bag of bones!" he shouted as the others began to pile into him. "Get dragged or get carried if you can't make better time than that. We're coming through!"

Samedi cast a look of amusement over his thin, black-suited shoulder, then of utter surprise as Clive scooped him up. "You tell us the way, and it better be the right way, too, or I'll drop you in the lake and hold you under, myself," he muttered to the frail, nearly weightless creature.

"Mammy, how I love ya!" Samedi grinned, folding his arms as the tatters of his suit flapped around Clive. "Go right, young man! Does you like Cajun food?"

They wound their way through a series of narrow pathways, the water lapping at their heels, running as swiftly as they dared. Geysers erupted on every side, filled with images, and bodies bobbed and floated to the surface near their feet. Things thrashed and splashed and screamed and called to them, but the company ran on, each man pulled by the next, and Clive leading them all as fast as he dared.

Samedi kept up an endless stream of meaningless chatter, but the only words Clive listened for were *right* or *left*.

Sooner than he expected they reached the far shore. Clive set Samedi down and sank to his knees, breathless. Except for Chang Guafe and Shriek, the others did the same. The sounds of panting made Clive look up. Finnbogg sprawled with his head in Annabelle's lap, tongue lolling.

"I thought you said he was hurt?" Clive said to Shriek.

*Clive being something needed did to focus energies.* There was laughter in her thoughts, but also apology and desire for forgiveness. *Concern for friend beings stronger than griefselfpity.* She hesitated, and he felt her searching her mind for the right words. *Lied, I,* she added finally.

Clive flopped on his back and laughed, and the sound rapidly spread to the others, who did the same. Shriek, too, chittered, and Chang Guafe made that weird mechanical sound that passed for laughter. Finnbogg set up a howl.

Baron Samedi looked down at them. "Come," he said, crooking a bony finger.

They got to their feet and followed their strange guide, still chortling and snickering. It was relief, of course, from the terrors they'd just experienced, and welcome, good-sounding relief it was, too.

The screaming and wailing had stopped as soon as they reached the shore. At Samedi's instruction they removed the earplugs. Clive cast his into the lake with a lazy sidearm motion and listened for the slight *plop* that never came. He scratched his chin about that. One more small, inexplicable oddity, barely worth noting in this Dungeon.

They walked now mostly in silence. Only a thin mist lingered on the land, which took on a radical change as they journeyed. Gone were the flames and the hot winds and the bubbling waters. A featureless black landscape confronted them now, not unlike the land they had found surrounding Q'oorna on the first level when they first arrived in the Dungeon.

Gone, also, was the light provided by the flames. A gray, misty twilight hung over everything, bright enough to see by, but depressing to the spirit.

The road led now toward a range of low mountains. Clive looked over his shoulder, remembering the beautiful Burning Mountains he had named at the Dantean Gate. He couldn't see them now, though he didn't understand how that could be. He only shrugged. Things changed down here too quickly.

At the first of the foothills, Samedi led them to a huge cave just off the roadside. "Come," he said, beckoning. Clive was just too tired to be distrustful anymore. He went without questioning.

"Food!" Neville cried.

"Smell food!" shouted Finnbogg.

Deep in the cave, a fire burned in a hearthplace, flooding a large central gallery with warm light. Before it, a lavish spread had been prepared and placed on a long wooden table. Candles burned in brass sticks, and soft, comfortable chairs ringed the table.

"Get us out of this rope!" Tomàs shouted, tugging at the strand around his waist. "*Pressa*, I can't break it!"

Clive couldn't break it, either. "Shriek, can you help?"

The arachnoid plucked one of her hair-spikes and scuttled to each of them in turn. The spike gleamed wetly with an odorless chemical that swiftly dissolved the line, freeing them.

They swarmed around the table. In no time at all every last morsel was devoured, every crumb eaten.

Clive carried a glass of wine to Samedi where their host stood leaning by the fireplace watching the feast. He hadn't eaten a bite, himself, but he accepted the wine and tossed it back.

"Our thanks, Baron," Clive Folliot said gracefully.

"Lemme tell you somethin', Jack," Samedi said with a leer toward Clive. "I get tired of all this 'come' shit, you know? I mean, lookit these threads, man! How you like to have to go aroun' in public in somethin' like this? Shit! But like, it's my job, you know. It's why I was put here. Don' mean I'm not a nice guy inside!"

Clive shrugged, confused. He wasn't sure he'd understood half of what his host had just said. He thought for a moment and scratched the growing stubble on his chin. "I like you," he answered finally.

"That's very white of you, Jack." Samedi turned the wine glass upside down on the mantel. "Now you better get yourself some sleep, 'cause tomorrow we got to make the Palace of the Morning Star. Big Dude hisself's waitin' on you."

Clive almost hated to ask. "Are there beds?"

Baron Samedi rolled his huge eyes and crooked a finger. "Come," he said.

## • CHAPTER FIVE •

# The Cave of Quiet Fears

Clive knew by now that Shriek didn't sleep; at least, not in any way that humans thought of it, and he felt perfectly safe knowing she stood guard while the rest of them caught a few winks. Nor had he missed the fact that she had set aside a few choice pieces of meat from the table to consume once she was alone, for she refused to eat in the presence of the others. All in all, she appeared as pleased to see them off to bed as they were to go.

Bearing a brand from the fireplace, Samedi led the way deeper into the cave. Numerous smaller galleries branched off from the main passage, and in each they found small pallets made from piles of thick, warm blankets. Beside each pallet stood a candlestick like the ones on the table. Samedi lit each candle with his brand as, one by one, the members of the company said good-night to each other.

Clive took the last gallery. So far into the cave, the air was still and close, but his belly was full and the pallet softer than he had imagined. He slipped off his boots and wiggled his toes, then wrinkled his nose at the smell. His feet had gotten wet inside the leather and needed a good airing.

He turned to say good-night to Samedi, but his host had already departed. Clive shrugged and stretched out for the night. He considered extinguishing his candle, then thought better of it. The tiny light it shed would hardly be enough to prevent his sleeping. He slipped off his khaki shirt and laid it aside. Then, folding one arm under his head, he closed his eyes.

Yet, as he lay there in the silence, it began to disconcert him how each of his friends had been separated from the others. Any of the galleries, though small, would have slept two or even three. He sat up suddenly, chewing his lip, his gaze searching the darkest corners of his chamber where the small flame did not penetrate.

At last, unable to stop himself, he slipped his shirt back on, picked up the candle, and padded barefoot back along the way they had come.

He found Finnbogg curled up around his lone candle, the blankets of his pallet rumpled and tossed into a designless mess that supported head and hips and little else. The canine creature yawned broadly and peeped out from under one droopy lid.

Clive shielded his flame and passed on.

Neville slept in the next gallery. His brother had peeled off his uniform and laid it in meticulous order on one of the blankets, which he apparently had spread upon the ground for the purpose. He lay naked with one blanket modestly across his middle, asleep as soundly as if it were his own bed in London he occupied. His thick blond hair made a mop around his face, and despite his size and musculature he looked ever so much the little boy.

Briefly, Clive felt a tinge of regret and frustration that he and Neville had never been close, never brothers in the fullest sense. But he still tasted the anger, too, and the bitterness. Neville had never made the least effort to close the gap between them, never done anything but ignore him while he lavished in the gifts and the favoritism their father showered on his so-called "firstborn."

A spot of hot wax dripped on Clive's hand, making him jump and curse silently. It was his own fault, he told himself, for letting his feelings run away with him and for clenching the candlestick too tightly in a fist that he'd much rather have used to give his brother the drubbing he so deserved. But that would have to wait until another time when they were all in much less of a fix. He gave Neville a last disapproving glance, then moved on.

One by one he checked his charges, for so he had come to think of them. Tomàs was curled fetally around his candle in much the same manner as Finnbogg. Sidi lay corpselike, stiff and straight with hands folded upon his chest, in what Clive guessed was one of the Indian's strange yoga trances. Annabelle tossed and turned restlessly on her pallet, but she didn't open her eyes when he lingered, so he passed on to the next gallery. Even his old friend Horace Hamilton Smythe, whom he might have expected to maintain an informal watch on his own, had surrendered to Morpheus' embrace.

Chang Guafe, though, was still awake.

"Can't sleep?" Clive asked from the gallery's narrow entrance. "Or don't you sleep, either?"

Chang Guafe stared at Clive for a moment, then turned his gaze on his own metal form. "My body does not require rest," he said with surprising softness in his mechanical voice. "However, my organic brain does. It eludes me, though, as you surmise."

Clive took that as an invitation to enter, reflecting on the incongruous sight that confronted him. The powerful cyborg had pulled his pallet next to the cave wall. He sat with his back against it, his legs sprawled open before him, arms at his side, looking much like a doll some child had placed there and abandoned.

"Ah, I know the feeling," Clive assured him. "Seems the more you need sleep sometimes, the harder it is to find. But can't you put yourself to sleep? With drugs, I mean?" Clive hesitated when Chang Guafe only stared back. "I mean, you had medicines inside yourself that healed your cuts and injuries. Is there nothing to help you sleep?"

It was Chang Guafe's turn to hesitate. He turned his head from side to side, and candlelight played eerily on his peculiar features. "I do not wish to," he answered finally. Then he reverted to his usual cold voice and added, "Alertness is a priority, observation an imperative."

But Clive wasn't fooled a bit. In fact, he was suddenly touched. Of all his strange new friends it was Chang Guafe who most unsettled him. Yet, now he found himself reaching out, laying a hand on the cyborg's shoulder. "Chang," he said, unable to keep the surprise from his tone, "are you afraid of the dark?"

"Negative!" the cyborg answered, then softening again, "And affirmative. Almost nothing can hurt this form," he said, rapping his metal knuckles on a metal thigh. "My sensors know this. The computer elements of my brain know this." He looked directly at Clive, his ruby eyes seeming somehow more human. "But there is still the organic brain, and deep inside it where the computer and the drugs do not reach, there lurk all the old archetypes and racial memories, the primitive fears and dreads that all beings know." He turned away and stared into the candlelight. The tiny flame reflected in his lenses. "Yes, Clive Folliot, in quiet moments such as this, even a Tin Man may know fear."

Clive thought for a long moment, silently recalling all the terrors he'd encountered in the Dungeon, able to face them with a sense of detachment because they were behind him. Then, he looked ahead and dared to wonder what still awaited them, and he bit his lip.

At last, he sighed and sat down beside Chang Guafe and leaned his back against the wall. "Well, I can't sleep, either," he said, setting his candle on the ground beside the cyborg's candle. "So we'll just bloody well look out for each other—how about that? Give me a blanket, will you?"

Two pairs of eyes met and looked away as the blanket changed hands, and two heads leaned back as one against the stone. Wordlessly, they waited for dawn, or whatever in hell passed for dawn.

\*　　\*　　\*

Clive did sleep, however, and woke with a start, chiding himself for doing so. He glanced over at Chang Guafe. The cyborg, too, had fallen asleep, braced against the wall, his head lolled to the side. There was no gleam at all behind the ruby lenses.

Clive rose as quietly as he could and stretched. The sitting position in which he'd slept had left him stiff in the lower back. He rubbed his neck, picked up the stub that remained of his candle, and slipped into the cave passage.

Returning to his own gallery, he couldn't resist checking once more on his sleeping friends. When he reached Annabelle's gallery, however, his faint light shone on an empty pallet.

Clive chewed his lip thoughtfully, then returned to his own sleeping place to recover his boots. They had dried quickly in the warm air, and he pulled them on, buttoned his shirt, and tucked it into his trousers. Then, light in hand, he headed back to the cave's huge main chamber.

Up ahead, the remains of the hearthfire cast a soft red radiance. Hoping to find Annabelle there, he increased his pace. His candle flickered out suddenly as the wind slipped between his fingers, but he didn't need it now. He focused on the glow.

Something brushed his ankle, and a huge, dark shadow suddenly blocked his way. Clive's heart skipped a beat. His hand lunged for the hilt of his saber and tugged the blade half-free as he leaped back.

*Being Clive.*

Clive let go a sigh of relief and let the saber fall back into the scabbard. He should have recognized the silhouette before him. He squeezed his eyes shut for a moment and rubbed his temples.

"My apologies, Shriek," he said wearily. "Guess I'm a bit on edge."

*Apologies mine for startlement,* she offered. *Nervous, too, am I. See? Trigger-web everywhere. On watch, am I. Anyone moves, informed am I.*

Clive glanced down. Stretched across the passage between the galleries and the main chamber was a narrow, glistening strand. It was that his ankle had brushed. Similar strands, he noticed, were strung at various points, and all of them were ultimately attached to one of Shriek's legs. If anything touched the strands, the vibrations alerted her at once.

"Have you seen Annabelle?" he asked, concerned.

Shriek repaired the damage he had done to the trip-web and scuttled back to the hearthfire. In the light of the embers her six eyes glittered like strange jewels. *Annabelle being outside has gone*, she answered.

"What?" Clive's hands curled into fists, and he beat his thighs. "You didn't stop her?"

No words, but genuine surprise blossomed in his thoughts as Shriek considered the very novelty of the idea of one intelligent being attempting to regulate the nonviolent actions of another. *Egg-new is Annabelle being?* Shriek asked abruptly, grasping for understanding. *Youngling is?*

Clive growled in frustration and headed for the cave entrance. Despite his irritation, he stepped carefully, avoiding the trigger-webs. No reason to destroy Shriek's work, he told himself. It was his fault. Sometimes he forgot he was dealing with an alien.

He moved up the short passageway to the outside. Even there Shriek had placed a pair of webs, one at ankle and one at chest height. He couldn't fault her diligence.

A blast of warm air greeted him as he emerged. His sleeves made a crisp snapping sound, and his blond hair whipped back. In the stillness of Samedi's cave he'd forgotten the strength of the wind outside.

He looked up and down the path for Annabelle, but there was no sign of her. He braced his hands on his hips for an instant and cursed. What did she think she was doing, separating from the group like this? At last, reasoning that she wouldn't have gone back down the way they had come, he started up the path.

Higher and higher the road went, and steeper, too, as it wound among the mountain foothills.

He heard her before he saw her. Her voice rang down to him, clear and poignantly sweet, and he stopped.

> *Oh, Fortune's Child, where are you now?*
> *Oh, Fortune's Child, where are you now?*
> *I'd cry for you, but I don't know how,*
> *Oh, Fortune's Child.*
>
> *Unfortunate Child, I'm gone away,*
> *Gone to hell, like momma used to say,*
> *Gotta make it on your own, the price you pay,*
> *Child of an Unfortunate Child,*
> *But I think about you every day,*
> *And try to cry, Unfortunate Child.*

Clive found her sitting on a small black boulder, her knees drawn up to her chest with her arms locked around them. She rocked herself as she sang with her eyes closed, and the wind stirred her short dark hair. He knew in her own time in her own world she had been a musician, but he'd never heard her sing, never heard her talk about her music at all. He couldn't bring himself to interrupt her, and his chest tightened as he listened.

> *Oh, Fortune's Child, where are you now?*
> *I'd cry for you, but I don't know how,*
> *Oh, Fortune's Child . . .*

She opened her eyes suddenly as if she had somehow sensed him standing there. For an instant, fear reflected in her gaze, but as recognition came, that softened, and Clive saw such pain in those eyes as made him sit down beside her and gather her in his arms.

She didn't cry, just rested her head in the hollow of his shoulder and sighed, her arms hanging limply, her legs slowly straightening and sliding down the sides of the boulder, letting him take all her weight.

Clive held her and stroked her hair, and neither of

them spoke. Dimly, he recalled how she had stirred his senses before he realized their relationship. But she was his great-great-granddaughter, and suddenly that meant more to him than anything else in the world. He missed his own beloved Annabella Leighton painfully, and he might never make it back to her side again. But their love, at least, had produced this wonderful child in his arms, and he would protect her, protect her with all his being.

"Sorry," she said after a while, straightening. "Guess I was feeling sorry for myself."

Clive was reluctant to let her go. "You sing beautifully," he said with gentleness. "Was that about you?"

She shook her head, slid off the boulder, and leaned against it, instead, as she stared outward. "For Amanda," she answered. "I couldn't sleep for thinking of her." She hesitated and swallowed. "I miss my daughter."

And he missed Annabella. He hadn't really allowed himself to think about it, but he missed her terribly. What must she think of him? All this time gone, and no word from him. And why hadn't she told him about the pregnancy before he'd left for Africa?

He hung his head. If what his granddaughter told him was true, then he would never see his Annabella again. She would bear his child and raise it alone in poverty, never marrying, embittered and solitary, probably cursing his name.

How could he bear it? How could he ever respect himself again?

"There's almost a kind of beauty to it," Annabelle said suddenly, gesturing toward the vista that spread before them. "You have to open yourself to it, but it's there."

They were high on the side of a hill. A perpetual twilight hung over the land, but still they could see a vast panorama. A featureless, gray ashen plain lay below them, marked only by the occasional rock or boulder. Beyond that, the Lake of Fire glittered blackly, threads of mist drifting upon its surface like ghostly snakes. Flaming spumes shot up through the water here and there, casting red ripples that whipped and lashed the maze of narrow road-ways, causeways really, that stretched from shore to shore.

Farther away, an orange glow lit the horizon, a dancing shimmer of heat and fire that marked the edge of the world on this seventh level. Like the sun at dawn, just as it peeked over the rim of the earth, it held the eye.

There *was* a kind of beauty to it, a terrible beauty that struck like an iron nail to his heart.

"Let's go back," he said, reaching for Annabelle's hand.

But she continued to stare outward. "That must be the Lake of Lamentations," she continued, pointing to a narrow inlet nearest them where the road met the shoreline. She glanced at him, then looked quickly away. "What did you see down there?"

He folded his arms as a lump formed in his throat and recalled that vision of Annabella lost in the fire with a squirming mass of souls, burning and rejuvenating, burning again as she screamed for him. It wasn't real, he reminded himself. Annabella Leighton was safe in London in her Plantagenet Court flat, probably reading to herself and worrying what had become of Clive Folliot. Or maybe by now she was cursing that name.

"Memories," he answered in a subdued voice. "Old friends."

"Old loves?" she prodded. "Did you love her, Clive? It's not my place to ask that, maybe, but it would matter to me to know."

"With all my heart," he admitted. "I wanted to marry her."

"Then why didn't you?"

Despite himself, he smiled at her directness. "Things must be so simple in nineteen ninety-nine," he said, laughing. "But in my time there is such a thing as propriety and responsibility. A man did not marry until he could afford to do so, and the salary for a major in the Fifth Imperial Horse Guards Regiment barely kept my horse fed and my brass buttons polished."

"But you did love her?" Annabelle Leigh persisted.

Clive looked her straight in the eye and answered with all seriousness. "I *do* love her. Present tense, for me, anyway."

She smiled and took his hand. "Let's go back, Clive Folliot." Then she added with a wink, "Granddaddy."

The smell of good English tea greeted them as they entered the cave again. Clive could hardly believe his nose. He forgot about Shriek's trip-webs as he rushed inside and nearly collided with the arachnoid as she jumped to investigate.

"Sorry, Shriek," he said, pushing past her, "but I thought I smelled . . ."

"Yes, it's tea, little brother!" Neville called, rising, cup in hand. "It seems even hell has a few amenities to offer."

The buttons of Neville's uniform gleamed in the light from the fire that their host had rebuilt in the hearth. For the first time Clive noticed it was all coal or some similar substance, not wood, that burned there. He usually prided himself on his observation of detail, and he took it as a sign of his fatigue that he had overlooked it. He should have slept longer.

But the tea refreshed him immensely, and Horace Hamilton Smythe poured a second measure of the precious beverage into the delicate china cups that looked so out of place on a rough wooden table in a deep dark cave in the depths of someplace someone wanted them to think of as hell.

"Almost like being home again, isn't it, sah?" Smythe said, setting the pot back on the table.

"I don't think I'd go quite that far, Horace," Clive said. "But it's certainly very welcome, isn't it, Annabelle?"

She looked into her cup and frowned. "Personally, Clive-o, I'd give anything for a Coke."

Granddaughter or not, Clive had long since given up trying to figure out everything Annabelle said. He shrugged and took another delicious sip and turned to Samedi, who stood by the hearth apart from the others.

"However did you manage to come by this here?" he

asked without setting his cup down. "Orange pekoe, I believe."

"Hey, Jack," Samedi answered with a snap of his sticklike fingers, "whatchoo need, baby, I got."

Clive took a second to figure that out. Samedi's speech was as odd to him as Annabelle's. Of course, why shouldn't it be? This was the Dungeon. "But *where* did you get it?" he persisted.

Samedi rolled his eyes and put on that big toothy grin that showed all his gums. "Friends in high places, baby, an' I done said too much. Ask me somethin' I can say straight."

But Clive wasn't ready to give up so easily. "What do you mean, 'friends in high places'? What friends? Did they provide the food last night, too?"

Samedi set his arms akimbo, leaned forward, and tapped his foot busily on the cave floor. "Look, man. What is it, rubber-hose time or somethin'? You itchin' or jus' bitchin'? Either scratch or get offn' my back, Jack, cause I ain't answerin' no more questions, dig it?"

Clive looked helplessly at Annabelle. "What did he say?"

Annabelle grinned as she swallowed the last of her tea. "He's running a limited function program," she said. "No queries."

Clive's brows knitted together in confusion. He turned to Horace Hamilton Smythe. "What did she say?"

Horace Hamilton Smythe leaned forward conspiratorially. "They said, 'Let's finish off the last of the excellent tea, sah, and get the hell back on the road.' " He picked up his cup and set it to his lips. "Wish I had a dollop of brandy, though—just for flavor, of course," he added over the china rim.

Clive drew a long breath and gazed at Shriek, Finnbogg, and Chang Guafe. He felt a lot closer to them, sometimes, he reflected, than to his own kind. Those three were aliens, after all. But sometimes he just wanted to set the others down and teach them the proper Queen's English!

"By the way," he said to Samedi, feeling a bit peevish about it all. "My name's Clive, not Jack."

Samedi strutted past, swinging his bony hips in a most foppish manner. "Clive," he responded, stretching the vowel to the point of breaking it, "no jive!" He sauntered on to the entrance, paused to adjust the top hat on his head, and turned back to face them.

Framed in the cave entrance, he crooked a finger. "Come," he intoned.

## • CHAPTER SIX •

# Deadly Echoes in the Hills of Hell

Higher and higher Samedi led them up the narrow mountain road. Jagged peaks rose like broken teeth on all sides. Sometimes, the road was little more than an uneven ledge that hugged the mountainside, and the tiny pebbles they kicked over the edge appeared to fall forever into a vast unending darkness. Other times, though, it was almost a lane, a broad ribbon of ebon stone, which took them through the highland-style valleys that nestled among those peaks.

> *What hills, what hills, so dark and low?*
> *Those are the hills of hell, my love,*
> *Where you and I must go.*

They were the words to an old British folk song, and they kept playing over in Clive's mind as he regarded their surroundings. He'd have to teach it to Annabelle someday. She'd sing it beautifully. Or—he grinned—perhaps he'd teach it to Finnbogg. Finnbogg would give it a distinctly different character.

He looked back at Annabelle, directly behind him in their single-file line, and two more lines came into his head.

> *And as they trod along the way*
> *She shimmered like glittering gold.*

Well, not gold, maybe, though she cut a nice figure in her red leather jeans and white camisole top with the black leather jacket tossed back over one shoulder. It occurred to him that she must be roasting in those clothes, yet she hadn't uttered one complaint. She was strong, his granddaughter, and she made him proud.

He reached inside his shirt and drew out Neville's diary from where it rested next to his skin. It was warm with his body heat, and the cover was damp with his sweat.

Neville claimed the book wasn't his, but could he believe his brother? He turned the diary over and over in his hands, rubbed off the moisture, rolled the balls of his thumbs along the binding as if he might discover some clue to the truth of the matter. The writing inside looked like Neville's, but Sidi's suspicions made sense. The thing had simply turned up in too many unlikely places.

So whose was it? Or rather, who was providing the messages and directions that kept turning up on the pages?

He stared directly ahead at the back of their guide. Samedi had mentioned "friends in high places." Clive tried to weigh the implications of that. What friends? Could he assume that someone somewhere was watching out for them? Were *they* the Dungeonmasters? Were these "friendlies" the ones providing the diary clues?

So many questions? He tried to turn his thoughts over, to look at the same questions from another view.

What if these "friendlies" Samedi had mentioned weren't the Dungeonmasters, at all? Did that indicate another faction in the Dungeon? Possible allies? Perhaps even something so unlikely as a brewing civil war? What if the diary entries were not the work of the "friendlies"? What if "unfriendly" forces sought to misguide and manipulate them? He fanned the pages with the edge of his thumb. Could he trust the entries at all or should he throw the damn thing away?

*The Ren and the Chaffri:* two names he'd heard on the second level, the names of two powerful alien races. He'd nearly forgotten them until now. The people on that level had suggested that one of them were the Dungeonmasters and spoke of both in fearful whisperings. But he'd learned nothing more of either race nor even heard the names again on any other level. Were they, then, just the products of local superstition, or were they, in truth, the architects of this fiendish place? He turned the names over and over in his head as he tried to make some sense of it all.

More than ever, he was convinced of this: He hadn't stumbled into the Dungeon by accident. He'd been brought here deliberately. So had Neville. So had all the others, probably. Annabelle, for instance. Could it be an accident that so soon after his arrival he'd found a granddaughter he hadn't even known about?

He put the book back inside his shirt. One question certainly remained hovering over all the others, and it made his head hurt.

What was going on?

He took a sip from the canteen he now carried. Samedi had provided several from his stores in the cave. Clive had one, and Smythe carried another. He mopped a hand across his brow and licked his lips. There would be no more drinking from the cyborg's mouth for him, or from anyone else's mouth. He took a second sip and put the canteen away. The heat and the searing winds had abated only slightly, and the exertion of the climb also exacted a toll. The muscles in his thighs ached, and he was glad for the sturdiness of his high-topped boots as he put one foot in front of the other.

> *What hills, what hills, so pale and high?*
> *Those are the hills of heaven, my love,*
> *But not for you and I.*

He tried to put the song out of his thoughts again. There were simply more important things to think about than folk songs.

There was Neville. What was he to make of Neville?

His brother seemed so quiet, almost cowed, not at all the Neville he thought he knew. Why, his Neville would be right up front with Baron Samedi trying to direct their course, himself, whether he knew the way or not, instead of following along docilely in line behind Annabelle. Why, from the first he'd expected Neville to wrest control of this little expedition away from him!

He glanced back over his shoulder. Filled with a sudden suspicion, he called back to his brother. "Say, Neville, remind me, will you? What was the name of Nanny's lapdog, anyway?"

Neville gave him a look of utter surprise. "Why, Tennyson, of course! Always thought the beast favored the old poet, she did. Strange notion, though, if you ask me. Whatever on earth made you think of that?"

Clive noted the expression of relief on Horace Hamilton Smythe's face. The quartermaster sergeant stood just behind his brother. Smythe knew the true intention behind his question. The Neville-clone they'd encountered on the sixth level had been unable to provide that simple answer, and so they'd discovered its pretense.

But this Neville had answered quickly and correctly. It was hard to doubt, then, that he was truly Neville Folliot, and Clive's brother. But he seemed so changed, subdued almost. Clive chewed his lip and thought and thought.

Gradually, the world became more muted. The gray near-light of perpetual evening segued down toward a more subtle and depressing shade that was not quite darkness. The mountains loomed all around them now like menacing giants unaware of the gnats that climbed their sides, and the sky closed in upon them like a hand ready to swat.

Still, Samedi led the way, unspeaking, never turning to look back, like Orpheus guiding nine Eurydices from the bowels of Hades.

"When will we get there?" Clive called suddenly. "How much farther?"

"Come," Samedi answered sullenly, stubbornly, lifting

one thin leg and setting it down, lifting the other, placing it carefully.

Clive wondered what time it was, day or night. It disconcerted him to look up and see nothing in the sky at all, just empty darkness, no sun, no moon, no stars, nothing by which to gauge the passage of the hours. He tried to count the seconds in his head and to order that count into minutes. It was a futile exercise, of course, one that left him frustrated and edgy.

For the first time he became aware of his shadow and of a gentle glow that cast it out like a thin line before him. He turned in wonderment and some relief, welcoming any source of light that might expel the cloying gloom.

Annie smiled wanly at him from within a pale green halo. She'd programmed the Baalbec A-9 for the effect despite the toll it would exact from her if she kept it on too long. But Clive could tell that the others welcomed the light, too, so he made no protest. Everyone knew enough to give her room while the Baalbec was operating, and the illumination, no matter how fragile, cheered them.

They reached the top of a narrow peak and rested for a while. The road wound down and down from that point into a mist-filled valley. Clive gazed that way, hands on his hips, his mouth in a pout. He wanted just to yell. They'd come so far, and there still seemed so far to go, and all around them nothing but this monotonous—nothingness!

Well, why not?

He set his hands to either side of his mouth, drew a deep breath, and yelled at the top of his lungs. It was great stress relief, he decided even before he'd gotten it all out.

"*Goddamn you, out there, Ren, or Chaffri, or whoever you are!*"

"You tell 'em, Clive-o!" Annabelle joined in.

"Good show, sah!" Smythe muttered approvingly. "Give the blighters what for!"

Finnbogg threw back his head and howled one long, loud note.

Samedi hurried to his side, his big eyes rolling. "Now you done it, boss. Done it good. Better get all your little asses movin' down this road fast now, cause the picnic is ovah!"

With that, Samedi gave a wave to the others, pushed his top hat down on his brow, and turned to run.

"Picnic!!!" Clive shouted, fury rising in him as he stared at the back of the so-called voodoo God. "What in God's name . . . !"

*GODDAMN YOU*

The volume nearly knocked Clive off his feet. He covered his ears against the pain in his skull and gazed upward, half-expecting to find the Deity, Himself, bending over them in all His glory.

*OUT THERE*

He staggered to one knee. Behind him, Tomàs lay rolling on the ground as he clutched his head. Sidi sat bent over, his head pressed between his knees. Annabelle sagged to the road, too, and Smythe bent over her, trying to shout over the thundrous assault, trying to convince her to turn off the Baalbec. Shriek had three of her arms around Chang Guafe, who looked awful even for a cyborg, causing Clive to wonder how high he'd tuned his audio receptors. Finnbogg, too, looked in terrible pain.

*REN OR CHAFFRI*

Neville looked white as a ghost, but he'd kept his feet under him. Clapping his hands to his ears, he sped past Clive in fast pursuit of the fleeing Samedi.

Now that was the Neville he knew, Clive thought bitterly, glaring at his brother's departing back.

*OR WHOEVER YOU ARE*

Those were his words, his own echo magnified tremendously and flung back at them. He felt his bones rattle as the force of it smashed at him.

*YOU TELL 'EM*

He struggled to get to his feet. He had to get up, had to get the others up and moving. But the pain! His head felt as if it were splitting!

## CLIVE-O

He half-stumbled, half-crawled to Annabelle's side. She had managed to shut off the Baalbec, and Smythe had his arms around her. "Get her up!" he ordered his former batman. Smythe got his arms under her arms and pulled her to her feet. "Down the mountain!" Clive shouted. "Go!"

Sidi Bombay had heard the instructions and taken charge of Tomàs. He helped the little Portuguese up, and they followed the others.

"*Não aguento mais!*" Tomas cried, shaking his head in a useless effort to clear the ringing. "I can't stand this!"

"Shut up, shut up!" Sidi Bombay hissed. "Every sound you utter is a missile that comes back at us!" He gave Tomàs a kick in the pants and pulled him down the incline.

## GOOD SHOW

"Oh, shut—!" Clive started to snap at the impossible echo. He caught himself. Sidi was right. Any sound was a deadly threat.

*Shriek!* he shouted in his thoughts, hoping she was there to hear. *Shriek! Can you handle Chang Guafe?*

In response, the arachnoid collected the cyborg in her four arms and scuttled downhill at astonishing speed.

That left only Finnbogg. The poor creature lay curled in a near-fetal position, its paws clasped tightly over its ears, emitting a low, pitiful howl of pain. Clive knelt down beside him and slipped an arm around his shoulder.

"Come on, Finnbogg, old boy!" he urged. "We've got to get out of here!" He kept his voice to a sharp whisper, his mouth close to Finnbogg's face. He forced the alien canine to look at him. "Let's go, Finnbogg!"

"Go! Leave Finnbogg!" Finnbogg cried, pushing him back with one powerful hand. "Owwww!" he howled, covering his ears again. "Clivefriend hurt Finnbogg!"

Rubbing a bruised backside, Clive crawled to Finnbogg's side again. "It's not me, Finnbogg!" he hissed, trying to keep his voice down. "I mean, it's me, but it's not really me. It's an echo." He tried to press a hand over Finnbogg's mouth. "Stop howling, Finnbogg!" he cried, forgetting himself. "It's all of us. Every sound we make comes right back at us. Now get up! Get up!"

But Finnbogg refused as thick tears ran down his cheeks. "Hurt too bad! Leave Finnbogg, Clivefriend!" He pressed harder still on his ears and squeezed his eyes shut.

Clive cursed and scrambled up angrily. "All right, pup!" he cursed, not bothering to keep his voice down. "I'm going, and you are, too! Cover your head if you must. This will do me just fine!" With that, he seized one of Finnbogg's legs and began to drag his whimpering comrade, bending all his strength to the task.

"Not leave Finnbogg, Clivefriend?" the canine moaned over one shoulder as he uncovered one ear.

"Not bloody likely!" Clive hissed between his teeth as he summoned his might and gave another massive heave. His heart hammered in his chest as he strained. *Good God*, Clive thought, *how much can the creature weigh?*

Finnbogg leaped up. "Then Finnbogg *must* go! Save Clivefriend!" He swept Clive up in huge arms before Clive could utter a protest and started down the road at a jostling run.

*GODDAMN YOU!* the echo started again.

"Put me down!" Clive demanded furiously. "I'm quite capable of running on my own two legs! I'm not a doll, you know!"

Finnbogg only squeezed him tighter and ran faster. "Save Clive Folliot!" Finnbogg repeated, panting. "Finnbogg's good friend! Yeah?"

"Yeah," Clive muttered helplessly under his breath, making up his mind to relax and enjoy the ride.

The road widened as they raced downhill. Their own voices rolled sonorously over their heads, shaking their senses and filling their eardrums with pins and needles. Finnbogg howled as he ran, no matter how Clive tried to convince him it only worsened the problem.

There was no sign of the others ahead, but Clive was sure he'd find them on the road somewhere. Down, down into the valley they descended, and the mist that Clive had seen rose up slowly around them.

It was a warm, damp mist that quickly permeated his clothing, a viscous fog that swirled in thick tendrils through the air and upon the road, obscuring it. At least, it muffled the voices that seemed to bounce unendingly among the peaks, muffled and diminished them so the pain left their ears. *How long can an echo last up there?* Clive wondered. He reminded himself this was the Dungeon, not his own native Earth. If the volume was so unnatural, how could he expect natural law to apply to duration?

Finnbogg slowed to a walk, but still he refused to set Clive down. *I am a doll to him*, Clive grumbled inwardly, *or a security blanket*.

The fog became a steam bath. The khakis were quickly soaked, and Clive's hair plastered to his forehead. Finnbogg's fur dampened, too, began to curl and hang in ropes. Clive almost barked a laugh when he looked up into his friend's face, but he held it back for politeness' sake.

They could see nothing ahead. Even the road beneath Finnbogg's feet had vanished. The air stirred like something alive when Clive blew a breath or passed his hand through it. "Nasty stuff," Finnbogg muttered. "Indeed," Clive agreed. He divided it with a sweep of his arm. It sealed itself again, leaving only a wispy vapor that clung to his sleeve momentarily before it diffused.

It was the fog of childhood ghost stories, exaggerated in the telling, surrealistically unreal. Impossible, like everything else in this Dungeon.

"Ooops," Finnbogg said.

Suddenly, Clive went flying through the air. He twisted and scrambled, uncertain exactly where the ground was. He hit it on his backside, on the same bruised spot he'd landed on earlier, and let out a yelp.

Unexpectedly, he began to slide. The road was steeper than he'd realized from above, and the mist had slickened the smooth black stone. *Where is the ledge?* a part of his mind screamed. *Was there a ledge?* He pressed his bootheels down to slow himself, with only marginal results until the left one caught briefly on some snag and he began to spin helplessly.

"Finnbooooogggggg!" he cried, but the fog absorbed the sound with an impersonal efficiency. He reached out to both sides. There was nothing to grab hold of. How wide was the road here? Was he still on the road?

Abruptly, the slope flattened out and Clive lost momentum. He spun a few more times before coming to a stop, then lay still for a moment. His heart thundered in his ears as loud as anything at the top of the peak, and he waited for it to calm. Only then did he get to his feet.

The ground was still smooth and slick and he stood carefully, as if he were on ice, nearly slipping, and recovering only to slip again with the next step. He held his arms out for precarious balance.

"Finnbogg?" he called softly. Then, more boldly, "Neville? Annabelle? Smythe?" He waited, listening for an answer, and tried once more. "Anybody?" he said hopefully.

He considered what to do. Reason told him Finnbogg, at least, should be close. On the other hand, the creature's weight might have increased his momentum, carrying him along a lot farther. Clive scratched his head and wished he had paid closer attention to his physics studies during his years at Cambridge. But no sense regretting that now. He had to make a decision.

He decided to walk. Clearly, no one was within sound of his voice, though, he admitted, in this fog that needn't be far away. Nor could he see anyone. His own hand at arm's length was an uncertain proposition. The damn stuff made pea soup look like broth!

"Neville!" he called again, and waited for an answer. It was best to call out, he decided. Maybe someone would hear him if he passed close enough.

"Annabelle?" he tried hopefully.

"Shriek!" Then, he stopped himself. There was a better way to try that. Maybe he could touch the arachnoid's thoughts if he concentrated hard enough. He squeezed his eyes shut and called with all his mind, *Shriek!*

There was no answer from anyone. Still, he shouted the names of his friends, hoping they might hear and respond. He began to worry, though. Where could they have gone? Was it possible he was alone? Could he have fallen into yet another level of this Dungeon? He felt for the hilt of his saber. At least he still had a weapon.

After a while he tired of calling out names, so he began to sing. That old folk song crept back into his thoughts, and he found himself intoning self-consciously.

> *Well met, well met, my own true love,*
> *Well met, well met, cried he.*
> *I've just returned from the salty sea,*
> *All for the love of thee.*

When Annabelle tapped him on the shoulder, he nearly jumped out of his skin. He hadn't heard a footstep or a breath or anything to warn him of her approach. Of course not, over his singing.

"Guess I got my talent from Grandma," she said with a smile.

Clive threw his arms around her. "Annie!" he yelled. "Annabelle, thank God!" He hugged her close and breathed a sigh of relief, admitting to himself how much the thought of being alone down here had frightened him. It was easy to admit, now that it wasn't the case.

"That really gave a new meaning to the Miranda warning, didn't it?"

He looked into her eyes, reluctant to let her go. "What's that?"

"The Miranda warning," she repeated, thrusting a finger skyward. "Up there on the peak. You know, 'Anything you say may be used against you'?"

"Oh," he said without comprehension. He knew by her tone, though, it was some kind of joke. "Yes, that's funny. Wasn't Sergeant Smythe with you?"

She freed herself from the embrace. "Well, don't laugh yourself to death on my account," she chided. "We got separated. Slipped on the road or something. One hell of a ride, if you want to know, or did you come by the same route?"

"Yes, the same route," he assured her, rubbing his backside. It felt raw through the wet khaki. She giggled and rubbed hers, too, but the leather had offered more protection. Still, her laughter lifted his spirits. If they had found each other, then they could find the rest.

He took her hand and held it tightly. "Don't let go," he warned her. "We've got to find the others."

"Will you teach me that song?" she suggested. "You really didn't do it that badly."

He grinned and started from the beginning. It was better than shouting names, and more fun, and Annabelle was a fast learner. They sang together and pushed at the fog with the power of their voices.

## ▪ CHAPTER SEVEN ▪

# The Goode Children
# of the Mist

"Clive?"

"Neville?"

"Major Folliot, sah!"

The voices of their friends drifted to them as if from a great distance, mere whispers that flowed ghostlike through the fog. Clive and Annabelle shouted back hopefully, but the voices faded without response.

Clive imagined all his comrades wandering around, blindly groping for each other, unable to see through the dense mist that filled this mountain valley. He wondered how long they had been separated, how they would find each other, if the fog would ever lift. He felt like a shade in some Greek Tartarus.

Annabelle squeezed his hand. "Sing it again, Clive-o," she said.

But he didn't feel like singing anymore. They'd done the same folk song three times until she'd got it right, and it had buoyed their spirits for a while as they searched for their friends. But after a while the words began to sting a little, cut a little too deeply, and Clive stopped.

They had lost the road, of that he was sure. The surface under their feet felt soft and powdery like ash. The road had been hard stone, and smooth, like basalt. No doubt the others had lost the road as well. They could be anywhere in the valley by now.

Damn Samedi, anyway, why hadn't he warned them about echoes and the danger at the top of the peak? Why hadn't he warned them about this valley? Where was he?

"Annie," he said, using the familiar form of her name, probably because Finnbogg was on his mind, "how much light can you get from the Baalbec?"

She frowned. "I don't know, Clive-o, I've never turned it up all the way. The limit would depend on the body heat I'm producing. I'm game to try, though. Here, keep tight hold on my hand and don't break the coupling. That way you won't get zapped."

She grabbed his right hand in her left, then began fingering the implants on the inside of her left forearm. Slowly, they began to glow with a soft greenish radiance. Clive could feel the pulse under her skin as the glow began to brighten and build. Annabelle looked up at him, and their gazes met. His lips drew into a thin line as the light pushed at the fog.

But the fog only threw the light back at them. The brighter they glowed, the worse vision became. "Forget it," he told Annabelle disgustedly. She might have continued to glow and become a beacon for the others, but he had no guarantee they could see her light at all, and the toll on Annabelle would have been too great. "Turn it off," he said with firmness when he saw she was considering the same idea, and gradually the light diminished.

"Englishman!"

That was Sidi Bombay! Clive whirled in the direction of the voice and pulled Annabelle along. "Sidi!" he called. "Over here! Annabelle's with me!" He groped through the fog with his hands outstretched. But if Sidi heard him, he gave no sign of it. Again came the cry of "Englishman!"— but from farther away.

"I'm dying in these leathers," Annabelle complained melodramatically. "I swear these jeans could walk by themselves."

"Then don't take them off," Clive grumbled. "The last

thing we need is one more life-form stumbling around in this murk."

She nudged him gently in the ribs with an elbow. "Careful, Granddad. You're developing a sense of humor."

"I'd prefer a more useful sense right now," he answered irritably. "Speaking of senses, where is Chang Guafe? Shouldn't he be able to spot us by our body heat? What did you call that?"

"Infrared," she told him again. "And I don't know. Maybe this hot mist is scrambling his receptors. It's like a steam bath. Must be nearly a hundred."

He stopped, sighed, and bit his lip. "I don't know whether to keep going or just stand still. We could be wandering farther and farther from the road."

He waited, hoping she might say something useful, but Annabelle kept silent. Clive wanted to kick something. There hadn't been a situation in the Dungeon yet from which he hadn't been able to think or fight his way out, but this damnable fog had him stymied. He'd never seen anything like it! Now all his friends were separated, possibly in danger, and it was his fault. Because of his infantile display of frustration back on the peak, they were in this mess. It was almost enough to make him scream again.

Then, the mist unfolded to reveal a figure coming toward them. At first, it was a shadow, barely a dark outline in the fog. It approached them slowly, bearing something draped over one arm, reaching toward them with the other.

Clive thought he knew that silhouette. "Neville?" he called hesitantly. "Is that you?"

Annabelle's grip tightened on Clive's hand.

Neville Folliot stepped out of the fog. He wore the look of a dead man. His eyes focused on nothing, and his jaw hung slack. Deep creases furrowed his forehead where the brows pinched together. Rivulets of sweat and moisture streamed down his face. He had removed his uniform jacket and carried it over his left forearm. The cuffed sleeves of his white dress shirt he had pushed well above the elbow, and the front he had unbuttoned to the waist-band of his trousers.

Seeing them at last, his features recomposed themselves. His brow unfurrowed, and the gleam of life came into his eyes. He smiled suddenly and shook his brother's hand. "Clive!" he exclaimed. "Good God, I'm glad to see you. Glad to see anyone. And I see you found Annabelle!"

"She found me, actually," Clive admitted, withdrawing his hand coolly, frowning at his brother's appearance. His own khakis were soaked with sweat, and his shirt clung uncomfortably to his chest and back, but he had not exposed himself in such a flagrant manner. He was embarrassed for Annabelle's sake, even though she obviously was not. "Have you encountered anyone else?" he continued. "What happened to the others?"

Neville wiped a sleeve across his eyes and stared at each of them in turn. "I haven't the foggiest notion—you'll pardon the expression, I'm sure. I think I've been wandering for hours down here. Called out until I was hoarse, I did." He rubbed a hand under his chin. "Still a bit of a sore throat. Worse than the bloody wharf district, if you ask me."

"Watch your vulgar language!" Clive snapped. But he agreed London had nothing to match this. "Take hold of Annabelle's hand," he said to his brother. "Let's not get separated again."

"My most charming relative," Neville said, lifting Annabelle's fingers to his lips. He planted a delicate kiss on her knuckles, winked, and smiled.

"You're slime, but you're my slime," Annabelle answered, putting on her best, most formally exaggerated British accent. Then, with a brother on either side she let go their hands and linked her arms through theirs, instead. "Now," she proclaimed, "let's go see the wizard."

Clive and Neville looked at each other over her head. They both shrugged at the same time. "Who knows?" Neville said. "Down here there may actually be one."

*Well*, Clive thought, *we are three now.* Three down and

six more to go. Seven if he counted Samedi. They moved slowly, peering into the mist seeking shadows and outlines, listening for voices. Every so often they called out a name and waited for an answer. The only sounds they heard were the soft scrapings of their own steps on the ground.

Clive began to feel lightheaded. He wiped the sweat from his eyes, from his face. He knew he was losing moisture too fast, dehydrating in the constant, relentless heat. He took out his canteen again, sipped, and offered it to his companions, who also drank. While Annabelle tipped her head back, he glanced at his brother. Their gazes met, and the message passed between them. Neville knew they were in trouble, too.

"Did you hear that?" Annabelle asked suddenly, passing the canteen back to Clive.

"Hear what?" he answered. "I heard nothing."

"Wait," Neville said, holding up a hand. "I thought I . . ."

They froze, straining to listen, and it came again like a plaintive cry. Out from the fog that single small sound issued, sending a shiver up their spines. There was no mistaking it, a tiny child's voice, weak and uncertain, fearful. And the single word it spoke was:

"Mommy?"

Annabelle slipped her arm from Clive's and covered her mouth. She stared into the fog, her eyes wide and bright with doubt and horror. She shriveled, drawing into herself. Her elbows pressed into her ribs, her shoulders slumped forward and down. Even her knees pressed together. She chewed a fingertip, then stopped. "Amanda?" It was a soft whisper and quickly swallowed by the fog.

"Don't be silly, Annabelle," Clive started. "It can't . . ."

Annabelle leaned forward as if in a desperate effort to see through the curtain of mist. "Amanda?" she said again, louder, more certain.

"Mommy?"

Perhaps it came from straight ahead, Clive couldn't be sure, but before he could do anything, Annabelle tore her other arm free from Neville and ran toward the sound, crying, "Amanda, baby! I'm here, Amanda!"

"Don't lose her!" Clive shouted at his brother, trying his best to keep his great-great-granddaughter in sight. A vague outline, a racing shadow, was all he had to follow, and the mist seemed determined to obscure even that.

Neville passed him. Neville always had been a better runner, winning at footraces and steeplechases and those sorts of things. He caught up to Annabelle easily and tackled her in a most ungentlemanly fashion. For an instant, they both disappeared as the fog rolled over them, and Clive's heart stopped. But then, they were on their feet, scuffling and struggling. One shadow kicked at the other and shouted angrily in Annabelle's voice. The low-throated curses were definitely Neville's.

"Amanda! Amanda!" Annabelle screamed hysterically as she kicked and kicked Neville's shins. He held both her wrists in unyielding fists, determined not to let her trigger the Baalbec A-9. He'd already had a taste of that.

"Pardon me, lady," he said suddenly just as Clive caught up. He let go of Annabelle's left arm just long enough to draw one hand up and slap her to the ground.

"Neville!" Clive cried in outrage. "Damn you, Neville!"

Both men knelt down beside her as she sat slowly up. Neville, Clive noted, was careful to keep a grip on the hand that would activate her self-defense unit, intent on stopping her if she tried to use it. "They weren't your shins she was beating on, little brother," Neville said unapologetically. "And she's a strong one, besides. The way she was twisting, she was bound to get loose long enough to turn that thing on. Where would either of us be then? I'll tell you where she'd be, all right. Running free and crazy in this pea soup, that's where."

He hated to admit it, but Neville was right. If Annabelle had used the Baalbec they wouldn't have been able to touch her, and it would have been only a matter of instants before they'd have lost her. He slipped one arm around her shoulders and bent close to examine her.

There was a darkening place on her left cheek where Neville's blow had landed.

Tears trickled from Annabelle's eyes as she looked into Clive's. "I was sure it was Amanda," she said weakly. "I heard her, I know her voice!"

Clive wrapped her in his arms. She trembled against him, even as her gaze darted frantically around. One hand clutched his shoulder, then she pressed her face against his and wept. Neville let go of her arm and sat back with a sigh, folding his legs under him. Clive looked at his brother as he rocked Annabelle and held her close and waited for her grief to pass. He wanted to tell her that they'd get out of here, find the way home, and that Amanda would be waiting for her. But he was no longer sure of that, himself, and he wouldn't lie to her. So instead, he held her and pretended to be strong and kept quiet. If he said nothing, there would be no quaver of doubt to hear.

"Mommy?"

He felt Annabelle lurch as he jerked his head around. Neville sprang to his feet, poised, ready, the saber already half out of its scabbard as he stared at the shadow emerging from the mist.

The child might have been four years old, not more. Dark, shiny hair hung down over her shoulders and into the glittery moist eyes that stared back so widely. Her naked little body shone palely in the shifting vapor as she reached out with one plump, stubby-fingered hand for Annabelle.

Annabelle screamed with delight. "It was Amanda!" she shouted at Clive as she pushed him away and reached for her child. "I told you I knew her voice!"

"Mommy!" the child said again. Then, as Annabelle's arms went around her, Amanda made a noise like an angry cat. The pudgy little hand she had carried behind her back in what had seemed a posture of childish shyness slashed out at her mother's throat.

Annabelle screamed and fell back, blood spurting dark between her fingers as she clutched the wound. Amanda leaped on top of her mother, spitting and hissing like a small, furious beast. Again and again those tiny clawed hands struck, and Annabelle rolled and screamed and tried to cover her face.

Then Neville grabbed the child from behind. It spat at him, making that terrible feline sound, and clawed at his bare arms as it also tried to kick him. He shook it angrily in an effort to make it stop, but it continued to spit and scratch, and blood ran thick into Neville's sleeves and soaked his shirt. At last, he gave a furious roar and heaved the creature away from himself.

"I'm sorry!" Clive shouted, his heart pounding in his chest as he came to Neville's side. "I was just too stunned to move. I couldn't move. It was a child!" He gripped his sword's hilt and shot a glance into the fog. There was no sign of the child, if it was a child at all.

Neville gave a moan and sagged to his knees, holding his arms limply out before him as he uttered a string of curses and oaths. Clive tried to examine the wounds, afraid some artery had been breached. But Neville growled and pushed him away.

"See to Annabelle!" he ordered. "That damn thing got her throat!"

Annabelle lay sobbing on the ground, curled into a fetal ball that Clive had a hard time prying her out of. Her arms and shoulders were a bloody mass of scratches. Clive felt a tightening in his gut as he bent over her, and tears filled his eyes. He wiped them away, though, as he ripped a piece of his khaki shirt and folded it into a useful square. Four jagged cuts pumped blood on the right side of her neck. Clive poured water from his canteen onto the square and daubed at them as he wept. Annabelle moaned and jerked at the touch of the cloth, but Clive kept up a pressure.

Neville crawled to his side. "Let me see," he said, and Clive lifted a corner of the wet square. "Good." Clive shot him a look that said how could anything be good about this, and Neville explained. "The carotid artery is here."

He drew a finger gingerly down the side of his own neck. Clive looked under the square again and realized the cuts stopped just short, but by only a hair's breadth. "She'll have a lovely set of scars, though, little brother, if you don't strangle her."

Clive frowned and eased off the pressure. The bleeding had slowed. He poured more water from the canteen onto the strip of shirt cloth and tried to wash her other cuts. Mercifully, Annabelle seemed to have passed out. She resisted and helped no more than if she were a doll as he worked. When he could do no more for her, he turned to Neville with the water and the cloth.

It was then they heard another, more familiar sound, the beating of great leathery wings. Side by side, the brothers looked up as Philo B. Goode, who now called himself Beelzebub, descended before them. His ankle seemed completely healed, nor was there any evidence of Finnbogg's teeth or jaws on his unblemished flesh.

In his arms, he cradled the child-monster who had attacked them.

Annabelle sat up. "He's got Amanda," she said painfully.

"That's not Amanda," Neville told her firmly, still on his knees as he regarded Goode.

Clive licked his lips as he noted how Neville and Goode stared at each other. "I never thought to ask after our last encounter," he ventured, "but have you two also met?"

"He did me a disservice back in Africa," Neville explained, never taking his gaze from their winged foe. "Passed me a note from one Lady Baker, wife of one Lord Samuel Baker, of whom you might have heard. They're on the social register. A charming couple, really. They were enjoying a safari in the Bukoba country, and I chanced to meet them. Anyway, the note suggested a, well, an amorous liaison to which I responded in person. Lord Baker found us and took great affront, though I assure you nothing untoward transpired. Not that it mightn't have," he added with a wink at Clive, "had we more time and a good bottle of brandy. The note, needless to say, was a practical joke, one of this chap's forgeries. He's quite good at them."

Clive glared at his brother. "You've done business with him?"

Neville shrugged. "I met him in a wharfside tavern after leaving the ship in Zanzibar, and we played a few hands of cards. Some blokes robbed us both in an alley after it was over. Took all my money, they did." Neville Folliot nodded toward Goode, who listened patiently with a big grin. "Goode, here, helped me obtain supplies anyway by, uh, charging them to certain other wealthy individuals."

"Such as the Sultan Seyyid Majid ben Said?" Clive suggested, recalling an unpleasant episode of his own stay in Zanzibar.

Neville shrugged again. "And a few of his relatives. You met the chap?"

Clive rolled his eyes and turned to Philo B. Goode. "You look better in this incarnation, Goode," he said. "It suits you."

Before Goode could answer, Annabelle slapped her head. "System malf! I've been on downtime! I know him, too!" She shot an accusing look at the archdemon. "Weren't you a roadie on my band's tour? Sure, I remember, chipchewer! You set up the equipment for the Piccadilly show!"

Philo B. Goode fluttered his wings, causing the mist to churn and swirl while he flung back his head and laughed. "Ah, my darling Ms. Leigh," Goode acknowledged. He licked his lips and ran his tongue over the tips of his fangs as he leered at her. "I'm a man of many places and many times. But come now, tell me how you like my little pet." He flipped the child over in his arms. The Amanda-thing arched its back and uttered a low growl as Goode ran a palm along its spine. "Mommy," it said, but there was nothing human in the sound.

"Bastard!" Annabelle muttered, her temper barely under control.

Philo B. Goode clucked, "My, my, Ms. Leigh, such

language. What must your grandfather and your uncle think?"

"Well, I, for one, think she's quite right," Neville volunteered offhandedly.

"Leave her alone, Goode," Clive threatened, low-voiced, rising slowly to his feet, laying a hand to the hilt of his saber.

"Leave her alone?" Again, Goode laughed, flexing his wings as he did so, stirring the fog and causing waves of damp heat to wash over them. He continued to stroke and pet the Amanda creature on his arm in an almost obscene manner. "My dear Major Clive Folliot, you fail to understand! It was a miscalculation that brought you here, an error which I plan now to correct." His catlike gaze shifted from Clive to Neville as, again, he licked the points of his fangs. "And you, Major Neville Folliot, you have been such a disappointment. Barely an entertainment. Your poor little brother, whom you referred to on the occasion of our acquaintance as 'inept and unprepossessing' has proved much more of a challenge."

Clive looked at Neville and raised an eyebrow. " 'Inept and unprepossessing'?"

Neville shrugged and tilted his head sheepishly. "I misspoke myself." It was the closest he'd ever come to apologizing to Clive.

Philo B. Goode sprang into the air. His pinions beat a powerful rhythm as he hovered just above their heads, still clutching his precious pet. "It's checkmate, Clive Folliot. Even with your friends you never really had enough pieces to play out the game."

"Whatever you think, Goode," Clive said, easing his saber from the sheath, "this is no game."

"Oh, but it is, Major!" Goode roared, laughing. "And I've an inexhaustible supply of pawns."

Without further warning, Philo B. Goode tossed the Amanda-thing at Clive's face. It came to him, screeching and hissing, claws reaching for his eyes.

Clive saw in plenty of time and drew back his sword.

Still, though, it was a child's face that he saw, and he couldn't quite bring himself to strike. At the last possible instant, he dodged it altogether. It gave an angry shriek, twisted, and landed on its feet. Hardly a heartbeat passed before it leaped at him again. He threw up his left arm to intercept it. Claws dug into his flesh; teeth tore his khaki sleeve. With a cry of pain, Clive flung the creature away.

Overhead, Philo B. Goode roared with mirth as from deep in the mists more shadows emerged, spitting and hissing, all Amanda-things, all identical, all reaching with razor claws. Clive stared in horror as dozens of little girls, all resembling Annabelle, rushed at them out of the fog.

Annabelle gave a scream of anger and dismay.

The children swept upon them like a wave, scratching and tearing, biting like little animals. Clive found his own moral code playing him false. He pushed and kicked at his small attackers, but halfheartedly. He couldn't bring himself to use the saber.

"Don't be soft, little brother!" Neville called, but before he could bring his own blade to bear one of the little beasts jumped up and sank its teeth into his wrist. Neville screamed and dropped his sword before he could shake free.

He heard Annabelle's cries, saw her rolling on the ground under the weight of half a dozen tiny Amandas. She didn't lash out at all, didn't even push them away. She tried only to protect her face and head as tiny fists pummeled her and tiny claws raked her skin.

Suddenly, Clive pitched backward under the onslaught. They pulled his hair, clawed at his eyes. Tiny teeth closed on his throat. Somehow, he lost his sword. With a furious roar, he swung out with his arms and sent his foes sprawling, but others took their places before he could catch his breath. Despite himself, he screamed in pain and threw up an arm to protect his eyes.

Then, for the first time, he heard the Baalbec. It sounded a second time and a third. Annabelle was fighting back! He knew what it must have cost her to make that decision, remembered how badly he'd felt about facing and slaying the Neville-clone on level six. But these were her daughters— that is, creatures made to resemble her daughter. Still, the emotional price . . .

With a wrench he freed one arm, caught the hair of the Amanda-thing nearest his face, and snapped its head back. It gave a screech of agony as he hurled it away and reached for the one that took its place. He punched and slapped and struck with his fists, elbows, any part of his body he could free, and managed to sit up.

A pile of stunned little bodies grew around Annabelle. All she'd had to do was activate the Baalbec. The children did the rest. They threw themselves mindlessly at her in wave after wave, touching her field. The sound of its energy whip-crack filled his ears.

Neville stood just beyond her, flinging the creatures right and left, a complete madman. He growled like an animal, himself, and his face wore a bestial expression. The shirt had been ripped from his body, and his trousers hung in tatters. As Clive watched, he lifted a child, broke it over his knee, and flung it away with all his might.

Philo B. Goode broke into enthusiastic applause. "Oh, this is delicious! Is it not special, Annabelle Leigh, as I promised you it would be?"

"You monster!" Annabelle raged, shaking her fist. The Baalbec A-9 implants gleamed with mingled blood and sweat on her bare upraised arm. "You think this is a game? That you can just play with us?" Hysteria burned in her eyes. Five more Amandas leaped at her, screeching, and hurtled unexpectedly backward to twitch and writhe before collapsing unconscious.

Goode clutched his belly with laughter as more and more of his pets swarmed out of the fog and flung themselves at Annabelle. The Baalbec's zap made a constant staccato as they reached out for her.

But Annabelle ignored them. Her gaze focused angrily on Philo B. Goode as she waded through the children to stand before him. "You fucking scrodhead!" she stormed. "I'm gonna crash your whole fucking program!"

Her right hand slapped against the implants.

Clive's horrified exclamation died before he could utter it as every inch of his skin crawled with sudden electricity and every muscle in his body convulsed. He hit the ground, his fall softened only by the bodies of several of the Amanda-things as they succumbed to the same force.

His chest burned, but he didn't lose consciousness. He saw the look on Goode's face as the force hit him as well. The huge leathery wings snapped out straight and locked, and Philo B. Goode fell like a very surprised stone.

Annabelle picked up Neville's saber and walked with hysterical calm to her tormentor's stunned form. Clive gained enough control over his muscles to ease up onto one elbow, but not enough to do much else. There was no way he could stop Annabelle from what she obviously intended.

She set the point of the blade to Goode's heart as a groan issued from his lips. "Shove this up your disc drive, you bastard!" she hissed as she leaned her weight on the saber.

Goode let go a sharp sigh of pain. His head lifted from the ground, then sank back. "Fool!" he whispered through clenched teeth. "The game goes on. I am but the servant who goeth before the master!" Another long sigh fled his lips, and with it his life.

Annabelle looked down at Goode. Slowly, she let go of the saber and stared, instead, at her hand. Then, she turned and stared in horror at all the tiny bodies that so resembled her daughter. She bit her lip, let go the meekest of whimpers, and slipped to the ground in a faint.

# • CHAPTER EIGHT •

# The Unexpected Ferryman

"I didn't realize she could push the field that far from her body," Neville said worriedly.

"Neither did I," Clive answered, grim-voiced, as he bent over her. "Her skin's cold as ice."

Every muscle in his body burned and ached, but he began to rub her as briskly as he could. Neville joined in. The hot mist should help to bring her body temperature back up, too, if it wasn't already too late. But such a tremendous power surge must have been a strain on her system.

"Thank God the thing shut itself off," Neville muttered as he worked. "There must be some kind of safety feature, an automatic shutdown point."

Clive massaged her left hand, then recoiled, appalled, as he noticed the smear of blood spreading on her pale flesh, his own blood that ran down the underside of his arm and into his palm. Well, he couldn't think of his own wounds now. He and Neville both were scored and lacerated with scratches and cuts. So was Annabelle. There simply was nothing he could do about them now.

He bent over Annabelle and listened for her heartbeat. "It's there, but faint."

"Take off your shirt, Clive, or what's left of it. We've got to get her warm."

Clive removed the tattered garment and spread it over

Annabelle's chest and shoulders as best he could, then settled back on his haunches and looked at his brother. Neville was nearly naked. Only his boots and strategic remnants of his trousers remained. His flesh was a bloody lacework, and blood matted his blond hair into ropes and knots. He appeared altogether a wild man. Nor was that an inappropriate description, perhaps. He remembered the vision of his brother hurling their attackers right and left, growling like a beast. It was not a pleasant vision.

Neville, too, settled back. "It's up to her now," he announced. "The air's hot enough to warm her fast." He picked up the arm with the implanted controls for the Baalbec A-9 and cradled it gently. "Unless this damn thing did damage that we don't know about."

The twins regarded each other then, their gazes locking, lingering upon one another. There was nothing of a challenge in those gazes. It was a mutual exploration on a very subtle level. Clive had thought he knew Neville. But he wasn't sure he knew this man across from him. Clive had thought that he hated Neville. But he didn't know if he hated this man at all. Clive had thought that he envied Neville. He wasn't sure if he envied this man.

All the childhood wrongs that Neville had done him, all the insults and injuries came rushing back into Clive's mind, and he tried desperately to fit them to the face of the man he saw now. Yet, he failed. The memories broke and blew away like a fine powder, like dust that he could see and smell and taste, but that eluded his grasp.

He looked away, confused.

Neville spoke first. "Hello, little brother."

Clive looked up. "I am not your *little brother*," he said stiffly.

Neville's lips parted in a slight smile as he nodded his head. "But you are my brother," he affirmed, "my twin."

Around them, the Amanda creatures began to awake. The brothers started and reached for their swords. Neville came up empty-handed, and he shot a look toward the corpse of Philo B. Goode. His blade stood at attention in the dead man's chest.

Slowly, the little girl-things sat up. They snarled and hissed as they shrugged off the effects of the Baalbec. "Mommy," they uttered in low, unnatural voices, "mommy, mommy." There was no love in the sound. It was a hunting cry, a lure, no more. They seemed uninterested in Clive and Neville and Annabelle as they stirred. They arched their backs and stretched, catlike, rose to tiny feet, and tottered toward the still form of their master. "Mommy," they whispered, the sound an eerie susurrus in the mist. One by one they moved toward Philo B. Goode, touched him, explored with their fingers, licked his face and hands, his chest and wings. They crawled over him in slow motion like maggots, and when he didn't respond, they eventually drifted off into the fog.

"What is that weird sound?" Neville snapped with some irritation as he rubbed the back of his neck.

Clive had been too awed watching the children to note the distant shrill ululation that barely penetrated the fog. "That's Shriek!" he exclaimed, leaping to his feet only to fall sideways. He looked at his right leg in surprise. A long rip in his trousers allowed the material to flop open, exposing a deep gash in his thigh that pumped a steady crimson stream.

He pressed his hand over the wound and squeezed his eyes shut in an attempt to ignore the sudden pain. He had to concentrate. Maybe Shriek had been too far away to hear him earlier, but she was closer now. He crossed his fingers.

*Shriek!* he called, firing his thoughts in all directions like warning shots. That was how he tried to imagine it, like a hunter alerting his comrades by shooting into the air. *Shriek!* he shouted silently over and over. *Shriek!*

"What are you doing?" Neville entreated as he stepped around Annabelle and knelt by Clive. He pushed his twin's hand away and looked at the gash. He made a face. "Nasty, that," he said. He tore away Clive's trouser leg and began stripping the fabric into bandages. Before he could bind the injury, though, a white silky spray snagged his arm. Neville gave a startled cry and sprang up, trying to rip free.

Before he could do so, Shriek appeared. Her eyes were unreadable as she glanced at the twins and hurried to Annabelle's side. The arachnoid kneeled on her front legs as she bent over the unconscious human female, chittering and clacking her mandibles.

It was then Clive saw the strands of webbing attached to her left rearmost foot. They trailed behind her and disappeared into the fog.

An instant later, Tomàs joined them. The strand encircled his waist and continued to snake back into the fog. He stared at them for an instant with horror on his face. "*Senhor* Clive! *Senhor* Neville! *Ai, Christo!* What has happened?" He glanced in all directions as if searching for danger as he knelt down between them. He spied the body of Philo B. Goode partially obscured now by the drifting mists. "Who is that?"

"The good Mr. Goode," Neville explained through clenched teeth. One hand rested now along his ribs. His expression betrayed the pain he had denied too long.

Clive tried to sit up. "How did you find us?"

Tomàs saw the gash on Clive's leg and gasped. Seeing the small pile of strips that Neville had started to make from the khaki material and discerning their intended purpose, the little Portuguese got to work. He washed the wound by pouring water from his own canteen over it, folded one strip, pressed it over the cut, and tied another around it.

"I found Shriek wandering in this cursed fog," he explained while he worked. "We wandered long time, very far from road, sometimes hearing voices, but finding no one."

Clive thanked the little sailor for the bandage, but he suspected it was Shriek who probably found Tomàs.

"*Ai,* you are a mess, so much blood!" Tomàs exclaimed,

dampening a strip and wiping at the scratches around the gash as he continued his story. "Suddenly, Shriek she go *demente*! Crazy!" He threw his hands up and made a face. "She catch me in her web and run into fog. I follow fast as I can, and she shoot her web everywhere blindly, just shoot it into fog!" He gestured again and rolled his eyes. "Once, she pause long enough I catch up and jump on her back. She not care. She stop again as if to look around. I relax one minute to catch my breath, and *ai de mim!* she start running, and I fall off." He smacked his palm against his forehead and smiled broadly. "But here I am!"

A shadow took form at the edge of the fog and merged into the familiar shape of Chang Guafe. The ruby lenses of his eyes burned at full intensity, causing a red glow that diffused spectrally in the mist that surrounded him. Shriek's webbing made a thick coil over one of his arms. "No apparent hostilities," he observed. "All sensors nominal."

Clive grinned, recalling the previous evening and his conversation with the cyborg. "Hello to you, too, Chang. Good to see you again."

Chang Guafe moved closer to the center of the growing gathering. "Monitoring accelerated blood pressure rhythms in both Majors Folliot," he reported, "accompanied by inefficient respiratory rates."

"We've had a little excitement," Neville explained with droll amusement as he winked at Clive. "But you'd better take a look at Miss Leigh."

Shriek's thoughts brushed into Clive's mind. *Problem her body is not, despite lacerations,* the arachnoid told him. There was a knife edge of fear in her thoughts that spread to Clive across their neural linkage. *Reach, though, her mind I cannot! Closed, she is!*

Clive pushed Tomàs back and crawled on his knees to Annabelle's side. He looked up at Shriek. "What's wrong with her, Shriek? Was it the Baalbec?"

Shriek clicked her mandibles and trained three of her eyes on him. The other three remained on Annabelle. *Shock, it is, Being Clive, deep shock. Even over great distance her mindcry heard I. Egglings, saw I. Her egglings. Then, madness, madness! Fear of Annabelle being*—she put two of her hands to her head as she shook it from side to side—*very powerful.*

Clive laid a hand tenderly on Shriek's shoulder. "Are you all right?"

Shriek swallowed as she nodded. *Frightened. Mindfear of Annabelle being lingers, but fades. Well, am I.*

He pointed to the webbing attached to her foot. "Do you have all our friends?"

The question seemed to trouble her. *Many beings in the web,* she answered. *Luck my spinning guided. Blindly worked I, casting my web. Much struggling, many vibrations. Too many beings, friends just to be.*

Clive rubbed his chin and winced, finding new cuts even on his face. "You've probably snared some of her egglings," Clive explained. "Shriek, we'll care for Annabelle. Can you backtrack and find the others? Samedi, too? Cut the rest loose. They seem to be harmless without Philo B. Goode to lead them."

*Can find all I,* Shriek answered, rising. *Vibrations lead I very fast.* She somehow slipped the strands of webbing from her rear foot, pressed them to the ground, and rubbed her spinnerets against them, making a firm anchor. Then she disappeared into the fog.

In no time at all the entire company was reunited. Finnbogg set up a grievous howl when he saw Annabelle. The others crowded around them. Cuts and scrapes were washed and bandaged with scraps of cloth. When the strips of khaki were exhausted, Smythe donated his shirt. Neville had a deep and very painful rake along his ribs and a serious trio of wounds down his back. There was no way they could bandage Annabelle's throat, but her arms and back were also severely clawed. Clive surveyed his own injuries and declared them minor, but the others pushed him back down when he tried to get up.

Baron Samedi hung sheepishly back at the edge of the fog, top hat in hand.

"Why didn't you warn us about this place, Samedi?" Clive demanded.

Samedi looked at his hat and shrugged. "Hey, Jack, everybody slips up now an' then, ya know? I panicked, okay, when you started flappin' your tiny Caucasian lips up high, right? So sue. If we'd taken it all slow an' kept together, things'd gone slick as satin, no problem."

Sidi frowned. "Tiny Caucasian lips?" he said pointedly. "Though you have been my gracious host and guide, I must insist that you, noble sir, are as white as my friends. Indeed, as white as any man I have ever seen."

Samedi looked at him as he tilted his head and cocked an eyebrow. "Well, *pahdon me!*" It was a perfect imitation of Smythe's voice and accent. Samedi donned his hat and patted it down over his brow.

Clive frowned at their guide. The creature still confused him with his funny speech, and more, with his elusive background. He claimed he'd been sent to show them the way. But who'd sent him? Could Clive trust him? Could he trust Samedi's employers?

Clive knew he'd have to answer those questions soon, but now it was best they get out of this fog. He had no more fear of the Amanda-things, but there might be other dangers lurking beyond the range of vision. "Let's get out of here," he said suddenly.

He started to rise, but Horace Hamilton Smythe pushed him back down. "No, sah," Smythe insisted. "You can't walk, yet. That leg wound is too deep and needs time to close."

Clive tried to push him back. "Don't be silly, Sergeant," he responded. "We can't stay here in this muck. The bandage will have to do. Now help me up."

But Smythe was adamant. "Shriek or Chang Guafe will carry you, sah, and Major Neville, too. Finnbogg will take Miss Annabelle."

Finnbogg looked enthusiastic. "Okay, okay!" he agreed. "Finnbogg carry Annie gentle as litterpup!"

"Don't be absurd, Horace!" Clive snapped, appalled at

the idea of being carried like a doll. After all, he was a grown man and an officer of Her Majesty's army. A certain decorum must be maintained. "I'm perfectly capable of walking on my own." Again, he pushed Smythe back and sat up, intent on rising to his feet.

"Better listen, little brother." Neville grinned weakly at him. "I don't think they're going to give you a choice."

Too late, Clive noted his brother's eyes, the way his gaze flickered to something behind Clive. He jerked around just in time to feel a new scratch on his right shoulder, followed almost immediately by a rapidly spreading sensation of numbness. He folded helplessly sideways into Smythe's arms. A moment of terror seized him as he resisted the chemical's effect, uncertain of exactly what had been done to him.

Shriek moved into his field of vision, a hair-spike still grasped in one hand. She'd drugged him again as she'd done twice before. Was that a smile on her alien face? It was so hard to tell.

"Shriek . . ." His mouth refused to obey, to form the words he wanted, and he tried to focus his thoughts enough for her to hear: . . . *you traitor.*

Something tickled his brain that must have been Shriek's laughter. *Fear you must not, Being Clive,* she said to him. *Powerful anesthetic have I made. But more subtle than last time, more human-suitable. No bad effects. Human blood from the Annabelle being have I tasted. On my hands it was when examine her I did. Blood having tasted, analysis my body does, new chemicals to know and produce.*

Clive forced himself to concentrate. His thoughts seemed to spin and tumble. It took an effort to think coherently. *What have you done to me?* He realized distantly just how much fear tinged his response. He had seen the effects of Shriek's hair-spikes before.

*Sedate, have I,* she answered, *and medicated, healing to speed. Same will I do to the Neville being and the Annabelle being. Care for you will all friend beings.*

He gazed upward at all those clustered around him:

Shriek and Sidi, Tomàs and Smythe. Samedi, too, with that funny, crooked grin. Beyond and above them, the fog swirled almost milk-white. For the first time, Clive thought, he knew real fear. Always before, whenever danger had threatened, he'd had his sword or his fists or his feet to run if necessary. But now he was helpless, completely helpless, and he didn't like it one bit.

Dimly, he heard a commotion and an outraged squawk that must have been his brother. That, at least, made him feel a little better. If he had to be carried like a sack of vegetables, it heartened him to know that Neville would share the same embarrassment.

Shriek's face appeared again above his, and he felt himself lifted with her lower set of arms. With her upper right hand she brushed a lock of hair back from his face. The gesture struck him as strangely, tenderly human, but he still didn't forgive her.

*Untrue forethought,* she said with a chiding, almost motherly tone. *Deepthought of Clive being forgives.*

From far away Clive heard a familiar word, but it oozed into his head with liquid slowness. "Cooommmmee." That had to be Samedi.

Horace Hamilton Smythe came to his side and squeezed his hand. "Don't you worry none, sah," he reassured confidently. "We're all going to be just fine, we are. You just rest."

Tomàs also moved close. *"Não se afliga,"* he said conspiratorially as one confidant to another. "Don't worry. I have your sword." He held the blade for Clive to see. "I give back soon when you are well. Now, though, Tomàs keep it and protect companions."

Clive could see Neville in the arms of the cyborg Chang Guafe. His brother wore a thoroughly idiotic expression as his head lolled over his bearer's huge arm. Likewise, Finnbogg carried Annabelle, but it was Finnbogg who wore the idiotic expression as he gazed with worshipful concern at his burden.

"Best be about it, lads."

That was Smythe's voice. Apparently, the sergeant had assumed the leadership role with Clive incapacitated.

They began to move. Shriek carried him with great care, and yet he chafed at his powerlessness and vulnerability. With a great effort of will he turned his head forward and tried to focus his vision. Samedi and Smythe led the way just as he'd figured. No one else walked in front of him. At least, he could see something of what lay ahead. At the moment, that was nothing but the mist.

Shriek had provided the way back to the road. They had indeed wandered far from it, but she had left a strand of webbing, which they now followed like Theseus from the labyrinth. In little time they were back on the smooth surface.

After a while, Clive thought he detected the smell of water in the air, and his ears began to pick up a dull rushing roar. *A river?* He sent the thought to Shriek.

*River, there must be,* she agreed, and indeed they shortly reached its bank.

From the sound of it he had expected a swiftly flowing body with a treacherous current, perhaps rapids. But the "rush" was not the rush of motion, of water between two banks. It was the bubbling and furious churning, rather, that he'd heard so far away, for this river boiled!

How would they ever get across?

The others gathered around in a tight group and stared with trepidation at this newest obstacle. It was then that Samedi reached inside the pocket of his jacket and extracted a small whistle, which he set to his lips. He walked as close to the water's edge as he safely dared and blew. A long, high-pitched note sailed evenly over the river's surface and faded into the misty distance. He returned to the group, then, and folded his arms expectantly.

Moments later, a similar note only slightly lower in pitch drifted back in answer. They stared toward the sound. A small ship crawled slowly out of the milky curtain of steam that hung over the river, powered by a pair of slender oars that rose and dipped with metronomic regularity. Long minutes passed before it finally touched the shore.

The oarsman sat with his back to them as the bow bumped the stony bank. Only when the oars were carefully shipped did he rise and turn to face them.

Gasps sounded from Tomàs and Smythe. Even through the sedative Clive managed to blink.

"Hey, Jack!" the oarsman said, grinning as he doffed his top hat. "High five!"

The oarsman and Samedi slapped palms with a loud smack.

They looked exactly alike.

## • CHAPTER NINE •

# Under the Shadows of Death

The journey across the river was steamy and miserable. Clive, Annabelle, and Neville were placed as comfortably as possible in the bottom of the vessel while the others seated themselves on small benches. The two Samedis took positions in the fore and aft.

The ship resembled a Viking Oseburg craft. Its prow swept upward in a high graceful curve, and a single sailless mast stabbed the heavy mist. Small enough to be rowed by one man, it nevertheless contained oars for three. Each of the Samedis worked a pair. Tomàs manned the third set.

The vessel's construction material fascinated Clive. It was not wood, not even metal. Completely smooth, it glistened blackly, and though the hull seemed quite thin, it conducted none of the water's terrible heat. There were no visible joints or seams. The entire ship, even the benches, the mast, the prow, all appeared molded from a single piece.

Shriek's potent anesthetic had begun to wear off. Clive could move again, but weakly, and that required concentration. Still, he wiggled his fingers on the bottom of the boat—he couldn't call it a proper deck—and marveled.

It was then he noticed the others. Food! They were eating! The sight instantly made him hungry, too. He tried to sit up, but he only made a thumping with his elbows and shoulders. It was enough to attract attention, though, and Horace Hamilton Smythe quickly bent above him.

"Sorry, sah!" Smythe apologized. "Assumed you were asleep like your brother, sah." Smythe slipped an arm under his shoulders and helped him to sit against the side of the boat as the others leaned closer. "Are you hungry, sah? Can you eat?"

Clive gave his sergeant what he hoped was a withering look. What kind of idiotic question was that? He forced himself to nod and stared pointedly at the strange concoction in Sidi Bombay's hand, something that looked like beef chunks between thick slices of bread. "Eat," he said, forcing movement into lips that felt like mushrooms.

Sidi Bombay twisted on his bench and reached into a box apparently made of the same material as the ship and withdrew some kind of packet. He unwrapped it carefully, and amazingly a tiny cloud of steam rose, bearing a potent savory odor.

Clive's hand came up shakily to accept it.

"That's what Samedi calls a sandwich," Smythe told him. He pointed toward the prow. "That Samedi there, that one," he added. "He's the one that brought the boat and the box of food. At least, I think he is." He turned back to Clive. "Don't look like any sandwich I ever saw in England, though, sah. Whatever that bit of meat is, it isn't ham, it isn't. And see, there's two pieces of bread, and not a spot of butter on either of them. It's hot, too. Tasty, though, I'll say that."

Clive Folliot didn't care what it was called or by whom. He brought the sandwich to his mouth, took a cautious bite, and chewed slowly. It tasted wonderful, and his brain seemed to clear with every passing moment. All he cared about right now was his stomach.

When he finished his meal, he licked his fingers. Then, he held out his hand again, this time toward Tomàs. "I'll have my saber back, if you don't mind," he said.

The little Portuguese continued at his oars, but the

blade lay ignominiously at his feet between his bench and the bulkhead. He pushed it with his toe toward Clive. "Thank you," Clive said. He looked back to Smythe. "How wide is this river? Is it the drug, or haven't we been crossing for some time now?"

"Some time, sah, yes," Smythe agreed. "It seems impossibly wide for these mountains, doesn't it? The bubbling and churning, combined with the effect of the river current, make for tough going. But Tomàs and our twin guides are doing their best."

"Annabelle and Neville?" he asked, gazing down on his relatives.

Smythe shook his head. "No change for Miss Annabelle. Neville finally went to sleep. The drug and the rocking of the boat, no doubt. We thought you had, too. Truth to tell, I was a bit envious."

Clive smiled. "Tired, Horace?"

Horace hesitated, then grinned. "Tired of the Dungeon, sah, that's for sure. What I wouldn't give to curl up by a fire in a London pub with a pint of stout."

A curtain of warm mist rolled over them. For a few moments it was impossible to see either end of the boat. Horace Hamilton Smythe drew nose to nose with Clive, and the two men stared at each other for an uncomfortable space, then glanced from side to side, anywhere but at each other.

Clive felt jittery, and the sudden thickening of the fog had actually made him jump inside. He knew that his sergeant had seen the brief flicker of fear in his eyes before he'd been able to suppress it. To his surprise, though, Smythe's eyes had betrayed the same momentary fear. It was an embarrassing revelation for them both.

A muttered curse in Portuguese caused Clive to look toward Tomàs. Except for Smythe, the little sailor was the closest person to him, yet a vague form in the mist was all he could see. It bent forward over the oars and pulled with a sure, easy stroke, but it could have been any spirit that rowed.

"When we get out of here, Horace," Clive said at last, wiping a hand over his damp face, "I'll join you at your pub. Damn it, man, I'll even buy. But I warn you, I'm going to have more than just a pint. A lot more."

"Be careful, little brother. You'll spoil your image."

It was a bare whisper, but Clive heard it plainly. A muffled scuffling accompanied the speech, the sound of uncooperative elbows and bootheels scraping on the hull.

"Lie still, Neville," Clive instructed. "It wears off slowly at first, then more quickly. "When the fog parts again, we'll sit you up and give you a bite, but right now let's not have anyone moving around and falling overboard."

"Thank you, brother," Neville answered stiffly, "but I am sitting up."

Clive peered hard through the mist and saw the dim form of his twin resting against the other side of the ship. He couldn't resist a frown. Neville would shrug off the effects of Shriek's drug just fine on his own without any help from anybody. Neville never needed any help. Neville always did everything just right.

Clive tried to straighten his injured leg, and a sharp twinge of pain shot up his thigh. A sudden intake of breath alerted Smythe, but Clive gently pushed him back when the sergeant leaned to see what was the matter.

Shriek's thoughts brushed against his. *Your painsong heard I, Being Clive. More healing venom need?*

"No, Shriek," he snapped aloud. "What I need is a clear head and a good leg!"

*Healing venom good make leg in time. Transparency of bone brain casement effect I cannot.*

Several snickers followed that, and Clive realized with some irritation that Shriek had generally broadcast her answer. Everyone had heard. Well, everyone had heard him snap at her. He sighed and laid his head back against the hull.

They emerged from the heaviest fog, and moments later the prow thumped solidly against the bank. They had reached the far shore. The Samedi at the front of the boat leaped over the side onto firm land and held the boat as steady as possible. Sidi and Tomàs followed.

Clive started to rise on his own despite the pain that screamed through his leg. Then, Shriek lifted him and carried him ashore. Chang brought Neville, and Finnbogg gently bore Annabelle. The thick mush of puppy-dog tears had matted the corners of his eyes.

The other Baron Samedi came last, bearing what remained of the box of food. He set it down on the ground and beckoned to his look-alike, and together they dragged the boat out of the water. Clive dismissed his pain long enough to marvel at how light the ship must be and wondered again at the material of its construction.

"Not wanting to be a bother, old boy," Neville said with polite patience, "but I could use some of whatever smells so good in that container."

Clive nodded and waved a hand at the box. Sidi Bombay dragged it closer, and they all made a circle around it. Only Shriek hung back as the Indian passed out the contents. Finnbogg accepted a bit of meat and munched it disconsolately as he cradled Annabelle's head on his lap and stroked her hair idly with the fingers of one hand. Tomàs devoured his portion wordlessly, licked his fingers, smacked his lips, and reached for more.

Neville Folliot ate with a pristine elegance that irritated Clive. As he swallowed his last bite and brushed crumbs from his mouth and mustache, he said, "Might I suggest we save just a little something for later?"

Neville looked at them all with that expression of utter reasonableness, and Clive mentally kicked himself for not thinking of it first. He stared at the untouched sandwich in his hand and frowned as he started to return it to the box.

"You my kinda man," said one of the Samedis, slapping the side of his leg. "Hey bro'! Ain't he my kinda man?" The other Samedi nodded and smiled. "Always thinkin'!" the first one continued, addressing Neville with a keen stare. "But you got to trust, man! Now, the palace ain't far away, an' the Big Dude hisself is waitin'. All you wanna eat, there, man. Pig heaven!"

The second Samedi bent down close and patted Clive's shoulder sympathetically. "So you jus' eat that, now, an' don' worry none 'bout savin' it. Get yo' strength back, Jack."

Horace Hamilton Smythe scooted next to Clive. "Shall I tuck some away, sah, just in case?" He nodded subtly toward Neville. "The major brother does have a bit of a point."

Clive thought about it, then shook his head. It wasn't just to spite Neville, he told himself, not just another instance of taking the opposite side. "No, Sergeant. Samedi has done well by us so far, and I think we should trust him as he says." He lifted his sandwich to his mouth and took a big bite.

Neville's gaze met his for just a moment. Then, his twin shrugged and helped himself to a second sandwich, too.

While they ate, Shriek filled all the canteens from the river and set them aside until the water cooled enough to drink. When everyone was refreshed and full, the company prepared to get underway again.

Shriek bent over Clive, but he thrust up a hand. "Wait," he said. "If you insist on carrying me, there must be another way. I am not a sack of potatoes, ma'am."

The arachnoid's brief chitter sounded embarrassingly like a snigger as she grabbed Clive with her top two hands and swung him high onto her shoulders. Two hands clapped over his thighs, carefully avoiding his worst wound, and the other two locked on his ankles. He caught his breath, then let it out. It was better than being carried like a baby.

Chang Guafe lifted Neville and placed him similarly on his shoulders. Clive didn't miss the way his brother flinched and caught his ribs, and he felt a twinge of guilt about some of the thoughts he had toward Neville.

"Where to, Samedi?" Clive asked.

Both creatures turned and smiled. "Movin' on up," one

of them said. "Outta this valley o' the shadow of death, man," said the other. They both raised an arm, looked at each other for a moment, and grinned. "Come," they said in unison, beckoning.

Clive rolled his eyes as Shriek lurched under him, and their two guides turned to lead. He stared at their backs, at their tattered black suits and worn old top hats. There had to be some way to tell them apart, but it eluded him. They were the same height, looked and talked alike, even walked alike. Their garments, too, were studiously identical.

*Clones.* He didn't understand how such a thing could be. Two living things grown from the same tissue. He and Neville were born from one womb, but that wasn't the same, Annabelle had told him. But what if they'd been identical twins instead of fraternal ones? Would the same egg, divided by whatever mysterious process at fertilization, have made them clones? Annabelle said no. He still didn't understand it, he admitted, and determined to quiz his great-great-granddaughter about it again later.

He twisted around so he could see Annabelle in Finnbogg's arms. She hadn't so much as stirred since her killing of Philo B. Goode. Finnbogg had wet her lips to keep them moist and continued to coo and whisper to her as if she could hear, but so far, nothing had reached her.

*Shriek,* Clive mind-whispered, *would you try again?*

*Touch her mind have I tried,* the arachnoid responded, her thoughts tinged with sorrow and concern. *The Annabelle being deep within herself retreated has. Find, I cannot, Being Clive.*

He looked at Annabelle and bit his lip. There had to be a way to help her, and he'd find it. "Take care of her, Finnbogg," he said worriedly.

The alien canine glanced up with sad eyes. "Okay, okay," he answered. "Finnbogg here, have no fear. Want to sing?"

Clive shook his head. "Not now, Finnbogg. No telling if there's anything else lurking in this damn fog. Let's not draw any more attention than we have to."

"Okay, okay," Finnbogg agreed. He looked at the woman in his arms and rocked her as if she were a child. "Let Annie sleep quiet, then."

They trudged onward, and the ground began to gradually slope upward again. Soon, the mist began to thin, and the path steepened. Clive locked his fingers under Shriek's chin to keep his balance. When at last they achieved a point above the mist, they stopped and looked back. A thick white sea stretched below, obscuring the valley and the river, swirling and eddying with a sensuous slow movement.

Samedi called them to look as he pointed to the highest peak that rose in the distance. "There rests the Palace of the Morning Star," he said with unusual formality.

They resumed the climb, picking their way carefully, for the path was still slick with moisture. Clive had hoped that once the fog was behind them he'd be able to look up and see blue sky again, or at least a normal sky full of normal stars. But there was only a flat black expanse. *Like the sky of Q'oorna on the first level,* he remembered, *but without even the spiral cluster to break the monotony.*

It grew darker as they climbed, too. The ridge of mountains behind them now obscured the fireglow from the east that had lit the earlier part of their journey. Perhaps they would rise above it in time, but there was no indication of that, yet. The two Samedis seemed unconcerned, as if they could see in the darkness, and perhaps they could.

But Clive was concerned. He didn't want anyone to get separated from the group in the dark. With Annabelle unconscious there could be no illumination from the Baalbec A-9. Maybe he should ask Shriek to web them all together again? He didn't care much for that idea, either. Even though Philo B. Goode was dead, the threat of attack still niggled in the back of his mind. He didn't want to be bound to someone if he had to fight.

"Chang?" he said over his shoulder, breaking the silence that had fallen over the company. The cyborg quickened his pace and came up beside him, bearing Neville. He glanced briefly at his twin before continuing. "We could use a little light."

The cyborg's eyes began to glow with a familiar red light. It wasn't much radiance, but at least the others could see it and follow it and know they were still all together.

"Perhaps we should stop for a while," Neville suggested. "Maybe this is night and it will get a bit lighter when morning comes."

It was Sidi Bombay who spoke up. "We've seen nothing to indicate there are such things as night and day on this level, Englishman. Only a perpetual darkness from which the flames provided a little relief."

Clive concurred. "Remember what it was like on the other side of Dante's Gate? It may come to that again."

"*Não agüento mais!*" Tomàs muttered. "No more of that!"

Horace Hamilton Smythe smirked. "Oh? You preferred the fire, then? Or the Lake of Lamentations?"

Tomàs grumbled something incoherent but undoubtedly rude.

"Come!" the Samedis insisted as one. "Not much further to the promised place," they chanted, slapping palms, "where milk an' honey gonna stuff yo' face!"

Clive used his vantage high upon Shriek's shoulders to keep a continual lookout. There was little to see, though. The mountain peaks were deep shadows against the general blackness, featureless and indistinguishable except for the tallest one, their destination. To fight the monotony he tried counting paces, but that, too, became boring.

At last, he sought out conversation. *Shriek?* She didn't answer at once, and he called again with his mind.

*What?*

The word cracked like a pistol shot inside his skull. Clive clutched his temple and waited for the shock to pass.

*Sorry, am I, Being Clive,* Shriek said apologetically. *Distracted, was I.*

But Clive sensed something behind the words, some puzzlement or concern that colored her thoughts. *Is something wrong, Shriek?*

The arachnoid shook her head. *Know I do not. Tense am I.* She chuckled, but Clive could tell she felt no true mirth. *Deep in your mind a phrase there is that fits, Being Clive.* She hesitated before continuing. *Itch have I, but scratch I cannot.*

She made a mental frown, and Clive withdrew. Whatever was bothering her, he sensed her desire for solitude.

The ground leveled out suddenly, and they found themselves atop a high plateau. The warm wind gusted over them as it had not done for some time. It blew Clive's hair straight back, and he dared to hope it might dry his tattered garments, which were saturated from sweat and from the steam bath they had left behind.

The Samedis led them to the far edge. A vast, black abyss yawned at the plateau's rim, and Clive felt a moment of vertigo as he peered down into it from Shriek's shoulders.

Smythe leaned outward precariously and stared, rubbing his chin. "Wonder how deep it is?" he said.

Neville was droll. "Personally, I'm not going to go crawling around for a pebble."

"Why bother with a pebble, sah?" Smythe retaliated. "We could drop you over."

Chang Guafe moved to the edge.

Neville gave an unexpected yelp. "Wait. I'm sure he didn't mean it!"

Even Clive gave a shout. "Chang!"

The cyborg stood with his toes right at the rim and extended a hand into space. A dull green light winked briefly on his palm, and a tiny, high-pitched *beep* sounded once. He balanced there a moment more before moving away from the edge. He looked at Horace Hamilton Smythe.

"In answer to your query, my sensors receive no sonar response at all from the signal tone."

Smythe looked around for help from the others. The confused look on his face was almost comical. "Do you mean to say there's no bloody bottom?"

"Affirmative," answered Chang Guafe, "or if there is a bottom, it is too far away for sensor detection."

"That means it's deep," Neville volunteered caustically.

"Do not sneer at my friend, *senhor*," Tomàs spoke suddenly. "But a moment ago you thought Chang Guafe meant to drop you. Your little yelp betrayed your fear. You are smug, but you are no better than the rest of us."

Clive grinned inwardly. Point to the little Portuguese! Neville didn't even have a good comeback. He looked away from his brother and stared across the chasm.

A tall shadow loomed above them, the peak toward which they had been journeying. At its summit they would find the Palace of the Morning Star and meet whoever had sent Samedi—the Samedis, he corrected—to guide them. Again, he considered the idea of warring factions in the Dungeon, one of which might at least be friendly. But which one? The Ren? Or the Chaffri? Or some other group, altogether?

Perhaps he'd find new clues at this palace. He considered its name again, turning it over and over in his mind. Clive knew mythology well, and he knew the only possible significance of that name in this starless place. He wondered if he should tell the others.

Finnbogg gave a low growl that made Clive twist around. "Finnbogg?"

The others noted it, too.

Finnbogg stared up into the empty sky and gave another throaty growl. Then, slowly, without taking his eyes from the air above them, he stooped and placed Annabelle on the ground.

Clive drew his sword. "Put me down," he told Shriek. "Put me down."

Too late, he heard the rush of air. Clive threw himself

backward to avoid the down-sweeping leathery wings and unbalanced both himself and Shriek. They tumbled over in a tangle. Clive managed to keep his grip on the sword, but the wind was knocked from his lungs. Still, he tried to scramble to his feet.

A pair of shrill screams ripped from the Samedis as they cowered at the plateau's rim. But two hideous creatures sank clawed talons into the clones' shoulders, and their folded pinions opened suddenly to beat the air. The clones fought and struggled as the monsters swept them up into the sky. They hammered with their fists as they kicked and flailed above the chasm, screaming and begging for help.

Clive stood helplessly at the edge, cursing, tears burning on his cheeks as he watched. The fight was far beyond him now. There was nothing he could do but clench his fists in bitter frustration and stare horrified.

Shriek drew back with an envenomed spike-hair, but he stopped her. "What good would it do?" he said despairingly. "If you kill the creatures, they will drop our friends."

*A quick death could I give,* Shriek insisted, drawing back again, taking aim. *Better than to fall endlessly.*

Clive caught her arm again as he reached out for the smallest hope. "Maybe they only mean to capture them!"

Shriek hesitated, her body trembling with indecision. In that instant came two long despondent cries that faded quickly into the depths.

Clive's own scream followed, long and anguished and full of rage as the winged demons turned their backs and flew away. He took a step as he shook an empty fist, calling curses, and his leg gave way and he fell toward the yawning blackness.

Smythe saved him from tumbling off the edge and pulled him safely back. The others quickly gathered around. Only Tomàs stayed where he was.

Something in the way the little sailor stood alerted Clive. "What is it, Tomàs? What's wrong, man?" He pushed at all the hands that tried to restrain him and sat up. "Tomàs?"

"Their faces!" the Portuguese said, unable to hide the trembling in his voice. "I got a look at them! *Impossivel*, but I know those faces! A man and a woman, they were standing on the dock in Spain when the *Pinta* set sail. Only then, they looked normal. I remember! They stared right at me!"

Clive clutched his leg and winced and he leaned forward. "Tomàs, are you sure . . . !"

Neville Folliot interrupted as he looked down from his perch on Chang Guafe's shoulders. The cyborg hadn't even had time to set him down. "I saw their faces, too, little brother, and I knew them. They traveled with the good Mr. Goode for a while when I first met him. A brother and sister, I believe. Twins, just like you and me. Ransome, the name was, Amos and Lorena." Neville scratched his chin and frowned. "I must say, her looks have certainly taken a turn for the worse."

# CHAPTER TEN

# Across the Black Abyss

The loss of the two Samedis cast a pall over the company. The black landscape seemed twice as black, and the mountain peak that was their destination seemed twice as far away.

Chang Guafe stood at the edge of the chasm and watched for the pair of demons with all his sensors at maximum. He blamed himself for the deaths of their guides. Had he attuned his audio sensors, he claimed, he would have heard their swooping attack in time to warn everyone, but he had foolishly given his attention to the argument between Horace Hamilton Smythe and Neville Folliot.

Clive alternately cursed himself, the Ransome twins, the soul of Philo B. Goode, and the unknown Dungeonmasters. The screams of the Samedi clones still echoed in his ears, and the vision of them tumbling into the depths burned inside his head. Maybe he didn't understand exactly what a clone was, but those final cries had been human.

And what did that mean, anyway? Would he feel any better if Shriek had been killed? Or Finnbogg? Or Chang Guafe? Though they were aliens, they were no less his friends. Their souls were as noble, their spirits just as fierce, their loyalties just as strong as any man's.

He looked at Sidi Bombay in that instant, as if for the first time seeing the black man from India, and he understood at last the depth of his own English-bred prejudice.

Dark skin or white skin, four arms or metal arms—what did any of it matter?

And why had it taken the deaths of two beings—he understood now the honorific and the honor inherent in Shriek's form of address—to teach such an obvious lesson?

Slowly, painfully, he pulled one foot under himself. With a rocking motion he rose and straightened, putting just enough weight on his injured leg to balance himself. The thigh muscle screamed, and he clapped a hand over the bandage, but instead of easing off he put more weight upon it and limped in a small circle. He squeezed his eyes shut for a moment to hold back the tears that threatened. Then he opened them again and began to force the pain to a dim back corner of his mind.

He glanced around at the others, unsurprised that Neville, too, had mastered his discomfort. His twin clutched his side as he moved, but he limped purposefully around the lip of the chasm as if searching for something.

"Being Shriek," he called aloud, and the arachnoid scuttled swiftly to his side. "Our guides are gone. We've got to find our own way to the mountain peak."

Before Shriek could respond, Neville sang out. He had wandered far from the group and stood barely visible in the darkness on the plateau's far side. "Over here, little brother. I believe I've found it for you."

Clive frowned, then chided himself for the misplaced sense of competition he felt toward his twin. This was no time for childhood rivalries between grown men. The lives of his friends were in danger every moment they remained in this open space. He unfastened the belt that held his saber and scabbard, wrapped the leather strap around his hand once or twice, and leaned on it. A bit of folded ornamental steel tipped the scabbard, which protected it from wear and scuffing, but that would make it somewhat unstable on hard stone if he used it as a cane. Still, if he was careful, it would do, and it was all he had. He hobbled toward his brother to see what he had found.

"Oh, not goody," Finnbogg said, creeping up beside

them with Annabelle cradled in his arms. "Not my idea of funtime, no."

Horace Hamilton Smythe came up on Clive's other side, stared, and made a face. "Good lord, sah! I'm really beginning to hate this place!" the sergeant muttered in disgust.

The others quickly gathered around.

"Do you think if we waited five or ten minutes you could find another route?" Clive said to Neville with some sarcasm.

Despite his injuries, Neville put on his usual grin and pulled himself erect. "Come now, chap, where's the spirit? It would be ungentlemanly of us not to take advantage of what our hosts have provided."

"I don't know about that, Englishman," Sidi Bombay said unhappily, "but this must be why Baron Samedi brought us here. It must be the way to the Palace of the Morning Star, if that is still to be our destination."

"Don't see that we have a choice, really," Neville said, heading off any argument. "The Ransome twins or demons or whatever they were deprived us specifically of our guides, so they must not want us to reach this palace. That's one reason I say we should continue. The most important reason, however, is that if there is a gate around here to the next level and hopefully, home, we stand the best chance of learning about it there. It may even be there."

Clive stared over the edge of the plateau and squirmed. He didn't like it, but Neville was right. Besides, he was too angry and too curious now about the architects of this Dungeon. He and his friends had wandered blindly through the upper levels, guided or manipulated by the authors of the so-called diary, escaping from one threat after another without ever really learning much about this strange place in which they found themselves.

Here, though, on this seventh level, there seemed to be a chance to change that, to gain some understanding of what was going on. Clive was quickly beginning to realize that such understanding would be crucial if they were ever to get home.

"I hadn't realized the Ransomes were twins," he whispered to his brother. "That's interesting, a new piece of the puzzle."

Neville nodded and answered quietly, "Actually, they made quite a point of it when I met them. Now here they are, twins, and here we are, twins again. I'd really like a bit of a chat with them about that."

Clive let go a sigh as he turned to the rest of his party. "I think Neville's right," he said finally. "We really have no choice but to go on."

Tomàs rolled his eyes. "*¿Por quê, Christo, por quê?*"

Clive stared once more over the edge. A narrow stairway of carved black stone descended into the abyss. Each step appeared barely as wide as a man's foot, and no end to the treacherous incline could be seen. The chasm wall flanked the left-hand side, but a careless misstep to the right spelled doom. A small doubt plagued him. What if they were wrong? What if this wasn't the way the Samedis had intended to bring them? What if the stairway went nowhere but ended in midair? For that matter, what if it wouldn't support their weight?

"Let's go!" Neville said, descending the first step.

"Not yet!" Clive caught his brother's arm and pulled him back, ignoring the wince of pain on his twin's face. He turned worriedly to Shriek. The narrow stairs might prove a problem for her four feet and greater size. "Being Shriek," he said formally, "can you navigate these safely?"

*Much care shall I take, Being Clive. For your concern, much thanks.*

Clive resolved to worry anyway and to keep an eye on her. He turned back to his brother. "Just get back, Neville. You're not going first. Chang Guafe's sensors will see where you cannot. If the stair just ends, I want to know before anyone drops off. And if the stone won't take all our weight, again his sensors stand the best chance of detecting the stress."

Chang Guafe stepped forward. "You choose logically, human, I will test the way."

"Everyone go slowly, and keep close to the wall," Clive ordered quietly as the cyborg took the first step. They watched as Chang descended, his ruby lenses burning into the dark. "Stay away from the edge and watch out for the updrafts," Clive reminded.

"For a brother," Neville interrupted lightly, "you make quite a mother."

"And you make quite . . ." Clive stopped himself and looked away. Childhood rivalries, he remembered, were things best left to children. "Quite a good second choice. Down you go." He tapped his twin on the shoulder and pointed to the stair.

Next went Sidi Bombay, followed by Finnbogg with Annabelle in his arms. Tomàs waited, swallowed hard, and crossed himself, then descended behind them.

"After you, sah," Horace Hamilton Smythe bade with a short bow. "And mind your leg. I'll be watching you, I will."

Clive had a different idea. He planned to stay next to Shriek so *he* could keep an eye on *her*. Despite her reassurances, such narrow stairs weren't made for four arachnoid feet.

"No, old friend," he said to his sergeant, "you go first, and if I stumble, I'll have you to support me, just as you've always done."

Smythe stiffened as if he'd been insulted. "If it please you, sah, with these steep steps the last thing we need around here is that kind of grease." He gave a stern glare that quickly turned into a grin to let Clive know he was kidding. "Besides, Major, you've never stumbled, yet, but what you didn't pick yourself up smartly."

"Now who's spreading grease?" Clive answered, returning his sergeant's grin. "Get going."

*After you will come I.* Shriek's thoughts brushed against Clive's, but with a strange saw-edge that he had never felt before. She tried unsuccessfully to mask some irritation by ignoring it. *The Smythe being watch you from the fore he will, from behind watch will I.*

Clive raised an eyebrow, leaned on his sheathed sword to ease the ache in his thigh, and wondered what could be bothering Shriek. "Now, wait," he said with a cautious grin. "Who's watching whom?"

He sensed the tickle of her laughter as she forced herself to relax. *Watch all, all watch,* she responded, *so live all safe.*

Clive regarded her for a moment and scratched his head. That sounded to him suspiciously familiar. Did her planet have its arachnoid equivalent of Alexandre Dumas? "Say it this way," he told her. "All for one, and one for all."

*All one, one all,* came her response.

No, no, he thought. Too existential that way. Voltaire, not Dumas. But he'd have to teach her later. The others were getting too far ahead. He limped to the first stair and began a cautious descent.

If only there'd been something to make into torches. As they dropped beneath the plateau's rim, the darkness began to approach that on the other side of the Dantean Gate. Clive pressed his left shoulder to the wall and took the steps one at a time, stepping with his right and bringing the left foot down to meet it and stepping right again. It eased some of the stress on his injury.

A few steps ahead he could see Horace. Tomàs before him, though, was a dim shadow easily identified by the string of foreign epithets proceeding from it. Beyond Tomàs he could see nobody, though he knew by the shuffling of their footsteps they were there.

He glanced back at Shriek. She leaned with three of her hands against the wall, using it for balance as she negotiated the narrow stairs. Her front two feet moved in unison, descending three stairs while her back two supported her weight. Then, she shifted her weight forward and brought her back legs down. The stairs were clearly not made for her kind. They were too narrow for her feet, putting her in constant danger of slipping, and Clive considered that perhaps he'd made a mistake in positioning her last, for if she fell forward, she'd sweep them all over the edge. The steps were also too narrow for her girth. Though she hugged the wall, her right arm and shoulder dangled in space.

She stopped suddenly and gazed upward.

Clive stopped, too. *Being Shriek?* he called silently.

She didn't respond, though she started once more down the stairs. Only two of her six eyes, however, appeared focused on her passage. The others darted upward, around, as if she searched for something in the darkness. Though it was hard to tell for sure, her mandibled mouth seemed fixed in a frown.

*Are you unwell?* Clive inquired, concerned, as he resumed his descent.

She hesitated before sending a response, and when she did, it came tinged with confusion. *Understand I do not, Being Clive*, she said at last. *Something . . .* She waved her free hand in a sweeping gesture toward the sky, then frowned again, and touched her temple.

*Oh, great,* thought Clive, *an arachnoid with a headache.* He clapped a hand to his mouth as if he'd spoken out loud and wanted to catch the words before they escaped. But Shriek read minds. She didn't react, though. Either she hadn't heard or didn't understand the reference or chose simply to ignore him.

*Should we go back up?* he asked, pushing his thoughts at her. *We can search for another way across.*

*No,* she answered firmly. *Only way this is. Certain am I, or the Samedi beings . . .* She stopped again, shook her head and rubbed her temple, then resumed. *A scratch I have, itch I cannot,* she said as if that explained everything.

*An itch you can't scratch,* he corrected, remembering she'd said something about that earlier. *Are you sick? Can you tell me anything more about this itch?*

She shrugged all four of her shoulders, a rippling effect that traveled up and down her torso, and again shook her head. Her frustration shivered the neural web that linked them.

He bit his lip, then gave his concentration back to the stairs. Again, he'd fallen behind the rest of the group. Smythe's back was barely visible. Clive quickened his pace, though it cost him in pain. He leaned heavily on the sheathed sword and against the wall.

After a while, he could no longer see the top of the plateau. Memories of the dreadful darkness they had first encountered on this level began to nag at him again. He hadn't realized or even admitted before now how the time they had spent wandering on the other side of the Dantean Gate had unsettled him. It had happened, and he'd survived it, and that was that. But now that he recognized the possibility of finding himself in the same situation again, it discomforted him all the more. It was shameful for a grown man to fear the dark, and he wasn't *afraid*, really. It just made him nervous. Not because he feared any fairy-tale bogeyman, either, but because he'd seen the very real things that crawled around in this Dungeon.

He snapped out of his reverie at the sound of voices. Horace Hamilton Smythe called his name, and the others ahead muttered and whispered in excited tones.

"Watch your step, sah," Smythe whispered. "It levels off quite suddenly, it does!"

The sergeant was right. Clive nearly stumbled when he tried to descend one more step and there wasn't one. The staircase had become a narrow ledge that continued on around the chasm wall. At least, he hoped it continued on and didn't just end somewhere. He pressed his back firmly against the wall and felt for the edge with the tip of his sword. Then he felt for it with his toe and caught his breath.

The ledge was maybe two feet wide.

"Shriek!" he called back. The arachnoid had stopped just above him before the bottom step. "For God's sake, be careful!"

The arachnoid nodded as she stepped cautiously onto the precipice.

Clive thought suddenly of Finnbogg, too. Finnbogg couldn't have much more room to maneuver, either, and he was further burdened with Annabelle. Well, at least, he only had two legs to worry about, and if he stayed flattened against the wall, he'd be all right.

They began to move again. This time, though, they stayed within reach of each other, sliding their feet sideways in a slow shuffle that took them around the rock facing at a snail's pace. A metallic scraping accompanied them for part of the way until Sidi Bombay paused long enough to shift the canteen he carried. Neville and Smythe took the opportunity to unfasten their sword belts, deeming it safer to bear the weapons in their hands than to risk tangling their legs, however remote that possibility.

Neville was first to break a long silence. "Any of you chaps read any good books?"

Clive recognized a gallant try at breaking the gloom that seemed to have settled upon them, but no one responded.

"Ummm," Neville continued. "An illiterate bunch, eh? Well, perhaps we can find more common ground for communication, anything to pass the time, eh?" He snapped his fingers. "I know." He paused, cleared his throat theatrically, then began, "There was a young lady from France . . ."

Clive felt his cheeks go crimson. If he could catch his brother's eye he might silence him with a look of disapproval. Of course, he couldn't see his twin in the dark, and he had no intention of trying to lean out to do so. "Neville!" he hissed.

". . . and if you should meet her, by chance, she might give you a wink, and for the cost of a drink . . ."

Clive's face burned. "Neville," he tried once more, outraged, extremely grateful that Annabelle, at least, could not hear.

". . . you could spend the whole night in romance!"

"You what?" Clive sputtered, surprised. "Why, that's not the way I heard that last line!"

Horace Hamilton Smythe chuckled. "Something about spending an hour in her pants, sah? Wasn't that the way you told it?"

"Sergeant!" Clive snapped.

Neville clucked his tongue. "I'm shocked, little brother, and I'm sure Father would be, too. You simply hold out with too rough a crowd."

"There was a young girl from New Delhi," Sidi Bombay started, "who sported a jewel in her belly. Some called it a sin how she danced for her men, as slowly she turned them to jelly." The Indian gave a little chuckle and called back to Clive. "It is a universal verse form, Englishman."

Clive gave a low groan, frowned, and shook his head. Then, Chang Guafe began, much to Clive's surprise. *Oh, no! Not the aliens, too?*

"There once was a cyborg named Sue," he recited in his coldest mechanical voice, "who wound up on the scrap-heap, it's true. What a vicious caprice—she was missing a piece, and perished for want of a screw."

Chang's laughter sounded much like a sudden crackle of static, but the others joined in heartily. Even Clive had to admit he liked that one.

"You see, Englishman?" Sidi Bombay said when the laughter died a bit. "It *truly* is a universal form."

They continued along the precipice, trading old limericks and composing new ones, and gradually Clive forgot his fear and surrendered to the mirth of the game. It felt good to hear his friends laugh again. It cheered him, and the pain in his leg seemed to lessen. The medicine of the gods, some poet had called laughter, and perhaps it was so.

The ledge began to slope gently downward, and they moved with great caution until it leveled again. Sergeant Smythe had just begun a new limerick when Chang Guafe's single word silenced them all.

"Alert," the cyborg said.

They stopped absolutely still. Clive listened for the dreadful sound of leathery wings in the darkness above, suddenly aware of their vulnerable position as his hand closed around the hilt of his sword. He didn't draw, though. There wasn't even room for a good fighting stance. He stared ahead, straining for a glimpse of Chang Guafe, and barely made out the cyborg standing at the very edge and looking downward.

"Visual receptors scanning at infrared," Chang Guafe reported when Clive called his name. The cyborg hesitated as he continued to peer into the abyss, then he spoke again. "Heat patterns of unknown origin or purpose appear along the lower wall opposite." He paused again. "Computing probabilities." Another pause. "At this distance, analysis must combine with logical supposition. They are vents."

"I say, vents?" Neville interrupted. "Whatever would anyone be venting down here?"

"Heat," Chang Guafe repeated, looking at Neville as if he were an inattentive schoolboy. "My readings, though subject to error at this range, suggest the probability of some underground industry."

Clive pursed his lips and peered over the precipice. The hot updraft blew his hair and stung his eyes, but he saw nothing in the yawning blackness. Yet, he had no doubts that the cyborg spoke truly. "How far below us are these vents?"

"As I understand your units of measurement," Chang Guafe answered patiently, "approximately seven hundred meters."

Clive chewed his lip. This new discovery intrigued him immensely. Yet, there was no way they could reach the vents from the ledge, and there was every possibility that all they would find there would be danger. It might even be home for the demons they had encountered.

"It's too far below us to bother with for now," Clive said unenthusiastically. "Let's move on."

"¡Sim, adiante!" Tomàs agreed. "But quietly, amigos, so we don't disturb our neighbors."

"He has a point," Neville concurred.

There were no more limericks, no more jokes. They proceeded around the ledge with their backs pressed to the wall as if to hide from unseen eyes that might be watching from below. They inched their way slowly, and the scuffle of their boots on stone made the only sound. Clive watched the sky and half-expected the wingbeats of their enemies.

Then, they stopped again. "Oh, you're going to love this, Clive, old boy," Neville said distastefully.

"Perhaps it's a good thing that Miss Annabelle is not awake for this part of the journey," Sidi Bombay added.

"What is it?" Clive whispered with some irritation, unable to see what they were talking about. "Can we go forward or not?"

"Affirmative," Chang Guafe responded. "We could go forward. The ledge continues as far as my receptors can detect. However, this span offers a route to the other side."

"Span?" Clive said, leaning forward. "You mean there's a bridge?"

Neville sniffed. "If you care to dignify it with that word. It looks like four ropes and a lot of old boards to me. Why the hell do you suppose they put it down here?"

"I've stopped asking 'why' about a lot of things in this Dungeon," Clive answered smartly. "But if it goes to the other side, then we've got to take it."

"Would you care to go first, little brother?"

Chang Guafe interrupted as his metal heel scraped on wood amid the creaking and straining of old ropes. "I am chosen to test the way," Chang told Neville firmly. More steps sounded along the boards. The ropes creaked horribly, then stopped. "Are you not chosen to come second?"

There was an unspoken care in the cyborg's voice that almost made Clive grin. Chang's ruby lenses and the twin beams of light he radiated illumined a small portion of the bridge, though, and he understood his brother's hesitation. Clive had seen such bridges only in picture books, and a part of his heart quailed at the idea of crossing this one. The ropes sounded ancient, and the boards looked rotten and riddled with wormholes. And yet, another part of his heart lifted with a kind of boyish excitement. He kept that part in check. This was the Dungeon, after all, and on that bridge they would be even more vulnerable than they were now.

Still, it was the way across.

"Either go, or get out of the way," Clive told his twin firmly.

"I'm going, I'm going," Neville snapped. "You're getting to be a bit of a pushy twit, Clive."

Clive ignored that. It was only Neville's way of summoning courage, and the sound of his boots on the boards was all that Clive listened for. Chang Guafe turned and moved farther along the span. His eyes burned like two glowing coals that seemed to float in the dark emptiness above the chasm. The line moved forward as Sidi, then Finnbogg, bearing Annabelle, and Tomàs and Smythe stepped onto the bridge.

The ropes creaked in his ears like a discordant music. Clive took the time to strap on his sword again, then gripped one rope in each hand and stepped onto the boards. There was a disconcerting moment as it sank under him, and the updraft swirled suddenly about him. He gripped the ropes tighter and gritted his teeth and took another step and slowly another. His heart raced around in his chest as it seemed to him the bridge took a strange pitch and righted itself. The boards bounced under him, vibrated with the tread of those before him, and the whole structure swayed frighteningly in the hot, rising winds.

Then his foot touched solid ground again, and Horace Hamilton Smythe reached out to steady him. "It's another narrow ledge, sah," his sergeant told him, but Clive was grateful for it, anyway. Narrow it might be, but it didn't shift or buck, and it didn't creak.

They crept along the edge, and the way at last began to rise at a gentle slope toward the chasm rim. The wind blew stronger on this side, though, and they hugged the rock face. Again, Clive unfastened his sword, preferring to carry it rather than have it slap his leg. But this time, as he undid the buckle, he felt something slip against his skin and catch in a rip in the side of his shirt.

*Neville's diary!* He made a grab for it, but the scabbard began to slide off its belt, and he made a grab for that. He didn't dare lose his sword. That motion, however, dislodged the diary from the rip, and the book tumbled out. "Grab it!" he shouted.

Shriek made a lunge for it. It bounced off her top right hand and went spinning, pages fluttering, its leaves opening like the wings of a precious bird as her lower right hand stretched out for the capture.

Then, the arachnoid gave a cry and teetered over the abyss. She fanned the air with all four arms, struggling for balance on a ledge barely big enough for her. Clive let go of his sword belt and tried to snatch her back. The scabbard clattered against stone, directly in the path of his foot as he moved, and went tumbling end over end into the darkness.

His fingertips brushed Shriek's, but it was too late. She screamed and pitched backward, following book and blade into the black emptiness as Clive and company stared in numbed horror.

# · CHAPTER ELEVEN ·

# Shriek's Flight

A billowy white substance blossomed far down in the chasm depths. Moments later, Shriek floated upward, borne aloft by the hot updrafts that filled the rippling, diaphanous strands of an immense sail-web. She hung limply, though, and the frivolous winds shifted and stirred and blew her away from the rock face where no one could reach her.

Clive screamed her name as she drifted higher above them.

*Well, I am, Being Clive,* the arachnoid answered without moving a muscle, *though fall I may yet. Violent, these winds. Tear my sail they may.*

"Throw out a line!" Clive called. "We'll haul you in!"

*Another web I cannot spin,* she replied, and a note of worry played among her thoughts. *Maintain this sail I must or fall.*

Horace Hamilton Smythe touched his arm. "But where will she go, sah? How high?"

So Shriek had sent her thoughts to all of them. Clive opened himself slightly and felt a jangling on the neural web that Shriek had spun about them at their first meeting. It was not a pleasant thing to him, nor to many of the others. It allowed far more than just silent speech if one didn't guard oneself carefully. But he reached out now and felt his friends, all but Annabelle, whose mind was closed, and all but Neville and Sidi Bombay, who had not been party to the arachnoid's mind-gift.

*Go I where the winds blow,* Shriek answered Smythe as she rose higher and higher on her strange delicate parachute. *Fly I where the hot breezes flow. Pass under me the land and sea. Freedom will I know.*

*A poem?* Surprise filled Clive's thoughts as Shriek ascended beyond sight.

*Translation,* came the arachnoid's answer. The worry seemed to have faded from her thoughts. A sublime joy filled her mind. *A song of my people at flight time, a special time for us. Not completely accurate, but close it is.* She paused, and everyone sensed the awe that consumed her as the winds bore her farther and farther away. *Drifting toward the mountain I am, Being Clive. Meet again we will. Meet again we will, friend beings.*

Clive didn't know if she simply stopped answering or if she had floated too far away to hear him. He called and called, but Shriek didn't respond. He watched helplessly as she floated away into the darkness and disappeared.

Horace Hamilton Smythe put an arm around his shoulders. "It's all right, sah, it is. She'll meet us at the top, you'll see, just like she said."

Clive Folliot looked his sergeant straight in the eye, then blinked and looked away. He let go a sigh. "I thought I'd lost her, Horace, just as I lost the Samedis, as I may have lost Annabelle." He drew a deep breath, held it, then sighed again. "I shouldn't be leading this outing. Let Neville do it. He's a natural leader."

"He's a horse's arse, if you'll pardon my saying so, sah!" Smythe whispered tersely. "Now you didn't *lose* nobody. The Ransome twins, or some mockery of the Ransome twins, killed the Samedis. As for Annabelle, she's right here, and we'll find a way to make her well if she doesn't snap out of it herself, as I expect she might when she's ready. And Shriek's not dead, either. She's alive because she's got the skills to keep herself that way, she has. It's all any of us have got, our wits and our skills. Well, it's your wits and skills that's going to get us out of this mess. Not Neville's. He may be your brother and all, but don't forget, he got himself caught by the Lords of Thunder, and he'd be last week's news, if you'll pardon the expression, but for you and Miss Annabelle thinking and acting so quick to save his hide."

Clive still wasn't convinced, but he put on a weak smile. "Good old Horace," he said, "always there to kick my backside."

"Only when it needs kicking," Smythe answered sternly.

Clive cast another glance upward, hoping for a glimpse of Shriek, but the darkness was unblemished. Well, there was no point in standing on this ledge debating the finer points of leadership with Horace Hamilton Smythe. "Let's go," he said at last. "We've got a friend waiting for us at the top."

They resumed their cautious trek and came to another set of steps just as steep and just as treacherous as the set that had carried them down to the ledge. After a long and arduous climb, they found themselves on the other side of the chasm, in the shadow of the mountain that was their destination.

"Okay, okay!" Finnbogg said with faint enthusiasm. "Not so dark as big pit. Easier to see." He shifted Annabelle's weight as he stared toward the mountain.

It was a subtle difference in the darkness, and the reason seemed to be the mountain itself. A nebulous halo radiated from it, as if the mountain obscured some greater light that burned palely behind it. The gloom was still pervasive, but they could at least see each other, and they could at least see their way. Yet, why had they not noticed it before from the other side of the chasm? The view of the mountain had been just as clear.

At Clive's suggestion, Chang Guafe searched with his electronic senses for some sign of Shriek. The cyborg found no trace of her, though. Who knew where the winds would carry her, or where she would touch down, or if in her strangely ecstatic state she even wanted to? He reached out with his thoughts and called her name, but only silence echoed back, bringing with it an odd loneliness.

The canteens were passed around and everyone drank. Clive's leg felt stiff and sore, and yet it bore his weight better than earlier. He limped ahead of the others and paused, the mountain filling his vision. At its summit rested the Palace of the Morning Star. That meant food, he hoped, and perhaps sleep as well. Maybe they would find the gate to the next level, too. He would welcome the chance to leave this one behind.

But would there be friends there? Maybe allies? Samedi had claimed he'd been sent to guide them to the palace. Philo B. Goode and the Ransome twins had seemed bent on preventing that. Why? One side for them, and one side against them. What did it mean?

Clive Folliot was beginning to feel more and more like a pawn in some kind of chess match, and he didn't care much for the feeling.

He turned and beckoned to the others to follow. "Come," he said automatically.

A short march across a relatively flat stretch of terrain brought them to the foot of the mountain. While the others rested briefly, Clive wandered a bit, searching unsuccessfully for Shriek. Returning, he knelt down beside Annabelle and took her hand in his. She still showed no sign of stirring. He lifted one of her eyelids. Her iris had drifted far up, and her dilated pupil was an empty well of blackness. He kissed her lightly on the forehead, then patted Finnbogg's arm. "Take care of her," he whispered.

"Annie okay, will be okay," Finnbogg answered with assurance.

Sergeant Smythe rose and came to his side. "You should let me check that bandage, Major, sah," he said.

Clive waved him off. "It's okay, Sergeant." But when his batman looked away, he pressed his hand over the wound and winced. The soreness was still there, and the stiffness. He'd succeeded in pushing the pain to the back of his mind for a little while, and he'd just have to do so awhile longer. If he sat down and rested like the others, he had a feeling he wouldn't get back up.

At first, it was an easy climb. The gentle slope took a minimum of effort and the footing was sure. They maintained less of a line now as each found his own path up the hillside. Horace Hamilton Smythe, though, stayed close by Clive's side, and Clive noticed with some reluctant gratitude how Chang Guafe watched over Neville.

The delicate light surrounding the mountain grew subtly stronger and illuminated the cracks and crevices that might have tripped them up, the rocks that might have turned underfoot. Clive began to reflect that he had seen no blade of grass, nor any living creature on this level except the demon-things that had attacked them. The other levels had been peopled with beings of all different kinds from all different times and planets. But apparently not this one. Why was that?

The climb became steeper. Now Clive felt the strain on his wounded thigh. He touched the bandage with his fingertips and found a warm wetness. Blood. The wound was seeping. He covered it with his hand to hide the fact from Smythe and kept climbing. Some of the inclines, though, were so sharp they had to lean forward and scramble up on all fours. He always tried to position himself so that the sergeant couldn't see his leg.

Halfway up they rested again. Chang Guafe and Finnbogg showed little evidence of fatigue, though the alien canine's tongue lolled a bit as he cradled Annabelle in his lap. Sidi Bombay also appeared fit and ready to continue, and Clive wondered if perhaps he'd spent some time in the mountains of northern India or some of the more rugged regions of Africa during his career as a guide and gunbearer.

On the other hand, Tomàs looked ready to drop, which was just what he did as soon as they stopped, just collapsing onto his back and throwing an arm across his eyes. He let go one long, miserable moan and fell silent.

Neville was the one he worried about most. His brother

refused to be carried anymore, but he looked pale, and his mouth had drawn into a taut lipless line. His right hand never left his ribs, and he was having some trouble breathing. Sergeant Smythe and Sidi Bombay both had examined him, though, and assured him that none of the ribs were broken.

Chang Guafe extended a slender tentacle from a small panel in his chest and passed it near Neville's ribs. Though he possessed numerous such appendages, the cyborg seemed to use them less and less, and Clive paused long enough to wonder if it was some latent aspect of Chang's lost mimicking power that he unconsciously relied more and more on his humanoid form as he spent more time with humans.

A tiny red light on the very end of the tentacle winked on and began to blink rapidly as it moved back and forth over Neville's ribs. "Difficult to be accurate," the cyborg reported, retracting the tentacle into his body again. "This sensor is calibrated for the study of alien flora. However, allowing for that, analysis indicates a higher-than-mean probability that Neville Folliot has torn cartilage between the ribs, which will cause pain, but will easily heal with rest and time."

Clive scratched his chin and wondered how much he should trust an alien's diagnosis of a human's injury. On the other hand, there was nothing else he could do, at least about Neville's ribs. Many of the cuts and scratches on his twin's shoulders and back, though, looked almost as nasty as the cut on his thigh. Clive thought they both probably needed stitches, but that, of course, was out of the question.

They sipped from the water canteens again, then after threatening and prodding Tomàs to his feet, they resumed the climb.

They ascended to another flat plateau and looked back the way they had come. It wasn't much of a view. The mountains they had already crossed looked like jagged shadows against a backdrop of night, starker and more ominous than when they had stood upon them. There was no sight of the mist-filled valley or of the river that had carved it.

Nor was there any sight of Shriek. Everywhere, Clive watched for the arachnoid. He missed her calming presence in his mind, and he missed the security of her fierce fighting skills. He scanned the plateau, thinking she might have been able to land safely there, but there was no trace.

Horace Hamilton Smythe stepped up to his side. "You're bleeding, sah," he said. "You should have said something."

"Get away from me, Horace," Clive whispered. "You're like a mother sometimes. And keep your voice down. We're high up now, and I don't know if there's an echo or not up here, but let's not find out, huh?"

"But your leg, sah . . ."

"It's all right!" Clive insisted quietly. "I'm keeping an eye on it, and it's all right, I tell you."

They crossed the plateau and began to climb again. The mountain turned more rugged. Sections of black rock shot up like splinters. Stone piled upward like stalagmites in a cavern for no apparent reason. Some toppled at a touch; others proved strong enough to lean against. Sheer rock faces loomed. Yet every time the trail looked too rough to follow someone found another trail conveniently close.

Tomàs complained of blisters, stopped, and massaged his feet. Smythe rubbed his palms together, wincing. Everyone's hands were raw from scrambling. Clive, too, felt the beginnings of a blister inside his boots. He wiggled his toes and let go a long, silent curse using words no true English gentleman should even know.

*A rude awakening, Being Clive.*

For an instant, Clive Folliot thought he had imagined it. Then, he snapped to alertness. He almost shouted but thought better of it. "Shriek!" he hissed, staring wildly about. "You're alive! Where the hell are you?"

The others heard him and regarded him with something

approaching the suspicion one harbored toward an idiot on the street.

*Up here, Being Clive,* she answered with a hint of sleepy amusement. *Above you, am I.*

Clive looked up sharply and caught his breath. Suspended between a tall, needlelike pinnacle and a cliff face hung the hugest web he had ever seen, and Shriek bobbed and bounced in the center in the gentle wind that rocked it. He pointed, and the others looked, too, with similar amazement.

"The barest hint of light on the strands," said Sidi Bombay in awe. "This is a work of art, my friends, a work of woven art."

Shriek stirred and stretched in her web. *The Sidi being kind is. Primitive, barbarous, disgusting this would be on home world of Shriek. Fly we do not on home world. Fly only ill-mannered or poorly raised egglings.* She paused, reached out with two arms, and plucked strands of the web, making it vibrate and to Clive's surprise, making it sing. Two musical notes shivered in the air. She plucked two shorter filaments and two higher-pitched quavers were the result. Then, her thoughts brushed against them all. *Yet, learning am I how much of our past, our evolution renounced have we. Sacrificed for affectations of civilization have we. Perhaps, basic nature of self rejected have we.*

Clive sensed something deeper under her thoughts, though. Suddenly, the back-and-forth motion the web made as the wind blew through it reminded him of a mother consolingly rocking her child. He reached out with his thoughts instead of his voice, offering the greater intimacy. *What is it, Being Shriek? What's wrong?*

After a hesitation, she answered. *Fear I do, Being Clive, and wonder. Home can I go? Fit there, will I? Learned much have I in this Dungeon. Changed much.*

A chill rippled down Clive's spine, and he looked at the others. They had all heard their arachnoid friend, and he knew by their faces they all felt the same chill.

Only Chang Guafe reacted differently. "Change is the nature of all things," he said coolly. "On my planet each new thing we touch we absorb into our beings. It becomes a physical part of us. Each new thing we learn causes us to change. We do not even look alike, but wear our changes and our learning as our skin." The others turned slowly to look at him, remembering no doubt his own story of his planet's evolution, of how life there had been just a primordial muck until the first spaceship landed there and both ship and crew were absorbed, giving intelligence and form that was both mechanical and organic. "I travel with you, fight with you," he continued, "because the Dungeonmasters have taken away my power to change, my power to grow and evolve. I want it back."

"Perhaps it is not the change we fear." Sidi Bombay spoke with a quiet wisdom. The little Indian turned his thin, dark face to each of them, and his eyes glittered with a sad compassion. "But the isolation. The veneer of custom, of civilization, locks us into certain patterns of accepted behavior. Shriek fears she has seen through that veneer, that the pattern is no longer acceptable to her." He looked at each of them again. "And so, I think, do many of us. And yet, if we do not conform to those patterns, whether they be English manners or Hindu beliefs, we face rejection and ostracism, perhaps even imprisonment, by our people."

"Or they lock us up in a bloody loony bin," Horace Hamilton Smythe added gloomily.

"How illogical and confining," Chang Guafe responded. "You are truly alien creatures."

Clive listened to the argument with one ear, but it was still Shriek's simple statement that struck him most deeply, maybe because with the mind-touch he caught something of the complexity of her fear, while Chang Guafe and Sidi attempted to simplify it with mere words. That was an important thing to understand, he realized suddenly, that language could only encapsulate. It could never express fully.

He wondered how he would ever fit back into Victorian society knowing that other planets harbored life in such an infinite combination of forms. What did that say about man's place in the universe and his relationship to God? Which of them, Clive, Shriek, Chang Guafe, or Finnbogg, was truly made in the image of the Lord? That was not the only question, though it alone was enough to rock the foundation of his culture, should anyone ever believe him and care to seriously debate the issue.

How would he fit knowing—*knowing,* not just speculating as did his friend George du Maurier—that one being might speak to another being with the power of thought alone?

How would he fit knowing the shape of the future to come, knowing of a nightmare world ruled by things called computers and populated by people who had harnessed themselves to strange machines in an obscene symbiosis, machines such as the Baalbec A-9. Chang Guafe was not the only cyborg he had met in the Dungeon. Chang, at least, came from another world, where other mores and customs were prevalent. It was not for Clive to judge Chang's world. But he'd met human cyborgs, too. Annabelle's Baalbec was an almost inoffensive example.

For that matter, how would he fit in having realized that women were not the fragile creatures he'd been taught they were, that they could plan and scheme and fight right beside any man if they chose to do so, that they didn't require a man's protection, let alone his supervision? Annabelle had taught him that much, his own great-great-granddaughter.

Yet, as he looked at his granddaughter, he saw suddenly the sad face of not Annabelle Leigh, but Annabella Leighton, the woman he loved and had unknowingly left in unfortunate circumstances alone in a flat in London.

He drew a deep breath and hardened his resolve. This time he spoke so the others would hear. "It's a fear we all have to face, Being Shriek, each in our own way and as best we can. But we have to go home."

*Why, Being Clive?* Shriek responded, the doubt in her thoughts easy to taste. *Perhaps here now belong we.*

"Then let me amend that," Clive answered stubbornly, moving to Annabelle's side and touching Finnbogg between the ears. Finnbogg growled appreciatively. "I have to go home. Matters compel me."

"Father?" Neville asked dubiously.

"Father be damned," Clive responded forthrightly. "I must get back for my own reasons, not for his. I've played his puppet for the last time."

"Puppet?" Neville said. "That's a bit disrespectful, isn't it? He sent you to find me."

"And I've found you," Clive snapped. "Now it's time to get home." He turned to the others. "For all of us."

"*Bom idéia,*" Tomàs muttered, "if we can."

## · CHAPTER TWELVE ·

# Annabelle in Wonderland

The source of the faint light was no longer a mystery. The mountain itself had obscured a familiar spiral of stars that floated up from some invisible horizon higher and higher into the sky. It was not the same spiral as the one that shone over Q'oorna, however. That one hung in the night, cool and picturesque and indifferent, like a faraway galaxy of icy diamonds. This one burned with the same cool light, but the stars swirled and danced in a cloud of churning gases. The entire mass seethed against the darkness with an unnerving and soundless fury.

Its light fell upon an equally unnatural structure that stood at the top of the mountain. The pinnacle, itself, had been sheared away by some great and inconceivable machine, leaving a surface like polished onyx that gleamed smoothly in the spiral's radiance. In the center of that surface loomed the strangest of houses, an immense dwelling whose lines and angles all seemed subtly wrong. It seemed to *lean* in three or four different directions all at once, and the roof sagged in some places, bulged oddly in others. The several chimneys tilted left and right, refusing to stand straight. None of the windows made a square or a neat rectangle either, but pinched in at one corner or the other.

"I say, the architect must have drawn his blueprint on a

napkin over drinks," Neville Folliot whispered to his brother.

"You mean *after* a couple of drinks," Clive suggested.

They crouched at the edge of the mountaintop, feeling nakedly exposed, almost afraid to stand. The hot winds blew in sudden gusts strong enough to sweep them from the edge if someone got careless. The final part of the climb had taken a lot out of them, for it had been the steepest and most difficult part, and the path had zig-zagged back and forth along a towering rock face.

Clive's thigh throbbed painfully, and the muscle trembled and quivered whenever he rested it. A thin trail of blood had trickled down into his boot, then clotted merci-fully. The bandage that bound his wound, though, was saturated. All his lesser cuts and scratches ached and stung, too, from the strain and from the sweat that contin-ually irritated them.

Neville didn't look any better. Neither twin said any-thing, though, or gave any complaint. They glanced at each other from time to time out of the corners of their eyes as if checking on the other. It was almost as if they were in a competition to see who would hold out longest, who would be the strong man and who would break. Annabelle had had some word for it, something shocking, but Clive couldn't recall what it had been.

*Macho bullshit,* Shriek thoughtfully provided.

Clive jerked around, appalled. "Thank you," he said dubiously.

"Who do you think lives there, sah?" said Horace Ham-ilton Smythe in a whisper as he crouched next to Clive.

"Oh, I think that's pretty obvious, Sergeant," Neville Folliot interrupted.

But Clive interrupted his twin. He'd solved that puzzle some time ago, and he was darned if he'd let Neville have the satisfaction of taking the credit. "We've had two very good clues, Horace. First, the diary entry when we first came here. "How will you feel when you meet Hell's Sire?"

it said. Then, there's the name of this place, the Palace of the Morning Star.

Neville broke in. "Obviously, it's—"

"Lucifer," Clive snapped before his brother could finish. "At least, that's obviously who we're supposed to think it is."

Tomàs folded his knees under himself and made the sign of the cross. "*Ave Maria, cheia de graça. . . .*"

Clive just frowned and tuned him out.

"Hell's Sire is an obvious reference," Chang Guafe agreed, "but my memory index provides no data on the second."

Clive explained. "Both my brother and I were provided with a solid education in the classics. Among the ancient Romans, a culture that once thrived in our world's past, the morning star bore the name Lucifer, or Light-bringer. Later, that name was attributed to the angel who led the revolt against God and fell from heaven. He became the ruler of hell, a place made specifically for his punishment."

"Your God punished him by giving him a place of his own to rule?" Chang Guafe looked from Clive to Neville and back. "He was victorious in his revolt, then?"

Clive and Neville looked at each other. Neville couldn't hold back a crooked grin. "You must introduce him to Milton sometime if we get out of this."

Chang Guafe looked at each of them again. "I register confusion," he said.

Sidi Bombay tapped him consolingly on the shoulder. "Their beliefs have always confused me, too, my friend." He tilted his head and made a face of mock-sympathy. "But they are English."

Chang Guafe turned his ruby eyes toward Sidi. "Are you not one of them?" he said evenly.

Sidi clutched his heart and put on a look of shock and offense so extreme they could not but know he was teasing. "I am Hindu!" he answered with exaggerated dignity. Then he waved a hand of dismissal and wrinkled his nose. "They are Christian."

Chang Guafe eyed them all one at a time as his eyes

brightened and dimmed, brightened and dimmed. "I register confusion," he repeated.

"It would take too long to explain," Clive responded, grinning at Sidi's antics. "Suffice it to say that although humans may all look alike to you, we have as many differences among us as your people. But none of this matters now." He rose slowly, cautiously with the aid of his sheathed sword to a half-crouch. The winds pushed against his chest, and he took a half-step back to catch his balance. "This is the place where Baron Samedi intended to bring us. I say we go knock on the door and see who answers."

"And if it's Old Nick, himself?" Neville said, also rising.

Clive cast a glance at their Portuguese companion, who still knelt muttering into folded hands. "Then we'll get Tomàs to scare him off with prayers."

The company clustered around Clive and began to walk toward the house. "Food, okay?" Finnbogg inquired. "Food for Annie, food for Finnbogg, food for everybody?"

"We'll hope so," Clive assured him.

"Probably devil's cake," Horace Hamilton Smythe grumbled.

"Or a fallen angel cake," Neville suggested.

Sidi joined in. "Or hot cross buns."

"Something from the oven, no doubt," Clive agreed. He looked up at the lighted windows that shone from the house and felt his gut tighten. He watched for shadows moving within, for a face appearing from behind a curtain. Wasn't anyone aware of them? He simple didn't believe they weren't observed. He was beginning to think every move they had made since entering the Dungeon had been observed by someone. He felt like a bug under a microscope. Or a student taking a test.

The house seemed even larger as they approached. An ornate trim of swirls and spirals bordered the windows and the eaves. Leering gargoyles jutted from the guttering. A kind of petrified hedge sprouted up on either side of the path to the main door, with ebony leaves and branches that sparkled in the light and shattered at a touch.

A huge knocker made of iron or some black metal hung upon the door. Clive reached out for it, then hesitated. He looked back at the faces of his friends and saw the same mixture of hope and anxiety in each of them. Only Chang Guafe's face remained impassive, yet in one night in Samedi's cave Clive had learned how to read his cyborg friend.

He grabbed the knocker and slammed it down twice.

The door swung back. A small, frog-faced creature perhaps four feet tall peered suspiciously out from a brightly lit entrance. Opaque membranes nictated over a pair of large round eyes that settled first on Clive's face, then on Neville's. An immense, toothless smile split the curious little face nearly in half and he flung the door open wide.

"You've arrived, arrived!" The creature began to spring up and down on powerful legs, and it clapped webbed hands gleefully. "We didn't know when to expect you, expect you! Come in, Clive Folliot! Come in, Neville Folliot! Welcome all! Welcome, welcome, welcome!"

The twins exchanged glances.

"Hardly my idea of Lucifer, little brother," Neville commented dryly.

"The Frog-prince of darkness, maybe?" Clive shook his head.

They followed the creature down the hallway. Their guide moved in tiny lurching hops, twisting its neckless head around to smile at them, maintaining a constant stream of chatter. Gold bracelets jingled on its wrists as it moved, and a robe of purple silk fluttered about its legs.

Horace Hamilton Smythe watched those legs with a gleam in his eye and licked his lips until Clive Folliot gave him a stern look. "It's devil's cake for you, remember?" he reminded his former batman.

"I don't suppose you have a name or anything?" Neville asked, interrupting their guide.

"Herkimer," came the rapid-fire answer. "I'm Herkimer, Herkimer. Now come this way, please. We have rooms for all of you, and hot baths and fresh clothes and everything to make you comfortable, comfortable! And later, when you're rested, there will be dinner. The master will be awake, awake by then. He's so looking forward to seeing you at last. You're all he's talked about lately, you know, all he's talked about. Oh, and your injuries, injuries! We'll send fresh bandages and medicine right along, along, along. Then, you must tell us all about your adventures. The master will know, of course. He knows everything. But he'll want to hear your stories in your own words, your own words. It'll be such fun!"

Clive followed but tuned out much of Herkimer's chatter. It surprised him as they passed from one hallway into another how the furnishings were from his own period. Here and there were paired overstuffed chairs, sometimes a delicate table or a framed mirror. Gaslight even provided the illumination. The walls were covered with a flocked, floral-patterned paper not unlike that in his very own home.

How strange, he thought, to find such Victorian tastes in such a faraway place. In many ways it reminded him of his own home, with many of the same finishing touches, and a moment of homesickness stole unexpectedly upon him.

They climbed a flight of steps to a corridor that was lined with doors. Herkimer pointed to the first with a mottled-green-and-brown hand. "Here's your room, your room, Mr. Chang Guafe, and there is yours, Miss Shriek." He indicated the door opposite from the first. Surprisingly, he knew all their names as he led them each to his room and opened the doors for them.

"Please," Clive said suddenly when Herkimer made Annabelle's assignment. "I'd like Annabelle to have either the room next to mine or directly across from it."

"Of course," Herkimer said with a smile. "That's easily arranged, easily. We'll just change her room, her room, for Mr. Smythe's." He turned his smile on the sergeant. "Since you're both of the same species there should be no problems, no problems at all."

Sergeant Smythe moved into the doorway but stood on

the threshold watching as did Shriek and Chang Guafe, Sidi Bombay, and Tomàs from their doorways. Finnbogg noted his room assignment but followed along after Clive and Neville with Annabelle in his arms.

There were exactly enough rooms to guest them. Clive and Neville took the last two at the farthest end of the corridor. Their rooms faced each other, and Herkimer flung back the doors, revealing a glimpse of lavishly furnished bedchambers.

Herkimer made a curt bow, his frog-smile never fading. "You'll find hot baths drawn and waiting, waiting for you," he said, "and fresh clothes in all the closets, closets. Never fear, the sizes are each yours. My master has seen to it, seen to it."

"I thought you didn't know when to expect us," Clive said suspiciously.

"Oh, we didn't!" Herkimer insisted. "But never fear, the water *will* be hot, hot. Trust my master. And when you are washed, dressed, and rested, then supper will be ready, will be ready."

"Will we meet your master then?" Neville asked casually, peeking around his door, surveying his room as he spoke over his shoulder.

"Most assuredly," Herkimer answered as he hopped back toward the stairway. "Most assuredly."

Clive watched him go and watched his friends as they glanced his way, then slipped into their rooms. He listened to the quiet closing of the doors until he found himself alone in the hall. He went to Annabelle's door, then opened it and passed inside.

The room was done in a rather Spartan military style reminiscent of an officers' quarters, and he remembered it was originally intended for Horace Hamilton Smythe. There was a bare desk and a chair with a small pile of stationery and an inkwell in one corner of the desk. A wardrobe stood in a corner of the room, and a wooden footlocker sat at one end of the bed. The odor of warm, herb-scented water emanated from a tiny side room.

Annabelle lay composed on the bed where Finnbogg had placed her. Clive sat down on the edge of the mattress, looked at her for a long moment, then drew one finger along her soft cheek. Wherever her mind had retreated to she looked so utterly at peace. He turned her head a little to the side. The wounds on her throat had scabbed over, but he feared they would scar and leave three fine, delicate lines. Her other scratches were relatively minor.

Clive felt a sudden fatigue wash over him, bringing with it a familiar guilt. Though part of him had learned better, another part chided him for failure. He should have taken better care of her, looked after her more closely, protected her. It should have been his hand on the sword that killed Philo B. Goode. He should have spared her that shock.

He drew a deep breath and cradled his head in one hand as he closed his eyes. No, even by then it was too late. He remembered the look in her eyes, the expression of terror as Annabelle waded through the creatures that wore her daughter's face, as she flung them right and left and drove them back with the machine that was part of her body. Even before she killed Philo, her mind had begun its retreat.

Well, if he had been unable to help her then, perhaps he could do something now. He had to, she was his own granddaughter, and his only link to another woman he loved in a world to which he might never return.

Shriek had provided him with a way. At their first meeting the arachnoid had drawn each of them into her psychic web so that they might all communicate on a speechless level with her, or by touching, with each other if they wished. It was not something they did often. Shriek, to whom such telepathy was entirely natural, was able to shield the passageways that led to her deeper thoughts and emotions, and her skill or courtesy was great enough that she didn't intrude too deeply into another mind when she initiated such communication.

But everyone else shied away from using the power without her guidance. It was too easy to tumble into the personality and secret intimacies of someone when you'd only wanted to say hello. In that first encounter before the shock made them all recoil, Clive had glimpsed not only the memories and personal experiences of all his comrades, but their biases and desires, even the bits and pieces of their own cultures as seen through their eyes.

It was all a bit too personal, and by unspoken agreement they had refrained from doing it again except in direst circumstances.

He touched Annabelle's cheek again, feeling the warmth and flush of his own blood under her pale skin. This was such a circumstance, he told himself. Maybe Annabelle would disagree, maybe she'd consider it the cruelest of all possible invasions. But he wasn't just going to let her lie there like that the rest of her life.

He was going to go find her.

He took her hand and pressed it firmly between his, then closed his eyes again. *Annabelle,* he called softly, *Annabelle.* But no answering thought stirred against him, no voice echoed gently up out of the black empty well that was all he perceived.

Clive opened his eyes and looked at her stubbornly. He wasn't at all ready to give up. He rose, moved around to the other side of the bed, and stretched out beside her, adjusting his body on the mattress so that their shoulders touched. He squeezed her hand again and pressed it down between their bodies. Again he closed his eyes.

*Annabelle,* he called, moving to the edge of the well, bending over it, shouting quietly down into it. *Annabelle, it's Clive.* He waited, staring down into the emptiness. Still, no reply. *All right, granddaughter, I'll come to you.*

He hesitated for the briefest of instants and stepped over the edge. An impossible wind rushed past his face as he fell straight down into the well, deeper and deeper, faster and faster. He began to tumble end over end. All Annabelle's memories, all her desires flashed by too swiftly to taste, all blurred, all tiny little images that cowered and trembled in cells and shallow tunnels that lined the sides of the well.

Either he fell for a very long time, or despite the evidence of his senses, he fell very slowly. Down, down, down—would the fall never come to an end? Down, down, down. *Annabelle,* he called, looking down past his toes into the darkness, though actually he might have been looking up into the darkness, he couldn't tell anymore. *Annabelle, if you're down there, look out below!*

Then, suddenly, *thump, thump!* He landed on something soft and firm. Unhurt, he got to his feet.

Annabelle stood with her back to him, crouched, and fingers extended clawlike. Her clothes hung in tatters, and her hair stood in a wild tangle.

*After this I shall think nothing of falling down a stair,* Clive said to her, trying to sound light and cheerful. She didn't even turn around to greet him. An animal sound escaped her lips. *Annabelle,* Clive called. *It's all right. Everything's all right. I've come to get you. You can wake up now.*

She whirled then, and a catlike scream issued from her mouth. Startled, Clive jumped back, stumbled, and fell on his backside. Only then did he see what he had landed upon. It was a pair of bodies—bodies of two of the Amanda creatures.

Annabelle gave another cat scream, and he looked up again. Suddenly, emerging from the darkness came scores of the furious little creatures, all looking sweetly childlike, all hissing and spitting, scratching and biting. Annabelle flung them away as they charged at her. She used the energy of her Baalbec and burned them to crisps. She sliced them in halves with a saber that seemed to appear and disappear in her hand.

Then the creatures simply vanished. Annabelle waited in exactly the same crouched pose as Clive had found her. He didn't even call out her name this time. She turned and screamed exactly as she had.

It all began again.

*Annabelle, don't!* he shouted. *This isn't real, it's a dream! It's all over! Wake up!*

But she didn't hear or didn't respond. Again and again she fought the same battle, slaughtered creatures who looked exactly like her little daughter, sometimes with her sword, sometimes with her machine, sometimes with her own bloody bare hands.

Clive couldn't reach her, couldn't touch her or run to her side. No matter how he ran or walked or jumped, he seemed to stay on the same spot. He could move, he just didn't seem to get anywhere!

But he had to do something. He thought of going back for help. Maybe Shriek would know what to do. Yet, when he looked up, he suddenly realized he had no idea how to get back. He tried to imagine himself back in his body, but that didn't work. He tried to imagine a well or a tunnel that would lead him back to reality, sort of a reverse route to take him out of Annabelle's nightmare, but that didn't work, either.

He was trapped!

With a sudden chill of fear he saw that for the first time the Amanda creatures were noticing him. They didn't attack him, yet, just watched. But he realized intuitively that the longer he stayed the stronger his fear would become, and the stronger his fear became the more Annabelle's nightmare would become real to him, too. Then the creatures would turn on him.

*No, Being Clive, not to be that is.*

The thought brushed against him with gentle reassurance, and immediately his heart lightened as he felt Shriek's presence nearby. Suddenly she stood beside him.

*Negative,* came another thought simultaneously with Shriek's, and Chang Guafe was also there.

*Finnbogg bite nasty-things. Save Annie, okay?*

Clive found himself surrounded by his comrades. Sidi and Tomàs and Horace Hamilton Smythe with saber drawn were there, too. They ringed him closely, and at once the Amanda creatures lost interest in him.

*Where's Neville?* he asked abruptly, spinning around.

*Yer bleedin' brother's not yet part o' the mind-web,* Smythe answered in his best cockney. It seemed to Clive an inappropriate time for such foolery, however.

*It's Shriek's idea, Englishman,* Sidi Bombay said, reminding Clive that every thought was open now. *We must maintain a good humor and allow no fear whatsoever. Then we must surround Miss Annabelle.*

Clive stared at the Indian. *But you're not part of the mind-web, either,* he said in confusion. *You were trapped in that damned egg-thing when we met Shriek. How can you be here?*

*Shriek brought him in just now for this, sah,* Smythe hurriedly explained. *Can't say the same for Neville, but we all trust Sidi Bombay. More importantly, Annabelle trusts him and cares about him. Shriek says that Annabelle needs us all right now.*

The arachnoid interrupted. *Caught in a memory loop the Annabelle being is. Find her I could not. Only to you a path did she open. Trust you most of all she does.*

*Then how did you find us?* Clive asked, his spirits buoyed by the presence of his friends.

*Trapped here you almost became, Being Clive. Called out to me you did. Closed your mind is not, so follow I did, bringing all friend beings. Friend beings it is can save the Annabelle being now.*

*How?*

*We must surround the senhorita,* Tomàs jumped in eagerly. *Shriek has explained it to us. The monstros would not attack you, and they will not attack us. When they cannot reach her the . . .* The little Portuguese hesitated and looked to Shriek.

*Memory loop,* she supplied.

*Si, the memory loop, the pattern, will be broken. Then, she may awaken.*

Clive turned back to Shriek. *May?*

She shrugged her four shoulders helplessly. *Try and hope. No more can we do.*

Clive nodded his head and put his arms around as many of them as he could and drew them close. *Well, let's do that much.*

With Shriek beside him, guiding his steps and all their steps, Clive found he could move toward Annabelle. He linked his right arm through one of hers and his left arm through Smythe's. Each of them linked with someone else, and they marched toward Annabelle, surrounded her, and closed a tight circle about her.

The Amanda creatures jumped about, making their obscene animal noises, slicing the air with their claws. They ran around the circle in agitation, long black hair flying, ragged blue pinafores fluttering about their legs. But they could not reach Annabelle. One by one they began to fade. Just an arm or leg at first, followed by another, then an eye or a nose. Always, the last thing remaining was a mouth. Then that, too, faded.

*I think she's read Mr. Carroll's new book, sah*, Horace Hamilton Smythe said with a grin.

Clive Folliot nodded to his old friend. Horace Hamilton Smythe never ceased to surprise him. *I didn't know you'd read it, sergeant*, he said. *It's rather recent.*

Smythe's grin widened, and he gave a wink. *A man's got to stay abreast of things, sah.*

Clive returned the wink, recalling Smythe's skill at disguise and his activities on the queen's behalf as an agent provocateur. *Especially a man like you, eh, Sergeant? I guess there's a little bit of Alice in us all.* He turned to see about Annabelle, but before he finished the movement his legs disappeared, leaving him hanging in midair. He looked at Horace in astonishment.

*Be seeing you topside, sah.* There was nothing left of Horace but his head, and that began to ghost away feature by feature. *Always wondered what a Cheshire puss was, anyway.* The sergeant put on his biggest smile. The corners of his mouth strained upward toward the tips of his ears, and he held it frozen playfully that way. It was the last part of him to go.

Clive looked over his shoulder at Annabelle. She stood with her eyes closed, but the terror was gone from her face. In its place he saw the same peaceful expression that her real body wore in the real world. He had a feeling she would be all right now. He'd come through for her after all. They all had.

*Me, too, Horace,* Clive admitted, putting on his biggest grin as he watched his right arm fade away. The others stared at him, uncomprehending. How peculiar they all looked half there, half gone. Chang Guafe had no torso at all, just two legs, two arms, and a head with lots of space between. Clive laughed. *The most curious thing I ever saw in all my life!*

*¡Ai de mim!* Tomàs exclaimed, making the sign of the cross with only three fingers and his smile showing. It looked like three little sausages teasing a hungry mouth.

*Indeed,* Clive laughed again. *Curiouser and curiouser.* Then he, too, was gone.

# CHAPTER THIRTEEN

# At the Palace of the Morning Star

Clive opened his eyes, immediately aware of the warmth of Annabelle's hand in his and of the softness of the bed upon which he lay. He rolled his head to the side to look at his granddaughter. She had a nice profile, such a lovely face.

With a start he sprang up. Whatever was he thinking of? It was a bed they were on, after all, and she was a lady, and he was a gentleman. It was no proper place to conduct business, or at least, to linger after business had been conducted.

"It's a nice blush yer wearin', guv, but don't be embarrassed." Horace Hamilton Smythe looked up at him from the floor and grinned as he still played the cockney. Clive had nearly stepped on him. "You did the right thing by her, sure."

All the company minus Neville sat on the floor around the bed, hands still enjoined.

"Is the *senhorita* all right?" Tomàs asked as he released the hands of Sidi Bombay and Finnbogg. He stood up slowly. It was plain he'd cramped his leg.

"I hope so," Clive answered, turning his attention back to Annabelle. Her eyes were still closed, though, and she hadn't stirred.

*Awaken soon she will, friend beings,* Shriek said to all of them as awareness returned to her six eyes. She released the hands of Chang Guafe and Smythe, and she, too, stood, rising to her full seven feet of height. She laid a hand gently on Clive's shoulder. *Find her I could not when before tried I. But a secret path unconsciously left she for you alone, Being Clive. This brave attempt had not you made, lost she would be still, perhaps forever.*

"Observation," Chang Guafe said in a cool metallic voice. "You are a hero."

"*Allons enfants de la patrie . . . !*" Finnbogg began to sing at the top of his lungs the French national anthem, and Clive decided at once he was going to have to chide Neville for the choice of songs he'd taught the alien canine at their first meeting. Before he could say anything directly to Finnbogg, however, Tomàs leaned over and clapped a hand around Finnbogg's mouth. Finnbogg's eyes rolled toward the Portuguese and they regarded each other for an instant. Then both smiled, and Finnbogg shut up.

"Oh, I've had such a curious dream!"

Everyone looked toward the bed at the sound of Annabelle's voice as she rose up on her elbows and looked at them all with an expression that beamed with joy. Sidi and Finnbogg and Chang Guafe scrambled to their feet and bent near the bed. Annabelle blinked at them for a moment, then her eyes twinkled.

"Why, it's the scarecrow, the lion, and the tin man!" she exclaimed, sitting up quickly and crossing her legs in the bed. "But that's another story." She reached out and patted Finnbogg on the head, and his ears pricked up. "Besides, you might be Toto," she said to him alone.

"I don't know about the other story," Horace Hamilton Smythe said, moving closer to the bed. "But Mr. Carroll seems to have made quite an impression on you. The major and I have both read his newest book, and I'm pleased to see it must still be popular in your time."

"It's one of my two favorites," Annabelle admitted. "But you wouldn't know Mr. Baum. I used to read both stories over and over when I was a kid, and later I read them over and over for Amanda." She looked down suddenly, and her face clouded over.

*Decorum be damned*, Clive thought, and he sat down on the bed beside her, put an arm around her shoulder, and drew her close.

"Guess I fell down a hole of my own this time," she said, looking up at them all again and forcing a little smile. "Thanks, everybody." She squeezed Clive's hand and gave him a kiss on the cheek. "Thanks, Grandpa."

Clive blushed again and stood up. Inside, though, he felt better and bigger than he ever had in his life, as if in some way he had just kept some unspoken promise to a lonely woman in a flat back in London. Emotions rushed powerfully upon him, and he knew he had to get away from everyone.

"If you can manage," he said quickly to Annabelle, "we're invited to dinner. There's a hot bath through there"—he pointed to the small side room—"and clothes in the wardrobe." With that, he stepped around the others and headed for the door.

"By the way, just where are we?" she said, but Clive didn't turn around.

Chang Guafe answered for him. "The Palace of the Morning Star."

As he stepped through the doorway, Clive heard her sigh and her comment, "I didn't think it was Kansas."

He closed the door and hurried to his own room. There, he sat down heavily on his own bed and held his head in his hands. Slowly, he mastered the emotions that had nearly caused an unseemly display.

Someone knocked on his door.

He hesitated but a moment, stood, and turned. "Come in," he called, expecting Horace Hamilton Smythe. His sergeant had a habit of looking after him, "mothering," he sometimes accused his friend.

It was Shriek who opened the door and stepped inside. She closed it quietly behind her. *Another problem there is*, she informed him.

"Of course there is," he answered, using speech. A smirk flickered across his face. "This is the Dungeon."

Her mandibles opened wide in what might have been her imitation of a human smile, and she shrugged her four shoulders. Clive started to wave her toward one of two overstuffed chairs that furnished the room, then realized wearily they wouldn't accommodate her four-legged form. For that matter, he had never seen her sit at all.

"Well . . ." He looked around helplessly, then gave it up. So much for Victorian hospitality. "What is it this time?"

Shriek paced to the far side of his room, looked around, then paced back. *No windows, Being Clive,* she pointed out. *None in my room. None in room of Annabelle being.*

She was right. Clive hadn't noticed, but she was right. His brow furrowed, and he ran his tongue along the back of his teeth. No windows, and only one door in or out of the rooms. The hackles on the back of his neck rose slowly. *Perhaps we've been careless, Being Shriek.* He sent the thought to her. No one could overhear their private thoughts.

*More there is,* she continued. *Irritated have I been. Distracted.*

*The itch you couldn't scratch?*

*Identify it could I not until linked in the psionic web were all friend beings. Not in myself could I see it. Too well it disguised itself. But in all of you burned it, glaring to my senses.*

Clive unconsciously ran a hand over his chest. *In all of us? What?*

*Scanned we are being, very subtly, by powerful telepath beings.*

"Well, who the hell are they?" Clive shouted and clenched his fists. So offended and angered was he by her revelation that he forgot himself and slipped into speech. Not that it mattered any goddamned way if someone could hear his thoughts as well as his words! A man didn't have any privacy at all!

*Know them I do not*, Shriek answered, projecting calm. *Find them I cannot. Far away they are and well-shielded. But no secrets can we be sure to keep. This I thought you should know.*

Clive thought. "Are they scanning us now?"

Shriek shook her head.

"Then it's not a constant scan," he said. He moved about the room uneasily. Even if Shriek said they weren't being monitored, he still felt like a bug under observation or under the shadow of someone's heel. "Is there any pattern? Anything in particular that they seem interested in?" He scratched his stubbled chin as he paced. "Could they be the Dungeonmasters—the Ren or the Chaffri—that run this place?"

*No time have I had to learn these things*, the arachnoid apologized. *Beyond my meager power are these telepath beings, but try will I.*

He stepped up to her and patted her left upper shoulder affectionately. Odd, how once he had considered her so ugly and strange. He saw none of that now. She had taken on a unique kind of beauty to him, an alien beauty to be sure, but something even his human senses could appreciate and trust.

And there was also about her a tranquility, a serenity that he tried to emulate. "There is no more we can do then, but bathe and dress and go down to dinner. You're sure our telepath isn't here?"

She clasped one of his hands and then released it. *Far away*, she assured him. *But more there is to do.* She pointed a finger at the wound on his leg. The blood had clotted, but traces of fresh red seeped around the edges of the clots. *Help I can, better than before.* She plucked one hair-spike from her body and held it up. On the tip a bead of clear fluid gleamed in the gaslight that illuminated the room. *Medicine for blood of human beings. More time have I had to assimilate blood-taste from the Annabelle being. Infection could I prevent and pain relieve the first time—*

"And Mickey could you slip," he interrupted, remembering a phrase he'd learned from Annabelle. He folded his arms and raised one eyebrow.

*Pain will this relieve again,* she continued. *And pain you have though deny it you do. Behind your every thought sense it I can. But heal this droplet will, also, and swiftly. Stop your bleeding, seal your wound, heal the scratches.*

"Can you do the same for Annabelle and Neville?" he asked, hesitating, then extending his arm.

*Accepted medicine the Annabelle being has already,* she told him. *The Neville being, too, if allow it he will.* She jabbed him quickly with the hair-spike. A drop of blood welled up around the puncture in his forearm and mingled with the clear droplet.

"I don't recall that you asked him the first time," Clive said with a teasing grin. He flicked the drop of blood away. A tiny hole marked the skin underneath, but no more blood appeared.

*Urgent it was that we move swiftly then,* she said, looking askance and shrugging. *Argument there was no time for.*

Clive barely heard her. The pain flowed out of his body as if he were a glass vessel with a crack in his foot. With it went all his fatigue. The tension in his neck and shoulders vanished. The sting of his scratches faded away. He flexed his thigh. There was some stiffness there and the mildest twinge, but even that lessened as he tested the muscle.

He beamed at Shriek. "Well, you ask him politely then and with all courtesy, but if he says no"—he winked at her—"jab him anyway."

His door opened and Annabelle entered wearing a disgusted look and a large damp towel. Actually, the towel wasn't *that* large. Clive let go a moan and squeezed his eyes shut.

"Oh, grow up, Clive-o!" she snapped. "And help me!"

With a patient sigh he opened his eyes again and looked. Over one arm she carried a man's khaki outfit. Over the other she bore a full dress uniform for a regimental quartermaster sergeant in Her Majesty's Fifth Imperial Horse

Guards. Her short black hair clung wetly close around her face, and her legs seemed to go on forever, and the towel just seemed to float there.

"My entire wardrobe is full of garbage like this!" she complained.

"Perhaps this would be more to your liking, miss."

Horace Hamilton Smythe appeared just behind her. He held up a white cotton dress in one hand and a pair of leather trousers in the other.

Clive rubbed his eyes and the bridge of his nose and sat down weakly on the foot of his bed. His own Annabella Leighton had never dared to appear before him in so little or in so much light! Well, that wasn't strictly true, he admitted wryly. There had been a very memorable night in her boudoir just before he left London. But there had been just a single candle, and she certainly hadn't been so brazen about it. His granddaughter, though, had made it plain that things were different in her century, but how different he hadn't guessed. Still, it was her life; she'd made that plain, too. Slowly, he let go the breath he'd been holding.

"Take your pick," Smythe told her, "or there's a lot more to choose from. We switched rooms while you were"—he paused, searching for a suitable word—"asleep. We can trade back if you like."

Annabelle dumped the two men's outfits in Horace's arms and turned up her nose at the dress and pants. "Just let me grab something else to wear—"

*Please!* Clive thought to himself.

"—and we'll switch after dinner. I've already used the bath, and I can tell you haven't, Sergeant." She patted him with mock condescension on the crown of his head and marched out of the room. Smythe followed.

"Well, she's back to normal," Clive said to Shriek. He rose to his feet. "I guess we'd better prepare for dinner. I'm suddenly eager to meet the lord of this manor." He frowned. "On second thought, 'lord' might not quite be the appropriate word. Well, no matter. I just hope his food is good."

Shriek moved toward the door and regarded him from the threshold. *That he knows the way to the eighth level hope I*, she said.

"You have a positive talent for the practical, my dear," he answered, making a short bow. Then, he turned serious again. "Let me know if you learn anything more about our mysterious monitors. If they're as powerful as you say, they may hold the key to this whole Dungeon." Then, he grinned again. "Now go give Neville hell." He made a jabbing motion with his hand.

Shriek made the soft chittering sound that passed for laughter and closed the door on her way out.

Alone, Clive turned and surveyed his room again. If it was a cell, it was a velvet-lined cell, and for now, at least, he intended to take advantage of it. He stripped off the rags that were once his clothes and kicked them into a corner near the wardrobe.

He stepped up to a full-length mirror that had been framed in an exquisitely carved antique wood and tilted it to an angle that best reflected his body. He had lost weight since coming to the Dungeon. Not that he had ever been fat, but the slight padding around his waist had disappeared. He'd grown thin and rangy in his time here, and his stringy muscles had strengthened.

He examined some of his scratches. They were no longer tender to the touch, and when he brushed a couple with a fingertip, the scabs fell off easily to expose patches of fresh pink skin. All the stiffness had left his thigh now, and a hard scab had formed over the wound. *Thank you, Shriek*, he thought silently.

*Welcome you are, Being Clive.*

He jerked around, covering his groin with both hands and blushing hotly, but there was no one else in the room. He relaxed, but kept his hands low.

*That's not fair!* he protested.

But she was gone already, in and out of his head almost

before he'd been aware of her. *Come on, old boy, you weren't aware of her at all,* he admitted. And if anybody else was prying around in his head, he wasn't aware of that, either, but just in case, he offered them a very rude thought having to do with the conduct of their mothers and strode into the bathroom.

The bath was still hot. He lowered himself cautiously into the tub, expecting to feel some stinging in the scratches despite Shriek's medicine, but he experienced only the delicious sensation of the warm water. Drawing his knees up, he sank to his neck. Undoubtedly, it was the closest thing to heaven he expected to find in this hell.

He found a bar of perfumed soap, along with some scented oils, on a small table at the foot of the tub. He disdained the oils, but the sandalwood odor of the bar he deemed not too unmasculine, and he scrubbed himself gently. Also on the table he found a small razor and hand-mirror. In fact, his host had provided for all his needs.

When at last he stood, he discovered more patches of exposed new skin. Toweling dislodged even more of his scabs. It amazed him how fast his body seemed to be healing!

He didn't stop too long to marvel, though. His stomach grumbled threateningly. He'd felt hungry before the bath, but now he was starving! A side effect of the arachnoid's medicine? he wondered. No matter. He hurried to the wardrobe, chose a pair of sturdy khaki jungle slacks and a loose shirt of white cotton. Everything fit him perfectly, even the boots he found at the bottom of the wardrobe.

He checked his appearance in the mirror. He barely recognized the man who looked back at him. He'd almost forgotten how blond his hair was, so long had it been since he'd last washed it. It shone now, as did his thin golden mustache, all the facial growth he'd ever allowed himself. He ran a finger over it, considering how it would look if he let it grow a little thicker. No, he decided. Then he'd be chewing on the ends, and a gentleman did no such thing. Better to keep it neatly trimmed.

He stretched one final time in front of the mirror, feeling better than he had in ages, then started to leave his room and join the others. He stopped, though, suddenly noticing a new sword, which lay upon the bed.

He picked it up and examined it carefully. It was an extraordinarily generous gift, a finely crafted blade. Yet a gentleman would not insult his host by wearing a weapon to dinner. It just wasn't done, not even if that host was Lucifer, himself. If anything went wrong he'd just have to rely on his wits and on his companions. He placed the sword back on the bed, then stepped through the door, and closed it quickly before he changed his mind.

Sergeant Smythe paced the hallway, obviously waiting for him. He cut quite a figure in his regimental uniform.

"I'd hoped to see you in the white, Horace!" Clive joked, clapping his batman on the shoulder.

"Hadn't the knees for it, sah," Smythe answered glibly, "and it pinched a bit in the middle, it did. So this will just have to do."

Sidi Bombay came out of his room. The Indian looked almost regal in white slacks and a white embroidered shirt. A sash of soft blue silk encircled his waist, and a turban of the same fabric perched upon his head. A small silver brooch sparkled in the center of it. "Ah, Englishmen!" he said by way of greeting. "My head is covered again. Perhaps God will favor me once more."

"In this place, old friend?" Smythe scoffed. "You're an optimist."

"Am I wrong," asked Clive abruptly, "or isn't this the first time the three of us have been alone together since we crossed the shimmering mist and found ourselves in Q'oorna?"

The three men looked at each other curiously. "I think you may be right, Englishman," Sidi agreed.

There was an awkward moment of silence. Then Clive spoke. "I'd like to thank you both. You've been good friends and stalwart companions. I consider it the highest honor to know you." There was another awkward moment before he asked to shake their hands.

"I also consider it an honor to know you, Clive Folliot," Sidi Bombay said. "You are, indeed, a credit to your race." He grinned broadly, showing lots of teeth.

Horace threw an arm around Sidi, clapped his back, and hugged him playfully, reminding Clive that the two had been friends for longer than he knew.

"Forgive him, sah," Horace begged, showing the same grin. "He's not a bad fellow, as dirty little fakirs go."

"I am quite clean after my bath," Sidi assured him defensively.

Smythe sniffed and wrinkled his nose. "You should have skipped the perfumes."

Sidi sniffed. "We Indians are unburdened by your English concepts of manliness. I find the floral oils quite pleasant." He sniffed again. "You certainly might have benefited from them."

"Enough!" Clive suggested, chuckling. He enjoyed their banter, though, and it felt good to laugh again. Still, it was time for dinner, and he was famished. "Where are the others?"

"Already gone down, sah," Horace informed him.

"Then what are we waiting for?" Clive made a bow and gestured toward the stairway. "Gentlemen?"

They descended together. At the bottom they looked up and down the long corridor. Not far away, Herkimer stood near a set of oaken double doors. Clive blinked and considered just how peculiar a four-foot frog looked in formal wear.

"This way, this way, sirs!" Herkimer said. The frog made a deep bow as they approached, and with one hand he pushed wide both doors. A red carpet led the way to an elaborate dining table. In the center of the carpet stood another frog who bowed, then smiled at them. "This way, please!" it said, and gestured toward the table where the rest of the company was already seated.

"Who are you?" Clive asked the second frog.

"Herkimer, sir," the frog answered politely. "You may choose your own seats, your own seats. Will you take wine with your meal, sirs?"

Clive grinned at Horace and Sidi. "That would be delightful, Herkimer, Herkimer," he answered for them all.

"We have a considerable cellar, sir," Herkimer continued. "May I suggest a claret, a claret?"

Clive deferred. "I trust your judgment, Herkimer."

The frog moved aside and made another bow as Clive, Horace, and Sidi took seats at the table. There were just enough chairs for them all, he noted, plus one at the head of the table for their host, who had not yet made his appearance. Then, he recounted.

"Where is Shriek?" he asked with sudden concern.

Annabelle waved him to a seat she had saved at her left hand. "She wishes to be excused," his granddaughter told him. "You know she doesn't like to eat in front of people."

Clive took the chair and sat down. The table settings were elegant by any standards. The silver had been polished to a high gleam. He could see his reflection in the china settings. The candelabra appeared to be gold, as did the butter dishes, the creamers, and the sugar bowls.

He turned to Annabelle. She had chosen the white cotton dress, after all, and she looked radiant.

"You look nice, too, Grandpa," she whispered.

Two more frogs appeared from a side entrance. One pushed a small metal cart with various covered dishes. The other bore a tray with three glasses of deep-red wine. Clive quickly noticed the others already had glasses.

"Herkimer, I assume?" he asked as the frog placed his glass on the table.

"Of course, sir, sir, sir," came the throaty answer, and the frog returned to other duties.

Neville sat directly across from Clive. He leaned forward now, placing his elbows on the table in unseemly fashion. "And where," he muttered conspiratorially, "do you suppose, is our host? I always expected to meet the devil someday, you know."

"And I expected the same for you," Clive admitted wryly.

As if on cue the double doors swung open again. Clive pushed back his chair and rose to his feet. Everyone except Annabelle followed suit and looked toward the entrance as their host appeared at the threshold, hesitated, and came toward them.

Clive's jaw dropped, and Neville, for once, was speechless.

Herkimer stepped to the edge of the red carpet. "My master, master," the little creature called in his best frog's voice, "and the lord of this manor. Also, your host, your host!" Then, he paused with needless drama before announcing the name.

After all, Clive knew his own father!

## · CHAPTER FOURTEEN ·

# Hell's Sire

"That don't look like *el diablo* to me," Tomàs muttered.

"Look again, sailor," Neville whispered. "It's the devil, himself."

Clive shot a look at his twin, surprised by the anger in Neville's voice and the poorly concealed contempt on his face. He'd never seen such a look before! Neville was Father's favorite, the chosen heir to the family estate and rightful heir to the Tewkesbury title as well. He didn't understand his brother's reaction at all.

Neville, though, noticed Clive's reaction, and his face went stony, then completely passive again as if nothing had passed between them.

Baron Tewkesbury walked forward, picking up speed with every step, beaming with paternal pride and joy as he approached the table. He cut quite an imposing figure in his brown velvet jacket and silk ruffled shirt. He was taller than either of his sons, and the years had not yet stolen all of the blond from his thick mass of curls or from his carefully trimmed beard. He still carried his broad-shouldered bulk with power and grace.

Clive stepped away from the table. "Father, what are you doing here?"

It shouldn't have surprised him at all when Baron Tewkesbury ignored his question and walked to Neville's side of the table. He'd had a lifetime of that kind of treatment.

Still, it smarted when, holding out his arms, the old man embraced his favorite son and clapped him on the back with enthusiasm. Clive's hand closed on the back of his chair and gripped it until his knuckles turned white. He was barely aware of it when Annabelle's hand covered his.

"My son!" the baron cried. "My prodigal son is found!" He embraced Neville again, wrapping him in great bearish arms. "Dear Neville, I thought I'd never see you again! But here you are!"

"So, kill the fatted calf," Neville muttered halfheartedly over his father's shoulder. He stared at Clive. Nothing but coldness filled his gaze.

"Sit down, sit down!" Baron Tewkesbury held Neville's chair for him and slid it under his son when Neville returned to the table. The old man patted him on both shoulders and planted a kiss on the top of his head, which brought a frown of annoyance to Neville's face. Though his father didn't see, it didn't escape Clive's notice.

He could wait no longer, though. "Father, how did you get here?" he blurted. "I don't understand. . . ."

"Of course you don't, Clive." At last his father acknowledged his presence. The old man looked at him strangely as he gripped the back of Neville's chair, and Clive trembled inwardly under that scrutiny, an old feeling that he remembered all too well. Automatically, Clive straightened his shoulders and drew in his stomach.

"Clive, Clive!" the baron said suddenly. He strode decorously around the table and opened his arms again to gather Clive in. Clive felt himself nearly crushed against his father's chest. He sputtered. In all his memory his father had never hugged him, never shown him any affection at all!

"Clive, can you ever forgive me?" His father pushed him back at arm's length and looked at him. "I've been an old fool. I've blamed you all these years for your mother's death, but I was wrong, Son." Tears barely held in check sparkled in the corners of his father's eyes.

Clive didn't know what to say. What was he to make of

such behavior? He'd wanted his father's love for so long, worked so hard for it until he'd finally given up. Now, at last, it was being offered unconditionally. His father had even asked his forgiveness. But could he forget so many years and so much indifference so easily?

Baron Tewkesbury kept one arm draped around Clive's shoulder as he turned to face Neville and the others. He made a sweeping gesture with his free arm. "My sons are home! I never thought to see this day! Welcome, welcome to all of you!"

He embraced Clive again, then moved to his seat at the head of the table between his sons. He sat down with great dignity, composing himself once more. "Herkimer," he called to the frog who had announced him. "You may serve now."

Herkimer bowed and clapped his webbed hands together. At once three more frogs, all exactly alike, came through the side door. Two pushed small carts, which they parked beside the first one. The other one carried trays of small steaming bowls, which turned out to contain rice. A dollop of green sauce rested atop each dish, along with several small shrimp.

The delicious smell crept up Clive's nostrils, reminding him how hungry he felt. Still, he couldn't believe his father was actually here in the Dungeon. He leaned forward on his elbows. "Father, how in hell—"

His father clucked his tongue and gave him a stern look. "Where are your manners, Son?"

Clive looked sheepish and took his elbows from the table at once.

"That's better," his father said, smiling again. "Now introduce me to your friends. By the way, isn't someone missing?"

"Our friend Shriek," Annabelle spoke up. "She preferred to stay in her room."

The baron frowned, then shrugged. "Ah, well. I'll see that a meal is sent up to her."

Horace Hamilton Smythe cleared his throat and glanced

at Clive. "Uh, she has rather peculiar needs, milord, she does."

"Nothing we can't meet," the baron assured. He picked up a spoon and tasted the rice dish. One of the frogs stood close by awaiting his approval. The old man chewed delicately, then smiled. "Please, everyone, we may converse as we dine."

Clive quickly made introductions, then took several bites from his own bowl. He had never tasted anything quite like it, but it was superb.

Abruptly, Tewkesbury put down his spoon. "Is the rice not to your liking, Mr. Guafe? You're not eating."

The cyborg had not touched the dish or the wine. He looked coolly at his host, and his ruby lenses glowed. "I do not need to ingest organic matter," he stated. "This body extracts single atoms from the air and converts them to the energy I require."

Clive looked at Chang over the rim of his glass. He knew, in fact, that his cyborg friend could eat and drink if he chose. He'd seen him do so, sometimes just to experience the pleasure of taste, sometimes as a means of analysis. But he said nothing now to contradict Guafe, though he watched him carefully.

The cyborg placed his hands in his lap and spoke to the baron with even more flatness of tone than usual. "You have repeatedly ignored the inquiries of your son, Clive Folliot. Respond to my inquiry, please."

The baron's eyes narrowed, and Clive saw the father he remembered sitting next to him. Tewkesbury's stare rivaled the cyborg's for coldness as he sat back and folded his hands across his stomach. He said nothing but waited for Chang Guafe to continue.

"Why do you attempt duplicity?" Chang said. "This dwelling structure conforms outwardly to the conventions of the period your son has described as Victorian." He touched a finger to the edge of his rice bowl. "Yet this food bears faint traces of microwave radiation." He touched the wineglass. "This vessel contains few of the minerals from which glass is usually made." He waved his hand in a casual gesture. "This structure, itself, the walls and floors, the ceiling—all seamless in construction, impossible for the level of technology Clive Folliot has described. Nothing here is exactly as it seems."

The baron relaxed somewhat. "And how do you know these things, sir?" he asked.

"His sensors are quite remarkable, Father," Clive interjected, "far keener than eyes and ears." He looked down the table at his friends. Everyone stopped eating, and all spoons were quietly set aside as they waited for their host to provide an explanation.

Tewkesbury picked up his glass and sipped the red liquid slowly. With great deliberation he set the glass back down. "You are quite right, Chang Guafe," he said. "And if we can allow the dinner to continue, I will explain how it is that I am here. We really have an excellent roast beef, and my servants get quite upset if they are not allowed to carry out their duties. Nervous creatures, really they are."

At his word, the frog-creatures rolled up the carts and uncovered plates containing steaming slices of rare and medium roast beef. Clive felt his senses reel at the fantastic odor, and despite himself, he picked up his fork and knife as soon as his plate was set before him. Alongside the beef were buttered small potatoes still in their skins and served with parsley.

From another cart came bowls of stewed tomatoes, corn, and peas. Another bowl of apples and oranges joined those. On yet another cart parked at the far end of the table sat three kinds of pie.

Two other servants, Herkimer and Herkimer no doubt, waited close at hand with wine and iced water.

*Iced water in hell*, Clive thought with an incongruous grin as he chewed and swallowed.

Then, he stiffened a bit as Annabelle's hand settled on his thigh under the tablecloth. "You were about to tell us how you came here, Mr. Folliot," she said, using a very improper form of address.

The baron pretended not to notice. "Thank you, my dear." He smiled at her, then reached out and caught the hands of each of his sons and smiled warmly at them, too. "I don't understand it all, myself, but I'll tell you what I can."

Tewkesbury sat back and twirled his wineglass between his palms. He seemed to gather his thoughts before speaking. Then, he looked up at Neville. "When you didn't return from Africa, I sent your brother, Clive, to find you and bring you home. You'd been missing for a year, and no one knew if you were alive or dead." He turned to his other son. "To my great shame, Clive, I waited two years after we lost track of you. Then, word came that someone had found some of your belongings in a shipwreck off the coast of Zanzibar, a suitcase or something with some of the articles you'd been writing for that unsavory scandal rag that your friend—Carstairs—edited."

His father paused and took a sip of wine to wet his throat. Clive didn't bother to explain that Carstairs was no friend of his, that the man had paid him for those articles, only enough to supplement the inadequate sum the baron, himself, had provided to outfit his expedition.

After a brief while, his father continued. "I don't mind telling you that, faced with the loss of both my sons, I set about to examine my entire life. Shortly after that, I set sail, myself, for Africa, determined to do whatever I could to find you both."

Clive felt Annabelle's hand tighten on his leg, and he caught it in his own hand. Anyone else might have misinterpreted her action, but he knew she only meant to reassure him. Still, he could hardly believe what he was hearing! His father, an esteemed noble of the realm, stealing through the fetid jungle like a common adventurer? Surely other lords and ladies had done as much. But his father?

He glanced across the table to see how his brother was receiving this, but Neville was uncharacteristically quiet. He listened politely, but his face remained unreadable, and he went through the motions of eating without consuming much.

"With some difficulty I traced your steps, until in Bagamoyo I encountered a Father Timothy O'Hara who remembered you both." He turned his gaze on Neville and shook a finger. "You with some consternation, I must tell you," he said to his son. "He charged nothing specific, mind you, but hinted at some highly improper behavior on your part." He sipped his wine again and beckoned to the frog-servant with the wine. "Thank you, Herkimer," he said.

"Father O'Hara," Neville said with a bemused smirk as he leaned back in his chair. "Now there's a man who knows more about this place than he pretends."

Clive agreed with a barely perceptible nod. "I suspect the same," he said. Then, with another nod and a wry tilt of his head toward his father, he added, "Though I charge nothing specific."

But the baron seemed to ignore them, lost, as he was, in his own tale. "Strange thing about Bagamoyo," he continued. "Never saw such lights in the sky in all my life." He thought for a moment, remembering, then shrugged. "Anyway, it was this Father O'Hara who told me about the Sudd. He said it was the last place anyone had seen either of you."

"You encountered the sparkling mists," Clive interrupted excitedly.

The baron nodded. "But not the first time. After I made it across the swamp—nasty place, that—I asked about you in a village on the far side and determined that neither of you had made it that far. I don't mind telling you I feared the worst then. If the Sudd had claimed you both, there'd never be a trace. I started back, intending to question the priest again or anyone else in Bagamoyo who might have seen you." Again, he took a drink of wine and dabbed at the corner of his mouth with his napkin. "I never made it back across."

"You didn't see the mists the first time?" Clive asked.

He'd forgotten his own meal as he listened to his father's tale. The idea that his parent had, indeed, come looking for him filled him with a rare and pleasing warmth.

"Not the first time, but there it was the second. I and two bearers were poling a small boat through the muck when the stuff suddenly closed about us. I tell you it came up faster than a London fog!"

"What became of the bearers, Lord Folliot?" Sidi Bombay inquired, speaking for the first time.

"They panicked and jumped overboard, I'm afraid. Whether they got away or died in the swamp I don't know. Perhaps the mist got them anyway and carried them to another part of the Dungeon. I wound up here alone. When the mist cleared, I found myself on the shore of the Lake of Lamentations."

Clive had met only a few people in the Dungeon who had not entered at Q'oorna, the first level, and worked their way to the other levels. None ever seemed to have any idea why they landed where they did, though.

Sergeant Smythe clinked his glass on the edge of his plate as he set it down. He glanced at Clive, then at the Baron Tewkesbury. "Pardon me, your lordship, but you said you waited two years after Clive disappeared before coming to look for him? But we can't possibly have been here that long!"

"I'm afraid it's true," the baron answered. "Certainly you realize by now that time in the Dungeon has a nature all its own. It's certainly different from time on Earth. It may even be different from one level to the other. I, myself, have been here for quite a while, I don't mind telling you." He waved a hand toward the other end of the table. "How about some pie, everyone? Herkimer is really a very good cook."

"Herkimer? Really?" Neville said with sarcastic liveliness. "Which Herkimer?"

The baron looked at his son with something of a frown. No one at the table had missed the note of unpleasantness or failed to notice how little Neville had spoken during the meal.

"All of them or any of them," his father answered quietly. "They are very talented creatures and learn quickly."

"They all look alike to me," Neville said curtly. He pushed back his chair suddenly and rose. "I hope you'll excuse me, but I'm quite tired. The dinner was excellent."

Clive watched his brother march stiffly away. Herkimer reached to open the door, but Neville beat the little frog to it, planting his hand against the smooth wood and giving a shove. Clive glanced at Annabelle, then, and she returned his gaze. There was a troubled look in her eyes that he'd learned to recognize. Under the table she squeezed his thigh again.

Finnbogg pushed back his chair and rose, also. "Finnbogg go make sure Neville okay. Maybe learn new songs." He followed the way Neville had gone.

The baron stared toward the door as Finnbogg departed. Then he rubbed his eyes and stood up. "I think I, too, shall retire," he said. A heavy weariness showed in his features as he pushed back his chair. "It has been quite a day seeing both my sons again, and an old man grows tired easily. But please, continue without me." He gestured toward the dessert cart and forced a smile. "There is still the pie. Herkimer will be disappointed if no one partakes."

None of the company spoke until Clive's father was gone. Then, one by one, they each pushed back their chairs and rose. Only Tomàs kept his seat. The little Portuguese sailor forked the remaining roast from Neville's plate and proceeded to devour it and anything else that was within his reach.

"Observation," Chang Guafe said, turning to Clive. "He did not respond to my inquiry. This technology remains unexplained."

"It may be worth noting, Englishman," said Sidi Bombay calmly, "that, as we have proceeded to the deeper levels of the Dungeon, the technology evidenced has become increasingly complex."

Horace Hamilton Smythe harrumphed. "You sound like our cyborg friend."

"But he's right, hacker," Annabelle agreed. "We should have noticed it before. Chang, what else have you observed?"

The cyborg answered without hesitation. "The gaslight is not gaslight at all. The food was molecularly reconstituted from other organic material—"

"You mean it wasn't real?" Horace blurted, passing a hand over his stomach.

"Real?" The cyborg shrugged. "The nutrients are perfectly balanced and without traces of preservative or pesticide or any foreign chemical contaminant. It is real, Horace Hamilton Smythe. It is wholesome. It is perfect. This can only be achieved through highly advanced nutriment design."

"Fake food!" Annabelle exclaimed. "No wonder the meat tasted a little bland. The vegetables were great, though. You know, they've just begun to dabble with this stuff in my time."

"What else?" Clive asked Chang Guafe.

"There are many energy patterns," he answered. He turned, and the candlelight from the table lent his armored body a burnished luster. "The walls are full of circuitry, some of it beyond my analytical capacities."

"I think we should be on our guard, sah," Smythe said quietly.

"But this is my father!" Clive protested. "Sure, he has to explain some things, but you all look ready to go to war again. I say let's grab some sleep and see what we can learn tomorrow when we're all fresh and rested. Coming, Tomàs?"

The little Portuguese looked at Clive as he chewed, then looked around the table with a frown. At last, he stood up, grabbed one whole pie off the dessert cart, and smiled. "*Sim*, coming, yes," he answered.

They filed out of the dining hall, leaving the cleanup for the frog-servants. There was no doubt they had just been served one of the finest meals set before them since coming to the Dungeon, and yet there was a strange air of quiet over everyone as they headed up to their rooms.

Herkimer, or at least one Herkimer, stood waiting for them at the foot of the staircase. From the smart dinner jacket he wore, Clive assumed it was the same one who had served as doorman to the dining room and who had announced his father. He looked down at the short little creature. Nothing but their clothes differentiated one from another. They were identical. *Clones*, he realized.

"Excuse me," Annabelle said to the patient-faced servant. "But I was wondering if there might be a program or something I could scan before powering down. There's really plenty of room left on my disk yet."

The frog put on a big smile that faded quickly. "Program? Scan? Disk, disk, disk?" He hopped up and down and a troubled expression settled across his features. "My master orders me to please, to please, but I don't know these things, don't know these things."

Clive was both touched and amused by the cute creature's near panic. He could almost hear the little being's heart hammering. "Calm down, Herkimer!" he said, setting his hand on its head so it couldn't bounce up again. "She means she's not sleepy, yet, and is there, perhaps, a book she could read?"

"Book?" Annabelle made a face. "Well, yeah, that'd do, too."

"Book, book!" Herkimer repeated excitedly. "Plenty of books. The master has a library. Want to see?"

The others had already gone up the stairs, so Clive decided to accompany Annabelle and Herkimer. The frog led them down the hallway and back past the dining room. They turned a corner and passed down yet another hall. Halfway, Herkimer stopped and pushed open another set of oaken double doors. He bounced twice and bowed with a sweeping gesture. "The master's library, the library," he announced grandiosely, and one webbed hand fluttered, inviting them inside.

It was a huge room, and a fire crackled needlessly in a great stone fireplace opposite the door. The house was too warm, already. The flames made the room a small inferno. Nevertheless, they went in.

The walls were lined floor to ceiling with books. The bindings looked old and worn, and a faint dust lingered in the air. An old wooden ladder hung suspended on hooks from an iron bar that circled the bookshelves, giving access to the higher volumes. In the center of the room sat two stuffed leather chairs on either side of a low wooden table.

"Shall I bring brandy, some brandy?" Herkimer asked. "Or a pot, a pot, of coffee?"

Annabelle and Clive moved to different sides of the room as they eyed the titles. Both muttered "no thank you" to the drinks, and Herkimer excused himself, leaving the doors open. The happy sound of his flat feet could be heard as he retreated down the hallway.

"He reminds me of a dashboard toy," Annabelle chuckled from across the room.

Clive turned around with a book in his hands. He glanced at the title on the spine, then at her. "A what?"

"A dashboard toy," she repeated. "In my time it's a little figure mounted on a spring. People stick them in the windshields of their vehicles, and they bounce around a lot."

Clive set the volume back in its place on the shelf. "To what purpose?" he called over his shoulder, choosing another book and opening it carefully. There was an audible crack as the dry pages separated. He shot a look guiltily over both shoulders and toward the open door, then shut the book, put it back on the shelf, and moved away from it.

"I saw that," Annabelle said accusingly. Then, "To no purpose, really. A lot of people in my time are pretty simpleminded. You know, easily amused."

"You mean their programs were buggy," Clive offered, moving the ladder out of his way. It scraped along the rail as if rust had formed where it couldn't be seen and it needed a good oiling.

"Hey, you're really hacking now, Clive-o, getting down to BASIC!"

She craned her neck sideways to read the spines as she moved around the room. "This is wonderful stuff," she muttered as she examined titles. "Just like home when I was a little user. Mother kept stacks of books in every corner of the house, and made sure I read them, too. Not diskettes, but real books. And old videos. She loved old classic videos." Suddenly, she stopped and pulled a book off the shelf. Lovingly, she ran a hand over the front cover, then looked at her palm and made a face. "Yucko," she muttered as she wiped her hand on her dress, leaving a smear of thick dust on the bodice.

"You've ruined a lovely dress," Clive chastised, selecting yet another book and placing it back.

"So, who cares?" she answered, moving toward one of the leather chairs with her volume. "There's like a whole wardrobe full of 'em. Your dear old dad really has a thing for virgin white, you know? And not much fashion sense."

She sat back and propped her feet up on the low table while Clive continued to peruse the titles. There were books on world history, English history, military history, ancient history. All the classics were there, and works on Plato, Aristotle, and Thucidides' *The Peloponnesian War*—another history. He found the plays of Shakespeare and Marlowe, and collections of poems by all Romantics. There was a book of colored plates by William Blake and next to it a volume of his poems. In another section he found Homer and Virgil and Ovid, the Norse sagas and the Pearl Poet, Chaucer and Bunyan and Jean de Meun.

He stepped back in awe and put a finger to his lips. He had not gone even a fourth of the way around the room. With a sigh, he turned back to Annabelle. She didn't notice, so deeply involved was she in the open book on her lap. He didn't get the chance to ask her what it was.

" 'It was many and many a year ago,' " said his father's voice from the doorway,

> " 'In a kingdom by the sea
> That a maiden there lived whom you may know
>     By the name of Annabel Lee;
> And this maiden she lived with no other thought
>     Than to live and be loved by me.' "

The baron walked into the library, a faint smile flickering across his face. He'd changed out of the brown velvet jacket and into a smoking gown of softly radiant blue silk. In one hand he carried an unlit pipe, in the other a small pouch of tobacco.

Annabelle closed the book she held, marking her place with her index finger, and turned a cool face toward her host. She didn't bother removing her feet, however, from his table.

" 'For the moon never beams, without bringing me dreams . . .' "

She spoke evenly, meeting the baron's direct gaze without flinching.

> " 'Of the beautiful Annabel Lee;
> And the stars never rise, but I feel the bright eyes
>     Of the beautiful Annabel Lee:
> And so, all the night-tide, I lie down by the side
> Of my darling—my darling—my life and my bride,
>     In the sepulchre there by the sea—
>     In her tomb by the sounding sea.' "

She took her feet from the table, then, and stood. "I never cared for Poe," she informed him, "and I particularly never cared for that poem."

Baron Tewkesbury settled heavily into the other leather chair and set the tobacco pouch on the table. He leaned forward, tapped the bowl of his pipe against the palm of his hand, and reached for the pouch. "But it's a beautiful poem, my dear, full of romance and mystery!"

"That Annabel dies," Annabelle pointed out, glancing at Clive as he came to stand opposite her by his father's side. "And her boyfriend is a sicko. Lie down by her dead body in its grave? Give me a break. Anyway, we spell our names differently." She backed toward the door, clutching her book to her chest with both arms. "Now, if you'll excuse me, I'm sure the two of you have all sorts of father-son shit to talk about, so I'll get out of your way."

She pulled the doors closed on her way out.

Clive took her empty chair. His father's jaw still hung open, and he still stared at the space Annabelle had just vacated. His hand had paused in midair, the reach for the tobacco pouch not quite completed. Slowly, he turned his gaze toward Clive, who forced a big smile.

"Quite a girl, isn't she?" Clive said innocently.

His father swallowed. "Uh, quite," he agreed. "Very colorful language. Very . . ." He swallowed again. Then he tilted his head quizzically and tapped his pipe.

"She'll grow on you," Clive assured him. "She's your granddaughter, several 'great's' removed."

His father looked at him. Again the jaw dropped, and again the hand hesitated as it reached for the tobacco. "You don't say," the baron finally managed. "The result of one of Neville's peccadilloes?"

# · CHAPTER FIFTEEN ·

# Home

Clive had never spent such a night with his father in his life.

Herkimer brought a bottle of brandy and two glasses with fine gold rims and left them alone while they sat facing each other over the library table, sipping the liquor, and talking as they had never done. The baron had never talked about Clive's mother. Now, he told his son everything he wanted to know: the color of her hair, her favorite flower, how his parents met, what they had hoped for out of life together. Lord Folliot described their wedding. They had married on the lawn of the Tewkesbury estate before hundreds of guests with not one but five wedding cakes, and all the notables of the realm had attended, including even the Prince of Wales, who bore a short congratulatory note from the Queen, herself. They had honeymooned in Lausserk, Switzerland, and spent an entire month in the sleepy little town nestled gently among the snowcapped mountains. They had followed that with a whirlwind tour of the capitals of Europe before returning exhausted to England and beginning the business of establishing their household.

It was upon their return to London that his bride had made her happy announcement. They could not have been more joyful over the news and set about preparing for a long and contented family life, as had always been the Folliot way.

By that point, the brandy was half-consumed. Clive stared into his glass, mesmerized by the rich amber contents as he swirled his drink round and round the crystal snifter and mesmerized by the soft sound of his father's voice. He felt incredibly warm and maudlin. For half of his life he'd wondered what it might be like to actually be close to his father, to feel that his father cared for him and about him as much as he did his other son. Clive could recall not one single time when his father had spent more than ten minutes alone in conversation with him unless it was to scold him for a bad grade or castigate him for some other real or imagined shortcoming. But now, all the barriers between them seemed suddenly to have collapsed, and they were talking for the first time man to man, father to son, and his heart felt simply too big inside his chest. He wanted to push away the table so not even that stood between them. He restrained himself, however. There was, after all, a certain amount of decorum they must maintain.

His father leaned forward and refilled both their glasses, then sat back and stared at his son for a long quiet moment. The baron took a swallow, then began again.

Clive knew instinctively that not even Neville had been privileged to hear what passed between them now. It could only have been the brandy that loosened his father's tongue. He spoke in a low whisper of the pain of losing his young bride in the first year of their life together, of how even now after so many years he dreamed of her and longed for her in the nights. He had never touched another woman, not even for a single night of pleasure, but kept himself for her, alone, when they met again in heaven. His hands reached out as he talked. One held his glass, but the other moved gently in the air as if he were caressing the face of a ghost that Clive couldn't see. It was a strange pantomime that made Clive lean forward, one elbow on his knee, and it was then he saw the tear that trickled down the old man's cheek.

Clive's breath caught in his throat, and the snifter nearly

fell from his numb fingers. He had never ever seen his father cry, and the sight sobered him for all of five or six heartbeats. Then he tumbled over that fine drunken line of self-control, set his glass down clumsily, and came around the table to embrace his father even as the elder Folliot rose to do the same. They clung to each other weeping before the fireplace.

"I've been such an old fool!" the baron cried. "Forgive me, son, say you forgive me!"

"I do!" Clive cried into his father's shoulder. "I forgive you! I forgive you for getting me so embarrassingly inebriated!"

The baron clapped his son on the back, still hugging him close, refusing to let him go yet. "Yes, we Folliots always had a taste for the grape, I'm afraid." He sniffed and ran a hand through Clive's hair. "To think it took a bottle to bring us to this. I never held you when you were little. You always wanted me to hold you. I saw it in your eyes. But I never did!" He put his face down beside his son's so their damp cheeks touched.

"It's all right," Clive whispered, when he could finally shape words through a throat too swollen with emotion. How odd it felt that he should have to console his father after so many years. "It's all right," he repeated again. "We don't have to speak of the past anymore. We can start again right here, Father!"

The baron lifted his head, sniffed again, and looked into the fire. "Yes, we can start again," he agreed, "right here." He backed away a bit, pulled an embroidered handkerchief from his jacket pocket, and wiped at his eyes and nose. "I'd like that, Son."

"I'd like it, too," Clive said, withdrawing a bit.

"It must be very late," the old man reasoned. "I think I'd better get Herkimer to see me to bed."

He didn't look at Clive again but stumbled to the library door. Herkimer was there without needing to be called. The little frog-servant took the baron's arm and helped him down the hall.

Clive stood by the fireplace for a long time and tried to sort out the jumble of emotions that whirled inside his head. He felt like a little boy who had just won his father's approval, and he felt like an old man who had needlessly embarrassed himself. All his life he had competed with his brother, Neville, for the old man's attention and always lost. But that was over, past, and all the old anger drained out of him as he picked up his glass and drained the last of the brandy.

His father's glass sat, empty, on the edge of the table beside the empty bottle. On an impulse he would never be able to explain, he leaned over and clinked the rim of his own glass to it. A pleasant ring floated upward at the contact, a sweet crystalline note that penetrated and stuck in his thickened senses.

He smiled, and the room spun a little, and he knew he had imbibed too much. He really had to get to bed before the others saw him. But first he would sit down just for a moment.

When he woke, a dull throbbing beat behind his temples. He peeled his eyes open slowly and recognized the room as his own. Who had put him to bed? Vague memories of a patient Smythe came to him. His former batman had carried him upstairs, then, if he remembered correctly. He touched his head and winced.

He practically oozed out of bed and into the bathroom. To his surprise, the tub was full again and hot. He eased into it and kneeled and filled his lungs with a deep breath. Then, he plunged his head under the water.

Fifteen minutes of soaking and scrubbing made him feel almost human again. A soft toweling and a fresh shave helped, too. He checked his appearance in the small hand-mirror by the tub and smoothed down the hairs of his thickening mustache.

Almost as an afterthought he checked the wound on his thigh and received his second surprise of the morning. There was nothing but a pink scar along the muscle, and no pain at all. In fact, he recalled now how Annabelle had squeezed his leg under the table at dinner, and there had been no pain. He hurried into the main room and to the full-length mirror. Most of his scratches were entirely gone, without trace.

He took clean clothes from the wardrobe and dressed and went downstairs. He found Herkimer in the hallway. The little frog wore an apron and brandished a feather duster. "You must be hungry, be hungry, Clive Folliot," the creature said. "I'll bring some breakfast to the dining room, dining room." With that, Herkimer hopped away.

Clive found the dining room easily enough and sat down alone. Herkimer came through the side door with a tray of hot rolls and butter and marmalade, a selection of cheeses, and a pot of hot tea. It was a different Herkimer who served him, though, at least to judge by the baker's whites and the chef's cap the small frog wore. He watched the awkward little servant depart and buttered his first roll.

"So you're awake at last, you are, sah." Horace Hamilton Smythe peered at him from the open doorway and ventured in.

Clive waved to him with the butter knife. "I vaguely recall your carrying me to bed, Horace," he said sheepishly. "Hope I wasn't too heavy."

"A gallon or so more than usual, sah," Smythe answered blithely. "But nothing to speak of."

"You're a paragon, Horace," Clive responded. He gestured toward the rolls. "Help yourself."

Horace explained that everyone had eaten breakfast early, a much larger meal than the one before Clive now. He launched into a description of the succulent piles of bacon and sausage, the eggs, the biscuits and gravy. Clive stopped him. Even the sound of such heavy fare made him feel queasy.

"Where is everyone?" he asked suddenly. Herkimer and Horace were the only ones he'd seen this morning.

"Well, sah, now 'morning' is a relative term, it is." He rose and moved to a huge curtained window at one end of the dining room and drew back the curtain. It was black as ever outside. "As for the others," Smythe continued, "they're all about different things, occupying time. Sidi and Tomàs are wandering around outside. Finnbogg's with them. Chang Guafe said something about running a systems check on his sensor circuits, whatever that means, and he's in his room. That's where Shriek and Neville are, too. Neville's been real quiet, he has, and Shriek hasn't come out since dinner last night."

"Leave her alone," Clive said quietly. "She's doing something for me." He'd already decided it wouldn't do any good to tell the others about the mind scans Shriek had detected. They couldn't do anything against an enemy they couldn't see, and it would just put everyone on edge. Right now was a time to relax, the first chance they'd had for some time. Soon he'd tell them, but not now. "What about Annabelle?" he asked.

Horace dipped one finger in the marmalade and put it in his mouth. He made a smacking sound with his lips. "Good as anything in London," he remarked. "Can't figure how he gets it here." He tasted another fingerful, looked around hastily, and wiped his hand on the border of the tablecloth. "Annabelle, now, she's been in the library ever since she woke up, sah. In fact, she took her breakfast in there. Still there as far as I know. In love with all those books, she is."

Clive buttered another roll and took a drink of his tea. "Have you seen my father?" he asked.

"No, sah, but then I suppose he had his own share of that brandy, and he's not as young as you, though he wouldn't like to hear me say it." Smythe hesitated, put his elbows on the table, folded his hands, and leaned his chin on them. "Did you ask him about the gate, sah? You know, to the next level?"

"No," Clive answered slowly. "Not yet. But there's time. I think we're going to stay here for a while, Horace. Not long, but long enough to rest a bit. We're all tired, and so far it's been one fight after another. We could use an interlude. I'll ask him tonight, though." They separated shortly after that. Since rest was the plan, Horace intended to get some, and he left Clive at the foot of the stairs.

Clive, for his part, took the opportunity to explore the rest of the house. He found a large sitting room filled with beautiful Queen Anne furniture. A heavy, brocaded paper of peach swirls covered the walls. A large window caught his attention, and he pulled back the drapes. Outside, the softly glowing spiral floated across the sky. He lowered the curtain and turned away. The smell of a clove-and-cinnamon potpourri wafted through the room, and he inhaled the rich fragrance.

Next to the sitting room he found a conservatory. Four concert harps occupied the center of the room. In one corner stood a piano. He shuffled idly through the sheets of music that lay open on the bench. Chopin, Brahms, Beethoven. He brushed his fingers over the keys. It had been so long since he'd played. He knew he wouldn't be very good. Nevertheless, he sat down and made a few runs at Beethoven's Piano Concerto Number Three in C Minor before giving it up in disgust. He looked around self-consciously to make sure no one had heard, then closed the lid quietly over the keys and left the room.

He returned to his room after that. The throbbing in his head had become a mild but persistent pressure. A nap, he figured, would relieve it.

Herkimer woke him with a knock on his door. His nap had lasted until dinnertime. He went down, eager to see his father once more.

The meal passed in quiet conversation. Almost everyone seemed occupied with their own thoughts as they ate. Annabelle had a book on her lap all the while she ate and answered questions only in grunts and monosyllables. Neville looked sullen and said next to nothing. Tomàs and Sidi and Finnbogg conversed among themselves, as did Clive and Baron Tewkesbury, while Chang Guafe hung on every word the old man said. Shriek again ate in her room.

"We have some small entertainment tonight," the baron announced when the last morsel was finished. At his direction they carried their teacups or wine glasses into the conservatory and took the seats that had recently been placed there.

When they were all comfortable, the four look-alike Herkimers filed in. They wore identical dinner jackets and sat down at the four harps. The instruments looked huge before them, but they touched the strings in unison, and the sweet strains of Beethoven's Sonata Number Fourteen in C Sharp Minor filled the room.

The music entranced Clive, who had long counted the *Moonlight Sonata* among his favorite pieces of music, but next to him Annabelle put down her book and hid the lower half of her face behind her cupped hands. She struggled not to laugh, but she convulsed with a fit of barely contained giggles.

"Don't you like Beethoven?" Clive inquired in a whisper, leaning close to his granddaughter. "I've never heard him on harps before. It's enchanting!'"

Another fit seized Annabelle as she looked at him wide-eyed over hands clapped tightly to her mouth. Merriment twinkled in her dark eyes. "Enchanting?" she dared to murmur. "That's the word, Clive-o!" She looked toward the four performers and uncupped her fingers long enough for him to overhear. "Pluck your magic twangers, froggies!" she whispered. Quickly, she picked up the book from her lap and hid her entire face behind its covers while she rocked with silent mirth.

On Clive's right side, the baron tapped the back of his hand with one fingertip and gave him a stern look. After that, Clive ignored Annabelle and settled back to enjoy the concert.

Midway through, Neville stood suddenly and left the room. Clive bit his lip as he watched his brother depart, but the first notes of Bach's *Arioso* made him forget about his twin.

When the music ended, everyone returned to the dining room for dessert and more conversation. When that was finished, the baron took them all on a tour of his home, apologizing for not doing so earlier. A mild headache, he explained. Smythe coughed and grinned at Clive, and Tomàs openly snickered.

After the tour Clive and his father drifted away from the others. Again, they began to talk as they aimlessly wandered the halls and rooms of the estate, cautiously at first, gradually letting down the barriers, this time without the benefit of alcohol. Clive told him about his years at Sandhurst, the friends he'd made there, and about his course of study, which had been literature and the classics. Then, he talked about his military life, his career in the army, the time he'd spent in Madagascar, and his promotion to the rank of major.

The baron listened attentively like a kindly father, shaking his head frequently, and chiding himself for ignoring his son for so long.

After a while, they wandered outside into the darkness. The spiral overhead lit the way as they drifted toward the very edge of the mountaintop. The wind blew against their faces as if to push them back, but they held their ground and stared outward. In the far, far distance, Clive thought he could just make out the hazy orange glow of the fiery land they had crossed. A vast sea of blackness spread between it and the mountaintop.

At last, Clive told his father about Miss Annabella Leighton and how he knew he'd found the love of his life in her. She was of a good family, he explained, but not of noble stock. He didn't care. She supported herself by teaching literature at a school for wealthy, aristocratic young girls and kept a small flat in Plantagenet Court, and Clive had wanted to marry her for a long time. Only his poverty had prevented it, for he felt life on a major's small salary too much of a sacrifice to ask such a lady to make.

"And yet you carried on a dalliance with this woman?" his father asked, brows furrowing.

Clive knew what he was hinting at, and he raised his

head proudly, if a little defiantly. "We were in love," he said defensively. "There was no sin in what we did, and certainly no shame." Then, he lowered his head. "The shame lies in my leaving her to find Neville. I didn't know she was carrying our child, I swear I didn't, and I admit that I was even eager to make the journey, for a chance to get away from England for a while. I thought I might be able to find my fortune and go back with money enough to wed her then." He looked away and shook his head sadly. "It just didn't work out that way. At least, as Annabelle tells the story."

"Your great-great-granddaughter?" his father said.

"Your great-great-great-granddaughter," Clive responded. He stared upward at the spiral, daring its swirling gases and dizzying stars to steal his senses, almost hoping they would succeed and leave him numb to the ache that suddenly filled him. "She says I never made it back to London, that I disappeared in Africa just like Neville. Neither of us made it back."

The baron reached out and laid a hand gently on Clive's shoulder. Then, he drew his son close and embraced him. "Because you found your home here," he said in Clive's ear. "We're together again, Neville and you and me. That's all that matters. There's no way out of the Dungeon. I know. I've tried to find it. This is our home now, Clive, right here, and we must make the best of it." He held Clive out at arm's length and peered intently at his son. "This is our home," he insisted.

Clive hugged his father with a trembling intensity. "Home," he uttered, half-believing it, wishing to believe it.

## · CHAPTER SIXTEEN ·

# Blood Relatives

Outside, the sky and the land remained black and foreboding. Only the pale spiral provided any light at all as it moved slowly, slowly across the sky. Clive learned to count the days by the cycles of dinners and sleeping periods.

He spent more and more time with his father. They talked and played chess in the sitting room, or he played the piano while his father listened, pleased at how quickly he improved on the keys. Sometimes, they shared wine in the library by the fireplace, or tea and crumpets in the dining room. Sometimes, they walked side by side along the rim of the mountaintop or along some of the easier trails that led down the far side.

"I can see so much farther now," his father confided. "To the edge of the world if I concentrate. So I saw you when you approached the Dantean Gate. I erected that myself, you know. A sort of jest to ease the loneliness I felt when first I came here." He touched his son's arm. "Now I will never be lonely again."

Clive saw less and less of his friends. Neville kept mostly to his room, coming out only to eat or to chat with Annabelle in the library or to wander solitary outside the house. When he spoke at all to his father, it was with brusque indifference or barely concealed anger.

Annabelle buried herself in some research. She showed

up for meals, usually with a book in hand. Otherwise, she could be found in the library or in her room reading.

Shriek did not show herself at all. The arachnid ceased even to eat the meals that Herkimer carried to her room. Clive dared to look in on her once and found her deep in a trance. She roused herself long enough to assure him she was well and to ask him to leave. He bothered her no more.

As for the others, he couldn't really say how they occupied their time. They milled about listlessly, and Clive began to sense a general restlessness in his friends. Still, he gave the matter little thought, and when Horace Hamilton Smythe came to his room after dinner one evening and said he might be gone for a while and not to worry, Clive merely shrugged. If his sergeant wanted to explore some of the other mountain trails, he saw no reason why he shouldn't. Smythe was a competent man.

At dinner the next evening Chang Guafe expressed his quiet dissatisfaction with the decision to let Smythe go. "There is still the matter of the implants in Sergeant Smythe's head," he reminded them. "We have not fully dealt with that. Instead, we have assumed, without evidence, that merely knowing about the implants would enable him to resist outside influence. But how can we be sure that leaving us was his own idea? We do not know who put them in his head, or why."

When Clive waved aside the objection, the cyborg raised a new, more sensitive, issue, openly questioning the clarity of Clive's judgment. "Perhaps, Clive Folliot," he challenged, "you are becoming too comfortable here."

The baron intervened to prevent an argument, though, and ordered Herkimer to serve the special surprise he had prepared—hot chocolate with marshmallow. No matter that the temperature of the air remained uncomfortably warm. It was a delicious treat.

The following morning Clive and his father passed Neville near the library. Neville closed the book he held in one hand and glanced curiously at the baron. "Tell me,

Father," he said with a lightness that made Clive hope his twin's mood had improved and the three of them might spend some time together. "I've been trying to remember the name of Nanny's dog."

Clive felt the heat rise in his cheeks, appalled at his brother's insinuation, but the baron answered nonchalantly. "Why, I'm surprised at you, Neville. How could you forget a thing like that? The poor woman fastened your first nappy! It was Tennyson, of course."

Their eyes locked for the briefest instant. "Oh, yes, that was it," Neville said, touching one finger to his chin and feigning a thoughtful look as he tucked his book under his arm. "How silly of me." His gaze flickered over Clive, full of something his brother didn't understand, before he turned away and went upstairs.

Later, Clive walked with his father along the petrified hedge. "I sent Samedi to guide you through the dangers to my side," the baron said. "I shall miss the little man. Because I was a baron, he decided to be one, too. Baron Samedi, he called himself, but I suppose you know that. And what did I care? What do such things mean in the Dungeon?" He looked sad as he remembered.

"Where did he come from?" Clive asked idly.

The baron shrugged. "We're not alone here, Clive. There are other creatures."

"The demons?"

Tewkesbury nodded as he whispered. "And more. But they stay away. They leave me alone."

What was it about darkness, Clive wondered as he hugged himself, that made men whisper? He took a step back and looked at his father, measured his huge silhouette against the shadows of the looming mountain peaks. When the old man turned toward him, the light from the spiral caught his eyes just so, giving them a weird catlike glow that made Clive shiver unexpectedly.

His father must have seen his reaction. "I am part of this world now, Son. I don't even want to go back to London. I'm changed, and there is no place for me there."

They stood again on the rim of the baron's high mountain-top, and the hot wind blew against their faces as he spread out his hand. "Your poor eyes cannot see," he said, "but there are lands beyond us. You've seen the Hell That Is Fire and the Misty Limbo, and you've crossed the boiling Phlegathon River to come to me. But below us there is the Kingdom of Ice, the Marsh Hell, and the Mud Hell, and more hells than Dante ever dreamed or imagined."

He took his son's hand and drew him closer to the brink. The darkness whirled about them as if it were alive, and the wind rushed in Clive's ears. "It is mine, my son. Ours, for whomsoever I will, I will give it."

Clive stepped back trembling, uncertain of the words that burned in his ears. Was it his father's voice, or was it the wind? Why couldn't he think? He had to think!

He untangled his fingers from his father's grip. "Let's go back inside," he said.

"Of course," his father answered. "I'm sure there's even a little chocolate left."

Clive felt strangely tired after their chocolate, however. He returned to his room without a word to anyone else and slept until dinnertime. Only once did he awaken. His sheets were drenched with sweat, and his head throbbed with a dream he couldn't remember.

A knock at his door awakened him for good. He called out, and Finnbogg peeked around the door. "Clivefriend awake?" he asked needlessly. Clive propped his back against the headboard and waved his friend inside.

Finnbogg wore a strange expression as he seated himself in one of the chairs. He glanced from side to side as if to avoid Clive's gaze. He tapped his foot and dragged the point of one claw nervously over the padding of the chair's arm.

"What is it, old friend?" Clive asked, for plainly Finnbogg wanted to talk.

The alien canine rubbed his nose with the back of one paw and cleared his throat with a deep *harummmp*. "Okay," he said at last. "Finnbogg promised Clivefriend to help find Clivefriend's littermate, Neville Folliot. Neville Folliot found now, okay?" He paused and cleared his throat again. "But we find not just Clivefriend's littermate, but Clivefriend's littersire. Happy for Clivefriend is Finnbogg at this joyous reunion!" He rose from his chair and began to pace at the foot of the bed. "But now Finnbogg thinks of Finnbogg's littermate. Finnbogg is lonely, too! Where is Finnbogg's littermate?" He stopped pacing directly in front of Clive. The look on his face was so sad and touching that Clive finally looked away.

"When do we go, Clivefriend?" Finnbogg pleaded. "When do we go?"

Clive got out of bed and went to his friend, placing both hands on Finnbogg's brawny shoulders. "Soon, Finnbogg, soon," he answered, feeling a band tighten around his chest as he spoke. "But not yet," he added. "A little more time. Just a little more time."

Finnbogg accepted that and left. Clive went into the bathroom and washed his face. Then, he picked up the hand-mirror and looked at his reflection for a long time. The mustache had grown out nice and full. Yet the face displeased him. On impulse, he reached for the razor and prepared to shave his upper lip bare. He looked at his reflection again, studying what he saw. It felt wrong. Everything felt wrong! He slammed the unused razor down, and the mirror, cracking it.

He changed into a pair of soft khaki pants and a white shirt and pulled on boots. Without meaning to, he slammed his door on the way out.

Annabelle was halfway down the hall coming toward him with a stack of books. "Clive," she called in a low voice. "We've got to talk now. I've overloaded my disk on this thing, and you'd better hear the voice-out!"

"Not now," he muttered, crossing to his brother's door.

"Clive!" she insisted.

He whirled on her. "I said, 'Not now,' goddamn it!"

With that, he pushed open Neville's door without bothering to knock and slammed it shut again.

Neville sat on his bed with his back to his headboard, much as Clive had sat earlier. But his hands were folded behind his head as he stared off into space, and a book of poems lay open on his lap. With an irritating self-assurance and calm, he rolled his head to the side and looked at his twin.

"Well, little brother—"

Clive didn't give him a chance to speak. "What in God's name is wrong with you?" he raged. "What have you got against Father, anyway? You haven't had a kind word for him, not one! You insult him at his table, and you're rude to him everywhere! And I want to know why."

Patiently, Neville closed the book and set it aside. He swung his legs over the side of the bed and rose.

"I just don't understand you, Neville!" Clive continued in a fury. "He gave you everything, and you treat him like this? You were always his favorite. He gave you everything you ever—"

"Stop it, Clive. You don't know what you're talking about."

But Clive wouldn't stop. His head felt as if it were about to explode, and his face burned as he shook his fist under his brother's nose. "He gave you every goddamned thing!" he continued. "And I got nothing! I didn't have a father, and I didn't have a brother, either! The two of you were too bloody busy having a good time to remember I was around! Now, we find him here. He came looking for us, for God's sake! And finally, for the first time in my life, he acknowledges that I'm alive, and you act like a silly prig about the whole thing!"

Neville's calm exterior began to melt. He clenched his fists at his sides, and his face colored. "You want him so bloody bad?" he said, trying to keep the anger from his voice. "Then take him. Keep him. It's time I was leaving, anyway. But I'll tell you this, little brother. You were better off when he ignored you. You didn't have his arm locked tight about your bloody throat!"

"And I didn't have my hand locked tight on his bloody pocketbook, either!" Clive shot back.

"He's a bastard, Clive, but you're too stupid to know it! You're getting your ears scratched a little now, and you think it feels pretty good, and maybe it does to a dog that's been starved for affection. But you damn well better learn to fetch his stick when he tells you to, and you damn well better bring his slippers."

Neville paced to the far side of the room, putting distance between them. "You don't know what he's like, little brother!" Neville shouted. "All you saw were the favors you think he did me. You don't know how he can push and drive and suffocate a man! Sure, he sent you to Sandhurst and me to Oxford. I got the better school, and that sticks in your craw, no doubt. But he picked the goddamned school for me without ever asking my opinion! He chose my course program, and my tutors. I studied what he wanted me to study! And when school was done, he pushed me into army service. He even picked my regiment and pulled the strings to see I wound up there. It didn't matter what I wanted! You think you know me? You think you know him? You don't know what my life was like. You don't know anything! You're just a stupid little sod who thinks he's been cheated out of something."

Clive trembled with rage as he faced his brother. He knew one thing, all right. He knew this had been coming a long time, and he didn't intend to back down now.

"I was cheated!" he shouted back, the words ripping out of him like sharp knives. "You might have turned around at any time and said, 'Father, let's take Clive fishing, too.' But you never did. You loved having him to yourself!"

Neville jabbed a finger at him. "You were lucky he ignored you, Brother! He left you alone. Yes, I probably flaunted the relationship a bit, I don't deny it. But it was because I envied you your *freedom*! You could do practically whatever you wanted. It didn't matter to him. But he was always breathing down my neck. Why do you think I started traveling so much? Even in the army I couldn't get free of him. Not until I volunteered for India. Not until I went to America. The world was the only thing I could find to put between us! Why do you think I went to Africa, you bloody fool?"

"Don't call me a fool!" Before Clive even knew what he was doing, he struck his brother. The impact tingled through his fist and up his arm, as Neville crashed backward over a desk, spewing blood from his lip.

Then, Neville came at him. His brother's momentum carried them into a wall, which shook beneath their weight. They fell over a stuffed chair and rolled on the floor. Bright stars flashed in Clive's temple, and he knew the taste of his own blood in the corner of his mouth. He lashed out wildly with both fists, pummeling his brother's face as he fought to push Neville off him.

Somehow, they both got to their feet. Clive's heart hammered furiously in his chest, and a red haze clouded his vision, but he saw well enough. As Neville straightened, Clive punched him again, sending him to his knees. But when he closed in, Neville struck. An incredible pain exploded between Clive's legs, and he sagged to the floor.

"This isn't the Marquis of Queensberry, little brother!" Neville hissed, spraying blood from his lip. "Get up! Let's see what they teach at Sandhurst these days!"

Clive's hand brushed against something, and he grabbed it and flung it. The pages of the poetry book fluttered like the wings of a terrified bird as it flew through the air and caught his brother in the face. It gave Clive time to get up. Neville, unhurt by the book, launched himself again, his arms reaching.

Clive grabbed the nearest thing at hand, a pillow from the bed at his back, and swung it with all his might. Neville crashed sideways into his wardrobe, bounced off it, and collapsed on the floor again in a shower of down feathers that swirled in the air. Clive looked stupidly at the ruined pillow and sputtered.

Neville rolled over just as the framed full-length mirror

teetered on its stand and fell on him. He swept it aside with his arm, and silver glass scattered everywhere.

The shattering crash was enough to make them stop. The anger drained from Neville's face. He raised up on one elbow and looked at the mess. "Well, that's seven years of bad luck," he said, and a grin spread weakly over his bloodied lips.

Clive felt out of breath and suddenly sheepish as he waved a hand through the feathers that swam around him. Then, he grinned, too. "As funny as time seems to be in the Dungeon, that should pass soon enough. And it's appropriate. It's been seven levels of bad luck, so far."

Their gazes met. They looked away, then looked at each other again, grinning.

"It was kind of fun, wasn't it?" Neville said. He picked up a piece of mirror, checked his reflection, smoothed his hair back, and tossed the piece over his shoulder. It shattered with a tinkling sound.

"Kind of fun," Clive agreed. He bent and recovered the book he'd thrown at his twin. He thumbed through the pages, then glanced at the title on the spine. "Didn't think you were the poetry type, big brother." He sagged down onto the bed as his breathing returned gradually to normal. *I'm going to need more of Shriek's medicine*, he thought to himself. *I hurt in a hundred places.*

"A small weakness in my otherwise completely manly self," Neville quipped with an exaggerated wave of his hand. He stood slowly and uttered a low groan. Then, he dabbed at his lip with the back of his hand. "I wonder if Shriek is in a charitable mood? I hurt all over. Not bad, for Sandhurst."

Clive nodded, acknowledging the compliment. "Not bad, for an Oxford softie," he returned.

"Shall we go down to dinner?"

"Let's."

"You know you look like hell?"

Clive looked at the rip in the front of his shirt and the sleeve that hung by a thread. All the buttons on Neville's shirt had flown off, and there was a tear in the knee of his trousers. As for their faces, Neville's lip was taking on a thick purple, but—Clive suspected—so was his left eye. "I look just like you," Clive countered with a wink. "And I'm starving."

They got up and went to the door, wearing their rips and bruises like badges of honor. They found their comrades waiting for them in the hallway. Even Shriek had roused herself from her trance. They all wore such anxious expressions. Annabelle was the only exception. She stood right in the doorway, her arms folded across her chest as she regarded them.

"Well, you're both still on your feet," she said with amused disgust. "You've got this macho bullshit out of the way?"

Clive looked at Neville. Neville looked at Clive.

"How she talks!" Neville said, clucking his tongue. "You really should have reared her better."

"It's her mother's fault," Clive answered disdainfully. "I could never do anything with her."

Annabelle half-turned and said over her shoulder to Shriek, "Isn't it cute? They're in the full ruddy glow of masculinity."

*Embarrassment, I thought it was.* Shriek's answer brushed them all.

Annabelle folded her arms again and tapped her foot. "If you two are finished playing in the sandbox, I've got an interesting pieces of news." She looked at them expectantly and impatiently.

Clive realized it was the first time in days he'd seen her without a book in her hand. She looked almost unnatural without one. "Something you found in the library?" he asked, suddenly serious. He knew that look in Annie's eye.

"I've been researching my ass off," she responded, turning eager again. "There's a lot of stuff down there about the Folliot family: histories, genealogies, biographies, that kind of stuff. Well, I've read it all now, and I've made a lot of notes and double-checked everything. I could have done it faster on a computer, but I'm finally sure I'm right."

Neville leaned on the doorjamb and folded his arms in imitation of her. "Well, what?" he asked.

Herkimer appeared at the top of the stairs, immaculate in a fresh tuxedo. He hopped up and down impatiently and called to them. "Dinner! It's time for dinner! My master waits, he waits!"

"Can it, froggie!" Annabelle snapped.

Herkimer looked stricken. His wide jaw dropped open, and his tongue lolled slackly while his eyes grew rounder and rounder and his shoulders slumped. He tilted his head quizzically, then turned and hopped back down the stairs.

Annabelle watched him go, then turned back to the others. "I didn't want the little critter to overhear," she whispered. "The two of you can decide whether or not to tell your father."

"Tell him what?" Clive said with some exasperation. He rather liked Herkimer, and Annabelle had plainly hurt the little creature's feelings.

She grabbed Tomàs by the arm and dragged him forward. By the look on his face he didn't know what was going on, either. The others gathered closer as Annabelle prepared to reveal her new-found secret.

"*Senhor e Senhor,*" she addressed Clive and Neville as she placed one hand over her heart. "*Eu apresento . . .*" Then a look of intense frustration crossed her face and she slapped her thigh. "Oh, damn!" she muttered to Tomàs and threw her hands up helplessly. "I still can't break down your verb forms! Well, never mind." She turned back to Clive and Neville and let go a sigh. "Oh, say hello to your long-lost cousin."

Clive looked at Neville. Neville looked at Tomàs. Tomàs looked at Clive. Then, they all looked at Annabelle.

"What?"

"What?"

"¿Qûe?"

Annabelle grinned. "Yep, it's true. The little scrodhead's a relative. I'll show you the research after dinner." Her grin faded and she turned serious. "Kind of brings us back to an old question, doesn't it? Who, exactly, is so interested in the Folliots?"

Clive looked Tomàs up and down and nodded gravely as he added, "And why?"

# · CHAPTER SEVENTEEN ·

# The Council of War

"I'll show you the details later, if you like," Annabelle said. "But one of your ancestors married a young woman of a poor Spanish commoner family in 1463 and took her to England. She apparently didn't fit in very well, though. Before a year was up she ran home to mom and dad with a small baby boy. Of course, since she'd shamed the family by marrying one of the hated English, they would have nothing to do with her or the child, whom they couldn't really afford to feed, anyway. She finally wound up living with some lowly relatives on the Portuguese side of the border."

Tomàs looked dazed as he stared over Annabelle's shoulder at the writing on the page. "*¡Pobre mãe!*" he muttered. "My poor mother! She never told me any of this!"

Neville pointed a finger at Clive. "Must have been your side of the family," he accused wryly.

Clive was silent for a long moment as he and Tomàs regarded each other. He couldn't quite read the expression on the little Portuguese's face, but there was no doubting his own confusion. He needed time to think, time to understand. "Let's go down to dinner," he announced quietly. "We'll talk more about this later, but for now let's keep it to ourselves."

*Also must talk we, Being Clive,* Shriek said to him privately. *Information have I to share.*

*After dinner, please, Being Shriek,* he answered. *We'll talk then. Will you join us now?*

*No, Being Clive,* she responded. *Repulsive you find my feeding habits. But grateful am I.*

Shriek went back to her room, and the rest went down to dinner. The Herkimers served yet another sumptuous feast, but the meal passed quietly. Clive and Neville studiously avoided their father's gaze while glancing surreptitiously at each other across the table.

"You seem to have a rip in your sleeve, Clive, my boy," the baron finally said between bites.

Clive swallowed a sip of the wine. "Um, I fell down the stairs, I'm afraid," he lied. To avoid his father's gaze he glanced at Annabelle. The scars on her throat, he noticed, were almost completely gone.

The baron rubbed his chin and glanced at both his sons. "I see. You also have ruined your shirt, Neville. Did you also fall down the stairs?"

Neville set down his knife and fork and smiled sweetly as he looked his father straight in the eye. "Why, yes, I did. Damn near landed on Clive, I did."

The baron crimsoned at Neville's epithet and leaned forward to chastise him, but at the last instant he appeared to think better of it and settled back in his chair with a glower. For the rest of the evening he watched them over the rim of his glass.

Again, Tomàs was the last to finish. The news about his family ties certainly hadn't harmed his appetite. Clive could only watch in amused appreciation as his Portuguese cousin wolfed half of an apple pie and washed it down with water. Fortunately, no one else had wanted dessert.

"Tomàsfriend eat like Finnbogg's littermates!" Finnbogg remarked at Tomàs's elbow. "Why doesn't Tomàs grow?"

"He's big where it counts," Annabelle answered from across the table.

Clive, in the process of taking a drink, started to cough, then sealed his lips tight to avoid spewing wine. Unexpectedly, though, it surged up his nose and down his throat, choking him. He spilled the glass's contents as he tried to set it down and get his napkin up in time, but some dribbled into his mustache before he could catch it. He coughed, trying to get air, and coughed again.

Annabelle watched him, grinning, and she tapped a finger over her chest. "His heart," she assured him ruefully. "He has a big heart."

Dinner ended quickly after that. The others retired to their rooms while Clive walked outside with his father. The spiral was low in the direction of the Dantean Gate now. Clive avoided looking at it, fearing its hypnotic effect.

He felt strangely uncomfortable in his father's presence as they walked between the pertrified hedges. They made the same idle small talk as they always did before turning to more personal matters. But this time Clive felt the old barriers erecting themselves once more. He looked sidewise at the figure of his father as they walked along the edge of the mountaintop where the winds blew on their faces.

When his father spoke, Clive barely heard. "Clive?" the baron repeated, touching his son's arm.

"Father," Clive said, turning away from his sire to look out into the vast darkness that enshrouded this world. Darkness, darkness everywhere. *I am half sick of shadows*, he thought, recalling a favorite line of poetry. It was one of the few things, the love of that poem, that his father had ever given him. "Father," he started again, "when I was a child you used to recite 'The Lady of Shalott' to Neville and me, and you'd get this faraway look in your eye." Clive hesitated, filled with a sudden realization. "It was Mother you were thinking of, wasn't it? She was your Lady of Shalott."

Baron Tewkesbury moved to the very edge. A sudden wind might have cast him to his death, yet he balanced there as if daring such a fate, and the only things the wind blew were his hair and the ends of his jacket. He didn't say anything, just stood there, lord of all he surveyed, or so he claimed.

"Recite it for me now, Father," Clive begged. He wanted suddenly to reach out and pull the old man back from the brink, to wrap his arms about him as he heard that deep voice and those lines he had loved so well when he was little, that he still loved. "Please?" he urged, taking a step closer to his father, his hands trembling to reach out and grab a jacket sleeve, but his hands remained strangely at his sides. "What was the first line? How did it go?"

The baron didn't move, didn't turn to look at Clive, didn't shrug even his shoulders. He might have been another distant shadowed mountain, a splintered fragment of the darkness itself, for all the indication he gave that he had heard his son.

Then, the Baron Tewkesbury raised a hand and extended it into the infinite, and his voice rumbled deep and rich as thunder though he spoke in only a whisper. "Whomsoever I will, I will give it. Stay with me, Son. Stay here with me."

Clive stared at the back of the towering figure. He trembled all over now, and his eyes stung as he blinked furiously. "How did it go, Father?" His voice was strained and fearful, and he thought of Neville and home and Nanny and her dog, Tennyson, and their mother he had never known. "How did it go, damn you?" His voice went up a note and quivered with emotion. "Don't you remember? Don't you know? 'On either side the river lie long fields of barley and of rye that clothe the world and meet the sky.' You remember, don't you? It was your favorite poem. You taught it to me. You couldn't have forgotten!"

Slowly, the mountain moved and turned and extended a hand toward him. "Stay with me, Clive," it said. "We don't need Neville. We don't need the others. Let them go. It will be just you and me, the way you've always wanted it. Stay with me."

" 'And through the field the road runs by to many-towered Camelot'!" Clive shouted, clenching his fists at his sides. "You know it! Why won't you say it? Why?" Even as he pleaded with his father he began to back away.

"I love you, Son."

The words struck Clive like painful blows and sent him reeling backward.

"I need you. Stay with me. Stay here."

Clive no longer felt fear or anger or desperation. He felt only empty and a little bit dirty. There was nothing more to say, for he knew the truth now. Neville had guessed it before him. He turned his back on the baron and walked sadly toward the house. When he reached the petrified hedge, he paused long enough to look up at the odd structure. *Four gray walls and four gray towers*, he thought wearily, recalling more of the poem his father had taught him. Then, he sighed as he started up the long walk to the door. "I am half sick of shadows," he muttered softly to himself and went inside.

He crept softly up the stairs and to his room. There he stripped off all his clothes and climbed into the bath. The water was cold now, but he didn't care. He wasn't even sure if it had been changed or if it was the same bath he'd soaked in earlier. He laved the water over his body, trying hard not to think of anything, seeking just a few moments of precious numbness before he had to start making decisions.

When he was ready, he rose, toweled himself, and dressed in fresh khakis from the wardrobe. He disdained the new boots he'd worn the past few days and reached for his old ones. They were scuffed and battered, but they were broken in well and would serve him better on the rugged trails.

Dressed, he stole from his room, crossed the hall, and rapped lightly on Neville's door. When Neville failed to answer, he twisted the knob and cracked it gently. A beam of light lanced across the gloom of the unlit room and touched Neville's empty bed. Clive closed the door quietly and wondered where his brother had gone.

He turned then to Annabelle's door. This time when he knocked, the door opened. Annabelle pulled him quickly inside and closed it again. All the others were there, too. "What's all this?" he said.

Annabelle shushed him, a finger at her lips. "Keep it down, hacker," she warned him. "It's a war council. We've been comparing notes, and none of us seem to care much for what we've learned."

Finnbogg got up from where he'd been sitting by the foot of the bed. He wore a child's troubled expression, which Clive found touching. "Smythefriend is missing," the canine said.

"I know that," Clive answered, moving into their midst. There were no more seats so he stood and leaned against the wall. "He said he was going exploring. The mountain trails, I think."

"Three days have elapsed since then," Chang Guafe said emotionlessly, "as you insist on measuring time by periods of ingestion and somnolence. We must consider that the implants in his head may have yielded him to someone else's control."

"Something has happened to Smythefriend!" Finnbogg insisted. "Finnbogg says we go look for Smythefriend, okay?"

Annabelle resumed her seat on the edge of the bed near Finnbogg. She reached up to scratch his back. That always seemed to quiet the excitable creature. "It's more than just Smythe," she reported in a low voice. She seemed to be in charge of this meeting, and Clive guessed it was she who had called it without bothering to wait for him. "Chang?" she said, turning toward the cyborg.

"Primary Anomalies, Report One," he responded, directing his ruby lenses toward Clive. "I have been in continual scan and analysis modes since we entered this structure. Though the artifacts of the interior appear familiar to your eyes in shape and form, they are each completely alien in molecular construction. They defy analysis of material and composition. All artifacts," he insisted. "Bed or bedsheets, clothes, chairs, books, walls. All are of unknown composite materials.

"Primary Anomalies, Report Two," he continued. "The interior of this structure gives the appearance of what has been referred to as 'the Victorian period.' Yet, I detect radiations and power fluctuations that are incongruent with such appearance. The walls, ceilings, and floors are interlaced with electronic circuitry of uncertain purpose. It is possible this structure is some kind of energy-receiving grid-station. But that is only speculation." He paused and ran the fingertips of one hand along the wall at his back. Clive knew the cyborg could sense the pulse of whatever circuitry lay behind the plaster.

"Report conclusion," Chang Guafe said formally. "On each level we have encountered increasingly advanced technology and increasingly sophisticated culture groups. Much of the technology on this seventh level reaches beyond even my knowledge, yet someone has attempted clumsily to disguise it behind familiar facades or in familiar forms. Of culture groups, we have observed few. Perhaps this is because so few of the Dungeon's captives ever survive to reach this level, whereas the gateways between the other levels were comparatively easy to breach." The glow of his lenses dimmed somewhat. "This is the general summary of Primary Anomaly Report. Details may be provided for specified areas of inquiry."

"That'll do for right now, Chang," Annabelle said. She twisted so she could see the other side of the room. "Shriek?"

The arachnoid had crouched down into a corner. All six of her eyes seemed to focus on Clive, but he knew that she directed her thoughts to all of them. *Under constant telepathic scan we are. Not word-thoughts, but images do they lift from our minds.* She turned three of her eyes toward Chang Guafe. *Believe do I in the Chang being's power grid. Believe do I that, at least in part, it boosts the telepathic powers of they who scan us.*

She hesitated then, but Clive knew her well by now, and he sensed before she could hide it that there was more. "Give it all," he said aloud for the benefit of the others. "Hold nothing back."

*Very hard it was for me,* she continued at last, *but this much more know I. They are two, our observers.* She hesitated again, then shrugged reluctantly. *And most interested are they in the beings Clive, Neville, Annabelle, and Tomàs.*

Neville sat at the top of the bed with his back against the headboard, but now he sat up. "In the four of us, you say?" He tapped Annabelle on the shoulder, and she twisted around. "I've been meaning to ask, but since everything in the bloody place seems to be fake, how can you trust what you read in those books? How can we know if the little sailor is really related to us? What if someone just wants us to think he is?"

Annabelle shrugged. "We can't know for sure, hacker. But whoever's got a modem hookup in our heads seems to be as interested in him as in us, so that lends some credence."

Sidi Bombay spoke up for the first time, rising carefully from his seated lotus position on the floor until he stood. "It is believed by some people in my land that God chooses special men for special testing."

Neville held up a hand and rolled his eyes. "Please, I think we've had enough religious nonsense. . . ."

But Sidi was firm. "If *you* please, Englishman. I brought it up only by way of example. I have meditated on this. I think the time has come to consider that this adventure— perhaps the entire Dungeon, itself—has been constructed as a test for the Folliot family."

"A test?" remarked Tomàs. He sat on the side of the bed between Chang Guafe and Annabelle. "*De qûe, amigo.*"

Sidi Bombay shrugged. "Of your character, perhaps. Of your courage, or your intelligence. Or perhaps through you, all of humanity."

"That's an awfully big burden for four pairs of shoulders," Annabelle said doubtfully. "Besides, where would that leave Shriek and Chang and Finnbogg, not to mention you, Sidi? Along for the ride?"

Sidi shrugged again. "Who am I to understand the ways of gods?"

"Whoever these Dungeonmasters are, they're not gods!" Neville muttered. "They're aliens! Maybe Ren, maybe Chaffri, or maybe somebody else. But they're not gods. Just damned inscrutable aliens!"

Annabelle got to her feet and began pacing back and forth at the foot of the bed. She held up the fingers of one hand and began to tick them off as she spoke. "Okay, here's the menu as I read it. First, Sergeant Smythe is overdue. Second, this whole place is a lot more than it seems. Third, someone besides Shriek is able to see into our minds." She stopped in the middle of the room, folded her arms across her chest, and looked at each of them in turn. "I think we've been sitting on our backsides long enough. Let's get some straight answers from Granddaddy Folliot, then go look for the sergeant. How about it?"

Clive shifted uneasily as he leaned against the wall. "I'm afraid you won't get many answers from him," he said quietly. "Granddaddy is a clone."

Neville sat up and slapped his thigh. "I knew it, old boy. I just had a feeling. But he threw me when he knew about Nanny's lapdog. How ever did he work that, do you suppose?"

"If our minds are being read," Clive suggested, "then maybe our observers heard you give the answer when I asked you the same question. Maybe they fed it back to their clone."

"How'd you trip him up, then, little brother?"

Clive's lips drew into a tight line as he remembered the scene on the mountain edge. "A different question," he answered curtly. He didn't feel the need to explain any more. The emotions were still too raw to probe now even with his friends.

Finnbogg sprang to his feet. "Okay, we go then. No safe place here. Go find Smythefriend."

"I guess that's one vote," said Annabelle, "and I'll add mine to it."

They all agreed.

"Then, everybody make a light pack of the things you'll need," Clive said, resuming his role as leader. "Neville, you and Finnbogg sneak downstairs and see if you can pilfer a little food to take along. We'll meet in the hallway. Let's go."

A few minutes later, Annabelle slipped into Clive's room. She'd changed into a pair of black denim jeans with a metal-studded belt and a white cotton sleeveless shirt. She carried her familiar leather jacket over one shoulder. "No matter how many times I open that wardrobe," she commented, "it has something new and exactly to my taste. I wish I could take it with me."

"Let's join the others downstairs," Clive said. He really had nothing to pack. He'd only come back to his room to retrieve his sword. He fastened the belt around his waist and adjusted the sheathed blade.

But Annabelle put a hand against the door. "Wait," she said gently. "Clive-o, I know you think you're hiding it, but the hurt on your face is as plain as a wart between the eyes." She caught one of his hands in hers and interlocked fingers. Her eyes were a misty blue as she forced him to look at her. "I don't know what went on between you and your . . ." She stopped herself before she said *father*. "I mean, I don't know what happened to you after dinner." She hesitated and bit her lip as she regarded him, and he felt her fingers tighten around his. Finally, though, she pressed on. "But Clive, how could they make a clone of your father? I mean, how would they get the tissue samples or the cell cultures to do it? I mean, he's back safe and sound in England, isn't he?"

He had already turned the question over and over in his mind, and he still only had one answer. "I don't know," he told her. "I don't know."

## · CHAPTER EIGHTEEN ·

# A Walk on the Deadly Desert

The Baron Tewkesbury met them at the bottom of the stairs. He blocked the door, flanked on either side by the four Herkimers. In his hand he held a weird kind of gun whose barrel appeared plugged with a small emerald jewel. It was leveled on Neville and Finnbogg.

Clive went cold with anger and hesitated halfway down the stairway. Right behind him, Annabelle stopped, too.

"Please, Son," the baron said evenly, "just turn around and return to your rooms. They should hold you quite securely. I had hoped to convince you to stay of your own will. But you will stay."

"You did a good job, whatever you are," Clive answered acidly. "You told me everything I wanted to hear, played your part just right. You bastard."

The baron looked pained as he waved the gun. "No, I'm not your father. But I could have been. Perhaps you'll understand in time, but now, please, return to your rooms."

Finnbogg gave a low growl and dropped his bundle, a stolen tablecloth apparently full of the supplies Clive had asked him to gather. But before Finnbogg could move, the gun shifted. A blinding green beam lanced forth lasting but a fraction of a second, leaving a smoking black scorch mark on the floor near Finnbogg's feet.

"Oops," said Finnbogg, touching the mark with the tip

of one toe and snatching it back. He forced a big smile that showed plenty of canine teeth.

"The beam is quite lethal, I assure you," the baron warned. "Now let's have no more unpleasantness."

The stern expression on the baron's face only made Clive angrier in its perfect resemblance to his father. The same expression and the same ruthlessness were in the voice that Clive remembered so well. He had no doubt that this imitation was capable of using the gun.

"Please, tell your arachnoid friend not to reach for a hair-spike." The baron raised the barrel of the weapon ever so slightly.

Clive ground his teeth. There was nothing he could safely do. Trapped on the stairway they made easy targets for the strange burning beam. One sweep of his arm and the baron could kill them all. They wouldn't be able to retreat quickly enough to get away, nor could they descend except straight into the beam. Someone would get burned even if the rest of them managed to overpower their host. He wasn't prepared to take that chance.

"Back up," he told the others over his shoulder, but his gaze didn't waver from the baron. Slowly, as the others gave way, he crept up the steps.

The baron motioned with the gun barrel for Neville and Finnbogg to follow. Neville placed a hand on the banister and took the lowest stair. "Now this is the father I remember, old chap," he said with a wink to his twin. "But instead of a gun to the head, it was a purse string around the throat."

Finnbogg gave another dumb look at the scorch mark on the floor, then stepped daintily over it. The smile faded from his face as he moved toward the stair.

The baron moved up behind him.

With speed that belied his squat bulk Finnbogg whirled. His hand closed swiftly on the baron's wrist, and the snapping of bone made a loud crack that was audible over the sizzle of the beam as it burned a scar in the ceiling.

The baron gave a sharp cry of pain and stared wide-eyed with surprise.

"Oops, your ass!" Finnbogg growled as he seized the gun from the baron's numbed grip. He passed it back to Neville behind him. He pulled the baron's face close to his and showed his teeth again. "Okay?" he asked.

"Okay by me," Neville answered lightly.

Finnbogg drew back a fist and sent the baron crashing backward into the Herkimers, who scattered like formal-dress tenpins. Amid much slapping and flapping of webbed appendages the frog creatures regrouped, and the baron rose painfully and leaned against the door that was their way out.

"Daddy dearest," Neville said nonchalantly, gesturing with the gun as he moved by Finnbogg. "I'm so glad we had this time together—"

"Just get him the fuck out of the way, hacker!" Annabelle interrupted, pushing past Clive to get downstairs. "And let's get out of here!"

The baron looked pleadingly up at Clive. "Son," he begged, giving another tug on Clive's heartstrings, "don't let him kill me."

Neville looked back over his shoulder and started to say something. As he did, the nearest Herkimer opened its mouth. A long, slick tongue shot out and snaked around Neville's hand. The frog jerked its head, and the gun went flying down the hallway. Neville leaped on top of the creature as it released his wrist and darted for the weapon.

The baron, spying the gun, dashed around the scuffling tangle of arms and legs that belonged to Neville and the frog. From halfway up the stairs Clive launched himself over the banister and landed in a crouch. Before he could chase after his father, though, something pink and slimy zipped around his ankle and pulled him off balance. He hit the floor with a crash that ignited stars in his head.

At the same time he heard another crash, a curse, and a growl. From the blurry corner of one eye he saw Finnbogg sitting astride the baron while the baron scratched and clawed after the gun, which was just beyond his reach. Finnbogg sniggered and smacked his captive playfully aside the head.

Clive started to rise to his hands and knees, and something leaped up on top of his back. He looked cautiously over his shoulder into the eyes of one of the Herkimers. Its tongue lashed out whiplike at his eyes. Reflexively, he threw one hand up to protect his face and caught the icky little organ in a tight grip. The frog looked at him in wide-eyed panic and grew quite still. "Oon'n oort ee!" it begged incoherently. Carefully, it slid off Clive's back and stood beside him. Clive held on to the tongue as if it were a leash.

He looked around as the others came down the stairs. In the corner by the door the two remaining Herkimers crouched side by side clutching their mouths behind folded hands and looking as if they'd swallowed something terrible. "What happened to them?" Clive asked as Annabelle came to his side.

She chuckled and fingered the controls of the Baalbec A-9. "They tried to trip me the same way they tripped you," she said, "but I had a low-power field on."

"Ouch," Clive muttered.

"Quite a pet you've got there," she said, laying a hand on the head of the Herkimer at Clive's side. The creature stood absolutely docile as she kneeled down and stroked it sympathetically. "They're so cute in their little tuxedoes. What do we do with them?"

"I saw a key in the library," Neville called from the hallway. He straddled the chest of his Herkimer and pinned both its hands in one of his. His other hand held its mouth pinched shut. A pair of little feet flap-flapped on the floor as the creature struggled helplessly. "We could lock them in there."

"¡Ora bolas!" Tomàs sneered. He had one hand on the doorknob ready to go. "Cut their throats and let's go, amigos."

Clive glanced at Annabelle. "¿*Ora bolas*?" he said. "Is that an insult?"

She frowned impatiently. "It translates roughly as 'baloney,' " she lied with a grin. "You know him by now. He only thinks in terms of food."

Clive thought for a moment. He didn't want to kill anyone, especially the baron. It still troubled him how easily he'd been able to kill another clone that resembled his brother. There was still a strange, lingering guilt about that. He wasn't at all prepared to deal with the idea it might be as easy to kill his father's look-alike.

"Get him on his feet, Finnbogg," Clive ordered. "We'll lock them up as Neville suggested."

He led the way to the library with his Herkimer in tow. Finnbogg followed with the baron, whose arms the alien canine held twisted up between his shoulder blades. Next came Neville, Chang Guafe, and Shriek, each carrying one of the Herkimers, all of whom were quite passive now.

When the baron and his frog-servants were safely within, Clive took the key from the inside lock and prepared to close the door. His father made one last appeal. "Stay with me, Son," he said quietly in a voice full of regret and despair.

Clive hesitated as conflicting emotions raged within him. "I wish you had been my father," he answered softly. "Maybe I would have stayed. Or maybe I would have come back." He shut the door before any more could be said, slid the key into the hole, and turned it. The lock made a solid click as the bolt slid home. Clive tossed the key on his palm for a moment, considering, then made a fist around it.

Finnbogg had gathered up his bundle again, and Annabelle had retrieved the baron's weapon. She offered it to Clive, but he shook his head and told her to keep it for now. When they were all outside, he drew back and hurled the key as far away as he could. In the darkness he had no idea how far that was.

Clive wiped his hand on his pants. His palm was sticky as the devil from the Herkimer's slimy tongue.

He gave a final look at the strange old house where for a short time he had realized a dream of getting to know his father as he never had. Only it hadn't been his father at all, and the dream had become another Dungeon nightmare. Someone had dug inside his head and found his heart's desire and turned it against him.

For that, he owed someone, and he intended to pay in full.

He called to Finnbogg. "Can you pick up Sergeant Smythe's scent?" he asked.

Finnbogg's face brightened. "Look for Smythefriend? Smythescent Finnbogg knows!" The canine set aside the bundle of supplies, dropped to all fours, and began to sniff the ground. For several minutes he ran back and forth before the door and along the petrified hedge, his nose twitching and sniffing.

Clive bent and retrieved the bundle and slung it over his shoulder.

"I will take it, Clive Folliot," Chang Guafe said, and he took the bundle before Clive could protest. "I do not tire as you humans do."

"Smythescent!" Finnbogg announced suddenly, standing erect again and waving his arms to attract the others. He had worked his way to the far side of the mountaintop rim to a trail Clive knew from his walks with his father.

*Not my father*, he reminded himself bitterly. *With the clone.*

Clive had absolutely no sense of direction on this level. But he knew that the Dantean Gate was behind him, so he thought of that as gateward. Whatever lay before them was unknown, and he thought of that as darkward. Everything else was left or right of the spiral, which seemed to cut a straight swath as it rose out of the darkness and descended toward the gate.

The downward trail on this side was not so steep as it zigzagged its way from the summit. Still, as they dropped beneath the rim, they lost the little light provided by the setting spiral at their back, so Annabelle took the lead and used the Baalbec to provide a faint illumination. Since the trail, itself, dictated the way Smythe must have traveled Finnbogg only made spot-sniffs and nodded his assurances.

At least they had had a chance to rest, Clive reflected as they climbed lower and lower. He felt fresher, stronger, almost glad to be on the move again. Everyone had recovered from their wounds and injuries. They'd had time to bathe and relax. They'd eaten well for a change. And it was nice to be wearing something besides rags. Maybe, all in all, they hadn't come away from the Palace of the Morning Star too badly.

Maybe.

At the bottom of the mountain they paused and shared sips of water from the canteens Neville had filled. Annie switched off the Baalbec at Clive's suggestion. It wouldn't do to tire her too quickly.

The hills and mountains loomed ominously in the darkness. The higher peaks still sparkled in the light of the spiral, but Clive and his company were deep in the shadows where no light ventured. The wind whispered through the valley in which they found themselves, a soft rustling susurrus that reminded Clive of dry leaves in autumn. But there were no leaves here and no seasons, only the darkness and the wind scraping against the stone.

"Smythescent!" Finnbogg announced. He had been sniffing about while the others rested. "We go, okay?"

Annie reached for the Baalbec controls on her left forearm, but Clive stopped her. The trail was smoother here and less dangerous than the mountain descent. There was less need for her energy-draining light.

He turned, instead, to the cyborg. "Chang, can you . . . ?"

"Affirmative," Chang Guafe answered. Instantly, his ruby lenses began to glow brighter, and the metal of his face and chest gleamed redly as it reflected the new light. Wherever he turned his gaze the black ground bled under his stare. It was a poor substitute for Annabelle's purer light, but it served, and it wouldn't tax the tireless cyborg to maintain it.

They resumed their march with Finnbogg leading the way. A narrow natural path wound among the hills, and they followed it, just as Smythe had done before them. In some places the ground turned softer, almost ashen, and Clive remembered the shores of the river they had crossed. It, too, had been ashen. Perhaps, then, these were antique stream beds, all that remained of the waters that had carved these mountains.

"Why ever do you suppose your man came this far?" Neville asked once when they achieved the summit of a rather tiring slope.

"He's not 'my man,'" Clive answered patiently. Neville's patrician attitudes could still be so annoying. "As for why?" Clive shrugged. "You had your poetry to occupy your time. Annabelle had her research. Sidi had his meditations, and Tomàs was busy stuffing himself. Shriek and Chang Guafe, too, found mysteries to keep them busy. But Horace is a soldier. He probably found himself with too much time on his hands, so like any good soldier he decided to scout the terrain."

Annabelle moved closer and took Clive's hand. "Do you think something's happened to him?"

"He's overdue," Clive answered tersely. "Good soldiers are never overdue without reason. If I hadn't been busy making a fool of myself, I'd have noticed sooner."

She looked at him sympathetically. "Hey, hacker, you weren't making a fool of yourself. There's never been a human born that didn't wish for the chance to sit down with his parents and really download, you know?"

He smiled secretly at her language but kept any further comments to himself. The episode was past. It was better if he put the whole thing behind him.

"Oops, bad news!" Finnbogg suddenly stood erect and sniffed. He looked around sharply in all directions, then bent down to the ground and sniffed again. "More scents, many scents, okay. All mingling with the Smythescent."

The glow from Chang Guafe's ruby lenses focused on Finnbogg, lending a weird spectral appearance to the bulldog features. "He encountered other sentients?" the cyborg inquired.

"Many scents, yes!" Finnbogg repeated in agitation. "They go this way together, all scents. We follow, okay?"

They continued darkward and sooner than anyone expected found themselves out of the foothills and on the edge of a vast plain. At least, they thought it was a plain. In the velvet gloom it was impossible to guess just how far it actually extended.

"The Deadly Desert," Annabelle whispered to herself. Her voice held a mixture of awe and dread.

After a brief discussion they decided to eat something from the bundle and rest at the edge of the plain, then resume the search for Smythe after a bit of sleep. It had been quite a trek from the mountains, and they'd made it in good time, but Clive didn't want to exhaust the company. They nibbled on celery, apples, and cheeses, a bit of bread, and washed it all down with a bottle of claret that Finnbogg had also appropriated.

*Sleep all,* Shriek said when the meal was finished. *Stand watch will I.*

They huddled close together on the hard stone. After the soft beds they had slept in at the Palace of the Morning Star, no one expected a comfortable sleep.

"*¡Ai de mim!*" Tomàs grumbled. He reached into his waistband and extracted a small wooden box. "Why did I steal these matches? There is nothing to build even a small fire."

"*¿Pequeno incêndio?*" Annabelle grinned, hugging her knees to her chest and rocking back and forth. "A small fire?"

Tomàs returned her grin and tucked the matches back into his trousers. "*Incêndio pequeno,*" he corrected. "You learn fast, *senhorita,*" he said with appreciation, and he clapped his hands in soft glee. "*¡Muito rapidamente!*"

Annabelle gave a lighthearted laugh. "Very fast," she

translated as she inclined her head. "¡*Obrigado, senhor!* Thank you!"

The little Portuguese smiled a crooked-toothed grin, and a twinkle came into his eyes as he answered shyly in his peculiar accent, "You have much high-speed ram in your hard-drive, hacker." He curled up, then, and lay back on the hard ground to sleep.

Annabelle stared at him for a moment, then hid her mouth behind her hands and gave a muffled chuckle. "He's so cute for such a little slime!" she whispered to Clive when she recovered herself. "You think he can really be a relative?"

Clive shrugged. "Since I never expected to inherit, I never bothered much with the family history. Beyond my grandfather I know very little about who did what with whom or when, if you get my meaning."

She lay back and folded her hands under her head while Clive sat beside her. Then, she rolled on her side and curled up into a fetal position. Then, she returned to her back. At last, she sat up again and glanced at the others.

Only she, Clive, and Shriek remained awake.

"I keep thinking about Sidi's idea," she said quietly, "that all this is some kind of testing ground. Why? Why would a race of creatures powerful enough to build all this be even remotely interested in us?"

Clive only shrugged. Tomàs, though, was right. He wished there was a campfire, not for warmth, but for the soothing comfort of its flickering light.

"And if they are interested in us," Annabelle continued in a low voice, "in the Folliots and their descendants and offspring, then what does that make everyone else, pawns?"

Clive drew a deep breath and let it out slowly. "Maybe it's Shriek, or Chang Guafe, or Finnbogg they're interested in," he suggested as he put an arm around her shoulder. There was a certain comfort and reassurance in the touch of another person that he had never appreciated before, and he pulled her close. Maybe it was even better than a fire. It didn't keep away the cloying dark, but he didn't face it alone. "Maybe we're the pawns."

She didn't say any more, but he felt a slight tremor run through her body. After a while, they both lay down. She put her head on his shoulder, and he folded one hand under his head for a pillow and they both stared open-eyed at the featureless sky. There was no other sound in the world but the ghostly stirring of the wind, which finally lulled them both to sleep.

# • CHAPTER NINETEEN •

# Down to the Underworld

"Are you sure Smythe came this far?" Neville complained. Sleeping on hard stone without blanket or pillow had left him stiff and grumpy. He walked along in a black mood, sullen and petulant.

Finnbogg lifted his nose from the ground long enough to answer. "Aye," he said. "The nose have it. Smythefriend have distinct odor."

"He'll be happy to know that," Annabelle quipped. She gave a toss of head and a light laugh as she patted Sidi Bombay on the shoulder. "He's your friend," she said to Sidi. "You be sure to tell him."

"This is hardly a joking matter," Neville snapped. "We could be very lost."

Annabelle caught Tomàs's hand and pulled him up beside her so that she, Sidi, and Tomàs walked arm in arm. "Well, you've certainly lost it, hacker," she responded. "You need to reboot your system."

Tomàs muttered under his breath, "*Sim*, I've got a boot for him."

"I don't mean to interrupt," Clive said patiently, "but has anyone else noticed those flashes to our right? You have to watch carefully. They're not very regular."

They stopped and looked where Clive pointed. After a few moments a short flicker of dim blue light colored the darkness. They waited as it repeated, one flash, two, a sporadic burst, then nothing, and Clive signaled they should move on, but they kept their gazes trained toward the phenomenon.

"What do you make of it, Tin Man?" Annabelle asked offhandedly. She had relinquished her grip on Tomàs and Sidi as her interest in the flickering grew.

Chang Guafe kept his gaze straight ahead as he walked beside Clive. The light from his lenses illuminated the ground at their feet and spilled around Finnbogg as the canine sniffed out the way. "All sensors scanning," he reported without turning to look either at Annabelle or the phenomenon. He hesitated, then added, "Monitoring a marginal increase in the number of negatively charged ions present in the air."

"Thank you," she said impatiently. "What's that mean?"

"Sudden violent electrical field fluctuations," Chang Guafe continued. An array of tentacles emerged from small panels on his face, chest, and left shoulder. Tiny lights at each of their tips activated and turned in the direction of the phenomenon. "Brilliant surges of luminosity," he reported. "Current discharges in excess of twenty kiloamperes. Specific flash temperatures vary from two times ten to the fourth power to three times ten to the fourth power in your Kelvin degrees."

"Never mind!" Annabelle muttered, cutting him off with a sigh. "Whatever it is, it's beautiful!"

"It looks like lightning to me," Neville said.

Chang Guafe's gaze left the ground for an instant and focused on Neville. "I believe that is what I indicated." The sensor-tentacles recoiled into his body, and the panel doors behind which they hid popped seamlessly shut.

"Is it coming this way?" Clive asked, suddenly concerned.

"Affirmative."

Clive exhaled slowly. "And me without an umbrella. Can we make better time, Finnbogg?"

Finnbogg stopped, drew himself up to his full four-foot height, and puffed out his considerable chest. "Very strong wind makes tricky task, okay?" he grumbled. "Must keep nose very close to ground to sort many scents. Not easy. Not human work. Let Finnbogg do it, okay?"

"Testy little beast," Neville mumbled in a low voice.

Annabelle glared at him. "I'm looking at the only beast around here, hacker."

"I apologize, Finnbogg," Clive said politely. "I know you're doing your best. Why don't we take a break and everyone have a drink of water."

"If that is lightning," said Sidi Bombay, "we may soon have more water than we want."

The flickering in the distance intensified. There was no longer a question that it was lightning, or that it was moving in their direction. The wind blustered about them and pelted them with airborne particles of ash and dust. A low thunder rolled ominously through the sky.

Finnbogg led them in a straight line across the plain. They moved at a brisk pace, fighting the wind. More than once, Clive nearly lost his balance as an unexpected blast caught him in midstride. Once, Annabelle gave a yelp and stopped suddenly to pick something from her eye. After that, she walked with one hand shielding her face.

The lightning drew closer. No longer was it a sheeting flash on the horizon. Blue-white snakes slithered with electric grace through the darkness. Tiny darting tongues licked groundward as Clive watched with growing concern. Every deadly bolt seemed to have a pair of eyes that stared in his direction.

Chang Guafe stopped so abruptly that Tomàs and Sidi Bombay collided against him from behind. "Scanning a heat pattern directly ahead," the cyborg announced, ignoring Tomàs's muttered cursings.

"What is it?" Clive said curtly, anxious to keep everyone moving. "How far ahead?"

"Unknown, but the pattern is similar to those I recorded in the chasm," Chang Guafe answered. "Distance approximately one thousand Earth meters."

"The vent shafts?"

Change Guafe shrugged. "Uncertain. But the pattern is similar."

Clive glanced again toward the storm. The cyan lace-work reflected eerily in the smoother gleaming patches of stone that dotted this world's surface, making ephemeral pools of blue fire that burst into existence and died in the space of a human heartbeat. He smelled no rain in the air, no moisture. Pure electrical fury bore down upon them, and it would catch them in the open without a hope of shelter long before they crossed a thousand meters.

Clive chewed his lip worriedly, and every hair on his neck stood on end. He knew better than to trust anything in the Dungeon, even the weather. "Finnbogg," he shouted over the rising wind. "Is there a chance Smythe headed for that heat source?"

Finnbogg didn't stop, keeping his nose close to the ground as he answered. "Smythefriend and many scents moving easy path straight for long time. Nose says still straight okay."

Clive called back to Chang Guafe. "Your heat source," he shouted, "it's also straight ahead?"

"Affirmative," the cyborg assured him.

The air sizzled suddenly, and the world rocked under them and turned stark white. Thunder exploded with deafening force, and the ground shivered as a crackling cobalt sledge smashed against the stone, sending fragments and splinters flying.

Clive clutched his face with both hands. The burning behind his eyes was an exquisite pain, and when he peeked out between his fingers, the world danced with shimmering afterimages.

"I don't come with a surge-protector, goddamn it!" Annabelle shrieked. "That was too scrodding close!"

The world screamed with whiteness, harsh and terrifying. Clive flung up his hands to protect his vision and felt the flesh on his arms crawl with galvanic sensation. All the world turned to thunder, and the thunder turned to a wave that lifted him up and dropped him on his back.

"Run!" Clive shouted, picking himself up and snatching for Annabelle's hand. "Chang, take the lead. Head for the heat source!" He waved to the others. "Follow Chang!"

Finnbogg straightened, looking sad. "Oops, Finnbogg fired!"

"¡Ai, Christo!" Tomàs muttered, crossing himself and looking to the cyborg. "¡Adiante! Go on!"

The next blast of thunder was as good as a pistol shot. With Chang Guafe in the lead, they raced across the plain. The sky hurled white knives that scarred and burned the black stone, that stabbed their vision and gouged the darkness from the world. They ran half blind, barely able to keep their eyes on the cyborg's back, which rippled blue and white and red as his metal body shimmered with the reflection of the storm.

A sudden bolt hammered the ground off to the right. Tomàs gave a scream and stumbled. Before Clive and Annabelle could reach his side, Shriek sped past them and swept the little Portuguese up in her arms.

Go! came the arachnoid's insistent thought. Carry him will I! Then she fell back again to bring up the rear while Tomàs cursed and clutched a bleeding cheek.

Since Clive couldn't see where they were running, it was impossible for him to judge how far they had to go. His heart pounded in his chest, and his breaths came in short gasps. His legs felt like lead, and too quickly he felt himself giving out. Still, he pushed himself, urging his limbs to greater effort as he fought to keep up with Annabelle, who ran tirelessly.

Then Neville stumbled. Without thinking, Clive caught his brother's arm and pulled him to his feet again. "We're almost there!" he lied encouragingly. He had no idea whether they were or not.

The lightning strobed with increasing fury. The world roared with thunder and wind.

Ahead, Chang Guafe and Finnbogg stopped. Sidi caught up to them an instant later and sagged breathlessly to his knees. Clive and Annabelle arrived next with Neville and Shriek and Tomàs close after.

Clive gripped the cyborg's arm and leaned on him for a brief moment. "What is it?" he asked between gasps. "Why are we stopping? Are we there?"

Chang Guafe pointed. In the lightning flash Clive spied a patch of blackness that remained black even under the brightest coruscation. They stood ten meters from its edge.

Cautiously, he crept toward it. It appeared to be a hole in the surface, perhaps five meters wide and perfectly round, and as he peered over the edge a rapid series of bolts illuminated the narrow metal ladder that descended into its depths.

Finnbogg sniffed around the rim. "Smythefriend and many scents go down!" he shouted enthusiastically from the top of the ladder. "Finnbogg not fail! Smythefriend come this way!"

Clive drew a deep breath and let it out. "Then we go, too," he said, stepping delicately over the side and setting foot on the first rung of the ladder. "Ditch that bag, Finnbogg. You can't negotiate this with your hands full."

"Wait just a bloody minute!" Neville objected. "Don't you think we should discuss it? I mean, we've got no bloody idea where this goes, or if it goes anywhere!"

Annabelle shouldered Neville aside and moved to follow Clive down the shaft. "You want to stand out here and get a galvanic haircut, scrodhead, that's your business. You and the barber can discuss anything you want. But get out of my way!" She dropped to her hands and knees and carefully explored with her toe for the first rung.

"Remember, Nevillefriend, what you teach Finnbogg!" Finnbogg slapped Neville on the back, practically knocking the poor man over the side. "Heigh-ho, and God save the Queen, and stiff upper lip! Let's go! Finnbogg after Annie!"

Down into the darkness they climbed with no bottom in sight until the lightning storm became no more than a round flickering moon above them, a silver-blue disk that grew even smaller as they descended. No wind blew in the shaft to menace them, though the air was as warm and close as ever.

"Never have I seen such a storm," Sidi Bombay said somewhere above Clive. "No clouds, no rain. It was as if the hand of Shiva had reached out for us."

A quietness settled upon them, and they concentrated on climbing. Clive felt gingerly for the next rung, always trusting it would be there.

Sometime later, Neville broke the silence. "Do you think this is the way to the next level?"

No one answered. There was no way of knowing for sure, though Clive doubted it. The deeper they descended through the Dungeon's levels, the more disorienting the transitions had become. A simple ladder from one level to the next seemed just too easy.

"I think I see a light," he said at last, keeping his voice low and calm and hoping the others would take the hint. If there was light at the end of the tunnel, there might also be someone waiting for them. Chang had mentioned back at the chasm the possibility of underground industry. He listened for the sounds of pumps, of engines, of any kind of machinery, and heard nothing. As he climbed lower, the silence made him edgy. He felt too much like prey. He could almost feel the gunsights on his neck.

It was definitely light—artificial light, in fact. The shaft in which they found themselves broke through the roof of yet another tunnel. "Stay here," Clive ordered the others when he estimated no more than twenty steps remained before they emerged. As quietly as he could, he moved toward the opening.

The ladder ended at the lip of the air shaft. Clive paused again and listened. Then, gripping his sheathed blade, he dropped lithely down to the floor. He blinked and shielded his eyes from the painfully bright light and waited for his vision to adjust.

It was not a tunnel at all, but a huge corridor. Glowing light panels placed at regular intervals in the ceiling provided an illumination that, after a few moments, proved soft and comfortable. The walls were perfectly smooth, and the floor tiled with great polished stone squares. To his right the corridor proceeded a short distance and turned a blind corner. To his left was some kind of crossroads.

Still, he moved quietly, nervously, with one hand at the hilt of his saber as he stole toward the crossroads and peered in all directions. Both ends of the new corridor curved out of sight. *Great,* he thought to himself. *Another bloody maze.*

He tiptoed back to the air shaft and whispered up to the others that it was safe to descend. Once down, Annabelle stayed close by his side, and Finnbogg began to sniff around. "Oops," he said apologetically, "no scent on this funnystuff stone."

Shriek emerged last from the air shaft, for everyone realized now that was clearly what it was. She looked both ways and chittered softly in appreciation.

"Hey, it's cooler down here," Annabelle noted, rubbing her arms briskly. "That's a welcome relief."

"Mechanically conditioned," Chang Guafe reported. "Olfactory sensors detect very faint traces of chemical coolant."

"Well, well!" Annabelle responded, brightening. "Civilization."

Clive looked around uncomfortably. "That's a word with a lot of different meanings," he warned. "Let's reserve judgment."

Suddenly, a soft purring noise vibrated in the air. As one the company turned toward it and saw a section of the wall rotate outward. Clive and Neville reacted as one, drawing their swords. Annabelle dropped into a crouch and brought up the business end of Baron Tewkesbury's strange lightbeam weapon. Shriek plucked a hair-spike and prepared to throw.

Someone moved behind the panel. "Hey, Jack! I know that voice! No-jive Clive, as I do live and breathe! Lay some skin, man!"

Baron Samedi pushed his top hat to a jaunty angle as he stepped into the corridor light and grinned his big infectious grin.

# · CHAPTER TWENTY ·

# Twisted Selves

"Forgive me for seeming ungracious, Samedi," Clive said, keeping the point of his saber level and steady, "but please stay where you are until you explain how you got here. We saw you die."

Neville also kept his blade high. "We saw two of you die."

"But don't you see?" Annabelle said, lowering her gun and relaxing. "That's the answer. This must be another clone."

Samedi let go a melodramatic sigh. "The last o' the line, I'm 'fraid, Jack."

Clive lowered his blade cautiously. "What do you mean?"

Samedi sighed again. "I mean, somebody's wiped the data bank containin' my genetic code and personality programmin'. There can't be no more Samedis. And there's a whole lot more you should know, but not here. Ain't safe."

But Clive was not yet quite ready to trust. "How'd you know we'd show up at this particular point? There are other shafts into this place, so why decide to wait at this one?"

Samedi put on a pout and braced his hands on his bony hips. "Hey, like I been hidin' out down here a long time, passin' as one o' the defectives an dodgin' the rat-catchers an' all, an' keepin' my eyes open. I seen 'em when they brought in your friend. They wander around on the surface sometimes, but they always come back, cause ain't no food up there. I figured odds were good you'd come runnin' along pretty soon to save him. Took your sweet time, though, you did. Thought I'd suffocate in that storage closet."

At mention of his sergeant Clive's brows knitted together. He lowered his weapon. "Save Smythe? From what? Who's got him?"

"A bunch o' defectives," Samedi answered disdainfully, "an' you better save his ass quick. Ain't pleasant what they're gonna do." He glanced back down the corridor suddenly. "Ain't pleasant what's gonna happen to us, neither, if we keep standin' here."

Clive sheathed his sword and gestured for Neville to do the same. Annabelle hid the gun again inside the waistband of her jeans and tucked her shirt over it so it couldn't be seen. "Can you lead us to Smythe?" Clive asked.

"Depends," Samedi answered, staring wide-eyed past the group.

"On what?" Clive snapped.

Samedi pointed. "On whether you can ditch the rat-catcher, Jack. Bye!" With that, he turned and ran.

Clive whirled in time to see a bright flash. At the same time, Chang Guafe spread his arms and swept them all to the floor as a searing beam scorched the air, barely missing them. Clive pulled himself from the tangle of bodies, ignoring the pain in his side where someone's elbow had smashed his ribs, and rose into a crouch to get a look at their attacker.

The rat-catcher was a robot, a legless metal monster that moved on nearly silent treads like a small tank. Its arms ended not in fingers but in yellow glowing lenses from which it had fired the beams that had so nearly claimed their lives. As he watched, those lenses began to glow again, and the creature's huge single eye focused directly upon them.

"Look out!" Annabelle cried, pushing Tomàs out of the

way with her foot as she tugged the gun from her waist-band. "Get out of the way!" She pushed Finnbogg out of her line of sight and brought the gun up to bear on the robot.

The emerald beam lanced outward, shattering the robot's eye-lens. Again Annabelle fired, desperately swinging the beam in a wide arc. Metal squealed and sizzled as coherent energy raked across the monster's throat. The head tottered for an instant, then fell forward and dangled from an array of colored wires and cables.

The rat-catcher went crazy, spinning on its tread, waving its arms and spraying the corridor with deadly force rays. The company scrambled for their lives, twisting, dodging, and rolling to avoid death.

Then, Shriek voiced her horrible battle cry and launched herself at the rat-catcher. Her seven-foot bulk struck the machine from the side and knocked it over. Its treads whirred uselessly as she stood on one arm with two of her four feet and ripped the other arm from its socket. In a fury she beat and tore at the machine until it crumpled under her fists like an empty can. Wires and circuits popped and shorted and sparked, and smoke exuded from joints and splits in the armor. Still, the treads continued defiantly to operate. Shriek gave another frustrated scream, lifted the broken robot in her four powerful arms, and heaved it against the wall. The crash made a terrible noise, but all that remained of the rat-catcher was a pile of junk.

Shriek stood victoriously over the rubble, breathing hard. Slowly, she looked at them and parted her mandibles in what served her for a grin, and Clive felt her in his mind. *Good that felt.*

"Hey, baby, I am *sooo* impressed!" Samedi peeked at them from around the corner far down the corridor. "I never seen nobody do that to a catcher before. But you all better haul ass now. Sound's what attracts 'em. That's how they locate the defectives, an' it's probably how they found us here."

"Then take us to Smythe!" Clive ordered, containing the urge to shout angrily as the others gathered around him.

Samedi grinned and beckoned. "Come," he said.

They moved quickly, but quietly, through one corridor after another, through closet-sized rooms and chambers as large as warehouses. The deeper into the complex they journeyed the more mysterious the place became. Crystalline tubes of various dimensions hung suspended from the ceilings. Within them coursed strange chemicals and viscous fluids. Some traveled in steady, streaming flows while others pulsed as if driven by an immense hidden heart. Some radiated with soft shades of golden color.

Another chamber contained vast numbers of square plastic boxes piled in orderly fashion from the floor to the ceiling. Each bore a series of unreadable symbols that Clive assumed were lot numbers. The seamless boxes defied all attempts to open them until Samedi showed them how. He approached the nearest container and touched the first two symbols simultaneously, and the top opened in a slow, controlled manner.

"What is it?" Clive asked, looking inside at a colorless mass.

Chang Guafe leaned forward and placed his hand on the substance. "In simplest description," he answered after a moment's pause, "raw organic compound. Do you wish a detailed analysis?"

Clive declined, and they continued on.

A short distance away they found another chamber full of the same cartons, but some of these had been opened. Empty containers lay scattered about randomly, and greasy smears stained the floor and walls as high as Clive could reach. A mildly unpleasant odor hung in the air.

An old shirt lay crumpled in a corner. A rusted set of keys lay discarded nearby. Neville found an old shoe. Annabelle slipped on a broken pencil. Sidi Bombay slipped in something else.

"Yuck," Finnbogg remarked, wrinkling his nose.

"Better watch your back, Jack," Samedi whispered in a low voice.

"The defectives you mentioned?" Clive inquired, and Samedi nodded. "What are they?"

"Defectives," Samedi repeated, straightening his raggedy suit jacket self-consciously. "Clones who couldn't cut it in the real world, you know? Clones who didn't grow right or whose programin' didn't take right." He shrugged and nudged one of the empty cartons with a toe. "Just meat, that's what they are, sometimes overcooked an' sometimes undercooked, but not fit for servin' up."

"You mean the Dungeonmasters make mistakes, hacker?" Annabelle said. She still carried her gun in her hand, and her eyes flitted now and then toward the shadows.

Samedi shrugged again as he looked at her. "Any assembly line has its share o' bad parts," he told her as he led them out of the chamber. "But some o' these parts can still think, an' they manage to avoid the regular disposal. Course, there's nothin' for 'em to do but hide out here. There's nothin' to eat on the surface, an' they can't get near the Gateway."

"The Gateway?" Clive said, catching Samedi's arm and jerking him around. "You mean the gate to the next level? Level eight? It's here?"

"That's right, boss. You'd o' found that out at the Palace o' the Mornin' Star, but I bet that turned into a bad scene, huh?"

Clive snatched Samedi's top hat and rubbed his sleeve against a spot on the brim. He hesitated, then passed it back. "You put it so politely," he said to the clone. "I suppose you didn't know it was my father, or rather his doppelganger, that we found waiting there."

"Didn't know what you'd find after I died," Samedi answered with a straight face. "Oh, yeah, you should o' found another me, but better dressed, like someone who lives in a palace an' talks better. But somebody killed him just like they dropped the other two Samedis into the chasm, the same people who wiped my gene bank. I felt it, you know."

"You felt it?" Sidi Bombay asked.

"Course, man!" Samedi answered. "How can you not feel it when your entire program an' all your copies get wiped? I mean, you can hear the scream down here!" He tapped his temple.

"Interesting," Sidi said quietly. "As if you were in touch with all your lives, past, present, and future. My faith speaks of something similar."

Finnbogg crept forward a bit and broke into the conversation. "Okay, how come Samedifriend still lives when littermates all die?"

"'Cause I hid my ass in a closet, Jack," Samedi answered honestly. "I was supposed to guide you from the palace to the gate in the central chamber an' send you on your way to the next level, but I'm jus' a walkin' dead man, now, a zombie, like what my original patternin' was taken from. But zombie or not, I didn't much feel like jus' walkin' into whatever trap was waitin' at the palace. I saved my skin, instead."

Clive stared into the creature's hollow eyes, then backed up a pace.

"That's right, Clive Folliot," Samedi said, meeting his gaze evenly, unapologetically, and dropping the inconsistent accent. "I resisted my programed task. I'm a defective, too."

"I don't give a bloody damn if you're Queen Victoria in drag, old chap," Neville said impatiently. "Just get us to Smythe and to the gate so we can get out of here."

"Wait," Clive insisted, cutting his twin off with a wave. He turned back to Samedi again. Everything the clone had said only convinced him that he was right about different factions operating in the Dungeon, perhaps warring with each other. "Who dumped your gene bank? Do you know who?"

Samedi shook his head, and a look of frustration flickered upon his pale face. "First, they grow us real quicklike," he answered, slipping back into his accent, "then they fill our heads with a preprogramed wet-ware personality and whatever knowledge they want us to have. But the more I resist that programin'—the more I insist on thinkin' my own thoughts an' doin' things my way—the faster their stuff fades. Course, the answer you want might never have been in my program anyway."

"Let's ditch this scrodding place," Annabelle suggested.

They started across the chamber toward the open door on the far side. Abruptly, the chamber lights went out, and they stopped in midstride. It was not completely dark. Light spilled in from the doorways before and behind them, enough to see their way. Cautiously, they moved forward.

A huge, hulking figure suddenly blocked the door, and a grotesque shadow stretched toward them. Two red eyes blazed, and the corridor light gleamed on powerful metallic shoulders.

"Back out the way we came," Clive said slowly without taking his eyes from the figure before them. There was something darkly familiar about it.

" 'Fraid not, hackers," Annabelle answered. "It's blocked, too."

Clive drew his saber and risked a hasty glance over his shoulder. Four figures shambled through the rear doorway. Two stood as tall as Shriek. One appeared much shorter, perhaps Finnbogg's height. The last seemed more reasonably proportioned.

"Forward, then," he decided. "There's only one."

He spoke too soon. Two more creatures joined the tall silhouette. Worse, Clive detected motion in the corridor beyond, and since none of the three turned to look, it had to be more of their friends.

"Looks like feeding time," Neville said, coming to Clive's side. He drew his saber as well.

"I don't mean to be depressing," Annabelle muttered, "but have you ever thought of yourselves as raw organic compound?"

"They won't eat you," Samedi said with assurance.

"That's a relief, *amigo*," Tomàs grumbled.

"They will strip you for genetic material and feed your pieces to the machines," the clone continued unpleasantly, losing his accent once again, "after they have drained your psyches and recorded your every memory and entered those in the master data banks."

"Why would they do that," Sidi Bombay inquired, "if their creators are trying to destroy them?"

"Not kill 'em all, Jack," Samedi answered quickly. "Just keep the numbers low. Some o' the defectives do menial service work, though most o' the clone bank is automated. But to drag you to the analyzers, the machines have to also give 'em access to central processin' where, if they move quick an' know what to do, they can punch up another copy o' themselves. Most o' the time the machines recognize the false command an' dump it, but not always."

"Reproduction with a cookie cutter," Annabelle commented dryly. "I don't mean to be pushy, hackers, but I think it's time to party. I've got the Baalbec, so Tomàs, you'd better take this." She passed him the beamer weapon.

Tomàs cradled it in his palm and looked up coldly. "*Obrigado*. I take out the big monster first, then." He brought the weapon up and pointed at the huge silhouette in the doorway.

"No." Change Guafe's hand closed firmly on Tomàs's forearm, and he pushed the gun barrel down. "He must be mine."

Of course, thought Clive. No wonder the shape seemed so familiar. Chang Guafe's visual sensors must have confirmed it immediately. "It's you, isn't it?" Clive said worriedly. "They've made a clone of you."

"Oh, the Dungeonmasters probably have genetic samples from all o' you by now. Drops o' blood, small skin samples. Easy enough to get, you know, especially what with all the scrapes you been in. It's your memories an' personalities they probably want most."

*Being Clive*, Shriek said quietly. She'd been silent for quite a while, but there was a sense of urgency in her thoughts. *More beings behind us there are. Numbers growing are.*

"All right, let's get out of here," Clive answered grimly.

Clive, Neville, and Chang Guafe advanced in a line. But as soon as they made a move, the defectives charged from both directions. Shriek made the horrible sound after which they'd named her as she hurled a handful of hair-spikes at the rear attackers. Five bodies gave equally horrid cries of pain and fell as their flesh swelled frighteningly, purpled, and split open, and pouring blood onto the floor. At the same time Tomàs muttered a hasty curse, leaped to the side, and pointed the gun. The emerald beam flared, but his aim was off. The deadly light missed the Chang clone but severed an arm from the creature right behind him. Its scream echoed in the vast chamber.

Chang Guafe and the Chang clone met with a crash. They struck the floor in a tangle of arms and legs and thrashed about until suddenly one of them obtained an advantage in leverage, planting armored feet in the chest of the other and shoving with mechanically enhanced power. A heavy form smashed backward into one of the neat stacks of plastic cartons and was quickly buried in the collapse. Almost instantly, though, containers flew everywhere as the cyborg fought free and attacked again.

Chang Guafe and the Chang clone looked identical to Clive, and he had no time to sort one from the other. He brought an arm up to sweep aside an empty carton that waffled through the air toward his head. Too late he saw the defective that followed it. Outstretched arms locked around his waist, pinning his arms and lifting him off his feet. He looked into a face that was almost human except that one eye was a good inch lower than the other, as if the flesh on one side had slightly melted.

Its strength, though, was superhuman. Clive felt the breath rush from his lungs as the creature squeezed, and his ribs started to give. Desperately and with all his force, he butted his head against the offered nose and heard it crack. Blood spurted, and his foe loosened its grip as it flung back its head in a gurgling outcry. Clive repeated the trick, smashing the tortured nose a second time, drawing another wail. The creature released him and clutched its face. Clive drew back with his saber and prepared to dispatch it, but at the last instant he uttered a low curse and slammed his fist into its exposed jaw, driving it to the floor, where it lay unconscious. Quickly, he looked around to see who needed help.

Four creatures cornered Neville against a pile of cartons. Unburdened by Clive's respect for Queensberry rules, his twin slashed two of them across the gut with smooth rapid strokes and kicked a third between the legs, which gave him time to thrust through the chest of the fourth. Barely breathing hard, he finished off the third as it sagged to the floor clutching its groin.

Tomàs's green beam blazed everywhere through the darkness as yet more defectives poured through the doorways. The little Portuguese had found himself a perch atop a stack of containers, and screaming strings of Portuguese epithets and curses, he raked the lethal ray back and forth across the entrances. Many made it safely inside, dodging his beam, but the bodies swiftly piled, and still he fired and fired.

Then, the two Chang Guafes, locked in each other's arms, encoiled in tangles of snapping tentacles that emerged from every part of their bodies, pitched backward like enraged juggernauts, and stumbled against Tomàs's perch. Cartons and Tomàs went tumbling.

Clive had no chance to help as a true monstrosity launched itself at him. It resembled a jellyfish on legs, and barbed tentacles snapped whiplike toward his face. He brought the saber up in a rapid arc, intersecting the deadly limbs, severing a few, which writhed and squirmed at his feet. But still the beast came on, forcing him to retreat even as he struck and struck again. Cold, malignant eyes regarded him from the mass as the thing advanced.

Suddenly, Clive dropped low, one knee actually brushing the floor, and swung his blade with all his might. The razor edge drew a deep ichorous line across the creature's knee. It gave an inhuman cry of pain and hesitated. For an instant, it stared uncertainly at Clive, then it came on again. But it moved more slowly now, more cautiously. Clive's foot nudged a carton as he backed. As he moved around it, he caught the open lid with his booted toe and flipped it upward at his unnatural attacker. He blessed his stars when the tentacle shot up to intercept the flying carton. He stepped in close, drove his blade deep into the central mass, and jerked it downward in a savage slicing motion as he withdrew. A pale vitreous humor rushed out through the rent in the skin-sac, and the thing deflated like a ruptured bladder and flopped hideously in its death throes.

Another carton hurtled toward him. In annoyance he reached up to bat it aside. Unexpectedly the full weight of its unbreached contents caught him in the face. Bright stars exploded in his skull as he crashed to the deck. The sword went skittering from his grip. Dazed, he struggled to reach it, but a booted foot pushed it farther away. He looked up into the eyes of Baron Tewkesbury.

"Father!" Clive cried in dismay.

The clone sneered as it reached a huge hand toward Clive's throat. "Forget it, human," it said in a horrible, rasping voice that in no way resembled his father's. "The programing didn't take! You're nothing to me but meat for the grinder!"

Clive crawled back a pace, seeking escape from that grasping hand and those almost mesmerizing eyes.

Then, Annabelle stepped between them and brushed her fingertips along the top of that hand. The baron gave a short, choked cry as the jolt from the Baalbec A-9 flung him backward off his feet. Immediately, Finnbogg pounced upon him and with a horrible growl, locked his jaws on the old man's throat.

A spurt of crimson shot across the floor, and Clive squeezed his eyes shut with a groan.

"Are you okay, Clive-o?" Annabelle said, turning. "I can shut off the field if you need help."

"You keep that thing on!" Clive shouted, recovering himself and scrambling to his feet. He looked around for his saber, spied it, and snatched it up.

"They're retreating," Annabelle informed him calmly. "The meat turned out to be a little too tough."

"Finnbogg heard, Annie!" the canine said, coming up behind them. His dark-stained jowls dripped blood. "We give them something to chew on."

She made a face. "Looks like you're the one who did the chewing, hacker."

Finnbogg turned away and wiped his face. Then, he wiped his hands on his fur. It was sometimes disconcerting how Finnbogg preferred using his teeth and powerful jaws in a fight to his equally powerful hands. But no one could argue with his effectiveness or his courage.

A loud crash made them turn. Chang Guafe or the Chang clone went hurtling through yet another stack of containers, smashed off its feet by a blow of incredible power from its opponent. Without hesitation the opponent dived after its prey. Empty cartons went flying. Full cartons burst open as the combatants rolled on the deck and grappled for advantage. Again, one flung the other off, and both rose to their feet. Arms and tentacle arrays reached out.

Suddenly, Sidi Bombay appeared between them. Annabelle gave a cry of warning, but the Indian ignored or didn't hear her. Instead, he pointed a small box at one of the cyborg warriors and it froze absolutely motionless, one foot advanced, one mighty fist caught in midswing. It resembled a horrible sculpture of some nameless god of war.

Clive had forgotten the stasis box that Sidi had stolen

from the Lords of Thunder, and he marveled as the Hindu dived and rolled out of the way with fluid grace.

The unaffected cyborg locked both its hands together, drew back, and smashed them into the face of its paralyzed foe. To Clive's horror flesh and bone and metal caved inward under the impact like so much melon pulp. The creature tottered for an instant and fell with limbs still locked in its last position.

The standing Chang Guafe turned slowly toward them as it retracted its tentacles into its body. Then, its shoulders drooped subtly as it advanced toward Sidi Bombay, extended a hand, and helped him up.

"How did you know which one?" Annabelle exclaimed. "I couldn't tell them apart!"

Shriek joined them, all six of her eyes agleam with excitement and cooling fury. She still held a handful of spikes, and her harsh breathing sounded like stones in a tumbler.

"I waited and watched," Sidi answered. He reached up and touched Chang Guafe on the arm in a gesture of friendship. "This one in the last moments risked a glance around to avoid falling on Tomàs. That's how I knew the difference. The wrong one would have had no such compunction."

"Tomàsfriend?" Finnbogg said in sudden concern. "Where is Tomàsfriend? Where is Samedifriend?"

"Right here, Jack," Samedi said, crawling out from one of the cartons where he had folded himself for hiding. "Hey, don' gimme that look. I got no weapons, an' these brittle bones break real easy. 'Sides, if anything happened to me, where would you survivors be without a guide?"

"Forget it," Clive said. "Where's Tomàs?"

Sidi Bombay led them to a far corner where the little sailor lay unconscious atop a mound of crushed containers. Clive recalled seeing him fall as his perch was knocked from under him. He must have been out since then. It was lucky the containers had hidden him from view.

Sidi Bombay dropped to his side, bent over him, and

began to massage his temples. Almost immediately, Tomàs's eyes snapped open. At first, a dull film covered the black pupils, but it quickly cleared as he came fully alert. "My gun!" he said, the first words from his mouth. He scrambled over on his knees and began feeling around for the missing weapon. He found it nearby under another carton and tucked it in his waistband as he looked around suspiciously. "Did we win, *amigos?*" Then, he backed a step and laid his hand on the gun butt. "*Christo!* Are you my *amigos?*"

Clive frowned. "What do you mean? Of course we're your friends!"

But Annabelle touched his shoulder. "I understand," she said, beckoning them to follow her. She pointed to the bodies of various clones as she walked. "Maybe you were too caught up in the fighting to notice. One of the advantages of this thing"—she tapped the controls of the Baalbec on her left forearm—"is that I don't have to fight, so my senses don't go all hyper. But look. Look at the faces. Almost everybody we've met in the Dungeon is here, several copies, sometimes. Almost every alien race, too. That jellyfish thing that attacked you, Clive. Remember the monster on the bridge at Q'oorna where you found Finnbogg? That might have been an early prototype."

Sidi Bombay cleared his throat. "Come to the forward door," he said, and they followed him. In the darkness to the side of the entrance stood a dozen or more clones all locked in stasis. Any of them would have made a fine addition to someone's sculpture garden. "I crouched here for a short time," Sidi explained. "Here are those who came through the door and turned my way. But look closely. Especially you, Missy Annabelle."

"Why, it's me!" Neville exclaimed, standing before his look-alike. He made a frame of his thumbs and index fingers and made a show of examining the face with his best artist's eye. "Technique's a bit rough, though. My jaw's much firmer, and my nose far more noble, don't you think? Those damned impressionists must be everywhere these days! Manet, you dog!"

Annabelle moved from face to face, peering closely. Then, she noted the two small doll-like clones deep in the darkness. She kneeled down and caught her breath sharply as she clapped a hand to her mouth. "Amanda!" she whispered in horror through her fingers.

"Not so, missy," Sidi assured her, going to her side and bending down. "Look closely. First this one"—he indicated the Amanda look-alike—"then this one over here." He drew her to the second clone.

It was hard to see in the gloom. Annabelle motioned Sidi back a little farther, then adjusted the Baalbec so that it gave off the faintest glow and lit up the tiny face. The hair was black like Amanda's, but straight and fine instead of curly. The eyes were subtly wrong, too, and the lips were too thin. "Why, it's me, sort of!" She looked to Sidi, then to the others as they all gathered around. "I don't understand!"

Chang Guafe bent closer as Annabelle scooted aside. The light of his ruby eyes put a blush on the doll face. Then, he straightened. "Microscopic scan reveals faint traceries of scar tissue at key facial points indicating surgical alteration." He looked directly at Annabelle as he continued. "Theory: Neither of these is a true clone of your child. They are clones of you, Annabelle Leigh, grown from or patterned on your genetic material. Your pattern would be similar, but not identical, to your daughter's. Cosmetic surgery, done with great skill and highly advanced techniques, corrects the differences."

"Then, it's possible the clones of my father are not made from him, either?" Clive interrupted excitedly as he sheathed his saber. "The tissue could have been taken from Neville. He looks enough like Father. And surgery did the rest!"

"Or even from you, Clive Folliot," Chang Guafe reminded him. "But I cannot be certain. I detected no scarring on the clone at the palace, nor will I expect to if I examine the one you fought." He waved a hand at the Amanda look-alikes. "These were made in great haste, obviously, perhaps as experiments toward the final model."

"It's not Amanda," Annabelle said with great relief. She closed her eyes and took a slow breath before she opened them again. "God, I was going quietly out of my mind for fear that they'd gotten hold of her somehow, that she was down here someplace in the Dungeon, too." She brushed a hand over her left forearm, shutting off the Baalbec. The light that surrounded her winked out.

"I know," Clive confided uncertainly in a muted half-whisper. "I keep wondering that same thing about my father." He bit his lip and glanced at his brother, feeling somehow that he'd confessed too much. But Neville's gaze betrayed nothing, no emotion that Clive could latch on to and share. How could he ever think of leaning on his twin's shoulder when it was cold stone? He might have gained a new respect for Neville, but he knew better than ever to look to his twin for that kind of support.

"Let's get out of here," he said.

· CHAPTER TWENTY-ONE ·

# The Black Factory

As they pushed deeper into the underground complex, they found each chamber increasingly fantastical. The crystalline tubes now made a chemical-bearing webwork overhead. Fluids of vibrant color, mysterious in nature, raced toward some unknown destination, catching and scattering the light from the illumination panels, casting rainbows on the walls, spilling swaths and pools of blues, greens, reds, and golds on the floors and ceilings.

If the outer chambers were given over to storage, the ones they ventured through now were filled with machinery. The muted hum of powerful engines vibrated the air, and the steady *thrump-thrump* of pumps and compressors created a constant, monotonous rhythm. Automated conveyors carried familiar cartons from the outer chambers to other destinations. Robot arms at the junctures scanned the symbols on the boxes and transferred each to the appropriate belt for the next leg of its journey.

Alerted by a sudden high-pitched whine, Samedi spun around. "Get back, Jack!" he said suddenly, waving everyone back behind the base of what to Clive's limited experience appeared to be a huge electric generator. Once under cover he dared to peek over Samedi's shoulder and around the edge.

Four small tanklike vehicles rolled into sight. At first Clive thought they might be rat-catchers, but they were rather transport carts of some sort. Four slender metal grappling limbs rose up out of each tank body to hold securely in place a huge piece of equipment, the purpose of which Clive couldn't even guess. On smooth treads they trundled through the center of the chamber and out the far exit.

"Why did we hide?" Clive whispered to Samedi when the four vehicles were gone. "Can they sense us?"

"Think so, yeah," their guide answered. "They don't do nothin' 'cept let the rat-catchers know we're around, an' you can usually get away 'fore they show up. Still, who needs it?"

"Right," Clive agreed. "Who needs it?"

Samedi crept into the center of the chamber, looked both ways, then beckoned them out of hiding. They stole quietly out and into the next room.

A wall of flame shot up on the left side. Clive threw up an arm instinctively to protect his face and jumped away from it, slamming into a close wall as the fire quickly faded again.

Annabelle looked at him with concern, then stepped to the left, reached over some kind of equipment console, and rapped her knuckles against a transparent substance that formed the other wall. "Protective glass, I'll bet, hacker," she said. "Indestructible." She turned, leaned on the console, and looked outward. "Some view."

The others gathered closer and looked, too. They found themselves on an observation deck peering down from a dizzying height, but what they gazed upon Clive couldn't guess. The chamber below was vast if it was, indeed, another chamber at all. They couldn't see the other side for the foul smoke and smog that hung over everything, nor could they be sure of seeing the bottom. Hundreds of smokestacks thrust up through a hazy fog and belched flame and thick noxious vapor into the air. Bright, burning geysers spewed upward in flaring outbursts. Apparently, such a geyser stood right below the observation window, as every few moments the same eruption that had so startled Clive occurred again.

"It's like an industrial version of hell, Clive-o," Annabelle said, low-voiced. "There are cities a lot like this in my time, whole metropolises turned into factories."

"That can't be a city down there!" Neville scoffed, but the doubt in his voice betrayed him. "No one could live in that."

Annabelle backed off a bit and began examining the console that ran the length of the window and the room. Luminous dials and instrument monitors gave readings in symbols similar to those on the cartons. "Look," she said, pointing to a series of indicators spaced at intervals along the top of the console. "These needles quiver each time a geyser goes off."

"I saw a factory once," Sidi Bombay remarked softly as he continued to stare through the window.

Finnbogg went to Sidi and put an arm around the Indian's shoulder, and they watched together. "Reminds Finnbogg of nasty place Clivefriend called Dante's Gate, okay?"

Clive felt as if a sledge hammer had dropped on him, then realized it was not his surprise but Shriek's that shivered along the neural web linking them. Apparently, too, everyone but Neville shared it as they turned to stare at her. The arachnoid stood with all four hands pressed against the Plexiglas, and while some of her eyes remained focused on the dirty panorama below, the others focused on Clive.

*Finnbogg being correctly speaks,* she sent to them, unable to withhold her excitement or the sense of unease that accompanied it. *Could it be level seven the power plant for this Dungeon is? Entire world a great factory is?*

Clive scratched his chin. "I don't know, Shriek, that might be part of it. But that wouldn't explain the visions we saw at the Lake of Lamentations, would it? In fact, since you told me that someone is lifting images from our minds, I've been wondering whether we can trust any of our perceptions. What if they've been recreating those images?"

"Scrod me!" Annabelle exclaimed. "That would explain it. I meant to mention it sooner. Remember, Finnbogg jumped into the lake when he thought he saw his brother, and we had to pull him out. But he wasn't burned or hurt or anything. The water was boiling!"

"And our good friend Philo B. Goode pulled him right through one of those fire spumes when he tried to shake Finnbogg off his ankle," Neville added, his eyes narrowing with suspicion and anger. "Maybe the fire wasn't real, either. Maybe none of this is real."

"*Sim, stupido,*" Tomàs grumbled with bare civility. "Maybe we are home safe in our beds. Maybe this is all a dream." He held two fingers up before his eyes as he glared at Neville. "These are all I got, *senhor*. All I can trust is what I see. When the fire goes up, you stand still if you like. Tomàs is going to jump fast."

"A very practical approach to life, my friend," Sidi Bombay said as he shrugged off Finnbogg's arm and turned away from the window. "If you cannot distinguish between real and false, then react as if everything is real." He folded his hands and touched the tips of his index fingers to his lips as he looked at Tomàs. "Yet that puts you completely at the mercy of our Dungeonmasters. We must, instead, look through the illusion to find what is real, peel away the impossible to determine the possible."

Annabelle tapped a foot and frowned. "Yes, yes, that's very Zen, Sidi," she said impatiently. "All that 'sound of one hand' claptrap is great on a mountaintop back home. But down here, a strange world with strange aliens, it's hard to know just what is and isn't possible."

A soft shuffling in the rearward chamber silenced them. They heard the sound again more clearly—bare feet padding toward them. Clive made a motion with his finger and they scurried out of the observation deck and into the next chamber. It appeared to be much like the other. Huge banks of generators and great machines filled the immense space, and they crowded quickly into the nearest shadow to see what followed them.

Ever so quietly, Clive unsheathed his sword.

"Careful with that, Jack," Samedi whispered in the darkness beside him. "I got nothin' that needs ventilatin'."

"Relax." He heard Annabelle's gentle reassurance as she nudged Samedi. "With that sword we call him ol' Doc Longjohn. He thrills ya when he drills ya."

Samedi twisted around to look at her. Then he tapped Clive on the shoulder and asked with a curious expression, "Where you come from is she considered a defective?"

Clive glanced at Annabelle and glanced away quickly, afraid she might see his grin even in the gloom. He thought it wisest, not to mention the most gentlemanly, to say nothing at all. It didn't matter. When a few moments went by and he hadn't answered, she kicked him anyway.

"Lout," she muttered.

He waved his hand suddenly, cutting off any more talk. Footsteps echoed clearly from the observation deck. They pressed deeper into the shadow and waited.

Four demons wandered through the doorway, defectives whose wings had developed improperly. As they passed, Clive could plainly see the twisted nascent pinions folded against their backs, wings too small or too malformed to lift them. Still, sharp claws and fangs gleamed in the faint light, and the creatures rippled with bestial strength.

"Do you think they were looking for us?" Clive asked Samedi when the defectives had passed on.

"Hey, what am I, the answer man?" Samedi shrugged, and used his palm to carefully redirect Clive's blade, which had drifted a little too close for his comfort. "Seems to me everybody in the Dungeon's after you folks."

"Okay, it's nice to be popular," Finnbogg muttered unexpectedly from his crouched position in the shadow. He rapped his claws impatiently on the floor. "But while everybody looks for Finnbogg, Finnbogg should be looking for Smythefriend." He stood up and squeezed out into the chamber light. "Why do Finnboggfriends hide? Fight! Bite, chomp, and scratch to find Smythefriend! No more hiding!"

Annabelle edged out past Clive and patted Finnbogg sympathetically between the ears. The dwarflike canine frowned but suffered her touch with barely a growl. "Finnbogg," she said gently. "Why do you always call me Annie, not Anniefriend or Annabellefriend?"

Finnbogg shifted uncomfortably as the others came out of hiding. It made an almost comical sight the way his squat, powerfully muscled body slumped as Annabelle towered over him. He looked like a schoolboy about to get a scolding. "Annie is more than friend to Finnbogg," he answered weakly. "Annie is like little littermate. Not just friend, more than friend. Smell nice. Smell better than anything in the Dungeon." He looked up at her with big round fierce eyes.

"She really does smell, doesn't she, Finnbogg, old chap!" Neville leaned against the end of the generator with arms folded and one leg crossed, a big smirk upon his face. He pushed back a lock of blond hair that had fallen over his eyes. "What a piece of work is woman," he continued, grinning, "how noble in reason, how express and odoriferous." His grin widened. "I think that's right, yes. Always loved Shakespeare, you know."

" 'Oh, what may man within him hide, though angel on the outward side!' " Annabelle quoted, turning slowly toward Neville, bracing hands on her hips as she stared him down. " 'That island of England breeds very valiant creatures: their mastiffs are of unmatchable courage.' " She took another step closer to Neville, taunting him as she threw another insult. " 'I had as lief not to be,' " she said, " 'as live to be in awe of such a thing as I myself.' "

Neville stared, his back stiff against the generator, the grin vanishing from his face as his arms slowly slid out of their fold and to his sides.

"Hoist on your own petard, brother!" Clive laughed as he sheathed his saber. "She knows the Bard better than you do." Still grinning, he explained for the benefit of the others. "She called him a phony, a coward, and a vain bastard all in one breath." He made an appreciative bow to Annabelle. "That was poetry, indeed, granddaughter, if a bit harsh. He may bleed from such wounds."

Annabelle put on a big smile and patted Neville's cheek with much sweetness. "Perhaps I was too harsh," she agreed, "but one must teach a child its place, don't you agree?"

"Indeed, I do," Clive answered, bowing again, eyeing his brother with bemusement. Neville had, of course, recovered his composure. His brother always landed on his feet, like all tomcats. Still, it was fun to see him pushed off a limb sometimes. And to his credit, Neville was good-natured enough to accept a certain amount of teasing if it was done with any style at all. "And I think," Clive continued, pointing toward the far side of the chamber where the demons had exited, "that our place lies somewhere through there."

"No more hiding?" Finnbogg grumbled, rubbing the tips of his claws together, causing a wicked little rasp that lent meaning to his question.

Annabelle returned to Finnbogg's side and took his hand in hers. "We hide only when we have to," she assured him. "The important thing is to stay alive long enough to find our Smythefriend, right?"

Finnbogg's only answer was a low, unpleasant growl.

"Come," Samedi said, taking the lead.

The next chamber was dark, but their guide knew the way across. Annabelle moved slightly apart from the others and used the Baalbec to provide a bit of dim light. Clive worried that it made her too easy a target for any unseen attackers, but she had grown too intrigued by the contents of each successive room to turn it off.

This room proved no exception. Curiously, she peered from side to side as her glow touched rows upon rows of tall glass cylinders, all arranged according to some unknown order as if to make yet another mazework of their passage to the other side. Clive glanced upward and noted that the strange chemical-bearing tubes that hung from the ceilings of other chambers had apparently taken some other route.

"Someone comes!" Samedi whispered in a panic, stopping so abruptly that Clive bumped into him as the raggedy creature spun around. "Get back! Get down!"

"Get stuffed!" Finnbogg muttered rudely. With a bound he leaped atop one of the cylinders, caught his balance, and bounded to the next. Quickly, he disappeared from sight.

Clive grabbed Annabelle's arm as she snapped off the Baalbec and dragged her back into a narrow aisle formed by the arrangement of the cylinders where the others were already obediently huddled. "I've been meaning to talk to you about your language," he whispered in her ear. "Finnbogg's picking up some bad habits."

He looked over his shoulder and hastily counted noses. "Hey, where's Shriek?" he asked.

Tomàs pointed upward with the barrel of the beamer weapon. "She's went topside after the *cachorro*."

Annabelle glared. "Finnbogg's not a *dog*, you scrodhead. You mind your manners." She touched Clive's shoulder and pulled his ear close to her mouth. "Maybe we'd better help this time, hacker."

"Just keep your head down, Jack," Samedi advised as he removed his top hat and hugged it to his chest. "It's a busy neighborhood, all right, but they'll go by. We just gotta be careful."

Before Clive had to decide, a brief commotion sounded nearby, and out of it rose Finnbogg's growl and a choked yelp. That was enough for Clive, who jumped to his feet and moved into the passage, forgetting his own safety. He whipped out his saber again as he rounded a corner and glanced down another aisle. Nothing there. He moved faster, aware of his friends behind him now. The passage twisted, and he cursed whoever had stored the cylinders in such an unreasonable fashion. Finnbogg had taken the right course by going over the top.

Then, he stopped short as a sound like a glass lid settling into place rang in the darkness. He pressed his back up against one of the cylinders, drew a deep breath, and concentrated. *Shriek?* he called silently.

Her answer came almost immediately. *Ahead come, Being Clive. Safe it is.*

He looked at the others and indicated with a tilt of his head for them to follow.

"We heard," Annabelle advised him, touching her temple.

Finnbogg and Shriek waited for them just a few meters farther up the passage and down one of the side aisles. Finnbogg sat atop one of the cylinders, swinging his feet to and fro, banging his heels against the side of his perch, and looking pleased with himself. The aisle was too narrow for Annabelle to use the Baalbec, so at Shriek's suggestion Chang Guafe turned up his ruby lenses. The red light gleamed weirdly among the cylinders.

"Herkimer!" Sidi Bombay exclaimed, pressing his palms flat against the cylinder upon which Finnbogg sat.

Inside, looking thoroughly miserable and forlorn, squatted one of the froglike clones. His wide round eyes regarded them in abject fear, and he trembled visibly as he crouched back on his naked haunches and thrust half of his webbed fingers into his mouth. Sidi leaned closer and put his face against the outside to see better. Then, reflexively, he jerked back as a long, thin tongue shot out with amazing speed and power and smacked against the glass, leaving a smear of sticky saliva. Immediately, the Herkimer resumed its pose of pathetic dejection.

Finnbogg jumped down and held out his arm. Even in Chang Guafe's red light they could see the bloody welts on his wrist and bicep. "Nasty tongue," Finnbogg mumbled, "but Finnbogg choked Herkimerthing a little and put it in big jar. Okay?"

Clive nodded and shook Finnbogg's hand. "More than okay, my friend. You did well. Can it get out?"

Finnbogg showed all his teeth as he scowled at the creature in the jar. It cowered on the farthest side, hugged its knees to its mouth, and shivered. "Lid is very heavy and fits tight. Holes on top, though, so Herkimer won't die."

"Holes?" Chang Guafe inquired. The cyborg moved closer to the cylinder and touched it with his palm. He trained his gaze upward.

*Holes and valves,* Shriek answered. *Tubes inserted through top are, believe I. All cylinders such lids seem to have.*

"Theory," Chang Guafe responded. His lenses focused on Shriek's face, and four of her faceted eyes glittered in the bloody glow. "These are tanks for the breeding and development of clones."

"Let's get out of here," Clive snapped. He felt a sudden deep-seated loathing for the whole idea. Beings who bred other beings artifically and programed them for roles or tasks! It smacked of slavery and slavers, by damn! And he'd seen enough of that in places such as Zanzibar and India. He hated it!

When they finally reached the exit, Clive had worked himself into a quiet moral rage. "Give me that gun," he demanded of Tomàs, and when the little Portuguese handed it over, he grasped it in both hands, turned back into the chamber, and swept a continuous emerald beam back and forth. Cylinders melted or shattered in an orgy of destruction, and the room sparkled as silvery shards and splinters caught and reflected the beam's light. There was no hope that he could destroy them all. There were far too many. But he played the beam as far as it would reach.

An odd high-pitched note trilled suddenly, and the beam ceased. Clive pointed again, fired, and nothing happened. In the unreasoning heat of his anger, he cursed himself and the gun. His finger fluttered pointlessly on the trigger.

"¡Asno!" Tomàs cried in dismay. His hands curled into fists. "You broke my gun!"

Chang Guafe reached out and took the weapon from Clive and studied it as Tomàs spoke, lifting it up to his ruby lenses, passing it several times between his palms, running his fingertips over all its contours and angles. "The tone may have activated a safety feature to prevent an energy overload," he stated matter-of-factly. "Or it may have indicated the exhaustion of the energy source, in which case it is now useless. Without dismantling it I cannot make a determination."

"Keep it," Clive ordered, returning the gun to Tomàs and moving on. "If it's just a safety feature, or some kind of automatic shutoff, it might work again. If not . . ." He hesitated, then shrugged. "Beat somebody with it." He grabbed Samedi's arm. "No more delays," he said, ushering his guide ahead. "I want to know where Smythe is, and fast."

Samedi flapped his wrists. "Oooo, I just love an authority figure," he purred sarcastically, but he picked up the pace as ordered.

# CHAPTER TWENTY-TWO

# The Clone Banks

They moved through another series of chambers, each more complex and puzzling than the last, then down a long spiral ramp to another level of the complex. Crystalline tubes again made an elaborate lacework on the ceiling and along the sides of the walls. Some of the tubes radiated warmth. Others felt cold to the touch.

They followed a wide corridor for a short distance. At Samedi's direction they pressed close against the wall and went as fast as they could. "Rat-catchers," he told them. "They don't like defectives in this place." Halfway down the corridor he led them into yet another chamber.

Annabelle caught her breath. "Computers!" she gasped. Thousands of blue-screen monitors filled the room with a flickering light. Clive's jaw dropped. Never had he seen such machinery. He couldn't even guess the functions of most of the machinery he stared at. Words and numbers and graph lines composed themselves at a speed no human hand could equal. He watched it fascinated and horrified, feeling for the first time like some kind of ignorant, outdated primitive. It wasn't that he couldn't read the language, which he couldn't, or decipher the alien symbols, which, like those on the cartons, he assumed were numbers. He didn't understand how words could write themselves on the small screens, or how colored light could take the place of ink. He didn't understand where the information came from, and it frightened him that Annabelle seemed suddenly so comfortable and excited.

"These are life-function monitors," Chang Guafe announced suddenly as he stopped before one of the many consoles. "Electroencephalographic," he said, indicating a series of screens. "Cardiographic, galvanic response, respiration." He paused and bent closer until his red lenses reflected in the screens. "Unable to deduce the functions of remaining monitors."

Annabelle went to the cyborg's side and bent beside him. "Time," she said a few moments later. She tapped a line of symbols with a fingertip. "See how this last one changes so rapidly? Twenty-two characters before this one changes." She pointed to another line. "And exactly twenty-two of these before this line changes. If we stayed here long enough I think I could figure out the Dungeonmasters' clock."

She peered at the screens a moment longer, then straightened suddenly and covered her mouth with a hand. She turned wide eyes toward Clive. "My God, hackers!" she exclaimed softly. "I know where we are!" She moved to the next console. "Each station has exactly the same set of monitors. Temperature, pulse, EEG, they're all the same." She turned in a slow circle in obvious awe. "This is the nerve center. Like a hospital nurses' station. From here they can monitor a clone's growth and development." She turned back to Clive again. "But there are thousands of stations, Clive-o, and all of them activated. Do you understand? Thousands of clones growing somewhere at this very moment!"

Thousands of versions of his father. Maybe thousands of Nevilles or Chang Guafes or Amandas. It seemed obscene to Clive, and it filled him with anger. Maybe somewhere there was a clone of Clive Folliot, too, a perfect duplicate, but a duplicate whose mind had been twisted and changed, who moved to someone else's commands with little will of its own.

The Dungeonmasters were monsters. It didn't matter to

him how many factions there might be or what their purposes might be in bringing him here. Good guys or bad guys, he didn't care. Both sides used and manipulated these poor creatures. Someone had sent demons to attack him, and someone had sent Samedi to help. But even Samedi had been programed.

Was this the gift of scientific advancement? High-tech slavery? That word kept coming back to him. *Slavery.*

"Maybe we can find out where they are," Annabelle said with sudden excitement. She whirled around and bent over the console. "I know computers, and if I can just figure out these symbols . . ." She touched the keyboard experimentally.

"No!" cried Samedi, crowding forward to snatch her hand away. But he was too late. The screen flickered and went black. "Now you done it, babe. That's burned the dinner for sure." He turned to Clive in a panic. "Everythin' 's cruisin' on auto here, Jack. Now she's fooled around an' messed with things, the rat-catchers are gonna know someone's in here an' come runnin'."

Annabelle looked up guiltily. "But we can't leave here! Clive, this is a treasure mine! Anything we want to know about the Dungeon is probably buried in these computers!"

"The only thing I want to know, *amigos*," Tomàs snapped, edging toward the exit with Samedi, "is the way out."

More than anything Clive wanted time to smash this chamber, to destroy the equipment before him and put an end to this horrible place. His previous action had been a senseless gesture, a childish shattering of mere bottles to vent his outrage. But wrecking these machines might deal a real blow to the Dungeonmasters.

There wasn't time, though. He had to think of his friends and of rescuing Smythe. Without the beamer weapon it might not be so easy to defeat a rat-catcher.

"Out!" he told everyone.

Maneuvering around the consoles, they ran for the far side of the chamber. Before they'd gone halfway, though, they heard the smooth, soft whine of a rat-catcher's tread and looked back to see the metallic torso of one of the monsters as it sped into the room. A second came close after it.

"Run!" Samedi shouted. "They won't fire in here. Too much chance o' damagin' the computers!"

They ran, but before they could reach the exit another rat-catcher entered that way, blocking their escape. It raised its handless arms and pointed at them. Golden energy coruscated behind the focusing lenses as the creature waited for a clear shot.

Shriek screamed with a savage anger and ripped an entire console from the door. Smoking wires and broken circuits spit fiery-colored sparks everywhere as she lifted the mass high overhead and heaved it through the air. It crashed into the rat-catcher, knocking it over on its side, crushing it.

"Look out!" Neville cried, sweeping Tomàs and Sidi Bombay to the floor as a golden beam sizzled through the space where they'd stood instants before and struck another console. An explosion rocked the room, knocking everyone off their feet, filling the air with smoke and a terrible acrid odor. Debris showered down about them as a second explosion and a third followed.

Shriek's console had made a mess out of the rat-catcher, but half-buried in the rubble, one arm lay twisted at a crazy angle, and its force beam smashed a straight line of devastation from one side of the chamber to the other as console after console went up.

Coughing from a lungful of smoke, Clive scrambled to his feet and pulled Annabelle to hers. The two rat-catchers on the far side maneuvered toward them, still unwilling to fire and damage more of the precious monitoring equipment. Shriek pulled Neville, Sidi, and Tomàs up. With her fourth hand she grabbed a broken keyboard from the floor and sailed it toward one of their attackers. It bounced harmlessly off the torso without slowing the rat-catcher in the least.

They ran for the exit, but Clive paused beside the

wreckage of the ruined rat-catcher long enough to deal several hard kicks to the still-firing weapon arm, managing to move it just enough to redirect the beam into another row of consoles. The rapid series of explosions that followed filled him with grim satisfaction.

"The door at the end!" Samedi shouted hurriedly when they were out in the corridor again. "Through there!"

They tore down the hallway at a breakneck pace, mindful of the rat-catchers behind them. It wouldn't take those robot assassins long to plow through the rubble, and in this straight corridor there was no cover. If they got caught in the open, a single beam shot could get them all.

Suddenly a panel in the corridor wall slid back. Yet another rat-catcher whirred into their path. As its arms came up Finnbogg put on a burst of speed, leaped, caromed from one wall to the other, and went feet-first into the deadly machine. It teetered precariously, then fell over. Instantly, Finnbogg sank his teeth into its metal throat, growling with a wild ferocity. He gave a violent shake. Metal ripped, and blue-white electric fire crackled.

Every hair on Finnbogg's body stood straight on end, and his eyes shot wide with surprise. He tried to open his jaws and let go, but he couldn't.

A turbaned streak launched through the air, and a pair of arms circled Finnbogg's shivering body. Sidi Bombay's sheer momentum tore his canine friend free, and they both tumbled head over heels and lay flat on their backs.

A shimmering arc danced around the rat-catcher's throat. It spun its treads but made no effort to right itself, nor did the arms make any movement. Chang Guafe, though, took no chances. Bending low, he drew a deep breath and punched his left fist through the rat-catcher's chest plating. Almost immediately, the treads slowed and stopped.

At the end of the corridor, Samedi slapped his hand against a door, and it slid back in response. They rushed through, breathless, into a dimly lit chamber. Five surprised demons whirled to face them.

"Damn!" Clive cursed aloud, flinging himself at the

nearest of the defectives as it brought its claws up. He smashed his fist against its hard-edged jaw with all his strength, sending the creature reeling into one of its comrades. Too late, from the corner of his eye, he saw talons rake down toward his face. Then, the point of Neville's saber slid over Clive's shoulder. The talons hesitated, quivered, and Clive jumped away. Neville spared him a glance as he withdrew his blade from another demon's throat and looked quickly around for the remaining two.

He needn't have bothered. The pair lay senseless at Chang Guafe's metal-shod feet.

"Through there!" Samedi pointed to a door, which the five demons had apparently been guarding. He pushed his way between Annabelle and Finnbogg, stepped over the fallen defectives, and pressed it. The door opened at his touch, and they dashed inside.

Horace Hamilton Smythe hung stretched upon some kind of cross, held in place by no visible means. He was completely naked. His head had been shaved, and his beard. The veins in his body stood out in blue tension, and though his eyes were closed his face was screwed up in a soundless scream. Thin silver wires sprouted from his flesh, three from his forehead, two from just below his ears, one each from the bends of his elbows and knees. Two were taped to the sides of his groin, two from his belly, and one from just above his heart. His palms, too, sprouted wires.

The wires fed into a huge machine directly behind him and to smaller consoles on either side. Monitor screens reported his brain and heart functions as English-written data flashed in scroll function over another pair of screens.

"My God!" Clive gasped, horrified. "Get him down from there! What have they done to him?"

"His memories are being recorded and personality samples taken," Samedi explained.

Clive, Neville, and Tomàs pulled the taped wires from Smythe's chest and limbs while Shriek stripped away the higher ones at his head. "I thought they couldn't record memories!" Clive muttered as he worked.

"Not deep memories, no," Samedi answered. All traces of his peculiar accent had once more disappeared. He moved to the console on Smythe's right side. "Not details. But the shallow memories. You know, habits, mannerisms, things you do without thinking about them. Speech patterns and the like. The machine probes those, records them, and feeds them into the central banks."

"To program other Smythe clones," Annabelle said.

"Any clone at all," Samedi corrected. "Once a record is made, his shallow memories can be impressed on any clone, whether it looks like Smythe or not. Or any part of his personality. Mix-and-match to suit."

"*¡Auxilio!*" Tomàs exclaimed. "Help! We can't get him down!" Try as they might, the little Portuguese, Sidi, and Shriek could not pull Sergeant Smythe from the strange cross.

"Oh, sorry," Samedi said, turning back to the console. "Have to throw this first." He moved a pair of switches, and the cross began to sink to the floor. "There's a specialized kind of presser field holding him to the platform," he added. "Be ready to catch him."

No sooner did the cross touch down than Smythe collapsed forward. Tomàs and Sidi caught him and eased him down to the floor. Smythe's eyelids fluttered briefly, then slowly opened. He looked up at Tomàs and let out a low groan.

"Are you in pain, *amigo*," the little sailor asked, "or don't you like my pretty face?"

Smythe rubbed his temples and gave another groan as he sat up with stiff effort. "What took you so long?" he asked, glancing around at his friends. Then, he saw Annabelle and shot a look at Shriek. "My God!" he cried suddenly, remembering his unclothed condition. He tried desperately to hide himself with his hands. "Ladies, please!"

"Please what?" Annabelle said sweetly as Clive, realizing the cause of Smythe's deep blush, quickly moved to block her view.

"Turn around, for modesty's sake!" Horace Hamilton Smythe pleaded. "I have no clothes!"

"But Shriek has six eyes arranged all around her head," Neville reminded him, grinning, leaning against one of the consoles. He folded his arms and smirked, obviously prepared to enjoy Smythe's embarrassment. "It won't matter if she turns around, she'll still see you."

"Well, close them, then!" Smythe snapped, staring at the arachnoid as his bare cheeks grew redder still.

*No lids have I*, Shriek answered generally, and Annabelle giggled.

It was Samedi who came to the rescue. "Here, take this, Jack," the clone said, removing his top hat and offering it to Smythe. "You just don't look right without a full head of hair."

Smythe turned an even deeper shade of red, and the color spread up past his eyebrows to darken even the top of his scalp. He gave Samedi an I'll-get-you-for-this look, but he snatched the hat and used it to cover his groin.

"Guess you better have this, too," Samedi continued, his widening grin showing all his stained teeth. He slipped out of his raggedy jacket, shook some of the dust out of it, and tossed it to Smythe.

"My thanks!" Smythe uttered through clenched teeth as he tied the sleeves around his waist and tried to adjust the garment for the maximum amount of coverage. And it wasn't much, Clive considered. Still, it would have to do. They couldn't afford to linger.

Clive went to his former batman, put an arm around his shoulders, and hugged him with relief. "You gave us a bit of a scare, Horace, wandering off like that."

"Sorry, sah," Smythe answered sheepishly. "Only meant to make a stroll of it, not a bloody holiday."

"Some holiday, eh?" Clive answered. He turned to Samedi. "You said you could lead us to the Gateway. Is it close?"

"Real close, Jack," Samedi answered as he hugged himself and rubbed his arms briskly. His thin translucent skin had a bluish cast in the dim light, and his ribs showed through unnaturally. Without his jacket he looked even more like a walking corpse, like the true Baron Samedi.

"Then let's go. But first," Clive added, turning to his friends, especially to Shriek and Finnbogg and Chang Guafe, "wreck this room."

It was pure, bitter joy for Clive to watch three such powerful beings go to work. And they so enjoyed their labor, too. In moments, they reduced the room to smoke and destruction.

In the outer room, two of the demons had regained consciousness and slipped away. They hadn't gotten far, however. Clive stepped out into the corridor in time to see the two rat-catchers he had eluded in the computer room. The mechanical killers moved back toward that room now, but behind them, by means of short retractable tentacles that grasped the demons' ankles, they dragged the ugly pair. A wide bloody smear that trailed along the floor proved the potential efficiency of the robots. Apparently, though, they were satisfied with any kill.

Clive ducked back until the monsters moved out of sight. Then he led the way into the hall. "Which way?" he asked Samedi, and the clone pointed and walked halfway up the corridor.

"Here," Samedi answered.

But Clive didn't see a door or any opening at all. He gave his guide a suspicious look and touched the wall where Samedi indicated. A section rotated outward a fraction.

"Remember my storage closet?" Samedi reminded him. "You couldn't see that door, either. The Dungeonmasters don't want defectives wanderin' around just anywhere, you know. So they hide some entrances. Most of us poor folks know about 'em anyhow." He pushed, and the door opened the rest of the way, wide enough to admit them two at a time. They crept inside.

Clive knew at once where they were. The vast chamber was dark, but thousands upon thousands of crystal tanks radiated a pale blue glow, and along the ceiling and descending into each vessel, crystalline pipes and tubes shimmered with vibrant chemical colors.

"It's beautiful!" Annabelle whispered in awe.

Clive shook his head. "It's monstrous," he answered.

They walked slowly, peering into the tanks at the life-forms within. Some were mere embryos floating serenely in amniotic ambivalence. Yet even in that simple stage Clive could determine which were human or humanoid and which were the cloned offshoots of more alien species. Some of the tanks contained infant children. On the tops of these machines sat small, boxlike machines. Wires from these boxes passed down through the glass lids and into the beings' bodies.

At such an early age, Clive realized, the programing began. It made him sick.

At one of the tanks he passed closest to, his heart skipped a beat, and he jumped back into Annabelle. "What's wrong?" she asked, concerned, and he pointed.

An apelike creature floated within the tank, but its eyes were open, and it watched them. The eyes were disconcerting, indeed. The being glared at them sullenly with a palpable hatred that sent a shiver up Clive's spine. It didn't move, it didn't threaten or gesture. Its face remained utterly impassive. But those eyes!

"A defective," Samedi commented quietly.

"How can you tell?" asked Sidi Bombay.

Samedi looked at him impassively, then looked back at the creature in the tank. Flat-voiced, he answered, "You can tell, Jack."

Neville came to Clive's side as the company moved on. "I feel as though I'm walking through a zoo," he whispered as he glanced uneasily from side to side. Neville's hand never left the hilt of his saber now, and his tension was almost tangible.

"Not a zoo," Clive responded, barely able to find his

voice. He realized how long it had been since he'd had a drink of water. "A garden," he continued. "A garden." He stopped before a tank. It contained a perfect young boy of, perhaps, seventeen whose perfect British features were crowned with an unruly mop of blond hair. Clive closed his eyes and drew a deep breath and let it slowly out. He looked around. So many tanks as far as he could see. "A garden," he repeated once more, "and these are just waiting for harvest." He swallowed. "It's obscene."

He caught Annabelle's hand and gripped it tightly. Her flesh was warm, real, and a part of him. His blood coursed in her veins, his history beat in her heart and soul.

She glanced up and gave him a tenuous, uncertain little smile and continued to walk along. Annabelle was real, his child, his offspring, at least. He loved her, his great-great-granddaughter. He couldn't help it. He felt that bond and knew how strong it was, how unbreakable.

But that thing in the tank with its boyish body and blond hair. A clone, unarguably, but of his father or Neville? Or was it Clive Folliot? What if it was his? What did that make it? Son? Nephew? Cousin? How did a proper Englishman define such a relationship? What was his obligation to it? Was there an obligation? Was it even true life, or just a blob of cells with a familiar form, without a mind of its own until some machine gave it one?

He felt sick. He felt angry.

"I knew a pub like this once, sah," Smythe said suddenly, coming up behind him. "In Liverpool it was. You wouldn't believe the odd sorts floating around there, either, soaking up a little nutrient solution, if you get my meaning."

# CHAPTER TWENTY-THREE

# Through the Looking Gate

"Audio sensors recording a disturbance," Chang Guafe reported suddenly, "approximately twenty meters to the left."

The company had gradually drifted into a tighter grouping as they passed among the clone tanks. Their faces glowed with the strange soft colors given off by the liquid coruscations of the chemicals, lending each of them a look as alien as any of the creatures in the vats. At Chang Guafe's warning they stopped and listened.

"Afraid I don't hear anything, old chap," Neville said, but he'd lowered his voice to a whisper.

Samedi tugged insistently at Clive's sleeve. "It don't matter, Jack," he said, shooting a furtive glance in the direction of the danger. "Our way's straight ahead. Nothin' over there for us."

Clive pushed Samedi's hand away gently, but firmly. He'd finally begun to note how his guide's accent thickened when he grew nervous, and there was no mistaking the look of fear in Samedi's gaze. Besides, Chang Guafe wouldn't have alerted them without good reason.

"What kind of disturbance, Chang?" Clive asked.

The cyborg hesitated as if listening again. "Weapons fire, shouting in many voices, pain cries, background sounds of destruction." He paused once more. "Analysis: violent confrontation on a considerable scale."

"If you don't mind my saying so, sah," Sergeant Smythe whispered at Clive's side, "if there's trouble that close, it wouldn't be wise to have it at our backs."

"But if it's that close, *amigo*," Tomàs interrupted, "why don't the rest of us hear it?"

"Apologies, human," the cyborg said to Tomàs. "My receptors are at maximum sensitivity. You are correct to point out the discrepancy. Nevertheless, the distance to the disturbance is as I stated." He looked from Tomàs to Clive. "It is an anomaly."

Clive sighed. All he wanted was to find the gate, but Smythe was right. He couldn't have trouble at his back without knowing its nature. "Let's check it out," he decided. "But keep down and out of sight. If they don't know we're around, let's keep it that way."

Chang Guafe led them through a maze of tanks using his sensors to choose the way. Clive kept his eyes on his cyborg friend and away from the tanks, themselves, having grown sickened by what they contained.

No one made a sound, not just to aid Chang Guafe, but for fear of being discovered by an unknown enemy. When they'd gone perhaps ten meters, Clive thought he detected a bare hint of sound from just ahead. Then came a solid *whomp* that vibrated the deck under their feet.

The company froze and looked at each other. Then, at Clive's direction they moved ahead. Everyone heard the sounds now, however faintly.

The southern wall of the immense clone chamber was made of clear thick Plexiglas that allowed a view of another chamber far below. Though the sound that reached them was greatly muffled, they could hear, as well as see, what Chang Guafe had warned them about as they pressed up against it.

"My God!" Annabelle murmured, leaning her forehead wearily on the glass as she stared outward.

No one else said anything.

There were light panels to see by on the lower walls, but no exits. Apparently, all doors had been sealed. Perhaps a thousand defectives ran in helpless terror from the ten rat-catchers that ringed the room. Beams of energy ripped into flesh. Bodies literally exploded at the touch of the golden light. There was no shelter, nothing to hide under or behind except a wreckage of open cartons in the very center of the chamber.

*Raw organic compound,* Clive recalled bitterly, and with a sudden horrible insight, he turned to Samedi. "What do they do with the bodies?"

"Recycle 'em, Jack," came the awful answer. "Waste not, want not."

"The goop in the cartons?" Annabelle asked with a sick look.

Samedi nodded. "Some of 'em."

Before Clive could ask another question a score of defectives turned and attacked the nearest rat-catcher. Some grabbed its arms and tried to hold on. Someone climbed onto its back and slammed fists against its metal head. Hands locked on to its tread and sides. With a heave they all lifted at once, and the machine teetered over on its side with a crash, and a cry went up.

But the victory was short-lived, as their action attracted the attention of the other rat-catchers. For an instant that portion of the room became a small bright sun as all beams trained on the group.

Annabelle spun away and covered her eyes.

Tomàs slowly drummed his fist against the glass. "I hate this place," he muttered like a man balancing on the edge of his sanity. "I hate this place."

Clive turned to Samedi again. The clone had slunk back from the glass to lean heavily against the nearest tank. Within it a tall, delicate creature with pointed ears floated apparently in blissful sleep. But its hands seemed almost to reach for Samedi's neck.

"What's going on down there!" Clive insisted, no longer bothering to whisper.

Neville turned around, too. "It looks like a cattle roundup I saw when I was Stateside."

"That's it, Jack," Samedi answered in a quavering voice. "That's jus' exactly what it is. You see, we're defectives, but some of us can think, an' all of us can hide. But they got to be sure of gettin' us so's we don' multiply too fast. So they put somethin' in the food cartons. The more you eat it, the more you want it until you got to have it an' you hurt real bad till you get it."

"Drugs?" Annabelle said incredulously.

Samedi nodded again. "They put a big supply of it in a big room like that one. Never the same room twice. An' everybody knows it's a trap, but you got to have the stuff. An' the first day the rat-catchers don't come, an' the second day they don't come, an' maybe they don't come for a bunch o' days, an' you think it's real safe, an' lots o' us finally come to get the food. O' course the rat-catchers show up 'cause they been waitin' the whole time jus' to get a whole lot of us at once."

Of a sudden, tears welled up in Samedi's eyes and streamed down his cheeks. He sank down to the floor with his back to the tank and cried. Then, the tears turned to soft sad laughter. He reached up and caught one tear on a fingertip and stared at it. "I'm free," he said without a trace of an accent. "I'm free of my programing. Just as they can't steal your deep memories, they can't give us the deeper emotions like love or grief or loyalty or compassion." He wiped away another tear and held it up. It sparkled in the pale blue luminescence from the tank behind him. "We have to find those on our own, and we can only do it when the programing no longer drives us." He looked up, and a hint of a smile flickered over his mouth. "I can cry now when I couldn't before."

He sat there for a moment more, his hands folded in his lap. At last he got up. "There's nothing you can do for those below, Clive Folliot, or for me, either. You see, I've eaten, too. But maybe you can find the Dungeonmasters, and when you do, think of us. Let's get you to the gate." He beckoned to the little Portuguese. "Come, Tomàs. I hate this place as much as you. Walk beside me." He put his arm around Tomàs's shoulder as he led the way.

"But Clive!" Annabelle cried as the company started to move away. "We can't leave them down there. It's a slaughter! We have to do something!"

"There's nothing we can do," Clive answered quietly. "Didn't you hear Samedi? It's the way of the world around here."

"If you want to stop it," said Sidi Bombay, pulling her gently from the glass wall, compelling her with his voice to look at him and away from the carnage below, "then you must stop the Dungeonmasters."

She looked at Sidi, at Clive, at them all. "I will," she said with a chilling fierceness. "Damn their souls, I will."

"We will," Clive amended, taking her hand in his, and with that contact he opened the neural link between them and let her glimpse just a portion of the pride he felt in her and the love he felt for her. In return, he tasted the flavor of her anger, which she had not yet mastered.

He backed out of Annabelle's mind as the company followed Samedi once more among the tanks. *Shriek*, Clive called silently, and the arachnoid's thoughts rushed open to embrace him.

*Yes, Being Clive?*

*When things are calmer*, he told her, *we must bring Neville into the web.*

Abruptly, Samedi stopped again. A huge metal cylinder stood on his right, and he looked at it thoughtfully. Familiar crystalline tubes rose out of its top and joined the lacework of pipes that supplied the chemical solutions that filled the clone tanks. There were symbols in black on its side, but if Samedi could read them, he said nothing.

He turned to Chang Guafe. "I have seen your strength," he said curiously. "Do you think you can punch through this?"

The cyborg stepped closer to the cylinder and touched it with his palm. A faint, high-pitched beep sounded, and there was a dim flicker of green light under his fingers.

Chang Guafe lowered his hand. "It is one-half centimeter in thickness," he reported. "I can breach it."

Samedi stepped back and made an inviting flourish with one hand. "Then please do so," he said.

But Clive interrupted. "Samedi, what is this?"

Samedi smiled, but Clive didn't like the look at all. There was something in the clone's eyes.

"I have served you well," Samedi said with the barest hint of a threat in his voice. "And if I, personally, have not, then my genetic material has. Three of me have died for you, Clive Folliot. If you cannot trust me now, then at least humor me in this. It means no harm to you."

Chang Guafe shrugged as he looked to Clive. "It is tensile metal of no great strength. I can breach it without damage to myself."

Clive frowned as he nodded. Everyone but the cyborg stepped back a pace. Chang's hand curled into a fist. With a single, sharp thrust he punctured the cylinder. A thin liquid spewed out around his arm, and when he withdrew it, a steady flow followed and spread quickly upon the floor.

"Yuck, nasty wet stuff!" Finnbogg yelped, leaping aside to avoid the flow. "Not okay!"

Samedi shrugged and turned to lead them away. "It's just a nutrient solution," he said over his shoulder.

"You mean, the clones in the tanks will starve without it?" Annabelle questioned.

Samedi didn't slow down to answer. "That's very unlikely. The monitors will record the damage and send repair machines. It will—how would you say it?—gum up the works. Possibly, they will even forget about the defectives below and dispatch the rat-catchers after us."

"Now there's a pleasant thought," Neville sneered.

"We'll be safely gone by the time they get here. You, through your gate, and me . . ." He shrugged. "By the way, Chang Guafe, here's another." He stopped before a cylinder identical to the first. "Would you mind?"

Four more times Chang Guafe punctured nutrient tanks

at Samedi's insistence. The floor became slick as the fluid seeped everywhere. A mildly unpleasant odor filled the air. Finnbogg held his nose and tried unsuccessfully to tiptoe from one dry spot to the next. "Yuck," he repeated with great distaste.

"It's not that bad," Annabelle chided, scratching him between the ears, but the look on her face said otherwise.

Finnbogg rolled big brown eyes up at her. "Annie have dead human nose," he told her defensively. "Finnbogg have very sensitive nose. All Finnboggs have sensitive noses." He pinched his nostrils again and said with finality, "Yuck."

Samedi stopped again before a panel of doors. They had reached the west wall. "This is the clone bank nerve center through these doors," he announced. "Lots of computers and machinery, but the gate to the next level is in here somewhere, too." He touched the panel with his palm. Nothing happened.

"It's locked!" he said with surprise.

"That's no problem," Clive answered resolutely. He was eager to leave this place, and no flimsy lock was going to prevent that. "Chang? Shriek?"

The door might as well have been made of tissue. The two aliens ripped it away with barely a pause, and the company rushed inside.

There were no computers, no machinery. In fact, the chamber was rather small and furnished like a Victorian drawing room with thick carpets and stuffed chairs, pictures that hung on the walls, and a fireplace with a crackling warm fire. A clock with a kindly old grandfather's face ticked loudly upon the mantel, and behind it, hung upon the chimney, was a large mirror, which reflected the entire room.

Before the fireplace two figures hunched over a table, a game of chess between them, and just behind them stood two more figures in heavy cloaks. The cloaked pair looked up at the same time and saw Clive.

"Drat and bother!" snapped the dark-haired female.

"Oh, shit!" said her brother.

"The Ransome twins!" Sergeant Smythe shouted, but before anyone could make a move, the pair shed their cloaks and with an astonishing leap, disappeared through the mirror.

Tomàs started forward. "*Pressa!* That must be the gate!"

But Clive caught his arm. "Wait," he said, approaching the two figures who had not yet looked up from their chess game. They seemed absorbed in their moves. One lifted a piece and carefully set it down on another square. The other had already prepared his counter and carried it through. Only then did they bother to acknowledge the intruders. Slowly, they looked up from the game.

Clive stopped as he stared at Philo B. Goode, once again in human form, and at his father, the Baron Tewkesbury.

"So, you've made it this far," Goode said appraisingly.

Annabelle tugged on Clive's arm. "Clones," she whispered.

"Are we, indeed?" Goode said with some amusement as he folded his arms over his barrel chest, grinning to his fellow player. The baron returned his gaze soberly. "So you can tell the real from the false now, can you? The illusion from the true? Have you learned that much?"

"Yes!" Annabelle snapped. "You're a clone, Philo Goode. You're both clones! And this room, it's fake, too, an illusion. You can take images from our minds. Shriek found that out. And this one's from mine. I've read *Through the Looking Glass*. The only thing missing are the kittens!"

*Meow! Murffff!*

They all looked toward the sound. Curled up on one of the overstuffed chairs sat a large white mother cat patiently cleaning the face of a smaller white kitten. At the foot of the chair a black kitten played mischievously with a ball of blue worsted yarn.

"You have learned," Philo B. Goode admitted grudgingly, "but you haven't learned enough."

Neville stepped forward, whipping out his sword in a

smooth threatening motion. "Then maybe we can carve some answers out of you, you bloody cob!"

"You, on the other hand, Major, haven't learned much at all." Goode reached into the pocket of his waistcoat and withdrew a stasis box like Sidi Bombay's. He pointed it at Neville and pressed the stud. Neville Folliot froze in midstep. "But then, that's why we gave up on you." He looked at Clive and grinned that hateful grin again. "Please don't reach for any of your weapons. You see, my friends, the game is far from over." He stared past them suddenly and his grin widened. "Aha. They're coming to take you away."

Clive spun about to see what Goode meant. Outside in the clone chamber three rat-catchers sped toward them, their arms leveled and glowing with a building golden fire. Then suddenly their treads began to spin uselessly as they encountered the slick fluid upon the floor.

"You're right, sir," Samedi said with mock civility as he leaned casually in the ruined doorway. "The game is not yet over." He opened a small box he held in his palm.

"Pickpocket!" Tomàs cried, patting himself. "He's got my matches!"

Samedi drew one of the flint-tips along the side of the box. A tiny flame flared, and a little puff of smoke purled upward about his face. He backed a step out into the clone chamber, and there was something in his eyes again that made Clive tremble.

"When at last you face the Dungeonmasters, Clive Folliot," Samedi said gravely, "then remember us. Remember me." He gazed again toward Philo B. Goode and hatred filled his dark, sunken eyes. "Checkmate," he said.

The match fell to the floor beside Samedi's feet. At once, the slick liquid caught the flame. With a rushing roar the outer chamber became an inferno. Samedi never even screamed as the fire rushed over him. He stood for a moment like a bright pillar, then just behind him, the nearest clone tank exploded in a ball of white-hot fury that knocked everyone to the floor.

Drops of burning liquid rained through the doorway. Smythe gave a shout as it touched his bare back. Frantically he rolled and beat himself. Finnbogg, too, gave a startled cry as a patch of hair on his rump began to smolder. Annabelle got to her feet, caught him, ripped off her blouse, and began to beat his backside with it.

More and more explosions rocked the outer chamber as tank after tank exploded. The heat raged through the doorway. The carpet began to burn where the liquid had touched it.

"I don't think that was a nutrient solution," Chang Guafe said.

"Are you trying to develop a sense of humor, cyborg?" Neville asked as he tried to pull Shriek to her feet.

"I have been analyzing the necessary elements," Chang Guafe answered dryly.

"Analyze them later," Clive urgently suggested. "Our friends have opted for the better part of valor. I think we should do the same."

It was true. In the confusion Philo B. Goode and the baron had made their escape, presumably through the mirror. Even the kittens were gone, if they had ever actually been there. As quickly as he could, Clive steered everyone toward the fireplace.

Then, as he dragged a chair from the table and set it before the mantel to use as a stepping stool to the mirror, he happened to glance at the chess game, and his heart skipped a beat. The fire and the danger vanished from his mind. He went cold inside.

It was not a normal chess set at all. Mingled among the white pieces he found small models of himself and all his friends. But among the red pieces there was a miniature of Sidi Bombay and one of Chang Guafe.

Suddenly, he remembered another chess set on an upper level—Green's set. That one had featured pieces modeled after Horace and Sidi. And—he remembered distinctly—his mother.

What did it mean? Could that set have any connection with this one?

The others, noting his strange reaction, bent closer beside him. With a cry of rage, he swept his arm across the board, sending the pieces flying in all directions. Had he acted fast enough? Had any of them seen? He whirled away from the table, breathing hard.

Without meaning to, he stared at Sidi Bombay, then at Chang Guafe.

Sidi noticed. "What is it, Englishman?" the Indian asked curiously.

Clive bit his lip. Then, the floor under his feet gave a strange menacing shudder. There were thousands of those clone tanks, he remembered, and vast stores of the chemicals that supplied them.

"Nothing!" Clive shouted over the growing chaos. He refused to believe the thought that crossed his mind. Maybe he couldn't tell real from false, but he knew his friends. He didn't give a damn about some pieces on a chess board. It was just another trick of Goode's meant to confuse him. Well, he wouldn't let it. *He knew his friends!*

"Through the gate!" he ordered, pulling himself together. "Let's get out of here!"

"Through the looking glass, you mean," Annabelle grumbled as she climbed up on the chair. "Come on, Finnbogg, let's go together."

Finnbogg climbed up on the chair beside her, and they each placed one foot on the mantel.

"That's a good idea," Clive agreed. "Everyone take a partner. That way, if we're separated, we'll at least have someone we can trust on the other side." He turned to his former batman and put a hand on his shoulder. "Would you go with Annabelle and Finnbogg? Keep an eye on them for me?"

"Of course, sah," Smythe agreed. "Though I'm sure we'll all be together on the other side."

"That sounds a little too much like a hymn, Sergeant," Neville said disdainfully. "Are you trying to be funny?"

Smythe sighed like a patient father with a petulant son. "The only thing I'm trying to do, sah, is pick up this cloak and cover my nakedness with it. If you'll kindly move your big foot?" Before Neville could move, he bent down and snatched a cloak one of the Ransome twins had dropped and jerked it out from under Neville's heel, nearly toppling Neville. Ignoring Neville's complaint, he fastened the cloak around his neck and hugged the folds of the garment around himself. "That's a little better," he said with a small, embarrassed grin.

Then, he climbed up on the chair and mantel with Annabelle and Finnbogg. Each with a hand out before them, the three leaned toward the glass and tumbled through.

Tomàs and Sidi Bombay went next, exchanging looks, then pushing off. Neville took one of Shriek's hands and stepped up on the chair. Gallantly, he tried to make room for the seven-foot-tall arachnoid. "She won't need it," Clive told his brother, and he felt Shriek's mirth over the neural web. She gave a jump and pulled a surprised Neville through.

"We go together, Clive Folliot," Chang Guafe said, stepping to the chair.

Clive eyed the cyborg, then took his hand. "That's right, Chang. There's nobody I'd rather have at my right side than you." *I don't give a damn about a chess board*, he added silently.

They climbed onto the chair and onto the mantel. The fire was halfway into the room now, the carpet nearest the door fiercely ablaze. Explosions continued to rock the complex, and smoke roiled everywhere.

"I'll remember, Samedi," he promised in a whisper. "I swear I will."

"We will," Chang Guafe corrected.

Clive looked up into the cyborg's face. Despite all the metal he found nothing frightening there. The ruby lenses were still windows to a soul, a soul he knew and trusted.

"You lose, this time, Philo B. Goode," he said aloud, "and every time."

"Is this an appropriate occasion for humor?" Chang Guafe inquired.

Clive rubbed a hand across his forehead to stop the sweat that threatened to run into his eyes. "Laughter is medicine for men and cyborgs," he admitted.

Chang's lenses glowed subtly brighter. "Then, 'There once was a cyborg named May, whose brother was certainly gay . . . '"

"Oh, no!" Clive groaned, and before Chang Guafe could utter another syllable, he pulled them into the mirror.

It was a long, long, long way down.

---

The following drawings are from Major Clive Folliot's private sketchbook, which was mysteriously left on the doorstep of *The London Illustrated Recorder and Dispatch*, the newspaper that provided financing for his expedition. There was no explanation accompanying the parcel, save for an enigmatic inscription in the hand of Major Folliot himself.

Our party united, we have traveled far from the terrifying chamber of the Lords of Thunder and tumbled onto yet another level of this blasted Dungeon! This level is most intriguing, filled with clones of ourselves and creatures we have encountered.

Now that I have found the real Neville, our major goal is a return to home and hearth. But before we can do that, there are two responsibilities yet to be discharged—finding Finnbogg's littermates, and vengeance against the masters of this hellish place!

DANTE'S GATE,
THROUGH WHICH WE PASSED TO EXPLORE
ANOTHER LEVEL OF THIS INFERNAL DUNGEON

ONE OF THE WINGED DEMONS THAT SERVED OUR OLD ENEMY, PHILO GOUDE.

UR MYSTERIOUS GUIDE
OUGH THIS HELL,
ARON SAMEDI.

THE VESSEL THAT CARRIED US
ACROSS THE BUBBLING WATERS.
NOTE OUR GUIDE HAS DOUBLED.

THE BRIDGE ACROSS THE CHASM;
THE ROPES ARE THREADBARE AND THE
BOARDS RIDDLED WITH WORMHOLES.

THE PALACE OF
THE MORNING STAR.

BARON TEWKESBURY, THE IMPOSTER!
LORD OF THE PALACE OF THE
MORNING STAR AND MY GREATEST BETRAYER!

INSIDE THE PALACE, WE WERE SERVED
BY THE FROG-CLONES, ALL NAMED
HERKIMER.

THIS METAL MONSTER CALLED A RATCATCHER
SHOOTS LETHAL RAYS AND CHASED US
THROUGH THE CORRIDORS.

HERE, WE ARE BESIEGED BY CLONES OF
EVERY CREATURE WE HAVE YET ENCOUNTERED.
I BATTLED A CLONE OF THE MONSTER OF THE
BRIDGE OF Q'OORNA...

...AND CHANG FIGHTS H
OWN CLONE.

IF THIS IS THE POWER PLANT FOR
THE DUNGEON, THEN WHAT MUST
THE DUNGEON BE?

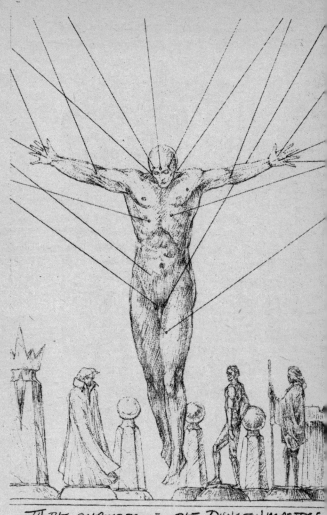

IN THE CHAMBER OF THE DUNGEON MASTERS,
SGT. SMYTHE'S MEMORY IS DRAINED AND RECORDED

AND IN A VICTORIAN-STYLED ROOM, A CHESS GAME
WAS PLAYED WITH REPLICAS OF OURSELVES.

THE HALL WHERE THE CLONES ARE
PREPARED FOR THEIR UNNATURAL BIRTH.

LEAPING THROUGH THE
MIRROR IN PURSUIT
OF OUR CAPTORS!

Catch the magic of Margaret Weis & Tracy Hickman!

# Rose of the Prophet

Here is the epic tale of the Great War of the Gods—
and the proud people upon whom the fate of the
world depends. When the God of the desert, Akhran the
Wanderer, declares that two clans must band together in
order to survive despite their centuries-old rivalry, their
first response is outrage. But they are a devout people
and so reluctantly bow to his bidding. Enemies from
birth, the headstrong Prince Khardan and independent
Princess Zohra must unite in marriage to stop Quar,
the God of Reality, Greed and Law, from enslaving their
people. *Rose of the Prophet* is their story—and much
more—packed with adventure, suspense and the kind
of magic that only Weis and Hickman can weave.

☐ Volume I: **The Will of the Wanderer**
  (27638-7 • $4.50/$5.50 in Canada)
☐ Volume II: **The Paladin of Night**
  (27902-5 • $4.50/$5.50 in Canada)
☐ Volume III: **The Prophet of Akhran**
  (28143-7 • $4.50/$5.50 in Canada)

Buy *Rose of the Prophet* now on sale wherever Bantam
Spectra books are sold, or use this handy page to order:

---